Ecological Memory

A Novel By
Caroline Ailanthus

ISBN 978-1-62806-221-2 (print | paperback)
ISBN 978-1-62806-222-9 (ebook)
ISBN 978-1-62806-223-6 (ebook)

Library of Congress Control Number 2019941026

Published by Salt Water Media
29 Broad Street, Suite 104
Berlin, MD 21811
www.saltwatermedia.com

Cover artwork and interior illustrations
by the author Caroline Aitlanthus

Acknowledgements and special thanks:
Passages quoted from *Practice of the Wild* by Gary Snyder
reprinted with permission of Counterpoint Press and Gary Snyder

Born To Be Wild
Words and Music by Mars Bonfire
Copyright © 1968 Universal Music Publishing,
a division of Universal Music Canada, Inc.
Copyright renewed.
All rights in the United States Controlled and Administered by
Universal Music Corp.
All rights reserved used by permission
Reprinted by permission of Hal Leonard LLC

For my teachers, Tom Wessels and Charles Curtin;
without you, Andrew Cote could not have come to consciousness.

All of us are apprenticed to the same teacher that
the religious institutions originally worked with: reality.

— Gary Synder, in *Practice of the Wild*

Table of Contents

Author's Note

I write books I would want to read. That includes writing author's notes I would like—I enjoy learning a little about what the author was thinking, the story behind the story. I'm guessing other readers might too. I also want to take this opportunity to correct a possible misunderstanding.

When I tell people I'm writing about the end of civilization, they often assume my book is a dystopia. It isn't. I write post-apocalyptic *optimism*.

Part of it is that I don't like civilization very much. Yeah, ambulances, antibiotics, vaccinations, and the Internet are all pretty cool, but then there is climate change, overpopulation, and other things that bug me. The end of all that doesn't sound too bad, honestly. But the other reason I don't write dystopias is that awfulness bores me as an artist. It takes a long time to write a book, and I don't want to spend years of my life thinking about how awful everything could become. I want to know how good things could be, despite the wounds in the world around me.

Anyway, we already have dystopias. The warning such works offer has been issued and does not need to be repeated. A siren that continues to wail ceases to warn and becomes mere noise. What we need now as a culture is hope.

Our civilization *will* end, one way or another. That is what "unsustainable" means. What we don't know is whether the end will be a bang or a whimper, a sudden cataclysm or a gentle transition. We don't know whether we will give up the old ways deliberately or have them taken from us by circumstance. We also don't know what will come next. Maybe if we can envision a good future, we will become more responsible about marching out to meet it.

We have some choices to make.

I'm sure I'm not the only one who daydreams about the end of civilization sometimes. Most post-apocalyptic stories contain more than a whiff of wishful thinking, going all the way back to the original story of the Apocalypse, the one in the Bible, in which the end of our world is but the first stage in the beginning of something new and better. On the secular side of things, consider movies like Mad Max, The Book of Eli, or The Matrix, all of which posit worlds that none of us want to live in, yet give us adventure of a type our world seldom provides. In these stories, bravery matters, and good guys win. Whatever virtue the daydreamer upholds, the end of civilization appears to clear the way for it. The trope of the cleansing storm is very old in our culture and very well entrenched.

The temptation is always to regard the people who die in such storms as collateral damage, tragedies that receive lip service at best while the real focus is on the adventure the disaster makes possible. I wanted to upend the trope, to take my personal version of the fantasy—which is unabashedly optimistic in terms of how the world looks afterwards—and pay attention to what it would actually be like to live through it, the shadow of the adventure.

And so a wandering scientist and his warrior student pitched camp in my mind one day, unbidden, and I watched her watch him shave in the shade of a hemlock grove.

Since then, the story has developed in directions I did not expect. I won't spoil anything by trying to tell you what the finished book is about. I will recommend that you read the two appendices at the end—and that you do so *after* reading the book, since they contain some references that won't make sense otherwise. The appendices are there to fill in some of the scientific background to the book, which is as accurate as I could make it. Even most of the places described are quite real. There actually *is* a large green map lichen growing on a vertical rock face overlooking Jackson Lab, for example. You can go visit it. While I have occasionally cut corners for practical reasons (I used arithmetic in order to calculate the pandemic progression, for example, rather than attempting to learn calculus), I have never once sacrificed realism for the sake of a good story.

Real life in general, and science in particular, are where the really good stories are, anyway.

For my first novel, *To Give a Rose*, I wrote a bibliography. After all, most people interested in fictional australopithecines (the creatures at the heart of that book) probably want to learn more about real ones and might appreciate the means to check my work. For this new book, I wanted to provide a similar opportunity, but I couldn't write a bibliography because I did very little of my research by reading. Instead, the story grew out of what I learned in grad school, supplemented by questions I addressed to various experts. So instead, I added the appendices—a list of recommended readings and a short, annotated essay on the science behind my fiction.

But the other function of a bibliography is to give credit to one's sources, and I still have sources to thank without whom I could not have written this book.

Tom Wessels is one of our finest living naturalists and a very kind and funny man. He has popularized, and to some extent created, the method of "reading" the history of a landscape that is so pivotal in my story. My characters' discussions of scientific concepts are also largely informed by his original synthesis of ideas as found in his lectures and books. His, too, is the habit of using ecology and physics as lenses through which to see every-day human affairs. He showed me that such comparisons are not metaphors, but rather a simple acknowledgment that human systems work by the same rules that all other systems do. Finally, I am a naturalist largely because of him.

Charles Curtin's influence is perhaps not so obvious, but I hope that something of his wisdom and passion have come through. He has always made scientific research seem like a huge adventure. His lectures and comments have made their way into the text in places, too, principally in the several discussions of islands and of disturbance histories and scale. He, more than anyone else, taught me that science is a human community with its own politics, history, issues, and the ever-present chore of fund-raising—a perspective that I hope my story preserves. And, quite unexpectedly, he became the best writing teacher I have ever had.

Tom and Charles also answered many seemingly random questions throughout the writing of this book. Neither knew much about the project, and both were and remain busy with their own work, and yet they graciously answered every question I sent their way, without hesitation. I hope they let me ask them questions forever.

Doug Tallamy is an entomologist as well as a champion of the use of native plants in suburban restoration landscaping. When my character, Elzy, asserts that even non-invasive exotic plants cause ecological harm, it is to his work that she refers. His treatment of ecological participation (resulting from shared evolutionary history) as the defining characteristic of a native organism is both practical and elegant—and serves as the jumping-off point for one of the central metaphors of this book.

Rowland Russell is committed to the concept of *place*, both as a scholar and as an artist. I have always responded viscerally to the differences among locations, but he showed me how to make that awareness conscious and deliberate. He gave me the language I needed to treat *place* as foreground rather than background, a character not a stage setting. Thanks also for many acts of encouragement, assistance, warmth, and inspiration, both large and small, over the years. Without him, I doubt I'd be the writer I am (I'd be a different, probably lesser, writer).

If Keene, New Hampshire *does* make it through the end of the Age of Oil intact, it will be partially to the credit of Steve Chase. Keene really is a transition town, and Steve was an early leader in its transformation and the person who introduced me to the concept of community sustainability (as opposed to either personal or national sustainability). When my character Andy says that there were people in Keene who thought a lot about fair distribution of resources, he is referring to Steve and his friends and colleagues.

Monadnock Ecological Research and Education, or MERE, an organization that makes a brief but important appearance in the story, is quite real. Its director, Peter Palmiotto, told me what the future Mount Monadnock should look like for Chapter 3. Additionally, he and Tom taught me my plants. Thanks to them, I can describe New England with all the detail that someone like Elzy would notice.

Kevin Egan put months into helping me design a fictional pandemic that is realistic enough to pass muster with actual virologists. I remain grateful. Thanks also to a ranger with the National Park Service—whose name I have unfortunately lost—who gave me a plausible location for Elzy's home as well as insight into why her family would go there. The staff of the Worcester County Public Library helped me locate Andy's study site (after several more obviously relevant experts could not—librarians rock). Will Broussard refreshed my memories of Pinkham Notch and the Presidentials, double-checked my weather, and helped me add birds. Monica Foley provided invaluable help with caterpillars for the Chapter 2 illustration. Kathrine Sheedy answered my geology questions and helped me get my ideas in order (she is also my mother). Diana Marsolek filled me in on the sorts of things ranchers in Arizona might be able to do if civilization ended precipitously. Scott Burnell, Public Relations Officer of the Nuclear Regulatory Commission, assured me that given my scenario, the nation's nuclear power plants *could* be shut down and stabilized before their operating staff died, meaning I did not have to include major nuclear disasters in the book's backstory (a great relief). Margaret Wander Bonanno helped me figure out how to to use fiction to explore ideas (something she does very well: you should read her books), even though we'd never met before. Allison Kramer helped me come up with a plausible smartphone game for my protagonist to play, so I named the game after her. Beth Gourley modeled for the cover (but doesn't really look like that), Susan Detwiler and Dan Schacter were my go-to sources for all questions related to American Jewish culture and history. Martha VanderWolk told me what a three-year-old burn zone in New England would look like and generally answered questions that no one else could or would. When in doubt, ask Martha.

To all of them, and to the innumerable others who helped enrich the story, I say thank you. The accuracy of this book is to your everlasting credit. Any mistakes are my own.

After research and writing, there is editing. Elizabeth Detwiler, Tasha Chemel, Reeve Gutsell, and Maggie Vinson served as my first group of beta-readers and each made the story a thousand times better simply by telling me what they liked about the story, what they did not like, and why. Tasha went on to serve as my developmental editor and made sure I gave the story a discernible plot. A second round of beta-readers helped me more clearly express the ideas hidden in the story; to Douglas Morea (my Dad), Kathrine Sheedy (Mom, again), Arabella Bianco, Ellen Womer, and Sean Wiley, my deep thanks. Joel Parthemore copy-edited Appendix A, and Rachel Brice took care of final proof-reading for me.

Then there is publishing. Stephanie Fowler and her colleagues at Salt Water Media did the honors, so without them you couldn't read this. It's nice having a publisher whose office I can bike to and who shares a dog with my neighbors.

And, finally, there is Chris, my Beloved, who in addition to everything else, brings me water so I don't forget to drink while I'm writing.

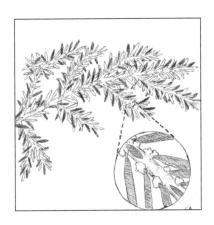

Chapter 1
Pathogens

"What's it like, having hair growing out of your face?" Elzy asked as she watched her ecology professor shave in the shade of a hemlock grove. He paused and looked at her.

"You have hair growing out of your face," he said. "You should know what it's like."

Elzy's cheeks grew hot and she looked away. She was sensitive about her few chin-hairs. But Andy didn't insult, and he rarely teased. He probably just meant her eyebrows. She turned back and watched him shave again. He let her watch, ignoring her gaze, as distant and professional as if they sat in his classroom back on campus. She felt safe with him. She didn't know why. She never played the little kid except with him, but she couldn't tell if he liked or merely tolerated the act.

Without his white stubble he looked younger, but Elzy could not guess his age. Personally, he remained a mysterious blank.

Professionally, she knew he was impressive.

Dr. Andrew Cote was one of the few scientists left from before the pandemic, and unlike a lot of survivors he hadn't left his old career behind. Instead, he and a very few colleagues had fought to save data and scientific literature from failing computers and then spent years reweaving professional networks and academic systems. Twenty years later he was still at it, crisscrossing the country on foot every summer. She planned to be an environmental educator, not a researcher, but she'd asked him to sponsor her application to the professional guilds anyway—nobody knew more than he did about how science functioned as a human community, and nobody was better than him at explaining how to work with people. That, and she admired his simple, fearless doggedness.

Everything else was a matter of rumor. People said he'd lost a wife and children in the pandemic, but of course a lot of people had—it was his refusal to discuss his family that lifted common tragedy to mythic status. Opinion split over whether he had remarried. Elzy had noticed, traveling with him, that he recorded video messages to someone every night on his little tablet computer. He didn't know she knew. She had overheard him once, just the tone of his voice, soft and gentle, and she had resolved to never overhear again. She'd defend him from anyone, if necessary, even from her own curiosity. She never asked him if the rumors were true.

She did once ask him to explain what "ten percent survival rate" really meant in human terms.

Andy had knelt beside her and asked her to put out her hands. She had laid them, all ten fingers, on the cool, brown needles of the forest floor. The man drew his pocket-knife and brought it down— hard—on her left pinky. Of course he didn't cut her, but it took all her will not to flinch. He repeated the motion with each of her other fingers and each time she felt a thrill of fear and the impression of the knife blade lingering on her skin. When he had mimed cutting off all her fingers but one, he folded away his knife and caught up that one surviving finger, her right pinky, in his own warm hand and gave it a friendly little shake.

"Now live the rest of your life like this," he'd said.

Andy was shaving because, after four weeks' backpacking up from Pennsylvania, they were drawing near the first of Elzy's speaking engagements. Andy had a rule against coming into town dirty from the road, the way most travelers did. He said if you want to embody the professional, you have to look the part from the minute someone first sees you. You have to manage the impression you make on the world.

"Why don't you just grow your beard out?" she asked. Most men did.

"I don't know," he answered. "Habit."

Elzy packed up the kitchen kit, getting ready for the day's hike. *When Andy was my age,* she thought, *he didn't have to walk everywhere.* He'd had his own car and flown to conferences on airplanes. But technically he didn't have to walk now, either—even without fossil fuels, there were other options. She'd once asked why they didn't ride horses or bicycles.

"Too much to keep track of," he'd answered.

Many people of his generation said things like that. Elzy knew it was because they'd become timid about having anything they might lose. But she had come to doubt Andy could be timid about anything, and anyway, he had a point. The pack had quickly come to feel like part of her body. She could forget its weight, take its contents for granted, and if she wanted to bushwhack up an interesting-looking ridge, or hop into somebody's horse cart at a road crossing, everything she needed simply came with her automatically. She and her teacher were free as turtles, needing nothing for shelter but their persons.

"So, tell me about this place," Andy said, quizzing her.

"This hill was once part sheep farm, part woodlot," she began. "I think there were some forest fires—small ones, like sparks from a larger fire somewhere else? This hill became protected land, some kind of park or preserve, before the pandemic. A family lived here during the transition, but they didn't stay long. Now it's protected again—a game sanctuary, probably."

"Do not say 'I think.'" Andy corrected her. "You can be wrong, but do not be unsure. How do you know all this?"

"The rock walls mean sheep, but some of the trees look old enough to predate the sheep farm abandonment and they aren't shaped like field-trees, so I don't think the whole hill was ever cleared. Multi-trunked trees and paired scars at the bases of some trees suggest logging, but that was also a long time ago, because those trunks are pretty big. The hemlock patches are younger than the trees around them, so they are growing in patches where the forest was cleared away. Even the leaf-litter had to be gone, because hemlocks need bare soil to sprout in. A fire could do that. Some of the hemlocks are long dead—adelgids, obviously, but no one cleaned up the snags, so this area was being managed as wild-land at the time. There are stumps from trees cut with axes. No one felled trees with axes before the pandemic, but there's no sign of recent logging, either. And the deer let us see them, at least briefly, so no one hunts here now, and no one has in the memory of the deer."

"Good. What's an adelgid?"

Andy knew perfectly well, of course. He was still quizzing her.

"A tiny bug, hard to see, introduced from...Asia? They eat hemlocks and the American trees had no resistance. Biocontrol—importing predator insects from the adelgid's homeland—helped some, but not enough. Some people thought we were going to lose eastern hemlocks completely, but then a new disease wiped out most of the adelgids. Since then, the predators have been able to keep them in check. So we still have hemlock groves, like this one."

"*Are* adelgids bugs?" This time Andy was probably not quizzing. He wasn't an entomologist, and there were things he did not know.

"I don't know. I meant bugs in the colloquial sense. I figured anyone around here who didn't know what a hemlock woolly adelgid is probably calls all arthropods 'bugs.'"

"Good thinking."

Elzy looked around at the forest. Nothing could grow in the deep shade of a hemlock grove except more hemlocks, and she could see nothing beyond the furrowed, reddish trunks but a few giant white pines. The short, irregular needles above gave the foliage a feathery appearance, but they hung in shadow and created shadow, all muted red and black, and suggested a different metaphor. The forest was a palace, a ruined palace, and the ragged, hanging foliage was just so much spider-web, spider-feathers gracing the chandeliers and the balustrades, the great arching beams of ballrooms still echoing with the dances of long ago. The whole forest was close and still, a dark silence that persisted despite the occasional singing of spring birds. Though Elzy knew hemlock forests supported dozens of species of insects and birds and salamanders, the place felt abandoned, melancholy.

"It's funny," she said, at last. "All this could have been gone, if it weren't for the disease that killed so many of the adelgids—and then the adelgids would have been gone too. They would have killed off their own food supply. Now both insect and tree have a chance. So diseases can be good sometimes. But the same thing happened to us, and the pandemic certainly wasn't good."

"Diseases aren't good or bad," Andy replied. "They just *are*."

Elzy could think of no response, so she let the silence settle.

Andy unpacked the charging kit for his tablet computer and glanced up.

"There's no sun here," he complained.

He followed a game trail out of camp, and Elzy followed him uphill, out of the hemlocks, to a hiking trail that led to a summit in a grove of red and sugar maple, red oak, and white pine. The April sunlight fell through the still-bare tree branches in lacy yellow patches, and the slope before them opened to a bright view of rolling hills and a wooded valley.

The overlook was artificial. Someone kept the rocky slope free of trees for several hundred feet. After a minute, Elzy realized why. Here among the remnants of last year's bindweed and a few leafless wine-berry canes crouched a crumbling square of stone, like another sheep wall, but one that turned and met itself, enclosing perhaps four hundred square feet. It was the foundation of a long-vanished house. The current land manager must keep the view open for the sake of visitors to the historic site.

Elzy sat nearby and considered the foundation. She was used to ruins, but this one was obviously older, predating the pandemic. *There's no one left who knows who lived here or why,* she mused. But she was wrong. The history of the house was easy to look up, and Andy had done so years earlier. She just didn't think to ask.

Andy hunted around on the open slope until he found a good, flat, sunny patch, and set up his tablet to charge. Then he joined her and they looked out over the valley together.

"Why is it important that the hemlock woolly adelgid came from Asia?" he asked, continuing the quiz.

"Because it's exotic," began Elzy, then realized that explained nothing. She started over. "Species with no evolutionary history in a place seldom do well. Either they don't survive at all, or they multiply out of control because nothing has evolved to eat them or to make them sick."

"Always?"

"I don't know. Often. Some plants naturalize without taking over, but they just sit there, ecologically. Nothing eats them. Or hardly anything, anyway. The exotics might as well be made of plastic. They take up space. They don't belong."

"What about us? Do we belong?" Andy asked, eyes suddenly shining. The rest of his face remained neutral, except for a hint of smile. His face was usually quiet, like that of one who through blindness or other circumstance had never known another's gaze, but his non-expressions varied. This one was quick, excited. Ideas were a game to Andy, and he wanted to see how well Elzy could handle a curve-ball.

Elzy smiled at him nervously, for just a moment. By defining nativity in evolutionary terms, she'd implied that people like the Abenaki or the Miq Maq were evolutionarily distinct from other New Englanders, a frankly racist idea. On the other hand, to deny that some people are native and others aren't seemed just as bad.

"Biological evolution isn't the issue for humans," she clarified. "We can learn how to form the relationships that make us native— how to find and use the resources we need and how to recognize and honor our limitations before we destroy so much. But it doesn't happen quickly. You have to get familiar with a place, everything that lives there and how it lives and how it affects you and you affect it. Maybe you have to grow up with the place, so it becomes part of you.

"I think—I mean—*it probably* takes multiple generations to develop a native culture. Maybe Yankees are native now. Or, maybe they're still...homeless, but they can start becoming native and get there in a hundred years or a thousand years." By *Yankees* she meant the cultural descendants of European colonists. It was an ethnic, not a racial term. "But I'm not a Yankee. I don't belong particularly anywhere." As she spoke, she dug her fingers into the soil, as though her hands were trying to grow roots. Trying and failing.

Andy glanced at her sharply for a moment. Elzy didn't notice. She was looking down the bare slope to where a fisher, a clot of animate shadow, hopped here and there under the trees at the far end of the clearing.

"I used to live there," Andy said at last, a gesture of his hand taking in the whole valley, even beyond where they could see. "There was a good-sized town."

"It looks like there is still a good-sized town," ventured Elzy, noting a few buildings and farm-fields in among the trees.

"No, I mean something bigger. You couldn't see it from here, but you could hear the traffic...."

"Oh. You mean Before." Elzy meant before the pandemic. If Andy minded his life being divided thus into two different eras, he gave no sign. He simply said yes.

"What was it like, Before?" she asked in a dreamy voice.

"Don't you remember?" replied Andy. "I'm not *that* old."

"No, I don't. I was alive, but I don't remember. I don't remember anything before I was around ten, a few years After the pandemic."

"That means you don't remember the transition period, either? This world is the only one you know?"

"Yes. I don't even know stories. My mother and her friends won't talk about it, and I don't want to ask anyone else." Her hands still worked the soil.

Andy looked puzzled.

"I'm a cop," she explained. "Was a cop, anyway. I didn't want it to get out that I have memory problems."

Andy nodded.

"Will you tell me?" she asked.

"Yes," he answered, but then the silence stretched on so long that he obviously wasn't going to tell her just then.

"Can we explore down there? The town?" she said.

"Sure. We're not due at Homestead till tomorrow. But we should get going, if you want to have time to look around today." He turned and headed back to camp. He'd pick up his tablet when he was done packing.

The way out to the trail-head was muddy and long. To minimize the chance of dirtying their good clothes, they waited until they were in sight of the gate before each stepped off the trail in opposite directions to wash up and change behind trees.

In the shelter of a large red oak, Elzy stripped off her wool trousers and shirt and wiped her body down with a damp, scented washcloth. Then she pulled on a pair of black flared slacks and a fitted, mid-thigh-length black tunic with a high French collar. She looked good and she knew it—slim, athletic, with clear, light brown skin and a funky mane of braids. The fit and flare of her professional clothes complemented her figure. For a bit of contrast, she added a bright beaded choker.

The only problem was that, try as she might, she could not reach to zip the back of her tunic. She'd tried it on only once before and only briefly. She'd hoped then that she'd reach the zipper if she tried hard enough. Now she realized she'd have to ask Andy. When she found him again back on the trail, he was dressed almost exactly as she was, except he wore straight-legged trousers. And he hadn't been able to zip up his tunic, either.

He helped her with courtly professionalism. Elzy returned the favor with equal decorum. He ignored the sight of her bra and she ignored the way his skin sagged across the muscles of his scarred and freckled back. The unavoidable intimacy of traveling together might have been awkward except that they had each decided to pretend it wasn't happening. It was a kindness, like all of Andy's kindnesses, that he could neither acknowledge nor bear to hear acknowledged—his knack of pretending he did not even see a person's vulnerable places.

Zipper fixed, he put on a red and yellow cowl, tipped the hood back off his head, and adjusted the fabric over his shoulders. The tunic and cowl were the uniform of their trade, a direct but more practical and more attractive descendant of old-time academic regalia. The colors and pattern of the cowl identified Andy's guild. A small silver pin marked him as a senior guild member, part of his guild's leadership and the modern equivalent of a PhD.

Andy was a very fit, but otherwise unremarkable-looking, middle-aged man. He had fair, weather-beaten skin and hair gone mostly to gray. But when he turned to face Elzy, dressed formally as he was, he looked again like the casually dignified academic she'd first met in a classroom four years earlier. She felt suddenly shy.

Out on the main road, they quickly dropped down into a wide, green valley. Far away, beyond the valley, a solitary mountain stretched the blue sky taut. Elzy stared at it for a few seconds, then walked on, past large, square plots of land piled with brick, broken cement, pried-up asphalt, the detritus of incompletely recycled buildings, architectural ghosts peering through very young trees. The town had shrunk, pulled in on itself. With the parking lots all torn up, Elzy supposed, there was a lot more permeable ground, and so less danger of flooding downstream. New England, she knew, flooded often.

Andy pointed out vanished landmarks as they walked—where grocery stores had been, where friends of his had lived. He didn't point out any places that were significant to him personally, but Elzy assumed he saw them. He hadn't been back here in over ten years, not since the early transitional period, and he seemed pleased to see that Keene had fared so well.

As he explained, Keene, New Hampshire had been a transition town, meaning its people had begun preparing for the loss of fossil fuel *before* the pandemic triggered the collapse. While the community had faced wrenching losses, the riots and general exodus that had destroyed so many of the old towns and cities hadn't happened here. Keene had re-made itself in place, and now goats and sheep grazed the old parking lots and the empty footprints of banks and chain restaurants. The few remaining houses were surrounded by fruit trees, some already with swelling flower buds. Vegetable gardens, patrolled for insects by black-feathered chickens, sat waiting to be planted in the sun.

There were very few stores, for the simple reason that without fossil fuel, most things that might be sold in a store were too expensive to buy. Biofuel production cost too much for the stuff to be used for anything besides emergency vehicles, so overland shipping moved only by oxcart or horse team. Biofuel or renewable electricity could power a factory, but again at a cost that had to be passed on to consumers. New manufactured goods, like Andy's little red tablet, were such rare purchases they had to be special-ordered by mail. In Keene, as elsewhere, most people made do with what they had or traded with neighbors at the weekend markets.

And yet Keene did have a small but thriving downtown commercial district.

The people here had managed to save their libraries, and from that seed had grown an adult education center and several small arts and entertainment venues. Recently they had even opened a boarding school for the region's few high school-aged children. All this cultural activity brought employees and visitors into town every day, and their money fueled the rudiments of a market economy. Businesses could stay open all week long.

Along the neatly graveled main street, shops sold dry goods, used electronics, non-perishable groceries, baked goods, even tobacco and cannabis. A thick canopy of young fruit and nut trees swayed above pedestrians, cyclists, horse carts, and wagons pulled by teams of oxen. The clean streets were a mystery until Elzy and Andy spotted children racing around to clean up the dung as it fell. Andy guessed that they sold the animal droppings to gardeners for pocket-money.

Elzy had seen such a cosmopolitan place only a few times in

her life. She gaped at the crowds and the store-fronts, at the lovingly preserved advertising from a bygone age—Coca-Cola, coffee, chocolate, things she had either never tasted or couldn't remember. Everything she saw hinted at the exotic glamour of the past. Andy looked around and grinned nostalgically. He bought her lunch in one of the little restaurants for the simple pleasure of make-believe.

Through all that afternoon, Andy began to tell Elzy about the past, what it had been like to live the old way, how it had all worked, how it had looked. He did not explain how one world had become the other, though he had obviously watched it happen. He did not talk directly about his own life at all. Elzy did not ask.

Then they went looking for the town audio-visual center so Andy could get online. Even when camping he spent a lot of time on his tablet, answering emails or editing papers related to dozens of projects scattered all over the country. When he could, he caught up on the literature. But there was no internet coverage between the towns, so he had to take what opportunities he found to upload his finished work and download more material for later.

Elzy had no such need, so she played around on a loaner machine while she waited. There wasn't much to do online, of course. Given the high cost of energy, which limited server space, most websites were periodicals, deleting old material after a few days. Multi-media centers archived content on efficient solid-state storage for patrons to either download or enjoy at the center. This place had once been a movie theater and still had an excellent main screening room and sound system, plus plenty of small, private screening rooms. Elzy's problem was that nothing on the center's menu looked interesting. She'd seen both *Gone with the Wind* and *The Best of Cable's Shark Week* three or four times already.

She sighed and wrote an email to Parker, her old college roommate, then clicked on a fashion blog from the center's archive. She was considering leaving to go exploring on her own when the text-chat icon flashed. It was Parker.

--*hey, u still online?*

--*Yep,* Elzy typed back.

--what's up? ur emails are always so short. Tell me what's up w/u these days?

--not much. Sorry.

--How are u? How's andy?

--He's fine.

--no, I mean, what's he like? To travel with? i don't know what u see in him, lol.

--I see tht he's brilliant, tht he can teach me what I need to know, and tht we get along.

--omg, remember what he did to chloe, tho? At the reception after she got accepted into her guild? He just vanished without saying anything to anybody. And he was her application sponsor!

--Parker, Elzy started to type some mild rebuke, but another line of text appeared before she could hit SEND.

--And that time Harper found him lurking in the bushes near the women's bathroom?

--Parker, the bathroom windows are frosted, remember? No one can see in. He likes to climb things. Everybody knows that. There's a tree there, he was probably going to climb it.

--omg, you're always such a cheerleader for him, lol!

Elzy stared at the screen in irritation. She guessed that Parker was literally laughing out loud and probably assumed they were laughing together. As students, they had spent many afternoons giggling over the foibles of this or that professor or classmate. Elzy didn't dispute Parker's characterization of Andy as far as it went, but to stop there and dismiss him as a weirdo was unperceptive and juvenile. Elzy felt no more affection towards her former roomie than she might have for a fun gaming app, and the app was getting annoying.

But if she alienated Parker, she might as well do the same for all her other friends, none of whom moved her deeply either. So, she politely typed out some witty come-back and asked after several mutual acquaintances, hoping to sound friendly and maybe solicit some interesting gossip.

"Andy? Andy *Cote*?" An unfamiliar voice spoke the name.

Elzy forgot utterly about the chat and turned in time to see Andy jump up and greet a tall, slim, long-haired man dressed in the tunic and hood of one of the other guilds.

"Saul!" Andy cried, "I thought you were dead!" The two men embraced.

Thinking somebody dead wasn't unusual—obviously, they hadn't seen each other since Before—but she was shocked by how glad Andy was to be wrong. She'd never even seen him hug anyone, and here he was chattering excitedly, obviously beside himself over this person. It occurred to her that she'd never seen him greet a friend before. She hadn't thought of him as having any.

Andy introduced the man as Saul Schaefer, an old college friend. The vaguely Germanic last name surprised her. His faintly brownish skin had made her think of her mother's friends and neighbors, and she'd automatically assumed that he was a fellow Mexican-American. But you can't really tell from looking, and she was a long way from home. She shook his hand and noticed that he, too, wore the silver pin of a senior guild member.

"Elzy Rodriguez?" Saul exclaimed. "*You're* the comedienne? You're our opening act on Wednesday!"

"You're the Greenfire Troubadours, then?" Elzy concluded, naming the storytelling troupe headlining at the market.

"*You're* in the Greenfire Troubadours?" Andy repeated the question, but with a different emphasis. "I didn't know that was you. That's amazing."

Saul turned out to be the troupe's manager. Elzy was eager to talk to him so she could coordinate her act with theirs, while he was curious about her blend of stand-up comedy and environmental education. The three of them arranged to have breakfast together and then walk out to Homestead as a group.

"Where are you two staying?" Saul asked, and suggested a nearby inn where a friend of his was hosting a semi-public party. Elzy logged out of the computer (she never got back to her chat) and left the two men to talk while she went off to do more exploring. The town was pretty and the weather fine. She'd meet them at six, when the party began.

But at six, at the inn, there was a problem.

"They put us in the same room," Andy explained.

"They *what*? Why?"

"It's a double, not a private," he reassured her, nervously. "They were the only two beds left. The dorm rooms are all full, everything."

Andy and Elzy were both comfortable enough in mixed-sex hostel dorms with strangers, but they had never shared a room with each other alone. They camped in hammocks, not a shared tent. They had never talked about why they took different rooms, so neither knew if the other actually cared, making the whole thing even more awkward. But there was nothing to do about it but go put their packs down.

By the time they got back downstairs to the common room the party was in full swing. Andy was recognized and pulled off into conversation, while Elzy looked around for cops or firefighters to dance with. She still thought of herself as a cop and felt like first responders in general were her people, but she didn't see many uniforms. Mostly she saw guild members, plus a few farmers in their leather vests and loose trousers.

"This is definitely a guild member party," she remarked to Andy when she saw him in line for food. He looked out at the crowd, trying to figure out what she meant, and noticed the sea of black tunics.

"You know," he remarked, "I can remember when you *couldn't* tell what people did for a living by looking at their outfits at parties."

"I've heard that," Elzy replied, and helped herself to a small quiche and a pile of sweet potato fries. "What changed?"

"Clothing got more expensive. It used to be you'd have separate outfits for separate occasions. You'd change after work…." His explanation trailed off as he considered whether to take a quiche or a bean burrito. He chose the quiche.

"But you didn't wear guild member garb to work Before, either," Elzy protested. "Where did *this* come from?" She gestured at her own black tunic and then grabbed a couple of onion rings.

"Sometimes we did. Ever seen a picture of a college graduation?"

"Black robes, I know. But that was once a year."

"Judges and priests wore very much the same robes every day. And doctors and lab researchers wore white, then as now." These professions also were represented by guilds because, like scientists, educators, journalists, and artists, their work did not fit well into a fee-for-service model. Instead, each town contracted with one or more guilds at sliding scale rates. Each guild then paid its members a salary to serve anyone in its network regardless of means. Andy grabbed two mugs of beer and handed one to Elzy.

"Thanks," she said. "But college professors *didn't* wear academic regalia to work every day." She grabbed a bowl of fruit cocktail and waited for Andy at the end of the food line, awkwardly juggling her bowl, plate, and beer bottle. He put his beer down on the table, grabbed a fruit cocktail, put the bowl on his plate next to his quiche and other items, reclaimed his beer with his newly free hand, and glanced at Elzy, raising one eyebrow. She rearranged her food following his example. "So, why do we wear this now?" she prompted, when he stepped out of line and joined her.

"Being recognizable is good for business," he explained lightly, and took a swig of beer. Then, more seriously, "when the first new colleges after the pandemic graduated their first classes, the students wanted to dress up for commencement, just like people used to. But they couldn't afford to wear an outfit just once. I've always thought it's kind of pretentious, personally, but it's what people expect now." He frowned slightly, as though confused, and sighed. A woman Elzy didn't know came up behind him, greeted him by name, and he was off in another conversation.

Another group of musicians took the stage and Elzy finished eating and wandered away to talk and dance with more people. The music was eclectic, a mix of songs of a dozen genres remembered and half-remembered from Before, plus some newer stuff, all of it fast and easy to dance to. But, since they used no electronic amplifiers, if you wanted to find a quiet place to talk, you could. Sometime after nine Elzy found herself talking to one of the Troubadours about her act and, to her complete mortification, she was pulled up on stage.

Unprepared and slightly tipsy, Elzy went through a rough version of her routine, a story about her travels, played for laughs. She brought the house down. She'd learned to be funny, first at home, then performing in the weekly markets of Lancaster Valley, as a teenager. It was easy. But somehow she forgot to put anything of environmental education into it and she stepped down amid thunderous applause, feeling all muddled.

Around ten, one of the Troubadours—Saul's friend—took the stage to explain, regretfully, that people upstairs wanted to sleep. Since no one, in his experience, had ever been able to keep quiet with an open bottle of applejack in the room, the party would have to disperse.

"Break out the pot instead!" somebody shouted.

"We already did, it didn't help!" someone else replied, but everyone was very cooperative about saying their goodbyes and clearing out. By eleven, the Troubadours and Elzy and Andy had gotten the common room all cleaned up to the satisfaction of the proprietor, who wished them all good night and went to bed.

This left Elzy and Andy nothing to do but retreat to their single room.

Elzy wasn't especially attracted to Andy. She assumed he reciprocated her non-interest, but she couldn't ask him. He was her teacher, and he was most likely married, and he was some unknown but large number of years too old for her anyway. The subject was closed. The sense of the forbidden, plus not actually knowing for sure, gave the whole situation an ambiguity that could have been sexy and exciting with the right person, but with Andy it was just awful.

In the dark, she could hear him shifting around in bed. He seemed uncomfortable with the arrangement too. She wanted to do something to reassure him, to dial back the ambiguity at least a little bit.

"Tell me a story," she said, in her little-girl's voice.

"I don't know any stories," he confessed. "I used to have to read to my daughter instead. I couldn't make anything up."

"That's OK."

"I don't know any stories except my own."

"That's the one I want to hear."

"It's not a great bed-time story."

"Tell it to me anyway."

And this time, to her surprise, he did.

Andy had indeed been uncomfortable. He knew there were men in his position who took advantage, and he didn't like to think that Elzy might fear him. But he felt no ambiguity, no attraction. She was just too young—if Sarah were still alive, she'd be about the same age. He'd been thinking of Sarah, not his living daughter, when he'd spoken of reading just now. He did not ask himself why. And so, when the girl asked, he gave in without thought, without caution, and gave her a bedtime story.

The first thing that came to his mind was the scent of the desert. The Sonoran Desert doesn't smell like anything else. It doesn't smell like a beach, though the soil is often sandy, nor is the scent exactly explained by its mix of plants, though they do contribute. If it rains anywhere within miles you can smell the creosote bushes come alive. A scent like an Eastern hemlock grove, only more so, flows along most watercourses, the perfume of invasive tamarisk trees. The cloying aroma of desert willow could distract a hiker in April. But underneath all that is something else, something delicate.

Andy thought it might be the local mix of soil bacteria, but whatever it was, twenty years later, when he cast his memory back, that scent was the first thing to greet him.

"When the pandemic came," he began, "I was out west, alone in the desert, working. I got the news online—"

"How could you get online in the middle of the desert?"

"There were cell-phone towers everywhere. There were *a lot* of people back then, so there were a lot of cell-phone towers. We had almost universal coverage there, at the end."

"Wow. OK, go on."

"So, on the news, there was just something about some measles cases in New York. Measles was rare, but not unheard of. No big deal. The strange thing was, a few days later, they said those people had already been vaccinated. The vaccine hadn't protected them."

"So the pandemic was measles? No one told me that before."

When Elzy spoke, he saw their small, darkened room around him. When he replied, he was back in the desert. The shift was jarring. He let himself slip back into his story again.

"No. See, that's the thing—measles isn't like the flu, where you need a new vaccine for every strain. With measles, the part of the virus that triggers the immune response doesn't mutate. If you're resistant to one strain, you're resistant to all of them, or it isn't measles. This wasn't measles. The symptoms were similar, but not identical. The biggest difference was that with the pandemic, pneumonia wasn't just a rare complication, it was an inherent part of the disease. That's part of why so many people died. They came up with a name for the thing, some acronym, but it never caught on. We called it *the pandemic*, same as now.

"Anyway, a few days after that, they said that the same thing, a measles-like pneumonia, was spreading in other cities around the world—London, Melbourne, Sao Paulo, there were a lot of places. But it wasn't that the other cities had caught it from New York. As far as anybody could tell, they'd actually all gotten the disease at the same time—it just took a week or so for somebody to realize the news stories in different countries matched."

"Wait, multiple cities, all at once? Was this thing *on purpose*?"

"Yes, probably, but nobody ever proved it. Nobody even settled on a really good motive. The people who did it are probably all dead by now."

"That's horrible!"

"Well, yes. It's a horrible story. Do you want me to tell it?"

"Yes, please. Sorry."

"The thing is, only a few dozen people were even sick yet. We'd had pandemic scares before, but they never really amounted to anything. As weird as this one was, I figured the public health people would just take care of it. Civilization seemed really remote to me that winter, and I had a lot to do. I had to map out potential bat roosts and nectar sources so I'd know where to put my interns during the spring migration.

"But I didn't know they were underestimating the scope of the disease. The public health services, I mean. A lot of people were misdiagnosed or just never sought help. And for the first week or so there were no obvious symptoms, you just felt tired, maybe ran a light fever, nothing you'd go to a doctor about, but you were already contagious. So however many people the CDC knew were sick, there were always many more. And those extra people each infected an average of ten more. So when the authorities tried to contain the disease? It was already outside the container. We never had a chance.

"But we didn't know, so I just kept doing my job. When I went into town for another month or so of groceries, I noticed people were freaking out, but that always happened with pandemic warnings, so I ignored it and went back out.

"But then my wife called me. She said the mystery disease, the pandemic, she said it was in Boston. It was in a lot of cities by then, Chicago, LA, Dallas, anywhere with a major airport—but we lived in Keene, right near Boston. And there were…little satellite infections springing up in smaller cities and towns all over. Everywhere they screened, they found the pandemic already there.

"But she didn't call to tell me all that. She had assumed I already knew. She called me to tell me not to worry about her, that she and the kids were fine, that I should stay out in the desert like a reverse quarantine for as long as I could, so I wouldn't get infected. She'd heard the disease was in Tucson, right near me. She wanted me to stay safe."

"What did you say?"

"I said *fuck* that, what would you think I'd say? I wasn't going to let my family face this thing without me. So I packed up my stuff and drove to Phoenix. I was going to catch a plane, get back East.

"But I got to Phoenix and there were no planes. They'd just imposed a travel ban that day, a few hours before I got there. The airport was full of people, there were still planes landing, but nobody was allowed to take off and everyone was shouting and waving money around. It was insane.

"I, ah, remember sitting in the airport, trying to figure out what to do, watching the TV there, all about the emergency measures, and then—my cell phone rings and—I'm sorry, this is just, I—"

"I know. Your wife. I'm sorry."

"And my daughter."

"I'm *really* sorry."

"Thanks." Andy said. He remembered, for a moment, not sadness, which he'd had no time for back then, but simply how surreal everything was. How the President on TV, calmly discussing the immanent end of civilization with the pandemic-rash already on his face, had seemed no more remarkable than the giant airplanes coming in to land outside. Neither had looked quite real.

His wife must have lied to him, he'd thought. She must have lied. He'd repeated the same thought, over and over, unable to focus well enough to finish with one idea and go on to the next. They had just said, on the news, they had just said two-to -four-day survival from onset of definitive symptoms. But he'd talked with her that morning and she'd said she was fine, she and the kids were fine. She must have been lying. She'd tried to save his life, the last thing she did, and she'd failed because here he was, in the middle of tens of thousands of probably contagious people, all for nothing.

But he would *not* cry with Elzy.

"I couldn't help my wife and daughter, but my son was still out there. I didn't know where he was. The man who contacted me said my son was at our neighbor's house, but when I called, the phone just went to voicemail. Same thing with most of our other friends in the area—most of them were probably sick already. Those few I could get a hold of had left town, so nobody could help me look for my boy. I tried the police, but they didn't seem to think a missing eight-year-old was an emergency! They thought I just couldn't find my babysitter's phone number or something. I couldn't explain it right. They were *polite* to me. I could have killed someone. I had to get back east and look for him myself.

"But I couldn't get a permit to get through the roadblocks. I started looking for ways to smuggle myself through, but somebody stole my supplies out of the back of my truck, and I couldn't replace it all at once—they were rationing food and gas so people *wouldn't* drive across country. I hoarded what I needed a little at a time. Days went by, a week. Everything was just ridiculously difficult.

"Things in Phoenix were falling apart. It wasn't that everybody was dying—only a few dozen people in the city were even sick yet. No, the problem was fear.

"People mobbed stores, buying up face masks, vitamin C, and duct tape, as if that would help. They bought up hand sanitizer, but that was just alcohol gel, and alcohol doesn't kill viruses, only bacteria. There were public dispensers for it all over the place anyway, people just weren't thinking. Any time someone would show up on the street with what looked like the rash, even if it was just a sunburn, everyone would panic.

"And some looked for someone to blame. You said you thought the pandemic might have been deliberately created. So did we, but we didn't know who. So some people guessed—it was a government conspiracy, it was the Chinese, it was the Arabs, it was white people, it was Mexicans—"

"Mexicans?"

"Oh, sure. There was a lot of tension because of the perceived competition for jobs between Anglos and Latinos, especially in the southwest. And there were always people in this country who didn't like immigrants."

"Yeah, my mother told me that. Her parents brought her here when she was little, without papers. Go on."

"The most ridiculous idea I heard was that Muslim terrorists from Syria or Iran had invented the virus and were smuggling it into the US inside infected undocumented Mexican immigrants. Guys went out into the desert with guns.

"You know, it's funny, when I was your age, we were all obsessed with zombies, I don't know why. There were movies and books and stupid little games on the internet, all about the 'zombie apocalypse.' And then it actually happened—we were all the walking dead, running around in desperate need of brains....

"But I still thought I was going to get out, I was going to be an exception. I was going to find some way through and go find my boy. Then I started coughing. I looked in the mirror and the rash looked back at me. On some level, I knew the pandemic wasn't a death sentence. Lots of people recovered. The real mortality was from what happened later. But I wasn't thinking survival statistics. I was thinking that's it, I've failed, I'm dead. I wasn't going to make it to New Hampshire—even with a car, the trip took almost a week. The hospitals were overloaded by then and they couldn't do much for you anyway, so I got in my truck and I headed north, to the Grand Canyon, to wait. I figured if I was going to die, I might as well do it somewhere pretty, away from the crowds.

"But then my stupid truck broke down on the way. I was starting to feel really bad at that point, really sick, and I thought, well, this is great, here I am about to die on the shoulder of the damned Interstate. So I rigged up my tarp for shelter and privacy, crawled into the back of my truck, got in my sleeping bag, and waited. Everything hurt, I couldn't breathe well, but the worst thing—I was *bored*. I couldn't sleep or even daydream because of the pain, and because I was out of my head with fever. Time passed, I don't know how much. Then the fever broke. Breathing got a little easier. I sat up, and it was like the fog had cleared. The virus was gone. But my lungs still felt awful, my truck still wouldn't start, and my sleeping bag was soiled, just soaked, so I figured I was going to die of exposure....

I had gotten up, gotten myself cleaned up and dressed, and I was trying to figure out what the hell I was going to do when, I am not kidding, three guys I knew came riding up on horseback and—"

Andy suddenly realized that Elzy hadn't asked a question in a while. He listened to her silence and concluded she was asleep. He tried not to feel slighted, but there was no way he was going to get to sleep himself.

He hadn't thought about these things in a long time—the way the desert smelled, the sounds of the riots in Phoenix, the cold, hard feeling of being sure he was about to die...and before all that, how it felt not to be a widower. He'd forgotten that one. He felt all jazzed up, ready for battle, but there was no one to fight, nothing to do in this silent house of sleeping friends.

He got up and went to the bathroom and then walked down to the common room, sat in the dark at the empty bar, and turned on his tablet. He hadn't meant to share so much. He'd planned to talk about his experience of the pandemic, not himself, but the two had proved inseparable. He had not been able to stop the feelings from coming up, and when Elzy somehow knew or guessed that his wife had died, he had been unable to deny it. He had managed to keep some things back, like the story of what happened to his parents and brother, but those thoughts and images too were all stirred up in his mind anyway.

Should he have shared any of his story? He told himself that Elzy had needed to hear it, and would need to hear at least an edited version of the rest, that he was giving her what her parents couldn't or wouldn't. She had a right to know where her world came from. So what if there were things he'd rather not think of ever again? Her need trumped his.

But he also scolded himself that he'd had no right to tell her, that she hadn't even really wanted him to, that she'd just been going through her stupid little kid routine for whatever reason, and he'd burdened her with his tale out of a selfish need for catharsis.

Mostly he thought about nothing in particular at all, just waited for exhaustion and the mindless rhythm of computer solitaire to calm him.

By the time he returned to his room, the moon, waning towards half, had risen high enough to shine across the roofs of the buildings on the other side of the street and in at the window. Its light shone on Elzy, sleeping with her mouth open and her dark braids splayed out all over the pillow. She looked very young. The moonlight reminded him of streetlights, the once ubiquitous sodium glow of another age, another house, another girl. He put out his hand to stroke the hair of the sleeping woman but didn't complete the gesture. He put his hand away and went back to bed.

Chapter 2
Native Organisms

Elzy woke mortified to find she'd fallen asleep in the middle of the story. The sun shone bright in the window and Andy was already up and out. She found him downstairs in the common room, reading.

"Oh, hi, Elzy," he said, as though nothing special had happened. "There's leftovers from the party, if you want some."

"Sounds good. Where's Saul?"

"Out for a walk. He should be back in a few minutes."

"OK, I'll wait for him. Does he like chicory?"

"I imagine. He liked coffee."

"OK, I'll make some."

She set water on to boil over the inn's ethanol stove and spooned a mixture of roasted chicory root and black tea leaves into a French press she'd found in a cabinet. Coffee, of course, which reportedly tasted similar and which everybody used to drink, wasn't economical to transport from the tropics anymore. She liked the chicory mix, but thought it funny that of all the things of the old world which were lost, the tradition of drinking some black, bitter, caffeinated thing for breakfast persisted. Odd, what people regard as important. So why wasn't Andy acting like her falling asleep on him was important? As if what he'd shared with her meant nothing?

She turned so he could not see her expression and frowned over the kettle. Should she say something? But before she could make up her mind, Saul returned bearing fresh corn muffins to share.

Over breakfast, Saul admitted that he'd liked her act, but that he hadn't seen any environmental education angle. Elzy blushed.

"That wasn't my real act," she explained. "I hardly had any time to prepare and I was really distracted."

"Well, it was a good party." His tone suggested his awareness that she'd been somewhat less than sober.

She blushed again and politely agreed. It was a good party.

"OK, so, what *is* your act? How does it work?"

"Well, it's got the same basic story line," she explained, "the same structure, but there's more to it. When I make fun of myself for being a newcomer here? In my real act, I talk about that in terms of place-based identity markers. Like, think of maple syrup and skiing—we don't have either, back in my part of Pennsylvania, but you have both. I want to remind people that part of who you are is where you're from. Then I can use that theme of identity throughout the workshops I'll do on Thursday and on Friday morning."

"What workshops are you doing?" Saul asked. Something about him was different. He'd changed, she realized, in the few minutes they'd been talking. Andy's old college buddy, generous bearer of muffins, was gone. Instead, she faced Dr. Schaefer, General Manager of the Greenfire Troubadours. The conversation suddenly felt like a job interview. Andy watched, silently, unobtrusively. He would use this, and all her other professional interactions going forward, to decide whether to put his name on her guild application. On that signature hung the rest of her working life.

She took a long sip of hot chicory and outlined her workshops, outwardly calm and confident, like Andy always was. She didn't believe he always felt that way, but somehow he could make whatever doubts he had irrelevant, and she followed his lead.

Saul listened attentively and without comment, until she mentioned using a loaned, miniaturized printer for her children's program on insects. With it and an app on her phone, she could convert a group of photographs from different angles into a scaled-up 3-D model of whatever arthropod the kids brought her. Saul asked to see the device, so she fetched it from her room.

"What does it use for print stock?" he asked, turning it over in his hands.

"Sugar! It prints *edible* bugs!" Elzy replied, grinning. "What kid won't like that?" Then she continued, more seriously. "All my programs involve insects, somehow. I just think about them a lot. You know, like the adelgids that killed the hemlocks? They didn't cause a problem back in their homeland in Asia, because the predators and the diseases and the trees themselves were all adapted to them there. They all kept each other in check. You lose that balance when you take a species—any species—out of its home and put it somewhere new.

"People ask how long does something have to be somewhere until it becomes native? It's not just 'til it naturalizes. There are plants that have naturalized just fine, they're not invasive, but places where there are a lot of them don't have many songbirds because there aren't enough insects to eat—because most native insects don't eat exotic plants. So, that's one answer to the question, right? A plant becomes native when the native insects evolve to eat it. And maybe, then, insects become native when the plants evolve not to be killed by them—when that balance re-establishes right?

"But I figure—if a plant is native when it has evolved relationships with insects and an insect is native when it has evolved relationships with plants and with various predators, what if *a place* isn't a spot on a map at all? What if it's all those relationships? Animals and plants and soil types and diseases and, I don't know, a particular angle of sunshine?

"I want people to know where they are, where home is, so I'm introducing them to their local insects. Among other things."

Saul smiled, approvingly.

"Sounds like you want to make those kinds of relationships conscious for your audience?" he suggested. "You want to make them more native?"

"Yes, exactly."

"So people won't cause havoc again, like the adelgids?"

"Well, yes. But I won't say that. It wouldn't be politic, considering."

"Oh, no, no, no. But I'm thinking, if a place is a network of relationships, is a person without those relationships really in a place? Or just kind of on the surface? Without that familiarity and interaction, you're estranged from *place*, you're a stranger."

"Yes! That's it! That's what I meant. You're not involved in the processes, so you're not here, because 'here' is the process." Very few people had ever understood her so immediately. For her third time in his company, she blushed, this time smiling.

"Are you thinking of this as a metaphor for social behavior, or just about human ecology?" Saul asked.

"Both."

He shifted in his seat thoughtfully and laced his hands together like a man at prayer, with his fingers hidden inside his doubled fists. Elzy had not thought of him as a large or imposing man—he was slim and rangy, and even somehow slight. He didn't take up space deliberately the way most men, including Andy, did. And yet he was by far the taller of the two. Elzy had to literally look up to him, even seated. If most men were trees, Saul was a long vine or an ancient shrub, a being of unfathomable roots.

"When two species come together for the first time," he began, "when they're strangers to each other, they have to relate to each other in a very generic way. If the insect can eat the plant, it's because that insect can eat pretty much any plant. It's a generalist. But over time, both adapt. The plant evolves defenses, the insect evolves ways through those defenses that don't work on all plants. They specialize. They develop that nuanced balance you're talking about, right? So in building those relationships, the species not only create *place*, they also create each other. Right?" He opened his fists

44

and showed Elzy his fingers, twined together, like in the children's game where the hands become a church, its steeple, and finally its wriggling parishioners.

"Yes," she said, nodding. "The predators and diseases were part of the adelgid's identity back in Asia. So were the tree species it ate. Here, the adelgid is less *itself*."

"Right. So, a few years ago I started to think what if humans are like that? You and I are strangers right now, so we have to treat each other like we'd treat any stranger. To me, you are a generalist, and I am a generalist to you. But if we had enough time together, we'd develop ways of interacting that we wouldn't use with anyone else. At least with each other, we would become specialists, and the relationship would then help define who we each are."

Listening to him, Elzy felt a sudden, strange longing and wondered if she were anybody's specialist, or ever would be. But she said nothing, only nodded and smiled to show she understood him.

"You're not just talking about place," he said, finally, "You're talking about home. You're talking about family."

Her smile fell before she could catch it. Somehow, Saul's words had landed as though he knew the thoughts she hadn't spoken, the real reasons for her intellectual interest, and everything she didn't have. Reflexively, she sought Andy's eyes, and he held her gaze a moment, his face unreadable. She wondered if he, too, were hearing Saul's words in personal terms, given what he'd told her last night. Maybe they were both lost, both estranged.

Saul listened to her describe the rest of her workshops, made a few more comments, and then said she should not try to adjust her program to the Troubadours. Instead, he would ask the Troubadours to adjust their stories to her. Inwardly, Elzy was astounded that a real professional would put himself out there for her like that, but outwardly she just nodded. Andy had once told her that to be treated like an equal she must act like one.

After breakfast, the three of them set out for Homestead with five out of the other ten Troubadours. The others had crops to plant that week and begged off.

Saul did not ask which of the several routes to Homestead the others wanted to take or when they wanted to start walking. Andy would have, if the trip were his to manage, though he would have made clear he wasn't ceding authority for a moment. But Saul neither gave orders nor asked for input, he just announced he was going and went. Elzy could not decide whether he was truly an autocratic leader or simply a fundamentally solitary person whom others insisted on trailing after.

In any case, the route he chose was lovely. They walked along a well-kept bike path through the forest beside the Ashuelot River, which looked narrow as a creek but had a ropy muscularity to it. It writhed across its floodplain, throwing loops and disjointed backwaters here and there, running usually out of sight behind the trees. The path, in contrast, ran mostly straight on an old railroad right-of-way, crossing the water on bridges several times as the river meandered under it. Sometimes the trail ran through riparian forest where silver maple overhung feeder creeks, their thin, curved twigs thick with tiny red flowers. In other places grew upland groves of white pine, black birch, and red oak, or the path passed through hedgerows of aging black cherry with plowed fields or horse pasture on either side. Here and there stood houses and barns. People passed, walking dogs, or riding horses or bicycles, and most of them nodded hello in a companionable way. Elzy could see that in another month or so the trail would become a long, green tunnel, but for now the skeletal trees still let in the sky.

Between the narrowness of the path and its traffic, only two people could walk comfortably abreast, so Elzy let Andy and Saul walk ahead together while she talked shop with one or another Troubadour. One of them, an attractive man named Jayden, helped her improve her imitation of a New Hampshire accent—she'd known about the transposed R's, but he taught her how to rearrange her diphthongs and harden her consonants.

They made good time and got to Homestead's town center around noon. The Troubadours planned to stay with friends about a mile farther on, but Andy and Elzy turned off to the right. They followed the road down a gentle hill, past a cemetery, to a dignified old house that looked like it had forgotten to stop. From the front the building seemed quite small, but then it went back and back, in a lumpy, added-on way, all of it quaintly elegant and set off nicely by gardens. Horses belonging to guests chewed hay companionably in a small, dusty paddock off to the side.

"I Am Siam's," declared the small, neatly lettered sign. "A Friendly Hostel, Private Rooms 3 Shares Per Nite." A *share* was the currency of the land, equal to about $20 in pre-pandemic money. The name reflected the fact that each square paperboard coin was a coupon for one person's daily share of food, water, and very basic shelter. Just as gold or silver had backed some of the currencies in the past, survival backed modern money. The inn didn't need to advertise its rate for dorm space because that was one share per night by definition.

Andy and Elzy had made reservations for private rooms, since Andy's guild would cover the bill. They stepped inside and the proprietor greeted them by name. Sort of.

"Dr. Coat! Elsa Rodriguez!" he exclaimed, shaking their hands.

"Cote," corrected Andy affably, pronouncing the "e" to rhyme with *bay*, "but please call me Andy."

"Andy Cote, I'm Siam Michaels." The man fixed his mistake graciously, without making a show of embarrassment.

"Call me Elzy," Elzy told him, as though she were also asking him to use her first name, rather than correcting his pronunciation. A lot of people called her Elsa, the name being much more popular than hers. The mistake irritated her, but she didn't want the proprietor to feel picked on. He was a big man, perhaps thirty, with a neatly trimmed black beard and green eyes. A red wool skirt sat low on his narrow hips and almost hid the musculature of his thighs.

"Are you actually Thai?" she asked Siam as he showed them around. He didn't look it, but you never know.

"No. My mother just liked the name."

The hostel was narrow but airy, with two large dorm rooms

upstairs plus half a dozen tiny singles. Elzy went into her room to unpack. When she came out, Andy was no longer in the hostel. She put her hands on her hips and frowned. She was used to him not saying where or even when he was going, and he always came back on time, but the problem was he'd left her with the laundry.

Andy normally vanished as soon as they checked in somewhere, resting, Elzy supposed, from his role as her teacher. She thought—she hoped—that he liked her and enjoyed her company, but he was at work whenever they were together. She accepted that. She normally accepted the domestic chores, too, because she was better at them. Elzy had a more detail-oriented mind and wouldn't forget to buy salt before heading off into the woods for a week, for example, as Andy had once done.

But today, she had things to do. She had to find locals to talk to in order to put the finishing touches on her act. She had to scout out locations for her workshops and learn her way around town. All that took time, but so did laundry, and she and Andy had both muddied their black professional clothes on the walk from Keene. She'd have to talk to him about this later and change their arrangement.

By mid-afternoon, arms aching from the laundry machine crank, Elzy finally hung the wet clothes on the line in the yard and got ready to explore the town. Of course, only her hiking clothes were dry, so she tried her luck in the hostel's lost-and-found and pulled out a rather nice vest. She could wear it over her spare travel outfit, the way farmers put on vests over their work clothes to go into town, and look presentable, if not quite professional. Actually, she'd look more than presentable. Modern men's and women's clothing might be alike in a general way, but the cuts and styles differed, and this vest complemented Elzy's curves wonderfully. The long fringe swayed when she shook her hips, and the neckline of the vest was low enough to show some cleavage if she undid the top two buttons of her shirt. Feeling pretty good about herself, she stepped out on the town.

Her first overall impression of Homestead was of greenness—

newly-green grass, stately green pine trees, and mostly evergreen shrubs around many of the houses. There was no true downtown, only a slight concentration of houses and some public facilities, such as a clinic, police and fire stations, two churches, and so on. The neighborhood had once been denser, since there were at least three driveways for every remaining house, but she guessed it had never been urban. Like most of the other towns that had coalesced After, Homestead was simply an area of farmland whose people all attended the same market. Its thin municipal powers were founded on that unity alone.

Because most new towns were named for the location of their markets, Elzy had assumed Homestead's would be somewhere along Homestead Highway, the street the hostel faced. Perhaps it had been once, but not anymore. After some searching, she finally found the place on the other side of the Ashuelot in a large flood-plain hay field beside a utilitarian-looking warehouse. The grounds were empty today.

She spent the afternoon exploring. She found micro-hydroelectric facilities, bio-fuel digesters, free-roaming chickens, and good cell reception. She needed to talk to locals, but couldn't connect with any. She hadn't expected to see many people out and about on a Tuesday, but the problem was that the few she did see either ignored her or stared at her from a distance and then hurried away. It was both inconvenient and bizarre.

The afternoon came to a head for Elzy when a policewoman stopped her and curtly asked her to identify herself, explaining that there had been some concerns.

"You don't look like you belong around here," the cop added, rather pointedly.

Elzy was indignant and explained who she was in terms that made clear she was both a fellow cop and the daughter of her town's police chief. She had no ID card to show. None existed anymore. In the small communities of the modern world, everybody knew everyone else, and travelers depended on references that could be checked right away by cell phone. Elzy gave two references, Katrina

Rodriguez, her CO (and mother), and John Suarez, the dean of students back at Tri-River College. She knew that Officer Diliberto (the woman wore a name tag) would not call either of them. The local cop had had no legitimate reason to stop her and would not be in a hurry to advertise that fact to another town's police chief.

Embarrassed to have hassled a fellow officer, Diliberto backed down. Elzy turned away, very much on her dignity.

But she didn't feel like much of a winner. *Did I really just threaten to tell my mother on a bully?* she asked herself. She'd been a good cop, and before that she'd been a good vigilante. She was smart, fearless, and cool-headed under stress. But she didn't feel like the competent professional everybody said she was. Law enforcement had never been her own idea for a career, and sometimes she still felt like a little kid who'd been inexplicably handed a gun.

She still didn't understand why the locals distrusted her. Whatever the reason, walking around town seemed like it might actually be counterproductive so, at a loss for what to do next, she went back to the hostel, read for a while, then checked on the laundry lines. Her tunic and slacks had dried, so she dressed and headed out again, with some trepidation. She still had to find some locals to talk to, so she went to Homestead's multimedia center but found no patrons there. The clerk gave her directions to the town's one pub.

The pub sat right on Route 10 and shared a low, gray building with a post office and a rather run-down looking hostel. Elzy guessed the latter catered mostly to pub patrons too drunk or stoned to bike home and travelers too tired or ill-informed to walk the half mile to the more upscale I-Am-Siam's. A man sat under a blooming crab-apple tree in front of the hostel's porch and smoked a hookah. When Elzy tried to greet him, he blew a smoke-ring in her face. She ignored him thereafter.

Inside, the pub was warm, dark, and almost deserted. The main room smelled very faintly of alcohol, tobacco smoke, old wood, and fried food. As her eyes adjusted, she spotted a couple of farmers and a preacher in one corner booth and three guild members in medical-white tunics in another. The farmers waved in a friendly way and went back to talking among themselves. The white-coats offered her a chair, so she joined them. They were playing chess.

The three were nurses just finished with their shift at the clinic. When Elzy confessed she did not play chess, they happily taught her. After losing one game and tying the next, she told them about her afternoon's confrontation. She wasn't seeking comfort so much as useful information, but her new friends misunderstood her and offered comfort anyway. That was OK. She had expected it, and learned useful things from their sympathetic anger.

"I still don't understand why they acted like that," Elzy said, toying with a pawn.

"People are idiots," said the female nurse, whose name was Mia.

"People are scared," explained Landon, one of the two men. "You know, five guys have been murdered this year? And they haven't caught the people who did it. It could be anybody. It *could* be you, for all Vivian knows. Not that I'm accusing you, it's just freaky." Vivian was Officer Diliberto. Of course they all knew her.

"Vivian is a jerk-wad," offered Ethan, the other man. "She needs to be out catching the killers, not hassling visitors. What would we do if people didn't want to come here anymore?"

"I think some people would like that, honestly," Landon replied. "Not me, but…."

"Couldn't it equally be one of you? A local?" suggested Elzy, who wasn't accusing anybody either.

"Well, yeah, of course. But nobody wants to think it's one of us." Landon seemed uncomfortable.

"You three seem friendly," Elzy remarked, allowing her comment to sound like a compliment. Really it was a simple observation. Everyone at the pub, not counting the obviously intoxicated man outside, had been very welcoming.

"You're a guild-applicant," explained Mia. "You're not just some random stranger."

Had the problem been that Elzy was dressed like a 'random stranger' earlier?

"You make it sound as though we treat outsiders badly," said

Ethan. "We don't. You come here, it's like you're our guest."

"Then what happened today?" asked Elzy.

"I don't know," said Mia.

"I don't know," echoed Landon. "Are you sure people *wouldn't* talk to you? That sounds weird. Maybe they didn't see you or something."

"Is it because I'm Mexican-American, do you think?" Back home, there had been some tensions among the various local ethnic groups. These people all seemed to be Yankees.

"No!"

"No!"

"You're Mexican? You don't look it. You're darker, and you have that hair."

Elzy fingered one of her braids almost reflexively. Her hair was dark, very fine, thick, and tightly curled. Yes, her hair and her color were both unusual, part of her inheritance from her mother, an Afro-Mexican originally from Vera Cruz. She stood out in New England, where everyone she had seen so far had European-type hair and (with the marginal exception of Saul) pink skin. As Landon set up for the next game, she grew quiet, wondering if she had just experienced something else her mother had told her about—racism.

Elzy did not think of herself in racial terms. Most people her age and younger did not. In the social chaos after the pandemic, communities had turned inward, and ethnicity had become much more important, overwhelming and supplanting color. Then, too, the collapse of all institutions and the entire economy had leveled most playing fields. Skin color just didn't matter much anymore. But she knew her mother had grown up in another world and that some of the old attitudes persisted in places, especially among older people. The thought that such bias might have reached out of the past and regarded her today gave Elzy a curiously vulnerable feeling. It was as though she had suddenly discovered she were naked in a crowd and had been so the whole time and hadn't known.

But was Homestead really some pocket of lingering racist animosity? Surely Andy would have warned her if it was. Or would

Andy know? Perhaps you had to be brown-colored to notice this sort of thing. And if Homesteaders were racist, why did they show it on the street and not in the pub? Or back at the hostel?

Puzzling over these things cost Elzy the chess game and she surrendered her spot at the table to Mia. She continued puzzling.

Perhaps it was only what the nurses had said, that the people here were scared by the recent, unexplained crime wave and getting jumpy about outsiders. When she wore guild member black, her tunic explained her presence and everyone was much friendlier. But then why didn't the nurses believe that her experience was real? They lived here and should know how outsiders were treated.

Maybe the problem was a combination of clothing, circumstance, and color? Maybe subtle bias worked like a multiplier, so that the people could honestly say they had no problem with brown people, they were only jumpy about strangers, but because Elzy was brown, they perceived her strangeness as somehow squared? When she dressed as a guild-applicant, there was no suspicion for bias to multiply so the problem was invisible. It would have been equally invisible had she not arrived in the middle of a crime-wave.

The idea had merit, and Elzy liked the thought that the day's confrontation was a result of an unusual combination of circumstances. She watched Landon and Mia play (Mia was winning) and started asking questions again, about chess and about the local culture.

She stayed at the pub all evening, letting the three nurses, and several other patrons who came and went, tell her all about the town and its people and how they honestly believed they always welcomed strangers.

That night, back at the hostel, Elzy wrote down everything she had learned and made adjustments to her act. Finding herself alone, she rehearsed in the common room and then read until Andy got back. She didn't like to go to sleep until she knew he was in safely. He acknowledged her with a wave and went to bed. The hostel was silent, but for the movement of a small, gray cat. She fell asleep in her chair.

She woke in the morning to the rumble of ox carts, people coming in to market. Most farmers seldom left their farms during the week, so market days were social occasions that attracted people whether they had anything to buy and sell or not. Over eight hundred people lived in Homestead, and most of them would pack themselves into the tiny town center for a few days. Families with young children, or some other reason to minimize travel, would stay over in town rather than commute a mile or three every day. Even as she showered and brushed her teeth, Elzy could hear people checking in downstairs. She had to weave her way through knots of people and piles of luggage to get through the common room on her way to wash her breakfast dishes in the kitchen.

Around nine, Andy came downstairs, freshly showered and looking handsome in his tunic and cowl, ready to get back to work.

The first order of business was to find the market coordinator and check in. They had no idea what he looked like or where he was, but they asked around the market grounds and found him at last, a busy and somewhat distracted man. He handed out a cloth bag full of round wooden coins, made a note on his tablet, and was on to something else.

The coins were credit counters, good only in their town of origin. Rather than asking guild members to document their expenses for reimbursement, town councils usually just issued the counters. Local businesses could then exchange the counters for real money later. The bag of coins Elzy held was therefore just a limited line of credit which no one expected them to exhaust, but—

"Andy, there's *twenty shares* here."

"Yeah, that's about right." He seemed a bit distracted, as though he were looking for something.

"Two people, for two markets, that's close to two shares a day and our lodging is *already covered*." She was used to the budget of subsistence farming where most wealth is never expressed in money. Her salary as a cop had been pocket-change.

Her incredulity snagged Andy's attention.

"Actually, I'd get that much if I were alone," he reminded her, smiling. Guild applicants didn't get paid, though Andy always shared with his apprentices. "And all of that's for today. We can get more tomorrow, if we want it."

Elzy's eyes grew very round. Andy wasn't personally rich, no one was After, but he obviously operated on a completely different financial scale than she did. He laughed and told her that when she joined a guild, she'd get that much herself.

Still laughing a little, Andy took a half-share coin for his own lunch and went off to attend the first of a series of meetings on predator/farmer conflicts. Elzy took the rest of the coins and went shopping.

Everything from spring greens to vintage plastic chairs to musical instruments was for sale somewhere among the rows of tables. Medical specialists, lawyers, barbers, and face-painters saw clients in brightly colored tents. Grilling foods sent their aromas across the grassy square, while street performers and corner preachers competed for the attention of passersby. The disparate melodies of half a dozen scattered musicians conflicted and harmonized weirdly as Elzy moved about from one row of stalls to the next. For Elzy, a farm girl and small-town cop in a rural age, markets always seemed dazzlingly cosmopolitan.

Mostly, she had to buy travel food, things that kept well, like instant bean mix and cornmeal. She also had to restock their store of basic medical supplies, especially NSAID pills and tape for blisters. But she had nineteen and a half shares in her pocket. There was no reason to limit herself to essentials.

She was busy admiring a pair of shearling slippers when the stall owner spoke to her.

"Two shares, Miss. And that's a deal. They're the last I made from a good hide."

He was right, it was a great price. The slippers were well-made and very soft.

"Oh, I'd love them but I can't," she explained. "I'm traveling. There's no room in my pack for extras."

"Too bad. See anything else you'd like?"

Elzy browsed through the man's wares, all high-quality leather goods. He let her look without trying to push her into anything, which she appreciated. He seemed to be about forty, handsome except for his skin, which was pitted and scarred from the acne of his youth. She liked his eyes and his rough, capable hands. She examined a row of women's leather vests, a decorative belt, and a couple of cell phone cases.

"You did all this yourself?"

"Mostly."

"Impressive."

"Thank you. What do you do? You look like a teacher or something. Except you don't have one of those hood-things."

"I'm only a guild-applicant." She looked over at the man and caught his blank look. "Sort of like an apprentice? I'm building up my resume under the supervision of my application-sponsor. When he says I'm ready, I'll apply to join a professional guild and get my very own hood-thing." She smiled a little, mimicking his phrase, teasing.

"You probably think I'm a dumb-ass for not knowing," the leather worker said, sounding touchingly vulnerable. "I've seen people dressed like you for years, now, and I've never asked how it all works."

"Are you kidding? I can barely sew! If I could do all this, I wouldn't care what else I didn't know!" It wasn't exactly true, but as intended it made the man perk up. He had a gorgeous smile.

"You still haven't told me what you do," he asked. "What are you apprenticed *for*?"

"Oh, I'm an environmental educator. I'm the opening act tonight. The comedienne."

"You're *Elzy Rodriguez*? Wow, they didn't tell us you'd be hot."

Elzy blushed and let him talk her into buying two small knapsacks for use around town, one for herself and one for Andy. They cost three shares each.

She shepherded her remaining coins more carefully but bought everything on her list, plus she helped herself to local specialties, like goat-milk fudge and blueberry chutney, and picked up a lot of the caramel candies Andy liked. The other merchants she dealt with flirted with her, too, just as the leather worker had. She wondered whether, now that she was dressed like a guild-apprentice, not a "random stranger," the multiplying effect of her color was making her seem strange in a good way—appealingly exotic. Either way, she flirted back.

Around five o'clock the vendors started to pack up. By six, all the tents were down and the market grounds were clear, except for a ring of carts around the edge and a low stage at one end. A trio of jugglers occupied the stage while technicians set up a network of wireless speakers and rows of folding chairs. The audience coalesced.

At 6:30, the market coordinator took the stage and introduced Saul to a big round of applause. They knew him here, Elzy gathered. Saul drew out his introduction of her for nearly a minute, building audience anticipation, while she searched the crowd. She couldn't find Andy. Was he not here? He was supposed to watch her perform, to evaluate her. That was part of his job. She finally asked a stranger beside her to guard her bags, Saul said her name, and she took the stage, heart hammering. More applause. She scanned the audience and spotted—at last!—Andy. Her body relaxed. She began her act.

"Hi, hi, glad to be here," she began casually, like almost any other stand-up comic would. "Anyone from *New Hampshire* here tonight?" She acted surprised—and vaguely alarmed—when everyone laughed and raised their hands. "Wow, *all* of you?" She ran a hand through her braids and chewed on her lip in an exaggerated show of nervousness. All her comedy was founded on such reactions. Her jokes would not have been very funny written down, without the accompaniment of her body language and timing.

She explained that she was from a place called Pennsylvania, as though her audience members might not have heard of it, and she started describing her surprise and disorientation now that she was in New England.

"I keep hearing this wild accent," she said. "It's like, you guys don't put your R's where I expect them to be. It's confusing, you know?" Making fun of a regional speech pattern would have been a cheap shot, but that wasn't what she was doing—she was making fun of herself for being a confused outsider. Her own accent was not exactly typical of Pennsylvania, being influenced by the softer Mexican consonants of her mother's friends, but she did not sound like a Yankee, and she exaggerated her out-of-state speech for effect. Within a very few minutes, she had worked herself up into a dialogue in which she played both parts, her outlandishly Mid-Atlantic self and a thickly accented New Englander, neither able to understand the other.

Of course, less than a third of the people in Homestead actually had the accent, which had begun to fade even before the pandemic. Those who did have it had no difficulty understanding Elzy, nor did she have any trouble understanding them. But she knew that the people here identified with the New Hampshire speech, whether they actually used it or not, and that it was the quickest, surest way she could tweak their regional identity.

From accents she continued on to food, the weather, and, above all, plant species, all of which she claimed to find worryingly different from what she knew at home. The idea that a traveler might feel overwhelmed and panicked by spotting too many unfamiliar trees was, of course, ludicrous—just as ludicrous as asking a crowd of locals whether anyone was from the state they were all standing in. She made her silly premise seem just believable enough to be funny (as opposed to plain bizarre) through her delivery and by carefully evoking a very real issue—the different regions of the country had been diverging culturally since the pandemic. Interstate travelers were rare and the information online was mostly either utilitarian or twenty years out of date. The people of Homestead had no real idea what someone from Pennsylvania would think of their town. Their ignorance embarrassed them. A seed of truth prompted laughter the way an irritating grain of sand can prompt a pearl.

And through the laughter and the bald ridiculousness of her

cartoon panic, Elzy's real message slipped through unimpeded— that a type of forest belonged to a people as much as their accent did. Those in her audience began to think perhaps there was something special about this landscape that an outsider from Pennsylvania wouldn't understand.

At the apex of her pretend anxiety, Elzy stopped, as though she'd had a new thought or some fresh revelation.

"But then, you know, I started to look closer," she began. And she described plants and insects and landforms all over again, but this time in fascinated, loving detail, eliciting fond laughter over familiar oddities. The research she'd conducted the previous day allowed her to set her plant and insect descriptions in local, well-known places and to weave in the cultural details the people were most proud of. Just as she'd linked the area's natural history to its accent and its cooking, now she made its spring wildflowers and the shape of its wooded hills seem like just another example of the pragmatic generosity Homestead offered even to strangers.

"You people really know how to make a girl from Pennsylvania feel at home," she finished.

The audience, warmed and charmed, erupted in applause. Saul joined her on stage and asked the audience, rhetorically, whether she was great or what, triggering further eruptions. When they quieted, he put in a plug for Elzy's workshops over the next two days, and she stepped down into the crowd, pleased with herself. Aside from a couple of mistakes no one else would ever notice, she'd nailed it.

None of it was true, of course. She had not felt overwhelmed by the local flora, obviously, and she did not feel at home here. She'd been treated like an unwanted alien, but even if she had not, she would still have felt out of place. She felt out of place everywhere. But she was used to that, and tonight, full of triumph, she paid no attention to sadness.

She went to find first her bags and then Andy. He offered her a word or two of congratulations and accepted the new knapsack with surprised pleasure, but by then the first of the Troubadours had begun to perform. Further conversation would have been rude.

They stayed to watch the story-tellers, both out of courtesy and out of interest, as the sky turned yellow and then orange behind the row of white pines along the main road to the west. Bats worked the air for insects stirred up by the many human feet. Along the river and in the flood control swales frogs began to sing. Each story lasted about twenty minutes. Some sounded like traditional retellings of ancient myths, while others were obviously contemporary. Two out of the five storytellers performed in poetry, and one of these sometimes broke out in song. Saul himself did not perform, except as master of ceremonies, but the others were fantastic and every one of them wove his or her story around Elzy's theme of belonging.

When the last Troubadour was done, there was a pause in the program while a group of musicians set up their equipment on the stage and tuned their instruments. The sun had just dropped below the horizon, and technicians activated colored LED lights on the scattered speaker stands against the coming night. Audience members helped put away folding chairs. Andy shouldered his new bag and turned to make his way through the crowd.

"You're not staying to dance?" Elzy asked, though she'd never actually seen him dancing. She didn't know if he could. He laughed a little.

"Entropy happens to us all," he told her. "You want me to take your bag back with me?"

"Sure. Help yourself to the caramels inside it."

"Thanks. Enjoy yourself."

And she did.

The next day, Thursday, there was little buying or selling at the market. Most vendors did not bother to set up. The day was reserved instead for social events, community group meetings, and education. The tradition of market workshops had begun as a way for survivors to trade skills after the pandemic and had evolved into a major institution, the most convenient and most enjoyable place to go to learn. For most young children, it was still the only option, other than their parents and the Internet.

Elzy taught five workshops, a grueling schedule, though she was pleased to get a decent turnout for all of them. Andy audited two of hers in his capacity as her application sponsor, plus taught two of his own, which Elzy was disappointed not to have time to attend.

Friday morning was similar, except that the two workshops each of them taught had to compete for attention with commerce. The vendors were selling off the last of their wares at a discount. By the afternoon, when the crowds finally headed home, Elzy was exhausted. She flopped down on the couch back at the hostel, dreading the pile of feedback forms she still had to review.

"I'm the one who's supposed to be tired," Andy said. "I'm the old guy." But he did not seem old—or tired. Elzy, shamed by her teacher's stamina, sat up and went over the past few days with him, reviewing her performance and her workshops for anything he thought she should improve. He agreed with her guesses about Officer Diliberto and bias, and suggested she email either Austin Hale, the agronomy professor back at school, or Alejandra Gonzales, the literature professor, since both had had experience as people of color in academia before the pandemic and might have some insight to share. She picked Austin, since she had taken his entomology class and got along well with him. The environmental education track didn't include creative literature so she wasn't sure she had even met Alejandra.

"What do you want to do tomorrow?" Andy asked her, finally. She was booked for a second market in Homestead, but they could do whatever they liked in the days between.

"I don't know, I hadn't thought about it."

"Want to climb Mount Monadnock with me?"

Andy had never before invited her to do something with him that wasn't obviously school or work related. She had expected him to vanish again and to stay vanished, more or less, until Wednesday. Yet here he was, inviting her on an adventure. Elzy's exhaustion evaporated. Of course she wanted to go with him.

Chapter 3
Differential Survival

Any solitary mountain created by the erosion of the land around it is *a* monadnock, but only one such mountain is *the* Monadnock, the one from which all others take their name, the pyramid of schist and quartzite Elzy had seen on her way into Keene. She had not hoped to climb it because it rose out of the rolling landscape ten miles away from anywhere she and Andy had any reason to be, yet here she was, on her way.

A little college crouched at the foot of the mountain, and Andy had contacts there. Either they had asked him, or he had asked them about visiting as a guest lecturer, she wasn't sure which. Either way, they both now had free room and board at the campus for a couple of days.

They traveled light, with only a couple of essentials packed in their new knapsacks, plus Andy's tablet and their season's supply of cash. He didn't trust the locks at the hostel. They stayed off the graveled main roads and stuck to public rights-of-way through newly plowed fields and old, still-asphalted streets pock-marked with neglect and whiskered by weeds. It was an easy day for a good mood, warm and sunny, with the wispy cloud streaks that foretell rain within two days. They ate a very early lunch in the ruins of a small airport because Andy thought it funny to sit and eat in the middle of a runway.

Two small airplanes, junk for twenty years but not yet recycled, sat on the tarmac waiting hopefully for long-dead pilots. Elzy chewed her sandwich and tried to imagine airplanes flying—not these little ones, hardly bigger than a glider or a drone, but those big airliners, white, shining goose-necked things taking to the sky with a roar that rattled the earth. She shook her head. She'd seen pictures.

"I learned a lot of my trees here," Andy commented, fondly.

"*Here?*" There weren't any trees on or around the airstrip, just crumbling asphalt and, beyond that, winter-flattened grasses and scraggly, leafless shrubs.

"Over there, on the edge of the airport property. There are a lot of different conifers planted, plus a neat little black spruce swamp. Want to see?"

"Sure!"

This is what they did, Andy turning every twist of their journey into a kind of never-ending field trip. He rarely taught field classes back on campus—his interests ran more to the abstract—but he did know a lot about the land. He repeated what he knew, usually by free-association, as they traveled, because Elzy needed to learn. As an environmental educator, she would need a detailed familiarity with the environment of her students. She knew that the next time they came upon a black spruce swamp, he'd quiz her. And she would pass the quiz.

Late that afternoon, after walking down a long, overgrown two-track through an oak and pine forest, they came out into a small clearing dominated by a single large house. A flock of variously-sized tents stood scattered through the woods nearby and clothes and table napkins hung drying from lines between the trees. It was the entirety of the Monadnock College campus. The mountain rose behind it, the slope faintly visible through the still-skeletal spring oaks.

Like most modern colleges, Monadnock was really a research

facility that took on students as a sideline. Andy's employer back in Pennsylvania was one of the few schools able to cover most of its expenses through tuition. There just weren't enough young people anymore for the old business plans to work. Elzy knew all this and wasn't at all surprised by the tiny campus.

They went inside and Andy showed her around and performed introductions. Elzy ate dinner with the two-dozen or so students and found them friendly and welcoming, but she and her teacher both bunked in the faculty dorms. In the morning they packed lunches from the school kitchen and headed uphill.

"This was once the second or third most-climbed mountain in the world," commented Andy.

"What rank does it have now?"

"Oh, I don't know. I don't know who climbs what mountains anymore."

"We climb this one."

"That we do."

"Andy?"

"Yes, Elzy?"

"This college is focused on forestry and climate change. That seems an odd pair. The mountain is forested, but why climate change?"

"See if you can figure it out while we're here."

"OK, I will."

The day was warm and the path gentle and scenic. Elzy kept an eye on her surroundings as she walked, expecting a quiz at any time.

She had grown up thinking of global warming as a problem of the past. No one used fossil fuels at all anymore, and most people ignored problems larger than their own farms and counties anyway. In college, though, she had learned that anthropogenic climate change was not over.

Warming takes time, so the carbon dioxide released twenty years ago was still heating the sky. And although the age of fossil fuel was over, old gas wells, landfills, and melting permafrost still leaked methane. Forest dieback set in motion by the changing climate and the large-scale logging of the past liberated unknown tons of carbon dioxide. On the other hand, at least in North America and probably elsewhere, some forests were re-growing, sucking up carbon, greening abandoned cities and suburbs. Did the rate of sequestration equal or exceed the rate of emission? No one could say. There were no research satellites left, few ground-based sensors, and very few people capable of analyzing the sparse data intelligently. And whatever the climate was doing, no one had a clear picture of how living systems were responding. There just weren't enough researchers or enough money to find out. But Elzy could think of no connection between all of that and a mountain in New England. She had a feeling the answer was staring her right in the face.

But then Andy wanted to show her one of the college's study plots and led her off-trail. He couldn't find the plot and then couldn't find the trail again, either. Climate change flew right out of Elzy's head.

"Getting lost can be a good thing," asserted Andy after a moment, half-smiling. "It's when the surprises happen." And he set out confidently uphill. It is difficult to get too badly lost on a mountain with only one summit.

As they kept going up, the forest began to change.

The first thing Elzy noticed was a kind of disorganization or ratty-ness. Somehow, the woods reminded her of an old, worn rug. The impression puzzled her until she realized that a lot of the trees around her were dead or dying. Most of them were spruces. There were living spruces as well, sometimes large clumps of them, plus old, tangled blowdowns of indeterminate species, victims of summer squalls or maybe Hurricane Odette. But the dead and dying spruces predominated, standing skeletal and broken, draped with lichen or sometimes still clothed in brown needles. And wherever the canopy was thus opened up, young deciduous trees, their buds swelling, were coming up, knee high, waist-high, or taller, according to the age of the opening. It was this variability, the seemingly disorganized decay and regrowth, which made the woods look ratty. Elzy would have asked Andy what had happened to the trees, but she knew he'd only ask her to figure it out.

Then, almost between one step and the next, they walked into an unusually large patch of healthy spruces, one so big that Elzy could not see any other kind of forest, except by looking back the way she had come. The place had an utterly different feel, all cool black shadow and primeval reserve. Thin patches of old snow persisted in the shade.

Elzy stopped and looked around, and Andy watched her look. After a moment, her eye fell on a particular tree. It was not a spruce, though its needles were just as short. It had smooth gray bark covered with small oval swellings.

"It's a sap-tree!" Elzy exclaimed. She reached up to grab a branch and inspect the twigs and needles. Back in Pennsylvania she had learned a lot of species in a herbarium from twig samples and drawings alone, so she needed the twigs to find the tree's proper name in her mind.

"Balsam fir, *Abies balsamea*," she announced. "I didn't know balsam fir was the same as sap-tree!" She reached for the trunk. "I used to love these! Me and my brother used to…"

But even as her fingers expertly found and popped one of the sap blisters, Elzy's eyes de-focused. Andy saw her face go slack in shock.

"My brother!" she whispered.

Andy watched helplessly as Elzy's mind slid away into the past. Her eyes weren't seeing, or at least they weren't seeing Mt. Monadnock. She stumbled away from the tree towards him, pawing at the air, blindly trying to find some sort of reference point. Andy caught her hand in his and sat down with her. She squeezed him so hard the shape of her bones stood out in her knuckles, but Andy showed no sign of pain.

"Don't resist it," he told her, "let it happen, see what comes."

Little by little, Elzy seemed to hear him. Her grip relaxed a little and her breathing started to normalize. Her eyes flooded but did not spill over. She could see again, but she did not look at Andy.

"I had a brother," she explained, wonderingly. "I don't know how I could have forgotten him. His name was Jamie. We played in woods like these."

"What do you remember?"

"His name, Jamie, that he was a little older than me, but not much, and we played in woods like these but—not on a mountain, I don't think. And then I played in those woods alone."

"What else?" Andy prompted. He was totally focused. If anyone else existed in that moment besides Elzy, he did not show it. He could have taken her entire weight in his one, stable hand. "What else do you remember?"

"Nothing!" She looked at him directly and her eyes showed fear, terror, not sadness. "It was all so clear a moment ago, but it's gone now, like a dream when you wake up. All I remember is playing with Jamie in woods like these and then I played alone."

He returned her gaze for some seconds. He didn't know what to say, but opened his mouth anyway. She looked away and spoke before he could.

"I had a home, but I don't know where it is."

"Did your parents tell you anything about it? Anything at all about your past?"

Elzy shook her head and shifted her position a bit. She was coming out of her fugue more fully, returning to adulthood and intellect.

"My parents divorced when I was very little. My Daddy got custody of me—and of Jamie, I guess—and we lived with him. We survived the pandemic, Daddy and I did, I mean. We lived together for a few years, but then Daddy got sick. I remember that part, at least the idea of it, Daddy being sick, knowing we would have to leave. Because there were no doctors. Or maybe there was no medicine, or something. No treatment for Daddy. And somebody had to take care of me, when he....I don't remember any details, where that was or what he said, but I remember knowing it. Daddy found my mother on the internet, and he brought me to her in Pennsylvania. He died before he could tell my mom where we'd been or what we'd been doing. I think in the beginning she was so excited to have me back she didn't ask a lot of questions. And they didn't...like to talk to each other. I could see that. My memories, my real memories, with scenes and images and everything, mostly pick up then, at Mom's place.

"The only thing Mom told me, other than about the divorce, was that Daddy must have taught me to hunt, because I could shoot straight. I could track. I knew how to be quiet. Mom taught me to hunt all over again—but she taught me to hunt people, human beings. The farm security team needed more members. I started training when I was eleven and joined when I was fourteen. When I was eighteen, they organized the town police force and I joined. I could have stayed there, been a cop all my life, but I've always been a science nerd. I wanted...something else. So, when the state gave Mom her education benefit and she transferred it to me, I went to school. Now I'm here."

"Now you are here." Andy's heart wrung for this strange woman-girl who thought nothing whatever of walking hundreds of miles just to get somewhere, who'd had to "hunt" human beings to protect her family, and who could also be as innocent and vulnerable as a child. But she would not thank him for noticing her vulnerability, she and he were alike in that way, and he did not know what to do about her sudden collapse. He felt so ridiculously awkward in the face of her tears. So he did nothing, except to continue to hold her hand and wait, for as long as she needed him. "How old were you, when the pandemic happened?"

"I was six. I was ten when I came to my mom's."

"That's—" Andy checked but did not explain his surprise and then continued in a different tone of voice. "That's young. And you don't...but you do remember your father?"

Elzy nodded noncommittally and sniffled. Andy handed her a handkerchief and she blew her nose.

"I remember his personality, the way he looked, the way he smelled—wood smoke and canvas. I remember what knowing him was like, but I don't remember any actual scenes with him in it, if that makes sense."

It was Andy's turn to nod. Elzy looked out over the rolling low country through the dark trees and shivered. Sitting so long, they were both starting to cool down in the mountain air.

"Why didn't I remember my brother?" Elzy asked. "Or at least remember him dying? I thought people usually keep traumatic memories?"

"You were probably very sick yourself, at the time," Andy explained, gently. "You probably had the pandemic as well. It brings a fever—you aren't aware of much. When you recovered, your brother was simply gone. You played alone. It's very difficult to remember something when the people around you don't act like it's real."

"You mean my parents wanted me to forget?"

"Maybe *they* wanted to forget. I think your mother did. I assume he was her child too, your natural brother, yet she never mentioned him to you. Tragedy is funny, loss is strange. Some people want to remember forever and others can't wait to forget."

Elzy turned at his words and looked at him very carefully for a few seconds.

"It must have been very tough," she said.

"Yes," Andy said, and swallowed hard. When he spoke again, his voice had changed, become intellectual and ordinary. "You know, there aren't very many places in the northeast that have spruce-fir forests at low elevations. And it must have been in the northeast, because if it wasn't, your father couldn't have emailed your mother in Pennsylvania—the internet was only regional sixteen years ago. The fact that you were in the same place both before and after your brother died suggests you are remembering the place where you lived then, the place where you grew up. If you could remember anything else, we might be able to figure out where you were. If that's what you want."

"Of course that's what I want! I'm tired of not belonging anywhere! But I don't remember anything else."

"You didn't remember this much twenty minutes ago."

"Has it been only twenty minutes?"

"Less."

Elzy shifted again and looked down at Andy's hand, still holding hers, as though she'd forgotten it until just now. She let him go.

"Are you ready to go on?" he asked her.

"Yes." She stood and stretched, stiff with the cold. He stood as well and looked at her a moment, unsure. She looked back, also unsure, and then decided for them both and hugged him. He held her tightly while she let him, but when they disengaged he turned and headed up the hill and she followed him, all professional decorum again. Neither of them spoke of the incident again, not directly.

Up on the summit cone, a cold wind swept around bare rock and shrubby, sapling trees. They ate their lunch perched on angular fins of gray stone, and Andy told Elzy about the fire that had killed the forest on the peak and the tourists whose trampling feet had kept it from re-growing for generations. It was starting to re-grow now, but the young trees were still small enough to leave an open view from the highest rocks, three hundred and sixty degrees of forest, farm-fields, and a few isolated clusters of buildings. Clouds were moving in, the weather starting to change. They found the trail they would have come up on if they hadn't gotten lost and headed back down the mountain.

It was only on the way down, when they walked out of the snowy spruce-fir forest and back into the deciduous woods of spring, that Elzy suddenly realized what the mountain had to do with global warming.

Red spruce and balsam fir are cold-climate trees, she had known that already. That's why they grow on top of mountains. So, of course, the dying trees she'd seen were the mark of warmer conditions moving up slope—climate change. The little college must be using the mountain to study the effect of climate change on ecological zonation or something similar. But, she also remembered that these species don't actually grow very well in cold climates. They dominate such places only because other trees can't grow there at all. Left alone, the spruces and firs would have prospered in a warmer world, but they could not fight the insects and the competition from the faster-growing broad-leaved trees and pines that the milder conditions unleashed. An entire community, the spruces and firs and all the plants and animals dependent on them, was collapsing in the new and gentler world.

Elzy thought about those plants on her way down the mountain, about who survives and who doesn't and why.

That evening and all the next day, Andy taught, lectured, and spoke with students and colleagues in the few big, artfully appointed rooms of the little school. Elzy audited every one of his classes, but he hardly interacted with her. In class, his glance swept over her as though he did not know her at all. She hadn't gone to the classes for his attention, of course, and she knew he was focused on his work, but for the first time his distance bothered her. She did not know what to make of his caring for her up on the mountain.

All night and day it rained, a cold, wet pounding she could hear on the roof right above her head as she slept. When the rain finally stopped around dawn Tuesday morning, Elzy woke in the sudden quiet and lay in her cot and listened to the soft breathing of the other women in her small room. She tried to wrap her mind around the fact of her brother and failed.

In the morning after breakfast, she and Andy headed back towards Homestead across wet ground under a sky gray as glue. The air still felt damp. A fitful breeze spat cold at them now and then.

"Is it just that we're so much farther north than I'm used to, or is this cold for April?" asked Elzy.

"It's within the range of normal, I'd say," replied Andy, looking at the sky. "You know, I can remember snow on the ground in April around here? A couple of inches."

"Did you have to walk uphill both ways to school, too?" she teased him. She knew perfectly well that he was right, the climate had been colder, but older people always said that sort of thing and, true or not, it had become a cliché.

He laughed. He had a wonderfully boyish laugh, like a grin that had boiled over showing a row of tiny, well-spaced teeth.

"Did you know there's a stretch of the Appalachian Trail that actually is uphill both ways?" he asked.

"Yeah?"

"Yeah. Well, on average, anyway. The Trail goes up and down a lot." He traced zigzag mountains in the air with his finger.

"How do you figure?"

"OK, so, the highest point on the Appalachian Trail is on top of Clingman's Dome, in Tennessee, right?"

"OK," agreed Elzy. She didn't actually know the relative elevations of the various Appalachian peaks, but she had no reason to doubt Andy.

"So, since Clingman's Dome is higher than the northern terminus at Mt. Katahdin, in Maine, a northbound hiker averages downhill from Clingman's Dome on."

"OK."

"Well, the *lowest* point on the trail is at the Hudson River crossing."

"That was the lowest point on the whole Trail?" They had followed that section of the A.T. on their way north from Pennsylvania.

"Yeah, it all averages uphill from there. But since the Hudson crossing is north of Clingman's Dome, that section is already averaging downhill, for a northbound hiker. So the section of trail from the Hudson River to Mt. Katahdin is both uphill and downhill if you're heading north, and is therefore uphill both ways."

"Brilliant. Is thinking up things like that what geniuses normally do in their spare time?"

"Well, we could try to take over the world, but that usually takes money."

Andy used to protest when Elzy called him a genius, but she'd noticed he no longer bothered. She grinned at him for a moment and then became serious.

"Andy, I'm sorry I fell asleep the other night."

"What other night?"

"In Keene, when you were telling me your story. I'm sorry I fell asleep."

"Oh, that. Thank you." His thanks sounded entirely genuine. Her sleeping must really have bothered him.

"Will you tell me more? The last thing I remember, you were sick in the desert, though obviously you must have survived it."

"Sure. Now?"

"Why not? I won't fall asleep, walking."

"No, you won't."

Andy tried to remember where he had been in the story, how much he had told her already.

"Yes, I survived. I woke up and the fever was gone, the disease was gone. But my lungs still felt like shit. And I was stranded in the middle of the desert, in February, with only a filthy, wet sleeping bag to keep me warm. I remember thinking, great, I've survived the plague, but now I'm going to die of exposure because of my stupid truck.

"But a couple of friends of mine had a ranch nearby, and they were out on horseback and happened to find me. I was still really weak, I could barely ride. Later, they went back to get the rest of my food and supplies, but my whole truck was gone. I hope that water saved somebody."

He thought about that truck and its contents sometimes. His whole remaining life, except his son, had been in it—his cell, his computer, his GPS, his notebooks...his wallet, with his driver's license and his bank cards, had been in the glove compartment, any way for anyone to contact him or for him to prove who he was or what he'd been doing, all gone. He had been a husband, a father, a brother, a son. He had been Dr. Andrew Cote, PhD., and he'd ridden away from all of it on a horse.

"Elzy, how much do you know about the pandemic and the early transition?"

"I know civilization collapsed, but I don't really understand why. Like, I know that without petroleum it was very hard to transport food and a lot of the people lived in cities, away from farms, so they starved. But I don't understand how a disease could end the Age of Petroleum in the first place or why the rest of civilization collapsed. Unless it was that everybody just went crazy from fear of the disease and rioted and the riots destroyed everything? I know there were riots."

"There were. Understand that we lived in a very big network—a network of networks—that had almost no resiliency. Do you know 'for want of a nail'?"

"I don't know, what is it?"

"I don't know, it's a Thing. Like a poem or a saying? 'For want of

73

a nail, the shoe was lost, for want of a shoe, the horse was lost, for want of a horse, the rider was lost, for want of a rider the message was lost, for want of a message the battle was lost, for want of a battle the war was lost, for want of a war the kingdom was lost, all for want of a horseshoe nail.'"

"I think I've heard that. Big things depend on little things in unpredictable ways."

"Exactly. Before the pandemic, we were like that kingdom, dependent on a lot of very specific horseshoe nails that couldn't be quickly or easily replaced. And the nails were, mostly, people. When too many people got sick at once, the whole system just collapsed.

"It wasn't just in the cities, either. Back then, most farmers grew only what would sell, and then bought all their food, a week's worth at a time, just like the city people did. The United States was a net exporter of food, but when the store shelves were emptied, farmers starved, too.

"It's that network, again. Even just to grow food, you needed the network.

"Like almonds. Almost all of the almonds in the entire country grew in just one area of California. They grew nothing but almonds there, so there was nothing for pollinators to live on, except when the almond trees were in flower. So they had to truck in bees, to pollinate the almonds. Eighty percent of the country's beehives were loaded on trucks and sent to California for two weeks every spring. The year of the pandemic, there wasn't anyone to drive the trucks, so most of the trees never set fruit. There was an area the size of Rhode Island of just almond trees not growing almonds. What do you do if you're in the middle of such a place? What do you do when the money you got selling your crops is suddenly no good? So you had people starving and food in storage, rotting, all at the same time."

"OK, I understand that, but why not just rebuild the system a few months later, after the disease had passed? Get the trucks running again?"

"Because we needed the network to create the network. The horseshoe nail needed the kingdom, so to speak. How are you going to pay people to transport and refine oil, instead of spending their time getting something to eat, if there's no money? And who is going to sell food in quantity to oil workers, or anyone else, if there is nothing other than food to buy? They can't buy fuel, there isn't any, because the refineries aren't operating, because there is no money. Complex economic systems take time to build, and we had no time. We needed to eat first. There was no food because there was no oil, and there was no oil because there was no food."

"Wow. *No* food?"

"In some places, yes, *no* food. But I'd say more people died of violence than starvation. The urge to live is very strong. Many people died, or killed and then died, fighting for what little food there was."

"OK, go on."

"I didn't know any of this was happening, at the time. I was sick in bed, recovering, for, I don't know, it seemed like weeks. Maybe it was. You said you don't remember—it feels like somebody sand-papered your lungs. And there wasn't a lot of news. None of us left the ranch without a good reason, and the news services kept cutting off. Cell service became intermittent. Or the electricity would be off for three days straight. We wouldn't know why. We guessed, and, in retrospect, we guessed correctly; that there just weren't enough people left out there to run everything.

"Not that so many people were dead, yet. The pandemic only killed about twenty percent of the people infected. But being infected knocked you on your ass, you were useless for weeks, and somebody had to take care of you. And every ten days, the number of sick people multiplied by ten. *Nobody* was immune. So, if a power line blew down, there might not be anyone to fix it for a week. There weren't enough police to keep order. If someone set a fire in a riot, like *three* firefighters would show up. The others were all sick. So there was this kind of sputtering, systems falling apart a little at a time. Then, maybe about two months after my friends found me, the internet and our electricity both went out and didn't come back on again. We were on our own."

"But you had nuclear power plants, right? And chemical factories? I don't understand how they didn't blow up if people were just not showing up for work. Were you worried about that?"

"The President had shut everything like that down, by Executive Order. That's part of why the electricity kept going out, the grid was under-powered. I was worried someone would get their hands on a nuke, in all the confusion, but turns out I didn't need to be. A few years later, investigators discovered that all the nuclear weapons had been permanently disabled. When did that happen? On whose say-so? Nobody's left who knows. It's not that people 'just didn't show up for work.' A lot of people *couldn't*. Those who could? How long does it take to do a cold shut-down of a nuclear power plant? How long does it take to destroy a nuclear warhead? To disable a missile's engine and launching system? How many people, do you suppose, never saw their families again because they stayed at work, keeping the rest of us safe? Most people are essentially good, when the big decisions have to be made."

"What do you mean, you were on your own?"

"No outside inputs. No electricity we couldn't generate, no food or water we couldn't source at home, no new tools or supplies we couldn't make, and no help from anyone outside of the ranch. No news from outside, and no way to tell anyone else we were still alive. But my friends, Rock and Jacob and Betti, had prepared for that, and not the way most preppers did. They had stockpiled food and supplies, but not to the same extent. Stockpiling is what you do to get through a gap in supply—it doesn't really help if civilization is just *over*. What do you do when your stockpile runs out? So, my friends focused on being able to *produce* food. They had the cattle, of course, but they needed more people to defend the land and to do other kinds of work. They started by calling their friends, inviting them in. I got a call, back when I was in Phoenix, but of course I wasn't free, then. Next, they went out visiting all their nearby friends who hadn't called them back, to see who was still alive and might like to join. That's what they were doing when they found me. They were on their way to go check on someone they hadn't been able to reach. They were on horseback because they were saving their gas for the generator on their well pump. They even took in some strangers. Eventually, there were about thirty of us, counting the children. They needed a large group of people who could live together, take care of each other, and fight for each other—yes, fight. Quite literally. That must sound a lot less bizarre to you than it did to me. I had never thought I'd have to make those kinds of decisions.

"The thing is, we had food and other people didn't. Not all of us could handle a gun, and not everyone who could was willing to kill, but enough people could and did. They patrolled the perimeter in groups. Anybody on the wrong side of the fence…they shot."

Even twenty years after the fact there was a catch in his voice when he said it.

"Did you ever shoot anybody?" Elzy asked.

"No. But I accepted the hospitality the others' violence won me." She nodded. He continued. "The rest of us built cisterns and dug more tanks so we could store more water when the monsoon came. We dug storage cellars and built meat-drying racks. We built new fences—there's a design you can use so wild animals can get through but cattle can't—around just enough land to feed the number of animals we needed. We took them inside and let the rest go. And then our security teams defended that fence.

"We weren't inhuman about it," he added. "If someone came to us for help, we gave it. Sometimes we let them stay, if we had enough room. But if someone came to steal, or to drive us off our land, it was them or us. And yet they weren't bad people, just desperate, just like we would have been. Do you remember species-area curves?"

Elzy blinked and didn't answer for a moment, evidently surprised by the rather academic-sounding term. He hadn't meant to say anything unusual.

"Yes," she said, finally. "The biodiversity of a given habitat patch is directly related to its size. There's an equation. Number of species times something or other."

"Yeah. Times something or other." He smiled fondly, mimicking her. "The thing is, living things need energy, and that energy needs to come from somewhere—ultimately the sun, through plants. So, the less land you have, the less sunlight you can collect, the less energy you can get. Less energy in a system means fewer members—fewer individuals, fewer species—and simpler structures. There is no getting around that. They used to create parks by drawing boundaries around some great wilderness. The land outside went for housing development, oil extraction, or whatever else, but at least the park was protected in perpetuity. Except it wasn't. It wasn't the whole system. Saving *just* the park was like eating the back half a steer and expecting the head to keep on mooing.

"Anyway, as soon as a park was isolated, it would start losing species. Different parks lost different species, it was partly arbitrary. What mattered was simply the number. Biodiversity would gradually drop down to what a patch that size could support. It's called *relaxation to equilibrium.* Less energy means fewer individuals, period, and some species would drop below their viability thresholds and die out.

"And that's basically what happened to us. Fossil fuel let us use a habitat patch that was larger than the actual planet, because fossil fuel is solar energy captured by plants over geological time—we had the Earth of the present *and* the Earths of the past. When that ended, our patch shrank, so our population had to shrink. It was mathematically inevitable. And I was on the inside of that fence and other people were on the outside. That was it. Random chance. There was no justice, no moral reason, to who lived and who died."

"Is it finished now?" Elzy asked, "the relaxation?"

"What? Oh, I don't know. Most of it is. People only starved for about a year. After that, all the hoarded supplies were used up or wasted somehow, and if you were still alive that meant you had a farm or a ranch or something. But nobody knows what the human carrying capacity is now—the land has been degraded through overuse. We might have to shrink again." But even as Andy spoke, his mind was drifting off into the past, the smell of the desert, the feel of its fine, crusted soil under foot, the voices and faces of his friends, and the lowing, always, of cattle, from somewhere. And most of all, the sound of knocking.

The knocking wasn't a memory but a visceral, automatic meta-phor. When Andy was a small boy in religious school, they'd read him stories, ancient tales from the days before children's fare was supposed to be sanitized and safe. Did adults even hear what awful things they were reading? And it had been obvious to his child's mind, logical and insightful even then, that Noah and his family hadn't been on the Ark because they deserved it and the rest of humanity did not. Perhaps *Noah* had been an exceptionally good man, but there were eight people on that Ark, Noah and his wife and their sons and their wives. If there had been only eight good people on the whole of the planet, surely chances were against them all being part of the same immediate family?

No, far more likely, Noah's family got on the Ark because Noah was obedient enough to God to build the thing, and his wife and sons and daughters-in-laws were obedient to him and so they went along for the ride. They weren't, therefore, specially chosen because they were good, *better* than the sinful crowds who stayed outside. They were just breeding stock, like the animals, two by two, on a lifeboat with limited space. And they must have known it. They knew their neighbors, and they must have recognized that their family didn't deserve anything more than the others.

So, when these eight people, obedient to God and to their pa-triarch, huddled inside the ark and listened to the rain on the roof and the rising waters sloshing against the hull and all the animals around them crying out and the people on the outside, their friends and neighbors, hammering on the hull and trying to get in—what had that sounded like?

The thought used to keep little Andy up at night, though even then he didn't like to tell anyone else what was bothering him. And then he grew up and stopped taking religion so literally. But still, every time he thought of that year spent defending his friends' ranch in Arizona, he heard hammering in his ears.

He shook himself out of his trance and went on with his story.

"At first, as soon as I got my strength back, I wanted to head East and go look for my son. The others talked me out of it. They said it would have been suicidal to travel on my own. They said that if my son was still alive then he was already somewhere safe. He could hold on until things settled down and I had a chance of making it. There was no point in my dying on the way to him. There's a certain kind of logic that happens at times like that. You do what you have to do.

"So I stayed with my friends, and we learned a new kind of ranching. New for us, anyway. I mean, how do you—"

Elzy interrupted the story in order to step off into the woods a moment. She might have waited, but not far ahead lay the open farm fields where privacy would be much harder to find. Here, a dense and mostly very young pine forest hid a person from the road almost immediately. Evidently, someone else had already taken advantage of that privacy, since a small, crude campsite lay hidden back among the trees. The ground was oddly free of twigs and fallen branches, probably because they had all been collected and burned for kindling, but whoever did it had carefully avoided breaking any of the dead branches still on the trees, apparently trying to keep the camp well-screened from the path. The whole thing seemed wrong to Elzy, who could think of no good reason why anyone would want to make a secret camp *here*. There was plenty of affordable, even free, lodging within a mile or two. But nobody seemed to be home right now, so she made a mental note to tell the local cops about the spot later, and found a good-sized tree to squat behind.

A sudden, cold anxiety bubbled up inside her.

Elzy knew from experience that her anxiety was wise. Something *really* was wrong, she just had to find out what. Listening carefully, she realized she could hear voices. Andy was talking to someone, and while she couldn't make out the words, his voice sounded too calm and reasonable, like a man trying to soothe a vicious dog. Elzy pulled up her pants and crept forward, carefully keeping the trunk of another large pine between her and the men.

Two men were quite clearly trying to mug her teacher at knifepoint. She saw all three almost in profile and was glad to note that Andy still had his backpack. There was so much cash in it, plus the valuable computer, that stealing it would count as *major theft*, a capital crime in most jurisdictions. The logic was that the victim might be deprived of the means to get food, something most people still saw as tantamount to murder. What cops like Elzy saw was that the draconian law made thieves desperate, inclined to kill all witnesses.

Even if Elzy's cell phone had service, which she doubted, the police were at least ten minutes away. There was no one to hear a scream, either. But she had trained to deal with badguys, and the old mindset reasserted itself automatically. It was an easier way of thinking, really, free of social demands and expectations, just a puzzle to solve. She drew her gun and considered her options.

She would have preferred to resolve the situation by talking, but Andy hadn't succeeded at that yet and he was probably a lot better at it than she was. If she showed herself now it would probably just escalate things, frightening the thieves into drawing the guns she could see bulging in their waistbands. And once those guns were pointed at her and Andy, her own gun would be strategically useless. She could kill any man before he shot her, she was sure of that, but then the gun already pointed at Andy would go off before she could aim again. Alternatively, she could kill Andy's assailant first, but then the survivor would kill her and do what he liked with Andy afterwards. That wouldn't do.

Just then, the robbers appeared to lose patience and lunged. Andy jumped backwards, narrowly missing being grabbed, and the man closest to him drew his gun. The air exploded.

The one robber fell, dropped as cleanly as a deer, while the other man spun on his heel towards Elzy and drew to return fire. He, too, fell before he could even aim. Two shots, two deaths, two or three seconds. Elzy stepped calmly out of the woods, her gun still held ready, scanning the trees and the path up and down for any more possible assailants

"That was amazing," Andy told her, his hands still reflexively held up in the air. Elzy could shoot the eye from a one-eyed jack if she needed to, but she was in no mood for boasting. She shrugged.

"I do what I can, and I can shoot straight," she told him. "We'll have to go report this. Do you think we're in Homestead's jurisdiction yet?"

"Yes, I think so." Andy moved to check the pulse of one of the fallen men, but Elzy stopped him.

"Don't risk blood contamination," she warned. "We don't know what they've got."

Andy straightened up, seeing her logic, but he seemed troubled.

"Are they dead?" he asked. "If they aren't, they'll need help."

"They're dead. I know where the bullets went," Elzy told him, but she checked the men anyway, using the back of her cell like a mirror to look for breath condensation. "They aren't breathing," she reassured him. He nodded, staring at the bodies, while Elzy turned on her cell, checking for service. He seemed more concerned by the deaths of the robbers than by his own close call. He could be shocked, Elzy noted, but not frightened.

"Hey, check it, I've got two bars," she announced. "I might be able to text Homestead police from here." While she fiddled with her phone, Andy carefully walked around the bodies, trying not to contaminate any evidence, and sat down a few yards away. When Elzy was done texting, she joined him, setting her gun down out of reach so it wouldn't scare the police when they arrived. "They're on their way. They said to wait here."

Andy nodded.

The wait wouldn't be long, since emergency personnel had bio-diesel cars. Elzy was a little nervous about the police. They should be able to see that she was telling the truth and had shot in self-defense, but since neither robber had actually fired it was possible she would be arrested, even tried. She looked at Andy. He was still staring at the bodies. He still looked disturbed, but that shocked expression was gone. He seemed as steady as ever. She felt better.

"Why don't you carry a gun?" she asked him.

"Because I'd rather die than kill," he answered. "It isn't an intellectual, moralistic thing. I've carried a gun, but when I was shot at, I didn't even think to shoot back. I don't think it's right to carry a weapon I'm not prepared to use."

"That's wise. I don't draw mine unless I'm willing to fire." They were quiet for a few minutes. "Andy," she began again, "you kept them talking for a long time. Did you expect me to fire?" He didn't respond right away.

"Yes," he said, slowly. "I just didn't expect you to do it *first*."

Elzy digested that, looking at the bodies.

"I'm not an immoral woman," she said finally. "I won't cause *extra* death, but someone was going to die here today, and I wasn't going to let it be you."

Andy looked around at her sharply, his face betraying, just for a moment, an entirely different kind of shock.

Chapter 4
Novel Ecosystems

The police let Elzy go without incident as soon as the preliminary investigation was finished. They even let her spend those hours unsupervised in the break room at the Homestead police station. Andy waited with her and they played cards for a while. Elzy mostly won, because she could count cards and Andy couldn't, but when he did win he won big because he could bluff well.

The desk sergeant brought them chicory and fresh muffins and chatted with them a bit. When he left, Elzy took out her phone and emailed her mother, while Andy read and reread a cracked copy of *Practice of the Wild*, by Gary Snyder. It was the only real, not electronic, book he bothered to carry with him—the only thing he ever read that had no direct connection to his work, so far as Elzy knew.

She felt no guilt or shame for shooting the criminals—and that itself disturbed her. They weren't even her first kills. Andy's concern for the dead men had not been lost on her. Even most other vigilantes hated to kill, and Elzy knew cops who had never discharged their weapons and hoped never to do so. She also knew a few sadists who got a kick out of being armed. Only Elzy didn't care one way or the other whether a stranger died.

Sometimes she wondered whether there was something really wrong with her. Was she born like this, or had some horror she couldn't remember killed something inside her? It was one more way in which she was a mystery to herself.

The investigative officer—Diliberto again—returned with her report in the late afternoon. Not only did she confirm Elzy's story, she had also discovered that the knives and guns of the dead men were the same ones used in the recent murders. The basic MO's of the attacks all matched, too. DNA evidence would take a few days to analyze, but the police seemed satisfied that they had their men. As a gesture of gratitude, they even left Elzy's name out of the report. She was still a fellow cop, at least nominally, and an off-duty killing would have complicated her resumé.

Elzy had worried a bit when she recognized Diliberto, but this time, whether out of gratitude or guilt, the officer was entirely respectful, even deferential to her—but not to Andy. Diliberto even seemed to take some strange pleasure in telling him that three of the five murdered men had been raped, implying that he might have been next. Elzy's blood boiled to see her teacher baited that way, but Andy calmly ignored the bullying and so she held her peace.

That market, Andy and Elzy returned to work as if nothing had happened. She tried a few variations on her act, and he led two more workshops that she had no time to attend. If either of them felt any lingering distress over the attack, they didn't admit it. Each knew the other too well to ask.

Friday night, Saul and some of the other Troubadours stayed at the hostel so Saul and Andy could hang out some more before life separated them again. The market crowds were gone, so they had the game room to themselves, and Andy played a ruthless game of pool.

Not that he *acted* ruthless. On the contrary, in Saul's company Andy seemed more relaxed, more purely playful, than Elzy had ever seen him. He laughed and joked and took swigs of hard birch beer between shots. He didn't act like he cared at all who won, except that he was damn hard to beat. When Elzy, no mean hand at pool herself, grew tired of losing, she left the game, flopped down on a couch, and fiddled with her phone.

Jayden, the Troubadour who had helped Elzy with her New Hampshire accent, also left the game and busied himself trying to work the antique jukebox in the corner. The other two Troubadours had already gone to bed. Eventually, Jayden managed to order up some happy-sounding song about a bullfrog named Jeremiah. Saul fished a joint out of somewhere and lit it, inhaled, and passed it across the table.

"I remember when this stuff was illegal," Andy commented, with some amusement, and took a drag.

"I don't," quipped Saul, and Andy giggled and choked on the smoke. Jayden accepted a toke as well, but Elzy declined. She seldom allowed herself to be less than sober when she was the only warrior in the room. A few minutes later, she noticed that the men had let the half-finished joint go out. Andy stuck it behind his ear for safe keeping, like a spare pen. When he leaned over to shoot, all compact, muscled grace, a tiny, silver Star of David swung free of his throat and caught the light. In that moment of concentration, his face was as calm and intent as a hunting cat's.

"Nice phone," said Jayden, suddenly standing next to Elzy.

"Thanks," she said. "Graduation present from my Mom."

"Yeah? What's your Mom do?" Not everyone could afford a phone, much less a phone as a gift.

"She's the Chief of Police of our town. Before that, she was head of our farm's security team. You know those transferable veteran's benefits the states gave out a couple of years ago? That's how she sent me to college."

"Lucky you. I couldn't go. Self-taught. Talking a guild into taking me seriously was a bitch."

"I didn't think you could get in without coursework?"

"Well, normally you can't," Jayden admitted, "not unless you're a musician, something like that. But I did have a secret weapon."

"Oh?"

"Saul was my application sponsor. He helped found our guild,

Earth Stories Limited. And he pulled some strings."

"Lucky you."

As Elzy spoke, Jayden did a double-take, suddenly realizing that she'd been using her artificial New Hampshire accent since he'd approached her. He burst out laughing, and she smiled at him quickly and sat up so he could sit down next to her.

"What are you doing?" he asked, and she showed him her phone.

The screen displayed a real-time image of what the phone's camera saw, as though she were about to take a picture. Except that in real life, the coffee table in front of the couch held only a few printblogs and an empty mug, while on the screen a small box also sat there. Elzy reached her hand into the camera's field of view and made an odd gesture. On the screen, she appeared to pick up the box and put it down again. The illusion was perfect.

"It's a new game," she explained. "Allison's Boxes. You're supposed to figure out how to open the box. In the beginning, it's all about noticing detail, but later on it's supposed to get into logic."

"Noticing detail?" asked Jayden, and reached into the frame and poked the box experimentally. It moved slightly.

"Yeah, see how this circle is a little darker? There's one like it on the other side. Maybe they're part of a locking mechanism?" She pressed the circle and it sank into the box under the pressure, while the circle on the other side poked outward. The dark circles turned out to be the ends of a long, thin tube, which she slid out of the box and dropped. The tube vanished as soon as she dropped it. With the tube gone, the lid opened up easily—and three more boxes flew out and settled themselves on the coffee table. The original vanished.

"More boxes," Jayden commented. "Do those have boxes in them, too?"

"Yup. The boxes have boxes, which have boxes. The whole structure of the game is fractal. Oo, look, these have a lot of circles."

"So, which ones do we press to open the boxes?"

We? Jayden spoke as if her game were now their game, an imposition she found she did not mind.

"That's what we have to figure out," she said.

They played for about half an hour, finding that the solution to each box provided a clue to all the more difficult boxes inside it, before Jayden suggested they get some air. They left Andy and Saul to their pool game and stepped out into the night of the courtyard together.

"I, uh, don't want to seem forward," Jayden began, and Elzy knew he was about to be forward anyway. She didn't mind. "But is that guy only your application sponsor?"

"That guy? *Only?*"

"Yeah, the pool shark? Is something going on?"

"Why?" she demanded, suddenly bristling. "You want to know if I'm *taken?*" As if she were property, to be reserved or released by some man. She felt irritable, quick to hear the worst in his words. Her hopes were making her anxious. She wondered if she were getting defensive of her teacher's honor, too. She couldn't tell. She felt muddled.

"No," Jayden replied in a patient, reasonable tone, "I want to find out if you're going to think I'm a jerk for even bringing the subject up. Because if you're with *that guy* then it's because you want to be, and you won't want *me* bothering you."

Elzy calmed, mollified slightly.

"Oh, you can bother me," she assured him. She sat down on the damp grass of the courtyard. Spring had advanced noticeably in the past week and a half, and the night was warm, even comfortable. Frogs and toads shouted musically from everywhere at once. "He has a name, you know. Andy. He's a very important man."

"Whom you're not with," Jayden added, as he sat down next to her. No light escaped the curtained windows behind them. Star shine alone lit the night. She could see the man beside her only as a vague and deeper darkness, but she could hear his nearness as a kind of auditory shadow.

"No! Of course not."

"Is he too old?" Jayden asked.

"No," Elzy told him, which wasn't entirely true. But Jayden looked to be nearing forty and she didn't want him thinking she only liked guys her own age. "Look, he's my *teacher*. Anyway, I get around him and I'm like *ten* all of a sudden."

"Ten is definitely too young for Andy."

"Definitely. Jayden? I just realized something."

"Hmm?"

"I am really terrible at flirting."

"You're no worse than I am, and here we are."

"How old are you? How old were you when the pandemic happened?" Most young people asked each other that, sooner or later. She lay back on the grass and looked up the stars. The sky was very clear. There was no moon.

"I was sixteen," he told her. "I was starting to look at colleges, but I couldn't figure out if I wanted to study mythology or astronomy. I'd just started writing poetry that year, too. You?"

"I was six. But I don't remember anything. Only that *my brother* died." It still felt strange to say my brother, which is why she said it—to practice. She spoke again to forestall further questions she couldn't answer. "Mythology and astronomy and poetry? They sound pretty disparate."

"Not really," Jayden replied, and he lay down, too. "Look up, and all the old stories are there." And he began to tell her about this constellation and that, weaving together scientific terms, like *main sequence star* and *blue-white supergiant*, with the names of heroes, animals, and goddesses from Greece, New Mexico, Polynesia, Japan. "No matter where you are or who you are or what you think or believe," he explained, "everyone in the Northern Hemisphere sees the same stars."

Hours drifted by and the Milky Way swung slowly across the night. Elzy wondered what it had been like to look up in a light-polluted city or town at night and not be able to see the stars. She wondered why the people of Before had stood for it, spending their money on wasted electricity and losing such beauty.

Then the stars appeared to jump and pale and Elzy knew she

must have slept. The pallor of the sky was moonlight, not dawn, but the sound of birds and the now-chilly air told her it was nearly morning. She stretched her stiffened limbs and found she was shivering. She knew what the others inside the hostel were going to assume, and at that moment she was only sorry they would be wrong. Jayden had asked if he could email her. Tonight was only a beginning.

After breakfast, they all hit the road again, the Troubadours heading north and Elzy and Andy going more or less east, headed for the Piscataqua River.

The distance would have taken barely a week of travel, if they'd been trying to go fast, but of course they weren't. They weren't even trying to go straight. Instead, they wove north and south, only gradually trending east, moving from one speaking engagement to the next.

The itinerary was Andy's. As the senior member of the expedition, of course he made all their major decisions—but he made most of their minor ones, too. Even the way he always asked for and considered Elzy's opinion presupposed that the final decisions were his. Elzy might have resented his need for control, but she wanted somebody else to be in change just now.

The deaths of the robbers played on her mind. She still felt no empathy for the men, but killing them had not been the act of a cop—it was the act of a vigilante, a role Elzy had thought she was done with. She'd forgotten how frightening it was to kill, how exposed she'd always felt knowing that no adult would come and take over the responsibility. It was nothing she'd ever discuss with Andy, though, and if he noticed that she was indulging in her little-kid act more than ever, he didn't say anything.

Through the end of April, then, and into May, they moved across the southern quarter of New Hampshire as the fields greened and the trees leafed out. The country was, for the most part, low and rolling but in an irregular, craggy way. Even greening with spring, New Hampshire was not a soft or gentle place. Hills, mostly glacial drumlins or slopes cut by stream erosion, rendered all roads curvy and most horizons short. Bare rock outcropped here and there, and most fields and forests were stony. Andy explained the geology as well as the natural history as they walked.

He seemed to have a giant, incredibly detailed, and fully annotated geological map stored inside his brain. If he knew where he was then he could key into his mental map and explain exactly what he was looking at—how it formed, and how it related to all the other geological features in the region. And yet he was not a geologist, not even on a hobbyist level. He could not tell one gray rock from another just by looking at it, something Elzy could do easily. He couldn't answer unexpected questions on the subject with his typical depth.

He was standing at the base of a road cut, going on excitedly about feldspar crystals, when Elzy asked him why he was telling her so much about rock. He looked at her, suddenly expressionless.

"Not that I mind," she amended. "It is interesting." He relaxed again.

"Because it's there," he quipped.

"No, I mean, you're an *ecologist*."

"Rock yields both topography and soil chemistry. To really understand something, you have to understand what's beneath." A chilly little gust of wind stirred his hair and the open front of his light jacket. He still didn't quite smile, but the expressionless expression he wore when he was being authoritative was gone. His face, his whole body, had grown animated, his movements quick and loose. Elzy, responding unconsciously, stood on the scree at the base of the cliff more or less at attention. She was no child now but an eager student.

"You mean like how different substrates support different plant communities?" she asked. He had taught her to think about substrate before looking to history when "reading" the land.

"Yes, but it's more than that," Andy replied. "It's not just an individual site and its soils—it's a whole underlying *pattern*, a necessary context. How does one site relate to another? How does each place fit into the whole? *Why* are the specifics that you see, soil types and so forth, *here*? And why now?" He made a curious gesture, as if catching something up between his thumb and fore-finger. He searched Elzy's face eagerly for signs of understanding, then he turned to the cliff, his hands on the rock, almost reverent.

"Geology is foundational to evolutionary biology too," he added, "and intrinsic to climatology." His hands inched up the stone, each finger exploring almost independently, as though he hoped to grow rootlets from their tips.

Elzy watched him and knew he wanted to climb the road-cut and probably could. She'd seen him go right up the brick wall of a defunct shopping center on a field-trip once, when she'd been the TA for one of his advanced classes. Student opinion, once he was out of earshot, had split over whether he was bad-ass or just plain crazy. She guessed that the only reason he didn't climb now involved the long lines of teamsters passing on Route 9 behind them. If he went up the wall, they'd rein in their animals to gawk and cause a traffic jam.

An early spring dragonfly, following the cliff for shelter from the wind, flew directly behind his head, and he turned at the sound and stumbled a little on the scree. The insect veered away at his movement, headed for the flies attracted by animal dung along the road. Its wings struck each other with a dry, papery sound as it turned. Andy looked at Elzy and grinned.

Over the next few weeks, the weather grew warm and the trees finished leafing out. Pastures and flood-control wetlands kept their winter drab a while longer, but fresh rhubarb and then strawberries appeared in the markets. The fields greened with seedlings, and birds argued musically from woodlots and from the forest buffers and wetlands along streams and millponds. Mosquitoes and black-flies appeared, and the scent of repellent joined that of flowers and growing things. Andy and Elzy switched out their wool traveling clothes in favor of cool cotton, hers in khaki, his in pale blue.

They seldom camped anymore. Walking between engagements rarely took more than a day. They seldom had any time off either, because while each town marketed only once a week, neighboring towns followed different schedules. Big places like Keene usually marketed over the weekend for the convenience of churchgoers, while smaller communities like Homestead went mid-week, when there was less competition for guild members. What down-time Andy and Elzy had, they used to adjust and improve Elzy's work. Not all her events went as well as her first, and no matter how well she did, Andy usually found something for her to improve. She had a particular issue with the one-on-one conversations necessary for networking and organizing.

"At least *pretend* to be interested in other human beings," he counseled her once, after a very long day. "Your Machiavellian is showing. That's not going to help you."

"Is that what you do? Pretend?" she shot back.

"If necessary, yes," he replied in the same tone.

But she knew she was being unfair. Whatever Andy's issues were, he didn't lack compassion. It was she who wished others' needs would go away when she wasn't in the mood for them. He kept insisting that it didn't work like that. She hated it, but she knew he was right.

And so, Elzy didn't have any time off. Andy might have given her a break if she'd asked, but she had resolved not to ask. She didn't know what he did when he went off alone, but guessed he was still working, and if he didn't take a break, she wouldn't. She once asked him how he managed to keep going.

"Rest from one thing by doing another," he advised her. "And never do anything you really don't like."

They rested from discussing her programs by studying natural history. Elzy didn't need much help with plant and animal identification—she had always done very well in those classes—but more abstract entities, such as forest types and successional stages, were harder for her. Andy questioned the validity of these concepts just as he questioned most established ideas, but said internalizing the categories would help Elzy notice patterns. He therefore drilled her constantly. And everywhere they went he asked her, as he had once asked on West Hill outside of Keene, to read the history of the landscape from the shape of the forest floor and the age and species of the trees.

None of these forests were like those she had known in Pennsylvania. The mix of plants was slightly odd. The chorus of birdsong was different. Often, she could not tell just what the difference was—perhaps the scent of the soil or the color of the light through the leaves. Sometimes whatever it was made New Hampshire seem deliciously exotic. Sometimes she just felt homesick.

But if she did go back, she would not be able to read the forests there. She would not be able to name most of the plant communities. She knew that each region had its own language of the land, founded on climate, soil chemistry, and land-use history—and that in learning the language of New England she had in some ways alienated herself from Pennsylvania.

But a part of her had always felt alien. She liked her mother's farm, but had never been able to shake the feeling that she should be somewhere else, she just didn't know where. She didn't know why friends and family weren't enough to anchor her someplace. Other people seemed to have some trick of human closeness that she just lacked—except with Andy. She couldn't explain that one, either.

Certainly, he did not encourage closeness. He was never rude or dismissive, just strictly professional. Elzy had known him for years now, and had essentially lived with him for weeks, yet with rare exceptions he remained politely impersonal. Despite his willingness to share on some topics, there were whole swaths of the most innocuously personal information that he kept to himself. He rarely spoke of his family and never said their names. She didn't know his birthday. He once grew very evasive when she asked if he were allergic to walnuts. He wouldn't even admit there was anything he wanted to keep private, as though even his secrets were secret. He was deliberately keeping Elzy at arm's length, she was sure of it. And yet there was his behavior up on the mountain. A certain fondness lit his eyes when he didn't realize she was looking. And he paid attention to her in a way no one else ever had. If she was tired or nervous or wanted something, he always knew.

Elzy had never been clear on what Andy did when he was not teaching. He knew the intimate details of what seemed like every ecological research or conservation project in the country, but which ones were his? Lately she'd wondered if maybe all of them were. Everywhere they went, Andy knew people. Some were former students or other colleagues he was actively collaborating with. Others had worked with him before or occasionally sought him out for advice. As with rock outcroppings or forests, the work of other scientists formed a pattern in his mind, a context in which he could place any given project. If modern science was a web, he was its spider, able to run out to any misplaced strand to help as needed.

He seemed to be quite deliberately inserting Elzy into the web because he made a point of introducing her to all of his contacts and colleagues, implicitly recognizing her as a professional worthy of their time and interest. On his advice, she wrote down every name, every detail she was given, took pictures where she could, and stored it all on her phone. She also emailed the lists, as a back-up, to her mother. She had a good memory for such things, but she wanted to create the illusion of an even better one.

"People are always flattered when you remember who they are years later," Andy said. "They don't have to know how you do it."

Andy himself relied on notes far more than Elzy had to. He knew a great deal about how to interact with and understand people, but he had learned all of it the hard way. What came naturally to him—recognizing and responding creatively to large, subtle patterns—he couldn't teach, except by example. He could teach the social component because he'd had to learn it. But because he did not have the same kind of difficulty with people that Elzy did, she assumed he didn't have any trouble at all. It certainly never occurred to her that anyone so confident might actually be shy.

Sometime in May, his habit of vanishing really started to bother her. So what if he was at work whenever he was with her? She was at school when she was with him, but didn't need to escape. She didn't need to cling to his company either, she told herself, but who wants to be avoided?

It wouldn't have been so bad if he wasn't friendly with her *sometimes.*

"Where are you going?" she asked. It was Sunday morning in a town of mostly ethnic Somalis, Muslims who marketed Thursday to Saturday around Friday prayers. Elzy and Andy had another day before they had to go anywhere, meaning Elzy could catch up on paperwork. She didn't need or want company, but a friend would have at least mentioned his plans. He hadn't.

He paused in the doorway of the almost-empty inn and looked at her, somewhat startled.

"I'm going to the multi-media center and then to lunch," he explained, as though her question were strange. "Why, do you need anything?"

"No. I don't always *need* anything, you know."

Andy frowned in frank confusion. Elzy was too angry at the moment to realize he had no idea what she was angry about. They didn't usually talk this way. He looked at her and waited.

"You could just tell me these things sometimes," she said.

"I just did tell you."

"I know."

"Well, if you have any more questions, shoot me an email, alright?" and he turned again to go. Elzy sighed heavily. He visibly suppressed a sigh of his own, turned back to look at her, and waited.

"There's no one to *talk* to in this town," she complained, even though she'd been talking to people almost constantly since Thursday. But she'd felt self-conscious among them, worried that they were staring at her bare head and arms.

"You could wear a headscarf," Andy suggested. "Many female guild members do in these towns."

"Not all of the *Muslim* women wear scarves."

"Yes, but you don't look Somali, so that changes how they see you."

"I know. I'm a godless American."

Technically, Elzy *was* a godless American, being an atheist, but this community, like all the others she had visited, welcomed guild members regardless of religious affiliation. She was just having a bad day. And on this day she did not want Andy's faultlessly professional responses.

"Elzy..." he began, and she looked at him. His voice had changed, grown kinder. "I don't usually spend that much time with my friends. It isn't personal." And he left.

That bastard, she thought. *I ought to act all clingy, it would serve him right.* But of course, she did nothing of the kind. She tried to distance herself from him emotionally, but after a few days that started to seem pointless, so she gradually reverted to her old habits. Andy, as usual, gave no sign of even noticing her turmoil.

Towards the end of the month, the first of the summer heat waves struck and Andy relented about always dressing in guild member black in public. Of course, Elzy still had to dress properly for her events, but he said that wearing vests over their travel-clothes otherwise was good enough.

"Heat-stroke doesn't look very professional," he explained. And indeed the heat sat heavily on him, in part because he refused to switch out his trousers for a skirt. He had grown up in a time when men did not wear skirts, and he said he could not start now. He might have worn shorts, except that to modern sensibilities they looked too much like underwear. At least his travel clothes weren't black, and the looser cut gave him a bit of a breeze. A new straw hat kept the sun off his fair skin.

"Jayden hasn't emailed me," Elzy announced one day, apropos of nothing, as they strode along through an apple orchard east of the ruins of Concord. The area had once been a park and a housing development, and old street-trees and patches of broken asphalt lingered. The branches of the young fruit trees arched over the right-of-way path, a long, flowered tunnel droning with bees. Andy frowned.

"Did you expect him to?" he asked, trying to put her comment in context.

"Yes. No. Maybe," she answered. She wouldn't normally have

discussed her love-life (or lack thereof) with Andy, and she was still trying, halfheartedly, to keep her distance, but there was just no one else to talk to. At least she heard no judgment in his voice. A lesser man would have sniggered about her night alone with Jayden. She wished she'd never left herself open to such assumptions.

"It probably doesn't help, but Saul hasn't emailed me," Andy offered.

"Did you expect him to?"

"No. He had no reason."

"You're right. That doesn't help."

"Sorry."

"Andy, Saul knew you'd survived the pandemic, didn't he?"

"Excuse me?"

"When he saw you in the media center he seemed surprised, but he didn't seem *that* surprised."

"It's true he would have seen my name if he's kept up with the literature," Andy acknowledged. "We had research interests in common, years ago."

"And he didn't contact you. He let you think he was dead for twenty years." A dangerous, protective anger welled in her voice.

"People have all sorts of reasons why they do what they do, Elzy," he told her, calmly. "I haven't contacted everyone I once knew." She didn't respond, stewing quietly for a few minutes. The sky above the apple trees had darkened with cloud. Andy changed the subject. "Have you given any thought to which guild you'll apply to?"

"Some. Yours?"

"You could. We don't have many full-time environmental educators, though. We might not be the best at representing you."

"I'd thought of Earth Stories Unlimited, but...."

"But that's the Troubadours' guild, yes. They do represent other troupes and a lot of independents. You wouldn't have to work closely with Jayden, if you'd rather not."

"I know. I also kind of like Trout Island."

"They have a very good reputation, but they don't contract with very many towns. It would depend on where you wanted to work."

"Here in New England, I think. I can belong to more than one, right? You do."

"I do," confirmed Andy, looking at the sky and walking faster. The temperature was dropping. "But you can only apply to one at a time, and when you apply to your second, they'll consider your reputation with your first guild, not so much your relationship with me. So you'll need a few years with whichever one you choose first, before you can add a second one."

Thunder pealed nearby and they looked around for shelter—a farm building, a ruined suburban house, anything—but found none. Everything had been recycled.

"There's got to be an equipment shed or something around here somewhere," Andy said. They jogged along the path as the air around them darkened to a soupy gray-green. The breeze died ominously.

"There!" cried Elzy, pointing through the trees at what might be a building off to the left. Just then, lightning struck a tree nearby, its thunder exploding with an almost tactile crack. They both shrieked reflexively and ran, frightened but laughing like children, slipping and stumbling under a sudden downpour through high grass slick and clingy with rain.

The building was just a tiny tool shed, fortunately not locked, but filled almost entirely with folded stepladders, pole pruners, and other equipment. There was no clear floor space. They threw their packs in on top of the pile and squeezed themselves into a void under the handles of a wheelbarrow. Andy pulled the doors shut against the wind.

"Did you *see* that lightning?" he said, out of breath and exultant.

"I thought we were *toast*!"

"Ha ha! *Soggy* toast!"

"Omigod, that rain!"

"I know! I don't think we'd have gotten soaked as fast if we'd jumped in a pond!"

"Omigod!"

"I *know*!"

It was hard to hear each other over the thunder and the drumming of the rain, so after a bit they quieted down and just sat together in the close, humid dark.

"It sounds like it's easing up," Elzy said at last. "Open the door so we can watch."

"OK."

The sky had paled to a roiling gray, but the rain still fell thickly enough to hide all but the two nearest rows of apple trees. Every few minutes thunder drummed again, more gently now, as the storm center moved gradually off to the northeast. Andy straitened his legs out through the door and let his sneakers get soaked all over again. He wasn't a very big man, but he was bigger than Elzy, and he could not squeeze himself in under half a wheelbarrow for very long. A fine mist of shredded, rebounding raindrops beaded on his face like sweat. She saw that he watched the storm the same way she did, with intent, rapt wonder.

Elzy looked at him and at the sky beyond him, and she had a new thought. Suppose that when he'd said "I don't usually spend that much time with *my friends*," he had not meant to contrast her with the set of my friends but rather to include her in it? Suppose he'd just been trying to tell her what kind of friend he could be?

In which case, she wondered, what kind of friendship did he need from her?

From the Concord area they trended south, stopping in one of the outlying Manchester communities, before heading east again. They had left the hill country behind and now traversed a low, very slightly rolling plain. Geologically, it was similar to the rest of New Hampshire, but it had long ago been worn flat by the ocean. The sea had not been higher back then, but the land had been much lower, pushed down by the weight of the glacier and slow to rebound after the ice melted. The modern sea was not far away. In that coastal country, Andy got them lost again. Elzy could never tell whether he let himself get lost on purpose, for the educational value, or if he just didn't mind being bad at navigation. She suspected the former but wished he'd ask first as she didn't always want to be lost. This time they found a footpath through a large game reserve and followed it in what seemed to be the right direction. They found both the path and the forest interrupted.

An irregular area many acres in extent was opened up to sunlight by trees missing or fallen or dead. Most of the standing dead trunks and stumps were visibly charred, yet there were green, thriving trees here and there as well, some actually leaning against the charred snags. Some patches of forest floor looked bare and burned, but most of it stood dense with raspberry bushes and young pin cherries. Green leafy sprouts crowned a few blackened stumps and a couple of quaking aspen seedlings shivered here and there.

Elzy stopped short, staring. Andy turned to her to make some comment, but saw her face and kept his silence.

"This. This," she said, in a strange voice. "I played here. In a forest that looked like this."

"You couldn't have played here in a forest that looked like this," he reminded her. "This burn zone is only a couple of years old."

She shook her head, as if shaking away a fly.

"A place *like* this, that looks like this," she clarified. "I don't know where it was."

"Do you remember anything else about it?"

"It's perfect." She was in her fugue state again, an excited, disoriented flashback. "Even the trees—" she knelt down for a moment, mimicking the height of a small child "—even the height of the cherries looks right. The aspens were all bushes, or smaller. There were standing dead—I can—almost—find my way around!" She didn't seem frightened this time, but she wasn't able to interact with Andy normally, either.

"Why don't you explore?" Andy suggested. "I'll be sitting right over there, OK? Come find me." Elzy nodded vaguely.

Twenty minutes later, she came to sit beside him, fully in the present again. She seemed dejected.

"It's gone," she reported. "It's the same as before, it was like I could remember everything, and now it's gone. All I know now is that I played both with and without Jamie in a forest that looked like this, too. Two kinds of forest. That's all. It's worse than before." She threw a bit of a stick at the ground.

"You know more than that," Andy told her, and showed her his tablet. It displayed a map of New England with irregular blotches all over. She frowned.

"What am I looking at?" she asked.

"When you were little," he explained, "much of New England burned. It was in June, in the second year of a very bad drought. Mostly lightning strikes and camp fires, though some arson, too, probably. When the pandemic happened, those burn zones were three years old. This, what we're sitting in, is also a three-year-old burn zone. You're remembering an area affected by the June Fires. That's what this map shows." Elzy examined the image.

"That's a lot of territory," she pronounced, finally. "I don't see how this helps."

"Yes, but…" Andy retrieved the tablet and swiped and tapped at its screen a couple of times. While he was waiting for her to come to her senses, he'd created a complexly layered map from data stored on his tablet. The little computer's software allowed him to hide and reveal the different layers almost at will. He held the machine out between them. The screen now had two different kinds of blotches on it. "This map also shows the regional distribution of balsam fir, and…" he swiped and tapped a little more. "Here are the towns." An irregular grid appeared over the map, the boundaries of all the little towns in the region. Elzy made a small, excited sound.

Andy tapped a few more times. The display changed to a table of names and numbers. "And here are the names and contact information for all ten of the towns within the range of balsam fir which were partially but not wholly burned in the June Fires. What was your father's name? We'll email them and ask who has a record of him." Elzy looked at him in amazement for a moment, but then her face fell.

"I don't know," she answered.

"You don't know?"

"Nope. All I can remember is 'Daddy.' And I don't think he

went by Rodriguez. I have a vague sense that my name is new, that it used to be something different."

"Can you ask your mother?"

"I can ask, but she won't likely answer. I've asked that one before."

"Hmm. We have something, anyway. We know it's one of these towns. Maybe you can remember something else to narrow it down."

"Yeah." Elzy was becoming dejected again. Andy's tablet beeped and he asked if she minded taking an early lunch so he could charge up. A high, thin haze was starting to thicken, and he wasn't sure he'd be able to later.

Elzy agreed and unpacked their little alcohol stove. A few minutes later she poured a cup of boiling water into a bowl full of instant re-fried beans, chopped dried tomatoes, bell peppers, and chilies. After two minutes to let the food re-hydrate, Andy added the fresh garlic and onion he'd been chopping and a tablespoon of seasoning mix, gave the whole thing a stir, and added sunflower oil and salt. They spooned the mix into corn tortillas.

"These were a good find at the last market," he commented. "I didn't know you could get good tortillas in Yankee towns."

"They're cornbread crepes. The last town was half French," Elzy replied. "What seasoning mix did you use? It's familiar, but….."

"Coriander, cumin, epazote, and a little mint."

"Epazote! Where did you get that?"

"Through the mail, actually."

When they were done eating, Andy poured the last of the hot water into the empty mixing bowl. With one finger, he scrubbed at the inside of the bowl until it was free of food residue, then drank the warm dishwater in one gulp and wiped the surface clean with a fresh handkerchief. Elzy put away the kitchen kit and the food. Ready to go.

But Andy's computer was not done charging yet, so they had to wait. Andy passed the time by reading Snyder, while Elzy fiddled with her phone.

"Hey, will you loke me that map?" she asked, after a minute. By *loke* she meant for Andy to establish a temporary local connection with her phone and email her directly, since they had lunched in an area with no internet reception. He didn't answer verbally, but he knelt by his tablet a moment and her phone beeped, requesting permission to accept the connection. A few seconds later it beeped again as the map arrived in her inbox. She thanked him and settled down to explore her possible hometowns.

"If this were a movie," she said, in a dreamy voice, "You'd turn out to *actually* be my real father." She was lying on her belly, chin in hand, kicking her feet idly. She was being ten again. Andy looked up from his book for a moment.

"I think I'd know," he said, dryly. Elzy was about to point out that, being a man, he might not—a man could father a child and not know—when she realized what such a comment would imply about his character. She shut her mouth. "I'd also know," he added, as though he could read her mind, "if there was a possibility I might not know."

Elzy's face reddened and she looked away. She would *not* apologize for thinking, however embarrassing the thought. Anyway, she hadn't meant that Andy *was* her dad, only that in a movie he would be, because movies are like that. He wasn't even her father-figure, not exactly. She didn't know what Andy was to her, or what she was to him. She didn't even know for sure if she was important to him at all. The silence stretched out for a while.

"I have some articles on insect host plant choices," Andy said, finally, "If you want me to loke you them, too?"

"Sure." Somehow, she had started to specialize in insects and how they interacted with human communities. She was researching now for a series of more in-depth workshops on the subject.

"You know," Andy began conversationally, "There is, or at least, used to be, a community of urban butterflies in the Northwest that aren't using *any* of the remaining native plants there. They are completely dependent on exotics in people's gardens. It's what's called a novel ecosystem, species that didn't evolve together but form a functional community anyway. If you got everybody to grub up those exotics and replant with natives, what would happen to those butterflies?"

Elzy happened to be facing away from him as he spoke, so she allowed herself to roll her eyes fondly. In her workshops she often stated, authoritatively, that non-native plants are inedible to native insects and so starve insect-eating birds—that living things need their evolutionary partners, the species they have grown up with, so to speak, to survive. So naturally, Andy had found a counter-example. He liked to do that. Questions interested him much more than certainty.

She made an interested noise.

"Relationships between organisms that do not share evolutionary history might not be as nuanced or as specialized," he continued, addressing the back of her head, "but sometimes they are enough."

Elzy turned to face him, surprised, but his expression was unreadable. Something inside her had softened at his words, but she wasn't sure whether it should have. Everything he said could be understood on more than one level, and she never knew which he actually meant—and couldn't imagine asking.

"What happened to those butterflies?" she asked instead. "Does anybody still tend those gardens?"

Andy looked away.

"I don't know," he said. "They may be extinct by now."

Andy's computer beeped. It was fully charged and ready for the hike to resume.

The first week of June, they made the old I-95 bridge over the Piscataqua River. Hurricane Odette had washed out a lot of bridges in New England, but not this one, and a steady procession of pedestrians and ox-carts crossed back and forth over it. Ospreys stared down skeptically at the traffic from the higher trusses.

Elzy and Andy did not go over that bridge. Instead, they went down to the ferry depot at its base where a fat, sturdy sailship awaited them. Their timing was good; the ferry sailed just a few minutes after they boarded.

The ferry was big and nearly as round as Noah's ark. It could carry three hundred passengers and their luggage, or two hundred people and a load of cargo, yet it had a shallow draft and so could manage almost any harbor. The round-bottomed boat rolled a bit, but could not tip. Speed it did not have, but its canvas square-rigged sails were coated with a dark blue solar membrane and it could proceed at a steady pace whether the wind blew or not.

The Maine Coast Ferries each took a week or so to make the run up and back between Piscataqua and the Bay of Fundy, because of all the stops on the route, but there were several of them, so each of their ports of call got a visit from a ferry going in each direction every day.

The plan was for Elzy and Andy to explore the Maine coast by ferry and water taxi for about a month. They would make the Penobscot River by early July and catch a river boat inland before the worst of the hurricane season began in August. From there, they would head south again overland.

After walking so far, it was a very novel thing to simply sit and be a passenger. Andy was happy to relax, but Elzy, restless, volunteered to help the sailors handle line. She would have climbed the rigging if they'd let her, but that required extra training. Andy watched her pestering them with intelligent questions and grinned.

But as evening fell Elzy slowed in her work and then stopped, leaning her elbows on the rail and looking out over the water towards land. Andy joined her, and together they watched the sun set behind the dark forests. Elzy seemed more relaxed than he'd seen her before. She smiled in greeting but said nothing to him, just watched the shoreline slide by. The breeze made her dark hair dance a little.

"It *is* beautiful," ventured Andy, guessing that was the reason for her strange, mellow mood.

"It is," she agreed, in a tone suggesting he'd guessed wrong. "It's *almost* right," she added. She seemed lost in thought.

Andy frowned a little, confused.

"'Right?'"

"Yes. *Right*." Elzy looked at him then, still smiling a little. "All my life, something's felt a little wrong, a little off, but this feels right. Or almost right, anyway. I don't know what I mean."

"Is it the sea? Have you seen the sea before?"

"Yes—I've gone to the beaches in Delaware with my mother, but that was less right than this."

Andy had seen Delaware's coast from shipboard and he remembered it as a vast complex of sand beaches, natural and artificial dunes, the ruins of various beach resorts, and then pine scrub, more dunes, and salt march stretching back away from the water as far as he could see. The beaches and marshes he had seen today were mostly darker, coarser, and interrupted here and there by rock ledges and slabs. There were no dunes, only grassy slope or forest, hurricane-wrecked vacation homes, and fishing villages. But he had no idea what distinction Elzy was drawing, or even if she was reacting to something objectively there at all.

"Some places are like that," Andy acknowledged. "The first time I saw the desert it was like I was home."

"Have you ever gone back there?"

"Yes, for a while. I met my second wife out West. Maybe I'll go again." He had never before mentioned his second marriage to Elzy, but he didn't realize there was anything odd about his doing so now. In the gathering dusk he didn't notice her startled expression. He never meant to keep secrets.

"You haven't finished your story," she told him. "I just realized. All these weeks and we haven't gotten back to it."

"How much of it do you want to hear?"

"All of it. However much you want to tell me."

"Alright. Where was I?"

"You were learning new things on your friends' ranch. You'd already decided not to head East and look for your son yet."

"Ah, yes. Yeah, there was a lot to learn. Like, when we slaughtered an animal we wanted to use all of it, but what do you do with a gallbladder? Or lungs? How do you preserve a whole carcass if you don't have either a working freezer or any salt to spare? Obviously, you dry it or smoke it, but which one? And that's a lot of meat. You have to work quickly before it goes bad. We had books and articles we'd downloaded and printed before the internet quit, but we really had to figure a lot of it out on our own.

"And it was all so…like, we were teaching ourselves to build these beautiful, high-tech wind turbines—they'd stocked up on parts—and at the same time we also had to figure out how to make sewing needles out of bone. The little steel ones we had weren't strong enough to pierce leather, which was all we had to make new clothes and blankets for everybody. So it was like high-tech and stone-age skills at the same time.

"Everything we had came from the cattle that first year. When we dug the third tank, we didn't have enough mattocks for everybody, so we made digging sticks out of bones. Almost all we ate was meat. We didn't know most of the edible wild plants and the cows wouldn't let us milk them. We lived on beef and water for eight months.

"After a few months, we stopped getting trespassers. By that point, either you had access to food and didn't need to steal, or you were dead already. And we had survived. That was the beginning. We've been putting our lives back together ever since.

"So, we rode out to make contact with our neighbors. We weren't sure they wouldn't shoot us. It was like a diplomatic mission or something, but we got a conversation going, compared notes.

"Most of the places around us turned out to be subsistence ranches, like us. Some had vegetable gardens, corn fields, or orchards, and some people knew more about wild plants than we did. We traded. Vegetables and dried fruit never tasted so good. And honey? One of our neighbors had honeybees. That was amazing. But we had more meat than most of them and we'd gotten better at making clothes.

"A group of us, about ten ranches, started to meet every month or so around an abandoned gas station—neutral territory. It was still like a summit of separate nations, separate tribes. I guess we made a treaty. We started calling ourselves Chevron Town, after that gas station, and we'd meet to trade and to discuss property boundaries or other issues. That was the beginning of our market and our town council. I think most of the other towns in the country went through basically the same process."

"Every month? Not every week?" Elzy asked.

"Out west there's less water, so you need more land to feed the same number of people. We were really spread out. Not everyone had horses, and it took them a long time to come in."

"What would you do at those markets?"

"The same things people do now: trade food and other goods, teach each other new skills, party.... The people with the bees were making mead, and a couple of folks had musical instruments, guitars mostly. We'd meet for business, then we'd camp together and take turns telling stories or singing. There were always birthdays to celebrate...." Andy felt himself smile, remembering those giant parties under the stars in the desert near the Chevron.

He remembered but did not say that a lot of the stories told around the campfires were about the dead or missing. A lot of the birthdays they celebrated were for people who weren't there anymore. Twenty years later, Andy could still recall most of the names he'd heard mourned by the people of Chevron, Arizona. And he was bad with names. It just felt like a duty to remember. As he'd told Elzy, it's hard to hold on to something if nobody around you does, so they'd helped each other by listening to and retelling the stories. And yet, he'd never told anyone about his wife, his first wife, Jenny. He still wasn't ready to share her with anybody.

"We had prayer services, too, sometimes," he added, quietly. "To pray for the missing."

It was completely dark, now, in the here-and-now that Andy had almost forgotten about as he told his story. The stars were obscured by a high haze and the moon had yet to rise. The shore slipping by before them was a full, rich black, and the open sea behind them was a vaster black. Most of the other passengers and half the crew were below deck, asleep. Some of the sailors of the watch moved here and there, quietly, working by the light of tiny, red LED flashlights, but most of them napped, sprawled out on the deck. A cool breeze hurried the ferry along and the only sound, when Andy wasn't talking, was the susurration of the waves slipping around the hull.

He was very aware, all of a sudden, of Elzy standing next to him, of the warmth and the weight of her body. It wasn't exactly sexual, this awareness, but she didn't seem daughterly at that moment, either. It was only that she was another human being beside him in the dark. For a moment he was sure she would touch him, offer some kind of comforting, friendly gesture, but she did not.

"I can't picture you praying," confessed Elzy. As an atheist, she tended to assume that intelligent people didn't.

"I do pray, sometimes," he said, quietly.

Just then, they heard bare feet running on the deck and turned to see the crew all in a rush of activity, each visible only by his or her red flashlight. One of them shooed the two passengers away from the rail so she could access the lines. The ferry had almost reached port and would stand offshore and let the passengers sleep till morning. The crew had to furl the sails before dropping anchor.

Elzy turned to Andy and he knew she wanted to leave off storytelling for a bit so she could help.

"Go ahead," he told her, and she was off, running barefoot across the wooden deck like one of the sailors. When the ship was secure he was going to suggest that they go to bed and get some rest.

Chapter 5
Islands

In the morning, the ferry motored into port, solar sails flying, and Andy and Elzy disembarked into an island of order in a sea of chaos.

Portland, Maine had once been an active, populous city. Now, of course, it was a wreck. Not only had it suffered through the convulsions of the early transition, like any other city, but Hurricane Odette had made landfall just to the south and driven a fourteen-foot storm surge, exacerbated by sea level rise, over every coastal community from Portland south to Boston.

But despite the wreck and ruin, the place still had a good natural harbor, and so a small community had carved out a space for itself to tend the rebuilt docks. Most of their food and other goods came from the sea, or from boats that served as mobile shops, but the people grew some vegetables on lawns or rooftops or parks and grazed goats and sheep at the old airport.

To raise money, the people made things. They were busy recycling the city.

Beyond the little clump of buildings where people lived were foundries, workshops, and small factories powered by landfill gas and by electricity harvested from the winds and tides. In those facilities, the people turned the trash and wrecked cars and other civilized detritus into tools, electronic devices, motor vehicles, and weapons—anything farmers couldn't make themselves. It was all available by mail-order. Elzy's cell had come from Portland, all the way to her mother's home in Pennsylvania.

And as the people of Portland worked, they cleared the land around them of raw materials, even to the point of breaking up the concrete and asphalt and sending it off for use graveling roads. Already a green circle, mostly goat pasture and young woodlot, surrounded the settlement. The soil exposed from under the ruins was very poor, of course, and would be for generations, but animal dung and leaf mold were gradually working improvement, and the green circle got wider every year. The little Portland settlement was soaking up the wreckage of civilization the way grains of salt pull in tomato juice.

Portland also took care of travelers. Its hostels and inns and restaurants were famous. Elzy was sorry she couldn't stay longer. At least she got to have lunch when they stopped to change money—each state had its own shares, and the restaurants and inns of borders and ports could handle exchanges. She ordered a lobster roll, her first, and enjoyed it, but Andy had trouble finding something he wanted. He spoke to the waiter and got an egg salad sandwich that wasn't on the menu.

Their next stop was a hostel in West Falmouth, a little farming town a few miles' walk up the coast. For reasons he did not explain, Andy chose a route through the heart of Portland's ruined city center, a broken landscape where people rarely bothered to go.

Almost every surface was concrete, asphalt, or glass, and everything was cracked, bent, scorched, or covered with mud from the hurricane and more recent floods. Junked cars sat rotting where riots had left them twenty years earlier, and no human voices spoke unless Elzy or Andy raised theirs.

But there were birds filling the silence, singing from the branches of young trees that grew with their roots splitting concrete. A coyote watched them pass from a tangle of grass and weeds, her triangular face calm but wary. The storm drains had all long since clogged, so small creeks ran through the streets between banks of broken asphalt, washed-up debris, and sediment stamped with raccoon tracks. Once, they came around a corner and startled a great blue heron into flight. Deer grazed in the old parks or darted across the wide and pitted streets. Elzy found and recognized bear scat, something she rarely saw in the farmland.

"The world is turning inside out," Andy told her, smiling. "It's the cities that are wild now."

Elzy smiled, too. She could see how some might find it eerie, but she liked the city. She did not like the outlying suburbs they passed through on the way out of town.

The riots hadn't touched these neighborhoods, nor had the storm-surge. The hurricane had lobbed traffic lights and tree branches through house roofs and the display windows of strip-malls, but most of the buildings looked intact. There was plenty of open space for gardens. Even just a few years earlier, the area could have been reclaimed, repaired, reoccupied, but the population was so small now that no one had bothered. The houses and shops waited, empty, year after year, gradually sagging and rotting towards oblivion.

The plucky, nascent wildness of the city had spoken to Elzy of beginnings, but the much greener suburbs spoke to her only of loss and waste.

The suburbs still seemed too human, that was the problem. On some of the old lawns, grown tall now with young trees, Elzy saw the remains of barbecues, trampolines, dog dishes, all lying where they'd been left long ago. Bleached out plastic toys sat, pale pink and blue, waiting to be reclaimed by children who would never come.

Elzy had seen such things before, but always she had seen them simply in the present tense, as trees with ruins and trash in among them. She had known they were from Before, but that purely intellectual understanding had had no hold on her. But since Andy had been teaching her to read landscape histories, *place* had acquired a fourth dimension. The past had become visible, and the past she saw here made her feel sad and lonely. The kids who had owned those toys would have been her age now, a generation of which barely one in twenty was left alive. She was that one.

"Andy, will this place ever *really* be natural again?"

"What's 'natural,'?" Andy asked, picking his way through a tangle of fallen, dead power cables.

"Like it used to be, before people got here and screwed it all up."

"Aren't humans natural?" Andy asked. Elzy could hear him smiling, though she couldn't see his face. She was busy watching her footing, too. "Humans have been here since the end of the glacier and it was the glacier that created the topography and soil chemistry of what we know as New England," he added. "There never was a New England without humans, and humans change the land—manage it. That's what humans *do*."

Elzy frowned and lapsed into silence for a long while.

"But that's not what I meant," she said, after so long a pause that Andy had to think hard to remember what they'd been talking about. "Whatever 'natural' means or doesn't, will it come home to itself? Will the forest that's supposed to be here come back?"

"I'd like you to clarify that question, Elzy. There are a lot of assumptions in there that are important to unpack. But as to whether a place can return to how it was before a profound disturbance? That, again, is a difficult question. It depends on whether the conditions that generated that original community still exist—climate, soil type, seed availability, and so on."

"Places are mortal, then. You change all that, and the old identity is gone, forever?"

"Yes. But places are hard to kill. You clear away a mess of exotic plants, restore an older fire regime or an older hydrology, and a lot of the time the old community does come back, or part of it does, anyway. It depends what's left in the seedbed, how far away other similar communities are, what kind of connectivity is left…

if there are enough hints of the original structure, the community can re-member itself. It's called ecological memory."

"The capacity of something living to reclaim itself, to heal, to become whole again." They had covered the concept in class, once.

"Yes. Not all memories are *good*, exactly. The seedbed can contain just a whole bunch of invasive exotics…and sometimes there are keystone species that are dead, extinct, so there is no way for the old community to re-establish. Or, there might be a loss of connectivity, so that even if the right species still exist somewhere, they can't recolonize. But even if the land has forgotten what it used to be, it can still heal following a disturbance, as happened after the glacier. It can still become a new kind of place and be whole. It just takes longer."

"I like that," said Elzy, walking along.

That night, in the hostel in West Falmouth, Elzy dreamed that she lay on her back while slim, young trees grew from her arms and legs and belly. Her breasts and the hollows of her armpits, the soft place at her throat, became the pillows and cradles of soil that form from old, uprooted trees long since returned to earth. She watched her branches turn green and heard birds sing from them, robins and phoebes and a rare warbler she'd heard once, but Andy hiked to the summit of her rib cage and looked down at her and said, "yes, but did this landscape even have an original condition?"

And then she woke to the sound and scent of an egg frying. Odd. They had the hostel to themselves, so obviously Andy was cooking, but normally she handled breakfast. She jumped out of bed and wandered into the hostel kitchen in her nightshirt, her braids still pointing every which way from sleep.

"I can do that," she protested.

"You *can*," agreed Andy, and continued to make breakfast. "There's chicory," he added. He was already fully dressed, shaved, and showered. Elzy poured herself a cup and sat down at the rough wooden table, feeling a bit confused. Andy scooted the egg from the fry pan onto a plate already loaded down with home fries, served her the plate, and sat down opposite with his own meal.

"Thanks?" said Elzy.

"I can be nice sometimes!" Andy exclaimed, rather defensively, which Elzy found odd, because he always was nice. He didn't always make her breakfast, though. "I checked the weather report," he added. "It's going to storm this afternoon. We've got to get out of here."

Elzy nodded, understanding. The old saying, *it doesn't rain except when it pours* had become almost literally true, at least in New England, where two or three weeks' worth of rain often arrived in a single cloudburst. This being June now, there might be hail. They planned to commute to her next venue by water-taxi, and being caught out in a storm in an open boat would be bad. She ate her breakfast in a hurry, showered, and threw on her clothes.

They made it. The first squall line rolled in just as Elzy's program began and the sound of the rain on the roof made her feel cozy and warm. Hers was one of several acts of a two-day cultural festival in a refurbished old barn, and the organizers happily let her and Andy sleep in the loft until morning. Storm waves lashed the coast that night but the pounding rain dulled the sound and Elzy slept safe and dry and happy.

Working and traveling in coastal Maine proved totally different from the weeks they'd spent in New Hampshire. For one thing, here the sea and not the land defined the distance from place to place.

The coast had its roads, but they were seldom the most efficient way to get any place. The Maine seashore can't go more than about twenty feet without crinkling itself into coves and headlands and inlets. Casco Bay, where Elzy and Andy planned to spend two and a half weeks, is especially crenelated. On maps, its peninsulas resemble a series of closely spaced icicles, each dripping islands off into the sea. At one time, a system of bridges had connected each peninsula to its associated islands, and most of those bridges still functioned, but no bridge could connect the long rows to each other. An island five miles away as a gull flies might be fifty miles away by road. Without petroleum, boats were a necessity.

But the sea connected the coastal people rather than separating them. The high price of biofuel limited most inlanders to the pace of human or animal feet, but a sailboat could harness either wind or sun for free. Islanders could commute twenty miles and back in a single day, so they had no need to wait for markets to get together. Elzy's bookings were scattered across the week.

The other big change was that Andy had abruptly delegated their day-to-day travel arrangements to Elzy. As he explained, in the last two weeks she'd shown new professionalism and confidence, so he'd thrown her another challenge. And a challenge it was. She had ten events in fourteen days and none of them were anywhere near each other. Successive days might give her events on opposite ends of the bay. If it had been up to her, she would not have made their itinerary so geographically complex, but Andy had not delegated event scheduling. He would not allow Elzy to collaborate on, or even question, any responsibility he reserved as his, though her job would have been easier if he had.

She asked him to at least tell her where *his* appointments were, so she could plan around them, but he evaded her effort to be helpful and changed the subject.

Eventually, she decided that finding lodging near each event was too much of a hassle. She booked their rooms in West Falmouth straight through to almost the end of June and told Andy they'd have to commute by water taxi from there.

The advantage of working small, isolated events was that she was often the only speaker or workshop leader there. Headlining, under whatever circumstances, would look very good on her resumé. Her confidence grew and, coincidence or not, her little kid-act receded. But the disadvantage was that a small crowd could easily become no crowd at all through shear bad luck, if a single family's boat sprang a leak, for example. Once, she spent over an hour by herself in a rented church basement, waiting fruitlessly for participants to arrive, reduced by boredom to reading insipidly rewritten children's Bible stories. After that, she always kept fresh reading material on her phone, just in case. And yet, once again, she had no actual time off.

Andy didn't always go with her. He had decided that her performances were already professional quality, and he had business elsewhere. He never told her what his other business was, but he put his black professional garb back on to go do it. When he turned up one morning at the dock in his blue cotton, she smiled because it meant he was coming with her that day.

"Do you think people know you're my teacher, dressed like that?" she asked him. She wasn't criticizing. He shrugged.

"You don't need me with you anymore, therefore you don't need other people to know I am with you," he explained. She took that as a compliment. He didn't give her many.

They chatted for a few minutes about this and that, and then Elzy checked the time on her phone and frowned.

"When's your taxi due?" Andy asked.

"I couldn't get a hold of the taxi last night. I hired a fisherman. He's four—five—minutes late."

"Maybe he got hung up on the tide?"

"He shouldn't," said Elzy, irritably. "It's not like the tide is a *surprise*. Maybe he ran off with my money."

"How much did you pay him?"

"Two shares."

"That's high."

"I know. I couldn't find anybody else. You'd think he'd want repeat customers at a price like that."

"Not necessarily."

"Wait! Is that him?" A little sailboat had just blown into view. Elzy waited patiently until it docked, but the man who hopped out of it was not the man she'd paid. He hadn't heard of the fisherman she was looking for, and he couldn't take her to Baily's Island himself because he was going in the other direction.

"Now he's thirty minutes late. Where *is* he?"

"I hope he's OK."

"I hope he didn't run off with my money."

"Can you call him?"

"I don't have his number."

"Can you call the event organizer?"

But no, Elzy couldn't do that, either. Her phone's battery had just run out.

"Can I use your tablet?" she asked.

"I left it in the lock box in my room. It's out of juice, anyway."

"Damn, what am I going to do?"

"Be late, quite possibly," Andy told her. She scowled at him behind his back, but as far as she could tell, he wasn't trying to be a smart-ass. He was just answering her question. And oddly, the response did calm her a little. No sense struggling against reality. She would have preferred a magic solution to her problem over a lesson in Zen, though. At least Andy wasn't giving her a lecture on the importance of punctuality. She scowled again.

Elzy paced up and down the empty wharf for a while, vaguely hoping that somehow a boat would appear, but all the fishermen had gone out for the day long since. She looked at her phone again, but of course the screen was blank.

"It's gotta be at least nine, now. I'll never make it, even if I did find a ride. I'd need a police boat or something. Something with a real motor."

"Like that one?" Andy asked, pointing. And indeed, miracle of miracles, one was putting along just beyond the wharf. Elzy ran out to the end of the floating dock and flagged the policeman down.

"Are you all right, Miss?" the cop asked her. Of course he thought she was having an emergency.

"Yes," she admitted. "I'm just late. My ride vanished. Can you take us?"

"What do I look like, a taxi driver?" but the cop was smiling at her.

"A little, yeah," Elzy replied, smiling back. "Anyway, the worst you could say if I asked is no."

"That's true," the officer acknowledged. "I'm not supposed to, but....Hey, listen, what do you do? Where are you going?"

"I'm a comedienne. I have a show on Bailey's Island. He's coming with me." She pointed at Andy, who nodded.

"You're a comedienne, huh? So, the show can't go on without you?"

"Nope. And it's my first booking with these people."

"Oh, that's no good." The cop thought for a moment. "OK, tell you what. Tell me a joke. If I laugh, we'll call it payment for the ride and I'll take you, both of you."

Elzy considered. She normally wasn't very funny one-on-one. Something about a crowd drew her out and amped her up—anyway human behavior was simpler, easier to manipulate, in large groups. People laughed because their neighbors did. Telling a joke to just one person? She had no idea what this man even found funny. Unless he *wanted* her to make him laugh? So he could give her a ride?

"OK, knock-knock," she started.

"Who's there?"

"Interrupting cow."

"Interrupt—"

"MOO!"

The officer laughed and tied the boat off to a cleat so they could hop aboard. Once away from the wharf he gunned the ethanol engine and the boat tipped back, skipping across the waves.

The day was beautiful, not so horribly hot as it had been, with a crisp, salty breeze. Streaks of cloud suggested rain on the way but didn't block the sun, which shone on the waves almost intolerably bright. Their way took them out into the open bay beyond the islands, past rocky headlands and forested islets and lobstermen checking their traps attended by gulls. Wind turbines spun smartly here and there, their arms white against the blue-and-white-streaked sky.

The cop tried to talk to Elzy a couple of times, but between the motor noise and the damp wind of their own passing, she couldn't hear him clearly. She and Andy just hung on to their sunhats and grinned at each other.

Finally, the boat turned into a big cove on a little island and pulled up to one of a group of wharves. The complex sat oddly low to the water, evidently a relic of the twentieth century and a lower sea level—already the floating dock rode only three feet below the stationary decking and the full moon tide still had at least an hour to run. And yet the place had survived Hurricane Odette. Elzy had to admire its pluck.

The cop tied the boat up and cut the engine. Andy shook his hand and thanked him before climbing over the side. Elzy went to thank the man, too, and he smiled at her almost apologetically.

"So, ah, is your grandfather going to kick my ass if I ask for your number?"

"Oh, he doesn't have to get protective," Elzy told him lightly. "I'm a former vigilante." She smiled at him, but something about her manner, her emphasis on the word vigilante, made the cop stop smiling and become very professional with her.

She had known he was probably going to ask for her number, and she'd been planning on giving it to him, but that last comment had rubbed her very much the wrong way. First, she needed protection from *nobody*. Second, her mother had taught her not to trust men who even so much as joked about her needing protection from themselves. At best, such guys were possessive. At worst, they were right. She shook his hand confidently, like a man would, and hopped ashore before he could insist on helping her. Then she thanked him again—no need to totally burn a bridge with a cop— and waved until he motored off.

"*Grandfather?*" Andy sputtered as soon as the officer was well out of earshot. "Do I really look that *old?*"

Elzy looked at him appraisingly for a moment, considering his worn, leathery skin and ashy hair. He looked like he might be sixty, sixty-five, and she knew she looked younger than her twenty-six years. Yes, in a pinch, he looked like he could be her grandfather.

At the same time, if Andy was old, he was the youngest old person she had ever met. His movements were efficient and vigorous. There was an eagerness, almost an innocence, to his face. Sometimes she forgot they were not of the same generation. Thinking of him that way, she couldn't believe he was much past forty.

"I don't know," she said finally. "Maybe he thought you were precocious or something?" Her joke made Andy smirk. "He probably just didn't want to think that you might be my boyfriend," she added, more seriously. Andy's eyebrows went up.

"Then I'd rather he think I am your grandfather," he said. Elzy glanced at him, stung. She didn't want him to find her *attractive*, per se, but she didn't want any straight man to think she was repulsive, either. Andy rolled his eyes. "I can't get fired on suspicion of being your grandfather, now can I?" he pointed out.

Elzy knew she was supposed to speak at a grange hall, but the address and directions were saved on her cell, which was useless at present. She looked around for someone to ask and noticed that the building on the wharf where they had landed housed an inn and a restaurant. She stepped inside and found a very old woman, evidently the proprietor, busily sweeping the floor. The woman explained that the hall was at the crest of the island, just off the main road, on the other side of the cove—at least a mile away. Elzy yelped, reflexively checked the time on her dead cell, and set off walking quickly. Andy followed, but they hadn't gone a quarter mile before she stopped again so abruptly that he almost walked into her.

"Andy, I forgot to ask the officer to pick us up. How are we going to get back to West Falmouth?"

"We'll ask someone else for a ride," he told her patiently. "Keep walking."

But after she had finished performing and fielding questions, there was no one else to ask. None of the people in her audience were headed that way, and no one who lived on the island was likely to go anywhere until the next morning.

"Joel has a water taxi," one woman commented, before remembering why Elzy couldn't call for a ride. "I'd let you use our cell, but my son has it today. I'm not sure when he'll get back."

No one else in the little group had a cell to lend, either. Some did not even own one. They all dispersed, sympathetically cluck-ing. Elzy felt her panic give way to despair and then to the reali-zation that she had no reason *not* to spend the night on Bailey's Island. This wasn't actually a disaster. She hid her face in her hands a moment and sighed, then let her hands slip down her face, pull-ing her cheeks, lower eyelids, and lower lip downward. She showed Andy the resulting ridiculous expression, and they both laughed.

They checked into the inn on the wharf and had dinner at its restaurant. Again, Andy had trouble with the menu. Maine's shell-fish were doing badly because of the warming, acidic waters, but there were so few humans left on the coast to eat them that there was still plenty to go around. Every restaurant in the region prided itself on food Andy couldn't or wouldn't eat—he didn't keep fully kosher, but did avoid the proscribed species. Finally he settled on a green salad with cottage cheese and a glass of blueberry wine. Elzy had no such problem and ordered lobster chowder, which tasted excellent but had no lobster meat in it. Apparently, the chef had simmered lobster shells in sheep's milk for flavoring, then added canned corn and fresh garlic, dill, tarragon, and fresh chives.

After dinner, the June sun was still high and golden. Elzy went outside to enjoy it, but ended up at the rail of the wharf, just star-ing down at the receding tide and looking glum. After paying the bill, Andy joined her.

"Still pissed at your ride?" he asked. She shrugged.

"Whatever," she answered. "Stuff happens. I'm mad at me. I didn't have a plan B. I had the directions on my phone and I didn't make sure it was charged. What if the grange hall had been on the other end of the island? I'm just lucky the whole thing worked out as well as it did."

"Yeah, well, a lot of people are lucky." The statement was am-biguous, so Elzy made a questioning noise. He clarified. "I mean, a lot of the things that work out do because of dumb luck. You do the best you can to be prepared and yeah, you can do better next time, but you're right, shit happens. People make mistakes, even you. It'll keep you humble."

Elzy grunted, a sort of half a chuckle. Humility wasn't her strong suit, though lack of confidence sometimes hid that fact. Andy asked if she wanted to go on a walk with him.

"Where?" She asked. Andy pointed back up to the spine of the island.

"When we were up there for your presentation, I heard surf. Might be some interesting tide pools."

Given Elzy's mood, the hill looked positively alpine—she would have rather crawled into bed and stayed there. But she knew the walk would cheer her up, so she agreed. Andy retied his shoelace and they set out. Within just a few minutes she started to perk up.

Their route took them along a sandy, grassy, spit of land that divided Mackerel Cove from a smaller cove behind. Together the two coves almost split the island in two, but the side with the wharf on it was low and mostly forested while on the other side a high hill rose. A steep earthen slope, almost a cliff, swept up from the water to the highest ridge of that hill, apparently the highest point on the island. The road climbed the hill at a shallower angle along a grassy, widening ramp that might have been natural but also might not have been. It was a curious topography, one Andy could not explain.

The little isthmus could clearly be over-topped by storm waves. There were no houses or gardens there, only the road, two piles of old lobster pots, and tangles of orache plants, beach pea vines, clusters of rose bushes, and a single crab-apple tree leaning far out over a wrack-strewn beach. A rope with a big knot in the end hung from that tree, for swinging. Elzy stopped to give it a try and sailed out over the sloping sand. Andy leaned against the tree trunk and watched patiently.

Elzy sang as she swung, a line or two she had heard somewhere about swinging on stars and carrying home moonbeams.

"Which is kind of what scientists do," Andy remarked.

"How's that?" asked Elzy. After her first few arcs the swing lost momentum quickly. There is no effective way to pump a one-rope swing, and her attempts to keep moving left her spinning around in an irregular way. She kicked at the ground when she could reach it, trying to push off.

"Well, there's Mystery out there—the star, starlight," Andy explained. "We attach ourselves to it, build our lives on it, swing there for as long as we can, and bring some of it back for other people."

"Aren't scientists supposed to bring back answers, not more mysteries?" Elzy asked.

"Answers are highly over-rated," he replied. "What's the point of a great answer if you don't have the right question?"

"You want a turn?" She would not have asked him that even a few weeks ago. Something had shifted between them since that day in the apple orchard. She didn't know whether he had changed or if just her perception of him had, but he seemed more human to her.

"Sure, why not?" He took the rope in his hands. Instead of sitting on the knot, as Elzy had, he jumped up and stood on it, swinging out, spinning as he went. He, too, tried pulling the rope this way and that so he could maintain his momentum, but his efforts only made his arcs even more unstable and he collided with the tree-trunk, hard. He hopped off, grimacing.

"Too bad you can't drop from the rope into the ocean," Elzy remarked, as Andy recovered himself. The cool water looked inviting. In fact, way down the beach, three middle-aged women enjoyed an artificial brick tide-pool under a big, blue umbrella. Slightly tipsy laughter reached Elzy's ears, but the women didn't look like they wanted company, nor did Elzy want theirs.

"Yeah, really," Andy agreed, and made ready to try the swing again. Launching himself, he swung out and at the apex of the arc he leaped free, spinning, seeming to hang, for a moment, in midair. He landed on the beach in a crouch, looked up at Elzy, and grinned.

They walked on and gained the ridge, where several small houses clustered, each with its garden of potatoes, peas, squash, sweet corn, tomatoes, and sunflowers. Everyone had a couple of crops their neighbors didn't, and the fences were all neatly trimmed hedges of the same *Rugosa* roses that had been growing semi-wild above the beach. They weren't native but had become iconic of the New England coast anyway, kept for both decorative purposes and for their large, fleshy hips that made excellent tea and jam. The main flush of flowers was past, but a few of the gloriously scented pink or white blossoms remained. Small orchards of blueberries or raspberries grew here and there, and everyone had an apple tree or two for shade and fruit. Goats and chickens wandered freely in the streets.

"How do these people eat?" asked Elzy. "There's no way these little gardens can provide all the produce for a whole family."

"They don't," Andy explained. "Each family owns two or three properties. They rent the houses in the summer to inlanders escaping the heat and keep the extra gardens for themselves. The inlanders bring a lot of their own food."

"Clever!"

"Tourism has been big in Maine's coastal economy for a long time. It's interesting that they've found a way to keep that going."

The grange hall was a barn-like building on a side road in among those houses, and Elzy and Andy returned to it as a landmark. From there, they wandered around for a bit, following the lane down a long, gentle slope towards the shore. A public footpath branched off and they followed it along the grassy top of a rocky escarpment some ten or fifteen feet above the high tide line. No beach faced the water on this side of the island, only shelves and fingers and cliffs of stone and miniature coves and bays filled with multicolored cobbles. The full power of the Atlantic Ocean curled and curled and curled against the shore, pounding and green without end. Elzy slipped off her shoes, tied them to her belt, and ran off to clamber around on the rocks.

Clearly she had no interest in scientific lectures at the moment, so Andy let her climb. Rather than trying to rein in his student, he joined her. He hadn't been bouldering in a long time, and the tide was on its way out, so there was no danger from the waves.

After a few minutes, he thought to offer Elzy some climbing tips, but when he found her again he saw she was already doing everything he would have suggested. She kept her hips centered over her feet, clung expertly to tiny nubbins of rock, and used counter-pressure in various directions to climb when there were no holds to cling to. The only mistake he saw her make—and she made it a couple of times—was not checking holds to see if they were stable. The weathered, gray-brown rock here was rotten in places. Some handholds came off.

Only when Elzy gravitated to a tide-pool on her own initiative did he approach her.

"What did you find?" he asked. The pool was not one he would have chosen, for it was small and high up, filled only with spray from the waves mixed with rain. Its water might be briny as the Dead Sea on a hot afternoon and all but fresh an hour later after a storm. Nothing could live for long in such an unstable place. Yet there Elzy was, curled up with her knees on bare rock, her face inches above the surface. She looked up at him.

"Little bugs," she explained. "Or...something, anyway. Look at them all!" There were indeed little gray dots, apparently alive, swarming upon the surface in a clump of several dozen.

"I don't know what those are, either," he confessed, sitting down. "I've seen them before...."

"That's the most important thing for an educator to be able to say," Elzy remarked.

"What?"

"'I don't know.'"

"That's very true. I say it very well, don't I?"

"Look," she said, presently, pointing to a pebble in the middle of the pool, "it's an island on an island." Indeed, the pebble did break the surface of the shallow water. Andy shifted his position. It was hard to get comfortable on the irregular rock. He didn't know how Elzy did it, but guessed being twenty-six helped.

"That pool is an island on an island," he told her.

"Really?"

"Sure. Think of it from the perspective of a fish. Or those bugs, whatever they are."

"OK, yeah."

"What makes an island an island isn't water per se, it's isolation. All the same rules apply to any isolated patch, whether it's a tide pool surrounded by land, a landmass surrounded by sea, or the top of a mountain somewhere."

"Or a park."

"Yes! Exactly!" He was pleased that she remembered their earlier conversation and could apply the concept.

"This is a temporary island," she said, of the pool.

"Yes, well, all islands are, if you wait long enough."

Andy looked to see Elzy's reaction to this counter-intuitive truth, and was pleased by her surprise. Of course, she must know intellectually that islands change, but viscerally, the ground seems as permanent as permanent gets. He thought her surprise was the beginning of an awareness of the non-obvious. He didn't realize that she was, in fact, amazed *by him*. She had understood that at geologic timescales, even a few million years could be brief. She had just never known anyone before for whom the small and the large scales were equally and simultaneously real.

She smiled back at him and looked away. After a moment, she returned her attention to the pool, splashing a little with one hand, playing with her reflection. It was a charmingly girlish gesture, but she wasn't doing her little kid routine. She'd been doing it less lately.

"Those parks were temporary," she remarked. Since the pandemic, there had been no Federal government, and therefore no Federal land management and no National Park System. "Did the parks get turned into farms or something?"

"Depends. Some did. Others are now protected locally. And a lot of the more remote areas have been abandoned, so the land around the old boundaries is re-wilding."

"Did they do any good?"

"You mean for conservation?"

"Yes."

"Yeah, I'd say so. They couldn't protect the land forever, but in some cases they worked for long enough."

"Andy, are the towns temporary islands? Each one seems so isolated. Some of the people I've worked with...they act like I'm so exotic."

He blushed a little at the question. He'd noticed the almost constant little glances occasioned by Elzy's brownish skin. There was no hostility, none he could see anyway, simply an automatic recognition of Other. As though skin color marked a person as different in a way that eye color did not. Watching older people especially notice *blackness*, and knowing that he still saw skin color that way too, Andy felt himself to be white and did not like it.

But Elzy was also exotic in ways more relevant to the isolation they'd been discussing. She was a stranger in an age when few people traveled, and a scholar and educator in a world where few people looked much beyond their own farm fields. He hoped that had been what she'd been thinking of, and he responded as if he were sure, keeping himself on solid conversational ground.

"Between the internet and people like you," he told her, "the towns are connected well enough culturally. But you're right, they may be islands economically."

"How long do the towns have, then? Are they...relaxing towards equilibrium, too?"

"I don't know," Andy said somberly. "I can tell you we have a chance now. We have a chance of not further exhausting our land and shrinking our resource base, and if we do need to reduce our population further, we have a chance of doing it by attrition only."

"Why? How? What changed?"

Andy considered.

"Without oil," he began, "cheap transportation ended. It used to be that economies operated on a global scale—if a localized resource was depleted, it didn't affect the economic system as a whole. Companies simply shifted to the next supplier, and nobody else noticed a difference. Meanwhile, the overall ecological deficit deepened. Systems, of whatever type—social, economic, political, ecological—have a lot of momentum at very large scales. It takes a lot of push before anything changes, a lot of damage. Even for those of us who knew better, environmental degradation seemed kind of unreal, because most of the time we didn't see it unless we looked. And political decision-making was mostly large-scale, too, so it wasn't very responsive, either. Now that transportation costs so much, we're dependent on local economies again. That shifts the relevant scale downward, so we'll feel resource depletion sooner—and we'll be able to do something about it."

"But the global economy predated the industrial revolution."

"It did to an extent," he agreed. "But the trade networks and imperial powers of the past are gone, too. Could those networks redevelop? Not in my lifetime. My generation is too scared of starving again to ever depend on somebody else's land for food. After us? I don't know. We have a chance."

"Now you're making it sound like it's *good* to be an island."

"I wouldn't say good or bad—but isolation protects, stimulates, *and* imperils. Island populations are vulnerable because they're small and because they can't easily be replenished from outside after a disturbance. That's another part of why isolated preserves don't work very well—going back to ecological memory, if an island 'forgets,' there's nothing to help it remember. Isolation makes recovery from disturbance slower and harder. Islands are where species go to die, as they say. But they also say islands are where evolution plays—weird forms develop in isolation, like flightless parrots or dwarfed elephants. Species that die out on mainlands persist and diversify on islands, like lemurs in Madagascar or giant tortoises in the Pacific and Indian Oceans. Lose the isolation, and all that ends, too."

"So the trick is to protect isolation where it's needed and prevent it where it's not?"

"No, the trick is to really understand a system before you fuck with it." His blunt language made Elzy laugh and lightened the mood.

"OK," she said, "so, my job as an educator is to make sure people know to keep their *economies* isolated *and* to pay attention to the systems they live with?"

"Yes, exactly," Andy agreed. Then he noticed that the sea was in shadow. The sun was setting sun behind the island. "We'd better get moving," he said. "We're going to lose light soon."

"Right!" said Elzy, getting up and heading out further along the rocks.

"Um, Elzy?"

"The path runs along the top of the rocks," she explained, "and there's a full moon tonight. So when the sun goes down, we can walk back along the path by moonlight. But we can't climb on rocks by moonlight, so we should go out as far as we can while we still can." And she ran off.

"I like how you think," he muttered, following along behind.

When he caught up to her again, she was sitting on what looked like a giant black staircase, its risers a foot and a half to two feet high, that ran down into the water some fifteen or twenty feet below. The stairs were the eroded end of a basalt or gabbro dyke, a *dyke* being a place where, millions of years earlier, back when all this stone was still deeply buried, molten rock had squeezed up into a crack and hardened there. In fact, the crack in the rock was still visible in the smooth straight walls on either side of the staircase—chunks of the dyke must have broken away, creating the steps and leaving an open gap five or ten feet across.

Andy frowned, puzzled. Why had the tough black rock eroded away so much faster than the material around it, when the latter was so soft that in places it broke like a cookie in the hand? He wasn't a geologist and could not guess. Waves surged dramatically against the lowest steps and beat themselves green and white between the surrounding walls of brown stone. Elzy kicked her bare feet like a child and stared down at the water. The tide had turned.

She looked up at his approach.

"Red sky at night, sailor's delight!" she said, pointing.

"I'd say that's more of an orange," Andy replied, and sat down beside her. The sky was clear and cloudless, but a little haze at the horizon caught and reflected the light of the setting sun.

"What do sailors think of orange?" Elzy asked. "It doesn't rhyme with anything."

"I don't know," he told her. The sea was entirely in shadow now, a deep blue under the sherbet sky. Had the sun set yet? The full moon would rise at the same moment, and he looked for its appearance along the horizon for some minutes, waiting—but the moon was already up. In the still-bright sky it did not glow, and he realized he'd over-looked it. There it hung, a finger's width clear of the horizon, huge and round and ruddy and dull as paint.

"Why did you take off your shoes?" he asked.

"Better traction," she replied offhandedly.

"Where did you learn to climb?"

"What?" Elzy seemed a little distracted. "Oh, nowhere. I climbed trees as a kid."

"Not rock?"

"Not usually. There wasn't a lot of it near my Mom's house."

"What about your Dad's house?"

This made Elzy perk up.

"What, you mean—but it couldn't have been *here*, or anywhere near here. This isn't right. I said that already."

"You did," Andy acknowledged. "But I don't believe that you've never been climbing before. You're too good."

"Maybe I'm a natural?"

"No, *I'm* a natural, and I didn't learn to boulder like that in a day. Let me ask you this. Did you take off your shoes because you *did* slip, or because you thought you might?"

"I took them off because the traction's better," she reiterated stubbornly.

"How did you know that if you've never tried it before?" He asked, and Elzy's eyes widened.

"OK, maybe I did learn to climb at my Dad's. But that just means it was somewhere with a lot of rock outcroppings. I already told you, this coastline is *not right*. It's beautiful, I really like it, but it's not home."

"All right, all right." They were quiet for a while. A clear blue line formed at the bottom of the sky, like another layer of sea, but it was the terminator, the shadow the planet made on its own atmosphere. As Andy watched, the blue layer widened, grew, and after some minutes it swallowed the more slowly rising moon. The first glimmer of moonlight appeared upon the water.

"Andy, you came East to look for your son, didn't you?" Elzy asked.

"Yes."

"When? What happened? Will you tell me?"

"Yes." But Andy waited as the blue rose up until the distinction between it and the orange above it was lost and the rocks grew almost luminous by moonlight. When he spoke, he watched the moon like a storyteller watches a campfire.

"I stayed with my friends for over a year. It was spring again when we left. I…was sorry to leave, especially as I wasn't sure I'd ever be able to come back, but I had to find my boy. Some of the others still tried to talk me out of it, they were afraid for me, but people were starting to travel. We had guests, sometimes, who told us news from other places. The roads were open again. So we argued about it, and I won.

"Two of them, Mike and Joni, came with me—there were people back East they wanted to find, too. The others gave us five horses, plus whatever gear we needed. And I rode away from everything I had on a horse. Again." Andy smiled, but Elzy wasn't looking. She was staring out to sea, listening.

"What was it like, that trip?" she asked.

Andy thought about it. The trip had been very long, so it was like a lot of things. There were scary moments and beautiful moments and boring moments, though not too many of those. There was a lot of talking as they rode along—more talking than he wanted, actually. There was something uncomfortably womb-like about traveling with the same people, day after day, for so long, and he'd missed his solitude. Yet he could not have explained to

Elzy, to anyone, what his companions came to mean to him.

But he didn't want to talk about difficulty and boredom. He was tired of talking about his own fear and pain, even in a veiled way, and anyway, Elzy already knew what long-distance travel was like. He sought a more interesting, but equal, truth.

"It was a blast," he said, finally.

"Really?"

"Well, not all of it. But I never thought I'd be able to just take a year and ride across the country. If you tried doing something like that before the pandemic, you'd end up with a hole in your resume you'd have to explain. Everybody could move around so fast, but that meant you *had to*. There wasn't much room in ordinary life for adventure."

"It takes a whole year to ride from Arizona to New Hampshire?" Elzy sounded surprised.

"Not now, it wouldn't," Andy replied, "but it did then because we couldn't just ride straight through. We had to stop for supplies, and we couldn't buy them because there wasn't any money. So, we'd have to work for a while, in trade. And we needed advice on where to go so we wouldn't stumble into some kind of violent craziness. Not all families liked strangers. So all of that took a while."

"What happened to the money they used Before? Dollars?"

"Oh, some people tried to keep using them, but dollars were always kind of an act of faith—they weren't backed by anything with any definite worth. After everything collapsed, people lost faith in the dollar pretty quickly. You could use them in one town for one value and in the next town over they'd have a different value, or they'd be worth nothing at all. People burned them for kindling, used them for toilet paper, or just left them places, in careful little piles on a flat rock with a stone on top. Or you'd find them stuck on cactuses by the wind. Some people tried gold for money, but that didn't really work, either. Gold is pretty, but it's not like you can eat the stuff or fix a fence with it."

"Is that how we ended up on the food standard?" She meant the share, the modern currency tied to the value of survival.

"Yes, but that didn't really start for another year or two—and it's only been ten years that all the states have been on the share system."

"What do you mean, violent craziness?"

"Racial and ethnic stuff, mostly. Gender, too. It wasn't always safe to be a woman—or to be queer or trans. Most people, if you needed something, they'd take care of you, no matter who or what you were. But the problem is that with no police, no larger society, any wingnut who could get a few like-minded friends together could become the law in a piece of territory. There were some towns starting up, but there were also dictatorships and theocracies. There were little empires twenty or thirty miles wide where one family had conquered its neighbors, and there were these enclaves where being black or Latino or Indian or queer could get you killed.

"The funny thing was, if you happened to be part of whatever group these people identified with, they were often the nicest people in the world. They'd stick up for you like family. So we heard, anyway. We never tried. One or another of us was always part of the wrong group. Joni was a woman, Mike was Indian, and I..."

"You're a Jew."

"No—I mean, yes, I am, but *that* wasn't usually the problem. I can pretend to be a gentile for a couple of days, if I have to. No, my problem is I'm a white guy. That could get you killed, in some places. Anyway, I didn't want to bet my life someone wouldn't think I'm gay.

"So we moved along. We'd stop somewhere, work for a while, get directions and supplies, and go on for another two or three weeks. Everywhere we went, we carried a list of survivors, the names of people we'd met. We'd show what we had to our hosts and add their names to the list. There was no internet back then, no way to check to see who was alive and who wasn't, except by meeting somebody who knew. Sometimes we carried letters. That's how news traveled then, with travelers. Some people let us stay and gave us food and supplies in return for the news and mail alone. It was really neat, heading east on horseback, not by train or airplane, and seeing the land change *gradually*, seeing the desert become prairie the same way summer grows out of spring."

"Did you see tornadoes?"

"Sometimes. Once we thought one was going to drop down right on our heads. There were these huge, swirling black and green clouds, the classic anvil-shape, it was damn scary. There was no cover at all, nowhere to hide. But it didn't happen. The funnel didn't come down. The tornadoes we did see were farther away, safer. All we got was hail, though sometimes that was bad enough. We'd unhook our saddlebags and hold them over our heads."

"Did you ever get sick?"

"Well," and so the tale went. Andy wasn't good at telling stories, as he'd said. He had no particular sense of narrative or drama, no way to structure the anecdotes and the information he remembered into a cohesive whole. He kept getting side-tracked by unrelated thoughts or stuck in the middle of his story, unsure of what Elzy might want to hear next. She helped by asking questions, and the answer to each question brought him farther and farther east, closer and closer to his son.

He told her about crossing the Great Plains, about his beloved little horse—a dark bay mare—about the people he had met and the things he had seen. He told her about whole counties where no one lived anymore except for herds of stray cattle or clouds of sandhill cranes. How most of the farm fields they passed lay fallow and either lush with herbicide-tolerant weeds or blasted by drought, depending on the local weather. The land had been broken and poisoned for the sake of people and now the people were all gone.

Except—

He remembered that one day, picking their way across an old field, he'd seen something else in among the weeds and the few dead stalks of last year's volunteer corn. No corn had sprouted this year, but there were new, young grasses here and there, coming up in bluish-green clumps that tugged at his memory somehow. He'd jumped off his horse and knelt to take a closer look—he wasn't especially gifted in plant identification, and grasses are difficult when not in flower. But he was pretty sure this was some kind of *Andropogon*. It might be big bluestem.

The prairie was coming back. He could almost have wept for hope.

Finally, he told her about crossing the Mississippi River at St. Louis on the massive Eads Bridge, which lay empty except for a few crashed cars. He did not tell her about walking through St. Louis and finding the bodies.

Most lay inside wrecked cars or clustered around burnt buildings. Some were clearly victims of violence, while others had been so torn apart by dogs and vultures that their original circumstances were impossible to discern. Most were rotted well past the point where race or sex or social station were visible, but some were big and others little. They lay singly or in groups and the horses shied and fidgeted to see them.

At first, Andy and the others calmed their horses and kept going. They had all heard rumors of what had happened in Phoenix, and in all the refugee settlements they had passed through on their journey the news had been the same—of the people still in the cities after the food trucks stopped coming, not one in fifty had made it out alive. Andy and his friends had thus had some warning about what to expect, so they continued on, sometimes leading their horses on foot through the empty, broken streets.

But mile after mile the bodies continued, and the scale of the thing began to press itself into their minds and drag at their legs. A stray breeze carried the echo of the scent of rot and they all stopped, horrified to near panic. Through the corner of his eye, Andy saw Joni cross herself, though she had never before mentioned being Catholic. The Kaddish repeated itself in his mind, even though he didn't know any of these people, but the once-familiar words brought no comfort. Andy had no stomach for praising God just then.

But he had no time to fall apart. If he panicked, his horse

would panic, and then all of them might as well join this wilderness of bones—they were too deep in the urban ruin now to make it out without the water the animals carried. He took a deep breath and forced calm and confidence into his chest, his arms. The little mare turned her ear in his direction, then looked at him, wondering, perhaps, if he really meant it. He did. He spoke kindly to the animal for a moment and walked on, leading the others out of the valley of the shadow of death.

"Andy? Sorry to interrupt, but it's getting late. The proprietor might think we fell in."

He was startled by her voice, startled by the present. He'd fallen into memory again, not as abruptly as Elzy sometimes did, but nearly as wholly. He agreed with her and stood up, surprised by how high the moon had risen and how far the tide had run. Another few minutes, and their seat would have been catching spray.

Andy felt stiff from sitting so long. Stiff and disoriented. He shook his head to clear it and followed Elzy up the path. She still had her shoes on her belt. She must be barefoot, though he couldn't see her feet because the path was overhung with sedges and the arching branches of small shrubs, all white in the moonlight.

The way ran sometimes literally along the cliff edge, but there was no danger of falling, for the night was brilliant. People said, of nights like this, that you could read by the moon. Of course that was hyperbole. The clarity of moonlight lay not in its brightness but in its directness, its ability to cast a shadow. Andy knew that the strange, silver beauty of the night was a result of there not even being enough light to activate the color-perception cones of his eyes.

Yet he thought that if anyone could actually read by moonlight, Elzy might. She seemed so sure-footed at night. He thought that perhaps her vision was better than his and that his had aged. She might be perfectly capable of rock-climbing by the moon and probably wanted to try. He wondered if maybe she was humoring his limitations by so willingly turning back. If she was, he hoped he would never know.

Even if she was humoring him, he knew the respect she had for him was quite real. He appreciated it. When Andy was honest with himself, he knew he craved it. Elzy saw him as he wished to be seen, as he wished to be—and, generally, how he was. He really was competent, considerate, and wise, but being so took deliberate attention on his part, and he couldn't do it all the time. He needed time alone to think, to recharge. He cultivated isolation, and still he knew he sometimes made mistakes.

The problem was that Elzy was no longer simply a student who looked up to him. Somehow, she had become his friend. Over the past few weeks especially, as she had started acting more mature, less needy—he felt almost safe with her.

The more time he spent with her, the more comfortable he became in their developing friendship, the more likely she was to see some of his shortcomings and failures. Would that change things between them? The depth of her admiration frightened him at times. It was a burden he sometimes wished he could escape.

Elzy, walking barefoot above the moon-brilliant sea, was, in fact, aware of Andy's poor night-vision. She was walking in front to make it less obvious that she was keeping track of his movements, listening in case he stumbled or fell behind. She always looked out for him and always hid her efforts. She didn't want to hurt his pride. She didn't want to let him know what he meant to her, either, but that was to save her own pride. She didn't realize there was any negative for him about her caring.

Chapter 6
Migrations

What Andy perceived as a deepening friendship, Elzy still found puzzlingly ambiguous. The connection she'd been so sure of back in May could have been wishful thinking. What she'd interpreted as small gestures of caring or solidarity might have been mere courtesy or coincidence. Nothing he said or did would have seemed out of place if he were speaking to an eager student he'd met yesterday—except for a subtle something that she might be imagining. Apart from his stories about the transition, he said almost nothing about himself, nor did he ask personal questions of her. She could recall each exception in detail, they were so few.

But since May, she had stopped caring how Andy felt about her. He might care, he might not, and her guesses on the subject switched every few days, but she was his friend either way. She enjoyed his company, looked after his welfare, and learned everything he could teach her.

Coastal Maine was still heavily settled, and much of its land was given over to vegetable patches, pasture, hayfield, and orchards. For all its rugged greenery, the country was garden rather than wilderness. And yet there were woodlots and hunting preserves and even little neglected patches of unmanaged forest, forests that looked nothing like those of New Hampshire.

Southern New Hampshire was mostly a mix of pine and oak—most forest types had at least one species of each—plus a varying admixture of hemlock, beech, red or sugar maple, and black, gray, or yellow birch. Coastal Maine, in contrast, was spruce country. Dark, short-needled spires stood massed above rocky headlands or hidden in narrow valleys, interrupted here and there by the feathery tufts of larch or by clonal colonies of big-toothed or quaking aspen. There were more familiar trees, too, like maples, cherries, and pines, but fewer of them. The land had a dramatically different look.

Elzy didn't notice such patterns easily—she could, quite literally, miss the forest for the trees—but she had spent enough time preparing for Andy's quizzes that at last she noticed the spruces and asked about them. Was it more geology? She knew that the rocks of coastal Maine had formed on the far side of an ancient ocean. That ocean closed and then the Atlantic opened slightly to the east of the old suture, leaving hills of different continents lying intimately together. Did it follow then that this geologic province, the Avalon Terrain, grew different trees than New Hampshire could?

"Good thought," acknowledged Andy, "but no. This time it's climate. The Humbolt Current is still relatively cold, so we get a lot of cold fog here coming in off the water. You'll see forests like this inland, but north of here."

And indeed, Maine *was* foggy, more so than any place Elzy had ever been. The sun could be shining brightly and the gray banks could still roll in as thick as shaving cream. Once, she and Andy were sitting on the porch of a charming little café when a dense fog came up the street towards them, for all the world as though it wanted to join them for lunch. The locals sometimes apologized for the bad weather, but Elzy liked it. The fog reminded her of something she couldn't place.

From Casco Bay, Andy and Elzy took the ferry north to Boothbay Harbor and from there explored a section of coast where the islands were fewer and farther apart and the peninsulas mostly broader. Some communities had real three-day markets here, and Elzy worked two of these. In the days in between, she and Andy returned to the mainland and she did one more natural history program in a church basement. They also attended two meetings of fisherman's associations because Andy wanted her to meet some community leaders and to get a better feel for the local culture. Both meetings were in dockside bars, where Andy surprised Elzy by seeming entirely at home. She still wasn't used to seeing him anywhere but in the woods or in professional settings. He offered no guidance but left her to observe or to mingle as she saw fit, while he sat in the back of the room, nursing a gin, chatting with the bar tender, and people-watching.

"You don't want to be the kind of expert who talks," he mentioned on their way out. "You want to be the kind of expert who listens."

In between things, Elzy actually had a few spare hours most days, and even a whole day off. She explored the shorelines, skipping rocks on stony beaches, swatting flies in mud flats and marshes, and climbing about the long fingers of bedrock that poked into the sea. She made good progress learning to identify the various seaweeds and shelled animals—barnacles, mussels, dog whelks, dog winkles, and three different kinds of periwinkle—that grew on or wandered over the wet rocks. Like plants, birds, and insects on land, these saltwater creatures existed in distinct communities, each occupying its own horizontal band defined by the dramatic tides of Maine. If Andy went with her, she'd ask him questions. If he did not, she'd tell him about her discoveries when they reconvened. He always listened, sometimes with grave, slow attention, but often with contagious intellectual passion. He might or might not care about her personally, she couldn't quite tell, but there were days when exploring with him rose to pure, joyous play.

They celebrated the Fourth of July at the mouth of the Penobscot River with an unavoidable day off. The little communities of the coast wanted to hire historical interpreters for their Independence

Day festivals, not ecologists and environmental educators, so there was nothing for Andy and Elzy to do in the town of Belfast Beach except to enjoy the spectacle. They wandered among stalls of carnival food, chatted with actors in character as Benjamin Franklin and John and Abigail Adams, and dodged children racing through the crowd waving sparklers and American flags, their cheeks covered in face-paint and ketchup. The United States, as such, didn't exist anymore, but even the children born After thought of themselves as Americans, thanks to festivals like these. The adults in the crowd talked optimistically about uniting the states again, as everyone did every year, but since a group of state governors were trying to organize a new constitutional convention, the talk seemed to actually have some basis.

That afternoon, a parade wound through the little downtown area twice, so that everyone could take a turn both marching and watching. Then, after the sun set, the whole town gathered on the lawns and docks and roof-tops above the water and watched teams of fire-eaters and jugglers perform on rafts and barges out in Penobscot Bay. After the show, the young people, Elzy included, sat up together drinking applejack and watching for shooting stars until almost dawn.

In the morning, Andy and Elzy boarded a river ferry bound for inland Maine and the Appalachian Trail.

The plan was to follow the Trail south, stopping every week or so to work the markets along the way. Around the middle of September they would, by river boat and coastal ship, begin the trip back to Pennsylvania in time for Andy's classes in early October.

The little solar-powered river boat had space for just twenty or thirty passengers and their luggage, but Elzy and Andy lost each other in the crowd anyway. Elzy tried not to worry that her teacher would be left behind. As the boat cast off and shoved out into the current, she found herself a seat by the rail, laid her head on her arms, and watched the river slide by.

The Penobscot River ran huge, ropy and muscular, divided here and there by big, forested islands. At first, mudflats and tidal marshes lined the banks and a rising tide helped the little boat along. Occasionally, the ferry stopped briefly to let off and take on passengers. Otherwise, there was nothing to do but listen to the quiet hum of the electric motor and watch over the side for herons and deer along the green and busy banks.

Somewhere in here, Elzy knew, the river crossed the Norumbega Fault, the joint between the coastal Avalon Terrain and the mass of metamorphosed mudstones and igneous intrusions that formed much of the rest of Maine and New Hampshire. She had hoped to see or feel something at the boundary, but either the fault was invisible here or she just plain missed it. She did notice when the river's estuarine character faded out near the ruins of Bangor. The scent of the river changed. She was back in the inland, freshwater world where no tide swelled, something she found vaguely disappointing, as though she were going the wrong way. She liked the rhythms of the sea.

Just beyond Bangor, a line of rapids stopped the progress of the ferry. The boat docked and everybody got off and walked around to another boat, identical to the first, waiting for them on the other side. The ferry service provided ox carts for baggage and for people with mobility limitations. A little restaurant offered food, drink, and the use of their toilets. Eventually everyone got settled again and the boat motored on up the river.

Because the two boats were identical, Elzy simply chose the analogue of her old seat by the rail. Andy found her and claimed the rail-seat in the row ahead of hers. Like her, he turned to watch the river and did not speak.

"So, you've been trying to study off-shore fisheries?" she began, after a while. She'd overheard him talking about it when he borrowed her cell earlier that morning. He'd been going on about proxy species, volunteer participation, and someone who might or might not be able to get a meeting with the leaders of a fisherman's association on Harpswell. It wasn't a secret, he hadn't bothered to step away from her to make the call, but of course he'd never told her about any of it directly, either. She still wished he could let her be more involved in his life. So she asked questions. "Is that what you've been working on all this time in Maine?"

"Yes," he acknowledged, "among other things."

"How many projects do you have going?"

"I haven't counted," he said. Elzy looked at him in surprise. He made an odd face and tallied on his fingers. "Seven, not counting students I supervise or sponsor."

"I couldn't do that," Elzy admitted.

"It is difficult," he acknowledged lightly, "but you learn to manage." Obviously he had learned, but Elzy thought there was something else too, something besides her relative inexperience that separated them. She didn't think she could ever learn to keep track of so many disparate ventures at once, but if she did, she'd damn well know how many of them there were.

"I never could do just one thing," Andy explained, perhaps a bit self-consciously. "It's boring. They tried giving me drugs for it, when I was a kid. They did that to a lot of people in my generation. But those drugs weren't any fun, so I sold them. I bought a nice mountain bike that way, when I was seventeen."

Elzy laughed. She liked getting these little glimpses of him. She wanted to ask what the drugs were, why there was a secondary market for them if taking them wasn't fun, and whether they actually worked—could a chemical really change the way Andy's mind moved? She wondered who would try to drug a young genius into normalcy and why, and whether Andy had resented or felt wounded by the attempt. Or did he truly regard the episode as simply an amusing and convenient way to get a mountain bike?

But she knew there were limits to what she could ask.

"So what did you do when you got to New Hampshire?" she said instead, and Andy looked at her, disoriented. She realized she had changed subjects too quickly—he might be able to keep track of seven different projects, but following the turns of Elzy's mind often stumped him. She waited for him to catch up.

"Oh, you mean, after the pandemic?" he guessed.

"Yes."

"I found some friends of mine in Keene who let me stay with them. I helped out on their farm a few days a week and I went looking for my son the rest of the time. I checked police records, when I could find those, hospital records, death notices, and different versions of the lists of living and dead. My son's name wasn't on any of the lists. I tracked down friends, thinking maybe somebody had found him and didn't know how to get a hold of me. But some of them were dead, some were missing, and nobody had any idea where my son was.

"Everything took so *long*. Before the pandemic, I could have talked to all those people in a couple of minutes, by phone. I could have visited all of them in a day. But walking...it took months, literally months, to follow all these leads. I mean, a lot of the people I'd known hadn't lived in Keene, they'd lived in Jaffrey or Antrim or somewhere and driven in to town to go shopping, go to parties, or whatever. When I came back, I had to walk to all those places to look for them, and that would take days. My in-laws lived in Boston. I knew Boston was gone, but I thought refugees might have gotten out and settled in outlying towns. So I took a week walking down there, two weeks wandering around asking questions, but no luck. Nobody knew anyone I knew. So I walked back. Another time I walked all the way down to the Berkshires because I'd heard someone I needed to talk to had moved there, but it turned out they'd died six months earlier, so I didn't learn anything.

"When I started all of this—when I first got back to New Hampshire—everything was still really primitive. There were towns, and most of the towns had laws, although not necessarily police—but electricity was patchy, there was no radio or cell coverage, there wasn't even mail—if you wanted to send a letter, you asked somebody to carry it for you. There was no money. There was, as you know, no medicine, although there were doctors. In time, all that changed, but in bits and pieces and not everywhere all at once. Some towns got radio first, others got a cell tower up and running....I remember when the Internet came back, how spotty it was in the beginning, and how different it was from what we'd had before. The new network was just regional, and most of the original servers either weren't in our network or had been destroyed, one way or another. Not that cat videos, porn sites, and Facebook would have done us much good, anyway. We built a new Internet and filled it with notices about missing people. Nobody ever responded to mine.

"I wasn't the only one doing this kind of work. A lot of people were out looking for friends and family, so we'd share leads, carry letters, exchange lists of the confirmed dead.... I didn't find my son, but I got very good at searching. Other people would give me lists of names to track down, and I'd find them.

"Two of my friends asked me to find some of their former colleagues. They had worked for an organization called MERE—Monadnock Ecological Research and Education. The group collected data, did Leave No Trace education with hikers, and so on. My friends wanted to see about reviving the project, or at least archiving it somehow. We found that most of the project's leaders had died, but we did track down some of their computers and a lot of the old field notebooks and original data collection sheets. So we started restoring and compiling what we had.

"In the beginning, I don't think we had any thought of doing any new research, we just wanted to make sure what we had didn't get lost—like monks copying books in the dark ages. But we needed electricity to get the computers going, and then we discovered we needed computer techs because nobody had turned the machines on in three or four years. Then we needed people to help transcribe the field notebooks and to cross-reference everything so we'd at least know what we had...we kept having to draw more and more people into the project and before long we had a little committed group going. A few of them wanted to get back on the mountain and check out the study plots. So, we found that house in what used to be Jaffrey--"

"Wait, so you founded Monadnock College?"

"I helped, yes."

"I didn't know that. It's not on your CV."

"You don't want to put *everything* on your CV when you reach this point in your career. You don't want it too long."

"What was your role? How did you help?"

"Mostly fundraising. Surprisingly, that didn't change that much, after the pandemic. It's always about finding ways to give the people with resources what they want, while at the same time making the project serve your own goals, too. The only real difference is we weren't looking for money in those years, we were looking for food, electricity, paper, and so forth. And we were dealing with farmers and town councils, not charitable foundations and government agencies. We did it by taking on students in forestry and game management—towns would pay us for that, as an investment in their future. And we trained and sent out environmental educators and charged a booking fee."

"So, you basically invented the guild system too?" Elzy asked. There was a hint of awe in her voice, but if Andy noticed he gave no sign.

"Oh, lots of people were doing the same kind of thing," he explained. "The guilds began as an organized version of traveling and working for your keep, just like we did coming East."

"There are people back on campus who say you saved science."

"Really?" He coughed or laughed a little in surprise. "Well, I've heard worse rumors about me."

"What *did* you do?"

"I kept doing the same things I did for Monadnock College, for different groups of people. I found the people who had been researchers and I put them back in touch with each other, helped them get new projects off the ground. If they didn't want to come out of retirement I found places—research centers or libraries— where they could archive their notes, their data, whatever they still had left. I talked them into recording their ideas, writing down what they could remember, so we could archive that. I found students interested in transcribing and compiling the archives. I fundraised. I problem-solved. I was a monk in the dark-ages, one of several."

"Why didn't some people want to come out of retirement? Be

scientists again?"

"Everything happens in context, Elzy, and the context in which most people did research was gone. There were no jobs, no grants... not a single university survived the pandemic. There were no *careers* left. Most people just preferred to say home, tend their farms, and get on with their lives. I might have done the same, if I hadn't had to come back East to find my son."

"Did you ever find him?"

"Not yet."

"You're still looking?"

"Not actively. I've done everything I can think of. I wouldn't recognize him if I saw him now, anyway. He's a man. I'll have to depend on his recognizing me." Andy stared out at the river as he spoke, not looking at Elzy, and she was glad he could not see her face. She wondered what it was like for a scientist to carry an irrational hope for twenty years. Was it heavy?

"Is that why you don't grow your beard out?" she asked.

"Yes."

"Is that why you're not mad at Saul?"

"What?"

"Saul. For not telling you he was still alive. Because he's proof some missing people still are."

"Yes, I suppose so."

"I'm sorry." And Elzy didn't just mean she was sorry to hear of his loss, or rather, his not-loss, although she was that. She felt powerless and she hated feeling powerless. She was much more comfortable with an enemy she could shoot, with a problem she could solve. She knew some people liked talking out their sorrows, and if Andy needed a shoulder to cry on hers was certainly available, but she didn't think he was the type to need that. He was too much like her that way, too practical and too strong. And here she'd asked questions because she was in the habit of asking him questions, and he'd opened himself up to her simply because she'd asked. His distance had always been a matter of avoidance, of redirection, of evasion, and Elzy suddenly wasn't sure if he knew how to say no to her directly. For that, she was sorry.

She looked over at him and saw his jaw tighten.

"It's nothing you can help," he said quietly.

"You said you went back to Arizona. When was that? And how did you get to Pennsylvania?" She was trying to change the subject.

"I went west when I'd exhausted all my options looking for my son. Maybe he left the area. Maybe he's forgotten his past, like you…. I realized I wasn't any more likely to find him in New England than anywhere else, so I went home. I went back to Chevron Town, to my ranch with my friends.

"I didn't just stay on the ranch—I'd gotten used to 'rescuing science,' as you put it. Really, I'd created a new context by which I, and others, could engage with research. That's probably the one important thing I've done. Because this is really a fantastic time to be a scientist. We've never seen the carbon dioxide concentration *fall* before. We've never seen the human population shrink like this. *Somebody* has to watch and see how all this plays out. So I'd ride up to Flagstaff and help the people restoring the university library there. Or I'd go down where Tucson used to be and see who I could find. Same thing, traveling around, putting people together….I even found my bats again! I'd wondered about them. I had no idea what was going on in their winter range in Mexico—anything could have happened to them. So I got back to my own research. It was a good life."

"Why did you leave it?"

"Things change. My wife got pregnant."

Elzy stifled a laugh. His wording made it sound like some inexplicable thing nobody bore any responsibility for—but she wasn't about to correct him.

"You said you'd gotten married again out there," she said instead. "How did you meet her?"

"Oh, she came with the mail." Andy waited a moment, straight-faced, to see Elzy's reaction, and then grinned. "I always say it that way. She was a letter-carrier. I really looked forward to getting mail there for a while," and his smile turned nostalgic.

Elzy grinned back, imagining him waiting, eager as a boy, by the mailbox.

"But both our ranches were at capacity," Andy continued, and Elzy frowned. She knew what he meant. Subsistence ranches and farms protected their members by not taking in more people than they were sure they could feed—a tradition that went back to the early transition and was becoming enshrined in modern financial policy and land-use laws. Andy was saying that if he and his wife had not moved, their child would have been born without a legal residence, without a home.

"Tri-River College was trying to recruit me at the time," he added, "so we decided to let them—the school's farm had room for us. That trip East only took a couple of months—we took boats most of the way, down the Rio Grande and then along the coast. That was just over five years ago now."

"And now you are here."

"And now I'm here."

Elzy had started college—the only formal education she could remember—a little over four years ago, which meant that Andy had brought his story up almost to the point where she entered it. She could remember the first time she'd met him, but she didn't know whether he remembered the same meeting—he'd been the only professor in the room, after all, while she'd been one of fifteen students. They must all have seemed interchangeable to him, at first. At what point had he noticed her? When did she differentiate herself from the crowd? She didn't ask.

They chatted about lighter things for a few minutes, and then Andy worked for a while on his tablet. Elzy watched the river bank slide by until she fell asleep. When she woke, the river had narrowed visibly, and Andy was reading his copy of *Practice of the Wild* again. The ferry hummed along steadily. Sometimes they had to get out and walk around rapids or rocks exposed by low water. The ferry company again provided ox carts and another ferry. Towns and forests, micro-hydro facilities and fishing weirs, the ruins of cities and breached dams, all slid by. The sun, veiled by a thickening haze, set. The boat hummed on through the night. She slept again.

Elzy woke in the darkness, disoriented. Her mind wouldn't quite get free of her dreams and it took her a few seconds to figure out where she was and why. The night felt warm, humid, and oddly still. The boat wasn't moving anymore. Was something wrong? Then the pilot turned on the deck lights and she worked out that the boat had stopped because they had arrived. Elzy shouldered her pack and followed Andy ashore and up the road to the hostel. By the time they stepped inside, her brain was clear of fog and she could pay for their lodgings like a grown-up.

"Hi, I'm Elzy Rodriguez, we have reservations?"

The proprietor found their names on his sheet and rummaged around in a cabinet for their room keys, chatting amicably all the while. He was tall and thin, with an asymmetrical mop of orange hair and no beard. He looked even younger than Elzy, but he said he owned the place.

"Name's Adric," he said, "and actually, I suck at math." Andy chuckled. Elzy frowned, but didn't ask either of them to explain the joke. "How long are you guys staying?" he asked, handing over the keys and a pair of clean towels.

"Just the night," Elzy replied, and this time Adric frowned.

"Oh, I doubt that. Data's likely to wash the roads out."

"Which data?" asked Andy.

"The hurricane—no, sorry, tropical storm. Tropical Storm Data. It's coming in tonight," Adric explained.

"There was nothing about a storm on the weather sites last night," Andy protested.

"Well, the weather forecasters don't *make* the weather," the younger man replied. "Nobody knew about it until it blew into the Gulf of Maine this morning. They sent drones out and everything today, and apparently the winds aren't too bad, but there's supposed to be a lot of rain in it and they think it might be one of those big, slow-moving storms that just sits on top of us—like what Mark did to the Cape the other year?"

"I heard about that," Elzy said. "That means we can't climb Katahdin," she added, turning to Andy.

"Depends," he told her. "You're in charge of travel plans now. Can we spare an extra week after the storm?" Katahdin could actually be climbed in an afternoon, but it meant a day's hike out of their way in each direction, plus up to several days of waiting for good weather. Bad conditions on the exposed summit could include anything from lightning to ice, even in July. With their next series of work dates probably already waiting in Andy's in-box, the wiggle-room in their schedule was sharply limited.

"No," she said, without hesitation, but pouted a little.

"Well, you won't be alone," Adric told her. "Half the people in here probably want to climb the mountain and can't because of the weather."

Indeed, a dramatic mural of Mt. Katahdin graced the wall alongside the staircase. Millinocket Dock was the closest place to the mountain to catch the ferry, and the town was a favorite of hikers getting on or off the trail.

As Elzy was brushing her teeth that night, she heard the rain begin.

By morning, the eaves of the old building were streaming with water. She opened the front door to smell the air and watched a fitful wind push curtains of rain down the puddled street. In the dim, dripping daylight, the neighborhood looked all but urban, whole rows of closely-spaced, multi-storied brick buildings. An illusion, Elzy knew—Millinocket Dock used part of an old mill town as its downtown area, but it was no more centralized than any other little farming community. The impressive old brick buildings housed only the usual clinic, tannery, fix-it shop, and so forth, plus some warehouses for goods coming in or going out by ferry. Even in good weather, there would have been hardly anyone on the streets.

"The storm's extra-tropical now," said Adric behind her. Elzy startled, embarrassed that she hadn't heard his approach over the sound of the rain. She was losing her cop's instincts, getting sloppy. The thought scared her.

"You've been online?" she asked, recovering herself.

Adric nodded.

"Weather radar couldn't find an eye overnight. They sent eye-wall drones out into the coverage gaps at dawn and there's no eye now. Looks like the storm merged with a cold frontal system."

"That's good, right?" asked Elzy, making conversation. She didn't actually morally judge the weather, but Adric, standing so close and so tall, flustered her. She could smell the damp wool of his red tartan vest. If he knew or cared that she found him attractive, he gave no sign.

"Not especially," he told her. "Up here the real danger's usually rain, and tropical or not, this thing's going to sit on top of us and wash all the roads and trails out. You coming to breakfast? I made grits and there's a little milk—I keep some goats out back."

Elzy liked grits, and willingly followed him to a long table already crowded with some twenty eager travelers. Besides the grits and two antique silver pitchers of milk, the table practically groaned under big ceramic bowls of apples and hard-boiled eggs, pots of honey and yogurt, and four carafes of hot chicory. Simple fare, but obviously good, and there was a lot of it. Twenty people couldn't possibly eat it all. She slipped into an empty seat near Andy and set to, serving herself and making introductions with her table-mates. Adric didn't join them but returned to the front office. A lot of returning holiday travelers had been caught on the road by the rain and when they came back into town to seek refuge, they would find a friendly, attentive welcome.

"Is there really only one of him?" one of the others asked when he was gone. "This is pretty incredible." The man was scruffy, bearded, and thin to the point of being gaunt. He wore no vest and had not showered. He had introduced himself as Loosianer but had not explained why.

"He *is* single," confirmed a similarly scruffy and emaciated man to his left. "So far. And you know, I make a *mean* pot of grits." His grin suggested he'd like to help the good-looking proprietor out with far more than breakfast.

Loosianer did a double-take.

"Dude, you gay?" he asked.

"Well, I wasn't before, but Adric turned me," his friend replied, obviously tongue-in-cheek. "Look at him! I mean *damn!*"

"I've hiked with you since *Georgia,* and you never said you're gay?"

"Why, did you want me?" The man countered. He had a weird nickname, too, but Elzy had already forgotten it.

"Fuck off," replied Loosianer, laughing good-naturedly.

"You like Adric?" put in another guest, who appeared to be an adolescent boy. "He's *way* too skinny for me." The "boy" had a woman's voice. Elzy frowned, puzzled.

"I thought you *were* gay," Loosianer said, addressing the mystery person. Apparently, he thought of the hiker as female, and was surprised to hear her express an opinion on a man. But he was evidently a poor judge of identity.

"Why do you care?" she or he asked, looking at Loosianer oddly. Seen as female, the hiker was definitely adult, probably older than Elzy. The very short hair and camo-print uniform meant an active-duty vigilante, what they called a private security specialist these days—not a cop, but still a sibling-in-arms. In the vigilante's presence, Elzy felt acutely conscious of her own long hair and her guild member's garb, as though she were pretending to be something she wasn't. Which of her identities was the real one, though, she couldn't say anymore. The person noticed her staring and turned towards her. Elzy blushed and looked away.

"What's your jurisdiction?" the vigilante asked conversationally.

"Octorara, Pennsylvania," Elzy replied, surprised and gratified. "How did you know I'm a cop?"

"You have the look. And you're carrying." There was no rule against civilians being armed, but most people who wanted a handgun also wanted to serve.

"I'm sorry, can I ask what your pronouns are?" Elzy asked. The voice was feminine only in pitch. It was masculine in cadence, and the more Elzy listened, the less sure she was of the speaker. She didn't want to give offense by accident.

"Oh, the female ones," the hiker replied, offhandedly. "Now, anyways. I lived as a boy the first couple of years After—safer, you know. Now, I guess I'm stuck like this. I suppose it's habit-forming, being a boy?" She laughed and began peeling another egg. Like the other hikers at the table, she could eat a fantastic amount and talk at the same time. The mountain of food Adric had served them was almost all gone.

Elzy just nodded. She didn't believe the vigilante had become boyish as a matter of *habit*, but of course she wasn't going to say anything. Actually, from Andy's stories it sounded as if being genderqueer might itself have been dangerous enough to warrant a disguise, depending on where a person found herself. But then, being virtually anything during the transition sounded dangerous. She wondered what risks she herself had run, in the years before she could remember.

After breakfast, there wasn't much to do besides read and talk. Normally, Elzy might have opted to read—not that she was shy, but none of these people had anything she wanted and none seemed like very much fun. But Andy had been after her for this sort of thing for so long that by now she could hear his voice in her head. She obeyed that voice, and set about getting to know her fellow guests.

Andy's voice in her head was, she knew, part of her own mind. He had evoked it, activated it, perhaps, and given it words. She had learned that, like him, it was nearly always right. But Andy himself wasn't telling anybody anything today. He was curled up in a big, upholstered chair with his computer, resolutely ignoring everybody. She didn't know whether he had pulled into himself in response to her prying questions on the ferry, or if this was just what his traditional "vanishing" looked like in bad weather. Either way, she let him be.

By lunch, several local families had come in out of the rain, joining an itinerant orthodontist and her assistant, a trio of musicians, and a pair of preachers. The musicians—two Wyandots and a Nordic Michigander—were on their way to help start a new music college on the coast. The two preachers, both women, also seemed to be traveling together, even though one was a Methodist and the other a Trib. The Society for Our Lord of the Tribulation, as they called themselves, was a new, rapidly growing religion with a reputation for intolerance, but this woman was generous and friendly to all.

The others, almost half the guests, were Appalachian Trail thru-hikers, either about to climb Katahdin or having just come down. For some, heading to Georgia, the mountain was the beginning of their hike. For others, it was the end. Not many people attempted recreational long-distance hiking anymore—among other issues, people who didn't live near an A.T. terminus faced an arduous journey just to get to the trailhead. Instead, most travelers used the trail the same way Elzy and Andy did, as a more scenic alternative to I-81 and its incessant and messy ox carts. The hostel held most of the season's exceptions.

The northbounders had been on the Trail so long that they had come to look alike, all skinny and scruffy in the same way. They all knew each other, too, and introduced themselves only by the nicknames they had given each other along the way. The vigilante who had once lived as a boy called herself Tank. The man who was so publicly lusting after Adric at breakfast was Cup-o-Chowder. He'd been obsessing about a cup of real New England clam chowder for hundreds of miles.

"No one has the heart to tell him clams don't grow on Mt. Katahdin," Tank confided in a stage whisper.

Cup-o-Chowder's longing for Adric might have been another joke, or it might have been quite real. Elzy couldn't tell. Certainly, he was seriously courting the man as a prospective business partner. The hiker was from Georgia, but had no intention of going back there. From the beginning he had planned his hike as a one-way trip, hoping to find someplace along the way he could settle. Adric's hostel had a great location and a lot of potential, and it was clearly under-staffed. By lunch, Cup-o-Chowder had volunteered to help serve meals. By dinner, he was outlining his plans to add a hard cider label to the business.

The hours slid by, gloomy and blustery.

In the evening, Adric persuaded Elzy to give a talk on some natural history subject. She chose insect migrations. The crowd was too small for her style of stand-up, but she did ask volunteers to act out various "bugs," so the evening was pretty goofy. Of course, she had picked the topic with her migratory audience in mind. She even tapped Cup-o-Chowder specifically to be a monarch butterfly so that she could talk about him traveling north on a one-way search for food and a mate. That got a laugh, especially since Adric was there and seemed to get the joke. Chowder blushed furiously and everyone laughed all over again. Later, the music teachers brought out their instruments: two small skin drums and a vintage handpan. One of the hikers had a harmonica and another carried a ukulele, so the five formed an impromptu band and the party lasted long into the night. But in the morning it was still raining.

The gloom outside had a greenish cast, the street being lined with young apple trees and planter-barrels and hanging baskets of growing tomatoes, potatoes, nasturtiums, and squash, all of which filtered and reflected the minimal, wet light. The air was hot and damp and heavy, starting to smell already of mold. Adric threw open what windows and doors he could in order to get some relief from the dank closeness, but every few minutes a fresh gust of wind would drive rain in under the awnings and spatter the sofas.

After lunch, he finally took a break and sat down next to Elzy in the open doorway.

"Mind if I smoke?" he asked.

"It's your hostel, of course I don't mind," she answered. "Smoke what?"

"Tobacco. You want any?"

"I've never tried it. It's addictive, isn't it?" She meant no disrespect, only that she didn't want to start something she might not be able to stop.

"Depends," he answered, rolling a cigarette. "I grow my own

out back, so this stuff's natural, not like it used to be. I only get the urge a couple of times a year."

"And today's the day?"

"Well, *yeah*." A gesture took in the rain, the spattered sofas, the over-full hostel, all reasons, apparently, why Adric needed a cigarette. "Hard to light in this weather, though." He finally got the thing to catch, inhaled, then exhaled theatrically. Elzy declined a drag. They sat in silence for a bit until the cigarette went out again. "Damn," exclaimed Adric mildly. "Sometimes I wonder if growing this stuff is worth it. Do tobacco hornworms migrate?"

"I don't know. I can look it up for you, if you want."

He waved away the idea and re-lit his cigarette.

"You know, I never thought about insects like that," he said. "I knew about monarchs, but not the others. Do all migratory insects do it across generations?"

"As far as anybody knows. No migratory insect returns to its birthplace, only its descendants do."

"And they do it to distribute their eggs? Seems a lot of work."

"That's the theory. But that's not what I think."

"Oh?"

"Yeah. I think insects never leave home, only their home moves so they do too. I mean *home* ecologically—the place defined by their relationships with other species and their environment."

"Like these hikers. Their relationships move. It's like a whole mobile village every year."

"Exactly."

"What do you suppose it feels like to do that, though?" he asked. "Do the butterflies know they're traveling? Or is it like riding in an ambulance, where you go thirty miles an hour and don't feel it?"

"I think they must feel it as some kind of draw. I don't see how they could navigate otherwise."

"How do they navigate? How do the monarchs all converge on the same few wintering grounds in Mexico?"

"I don't know. No one does. There are a couple of good ideas, but the evidence is conflicting. I like to think they're just on their way home."

"They're looking for a home they don't remember."

"So am I."

"Oh?"

"My Daddy took me to live with my Mom when I was ten. Then he died. He didn't tell Mom where we had been and I don't remember. My entire *life* is a result of changes I don't remember. And I want to."

Adric listened attentively and then knocked the ash from his cigarette into a nearby puddle.

"I don't remember transition, either," he said.

"Oh?"

"I'm too young. I'm only twenty."

"You're *twenty?*" Elzy was shocked. "I thought all the babies died in the pandemic?" Indeed, the disease had affected the very young and the very old disproportionately, and the few young children who had survived the pandemic mostly died during the transition. Then, no one had risked having any more kids for about five years After. There was a demographic hole in the world ten years wide, and Adric had grown up right in the middle of it, an only child in a heartbreakingly literal sense.

"All of them except one," said Adric. He took another drag on his cigarette and exhaled a long, visible sigh of smoke. They were both silent for a while.

"Adric, do you ever think about what you were born to?"

"Born to?"

"Yeah, you know—born to rule, born to run...."

"*Born to Raise It.*" He quoted a current pop song and they both laughed.

"Yeah. I dunno. Like, when your mother was pregnant with you, that was Before. They didn't know about *this*." A wave of her hand evoked the whole rainy, modern world. "She must have had all kinds of plans. For you to...attend a liberal arts college and get a drivers' license and whatever else they did back then. We were born to a world that doesn't exist anymore. What does that make us?"

"I don't know what *it* makes *me*, but *I* make *it* my world. I bought this place about a year ago, after my father passed, and I've made it my own. It's a pretty good place."

"It is. I wish I had somewhere of my own to belong to," said Elzy. She had no idea why she was unburdening herself to this stranger. Maybe she was just leaking.

"You know what I think?" he asked.

"No."

"I think we're like your butterflies. We're born at one point in space and time, live at another, and eventually we'll die in a third, but we never really leave home. We never really go anywhere we can't connect with."

"Maybe you're right."

Adric tried to inhale again but found his cigarette had gone out. It was little more than a stub now, anyway. He stared at it for a few seconds, then got up.

"Hey, nice talking with you," he said.

"Yeah, good talking with you," Elzy echoed, and he was gone.

A few minutes later, she went back inside and engaged the Trib preacher in a game of chess. The other hostel residents orbited around them, fetching books, huddling around tablets, sharing snacks.

Hope, a ten-year-old girl, occupied herself by talking.

"When you go hunting," she was telling Tank, "it's really, really important not to stink. A lot of people think it's OK to use scented soap, fancy shampoo…animals can smell that stuff, so don't use that. Keep the wind in your face, that keeps them from smelling you too. Oh, and it's really, really important to keep your feet dry. It's really important to take care of your feet…." She was the youngest of the group, the daughter of a family that lived largely by hunting and by selling leather, bone, feathers, and specialty woods to artists. The storm had interrupted her first trip with the adults, so instead of using her skills she was talking about them.

Tank invented some excuse to go elsewhere, and within a few minutes Hope had moved on to the Wyandot handpan player.

"Don't look for an animal, look for *parts* of animals. Look for vertical lines. Look up! Don't just look at your feet when you walk. And you have to use your ears as well as your eyes. You have to listen. And you have to be quiet, that's really, really important. Hunting time is *not* talking time, not if you want to catch anything. *Some* people...." The man's eyes glazed over. Elzy attended to the chess game. Twenty minutes later, Hope was still talking shop, this time with the Methodist preacher, who actually seemed interested. "So you have to understand animals' behavior, their habits, not just their sign. That's really, really important. And if you're hunting with a bow you need to inhale when you draw, but if you're using a gun, *exhale* before you shoot...."

All of it was correct, but Elzy too had known how to hunt when she was ten, so she was not especially impressed. *Silence—now there's something that's "really, really important,"* she thought, uncharitably.

At the same time, she noticed the child's intelligence and her eagerness to learn and to teach. She hoped the girl would get a chance to go to college or, failing that, that someone would train her up for a citizen science project. Either way, Hope had potential that deserved to be developed.

Such thoughts were new. Elzy had never put much energy into thinking about other people's careers, and now here she was, beginning to daydream about taking Hope under her wing. One part of her mind was now constantly thinking about networking opportunities and communicating science. With another part of her mind, she was still keeping track of security vulnerabilities and looking for suspicious, anomalous behavior. The two parts of her mind didn't seem to have anything to do with each other.

After the chess match, Elzy distracted Hope by teaching her some environmental education games. The preachers and some of the hikers soon joined in, and the girl reciprocated by teaching the group a couple of games she knew, like "This Is a What," and "Going to Kentucky." The latter was more of a goofy dance than a game, with each person taking a turn in the middle before pointing to the next dancer.

Another day passed.

The hostel had good internet reception, so Elzy used some of her time stuck inside to do a little research. She still had the list of possible hometowns Andy had given her. One of them had to have good rock-climbing possibilities, a lot of fog, and the other details she'd noticed as familiar in recent weeks, but nothing jumped out at her. Nothing ever did. She'd done these same online searches before. She emailed her mother too, asking again for information about her father, but knew she'd get no response. She entertained the possibility that she and her father had been migratory, that her memories actually referred to a series of separate places—that there was no answer to the puzzle at all.

Adric might say that wasn't so bad, wasn't so different even, than having a distinct, geographical home. She wanted to believe it. She'd found she liked these people, liked the fleeting fellowship of travelers. She could *almost* believe this was home. Except she didn't.

By noon of the third day, the whole hostel smelled strongly of apple cider vinegar as Adric and Cup-o-Chowder fought back valiantly against the humidity-fostered mold. People were getting irritable. Tank threw herself down on a couch and covered her face with a musty pillow.

"I can't remember when it wasn't raining!" she announced, voice muffled.

Elzy felt so bored that her hair itched. Logically, the storm couldn't last much longer, but, like Tank, she was starting to think of the rain as eternal. There was *nothing* whatever to do. They could have gone to the pub across the street to play darts or down the street to the multimedia center for a movie, but not without getting soaked. No rain poncho could hold up beneath this fitful, windy rain. And nothing could dry in the humid, moldy air. The hostel guests were imprisoned by the rain and by sensible practicality.

Finally, Elzy had enough. She threw down the book she was reading and jumped up.

"Fuck it," she said, and ran outside.

She was instantly soaked and did not care. The muggy stick-iness was gone. Her body accepted the warm rain as easily as a sounding seal might accept the sea. She raised her hands to the wild, gusting sky, grinning and spinning in circles, barefoot on the broken pavement, ankle-deep in water sluicing clear and fast out to the Gulf of Maine.

Hope ran out to join her. The girl's mother tried to get her back inside, but gave up the attempt as pointless and joined in the dance instead. Tank and Loosianer and the Methodist preacher followed, kicking water at each other and laughing. Suddenly it seemed like everyone from the hostel was out in the street together.

"We're going to Kentucky," sang Hope, and the others joined in, circling around first one dancer and then the next.

We're going to Kentucky
We're going to the fair
To see the señorita
With the flowers in her hair

Elzy, the señorita of the moment, danced until rainwater flew from the ends of her braids. As per the rules of the game, when the song ended she pointed to the next dancer and stepped back into the circle. And suddenly she realized she didn't know where Andy was.

Had he vanished again? Had he made a dash for the multi-media center down the street, or holed up in the dorm-room for some privacy? She'd seen him curled in his chair after breakfast that morning, but she hadn't really spoken to him in days. She felt disoriented. She looked around, surreptitiously panicking, then noticed with a start that he stood less than ten feet from her. He was like the moon that evening on Bailey Island, plainly visible yet oddly hard to see.

His eyes were closed. In the midst of people, he maintained his solitude. He would not see her staring. He stood under the edge of the overhanging roof, letting water from a break in one of the gutters pour over him. He could not have been standing there long because the shoulders of his travel shirt were still partly dry. The fabric darkened even as Elzy watched. He turned his face up towards the streaming sky, his hair slicked flat to his pale scalp, his chin and the slight hollows of his cheeks whitened by two days' worth of stubble. She'd never before noticed how thin his hair was. It made him look older, almost frail, but under the deluge he stood unbowed.

His expression, unreadable as ever, betrayed just a hint of something. It might have been joy. It might have been pain.

Chapter 7
Bifurcation Events

Eventually, the rain let up and the remnants of Data moved off to the north. Sunny, crisp blue took its place, and the temperature didn't rise above eighty degrees for days. In the lovely and unusual weather, Adric and his guests opened doors and windows and hung out clothing and gear to dry.

With the change in the sky, Andy's mood shifted. He came out of hiding, chatted pleasantly with the other hostel guests, and generally acted like a normal, social human being. Privately, he made a startling confession to Elzy—there was no work for either of them in the woods of inland Maine. Not in July, anyway.

Like most itinerant professionals, Andy left scheduling to the last minute. He had to. Foot travel was just too unpredictable. He'd filed a rough itinerary before he left, relying on his guild to find and book appropriate events for him as he walked. He'd review and approve the tentative schedule a week or two at a time, when he was close enough to be able to commit to arrival dates. But when he checked his email in Millinocket, he had found no new list of bookings. Instead, he'd found a note—the forest families of inland Maine had all marketed on Fourth of July weekend and would not meet again until August.

He had known that the few, scattered people of the forest met only once a month, but other monthly marketers staggered their schedules, no town meeting in the same week as its neighbors. Andy had built his plans for the summer on the assumption that Mainers followed the usual pattern. He'd been wrong.

"You're telling me I'm going to have a hole in my portfolio," Elzy stated, trying not to sound angry.

"Not necessarily," said Andy calmly, as though he'd had no role in the mix-up. "We could change our route and go work somewhere else, further along the Maine coast, for example. We have options."

"Not good options, though. We can't explore both inland Maine and northern New Hampshire if we spend July on the coast. We'll run out of time. And that was your whole plan for the trip, right? You've never networked in those areas before."

"My plans are flexible," he stated flatly, in a tone precluding any discussion. For all that he usually treated Elzy as his equal, he would not admit to needing her help or consideration. His business was his own, period.

Elzy kept herself from rolling her eyes.

In the end, Elzy decided to stick to something like their original plan. As she explained, more time on the coast wouldn't give her anything she didn't have already, and by talking with locals at resupply points, she could lay the groundwork for a later trip to the area. Plus, by hiking through Maine without stopping, they'd have several extra weeks to explore New Hampshire. That her plan also took care of Andy's needs wasn't a coincidence, but she didn't draw attention to the fact.

In a couple of days they were back on the Appalachian Trail for the first time since Massachusetts. The storied AT looked surprisingly modest, just an ordinary footpath in the woods, but as they stepped onto it, Elzy fancied she could feel a familiar current, a friendly warmth, hurrying her feet onward, north. But she and Andy turned south.

After over four months of travel, they were as far from campus as they would get, and like a comet in the reaches of space, they turned and began the long, slow trip home. That had been the plan from the beginning, but somehow Elzy wasn't comfortable with it now. She kept looking over her shoulder.

"It feels like we're regressing," she said, puzzled. She was embarrassed to admit how irrational she was being.

"Progress has no inherent direction," said Andy, a hint of a smile in his voice. It was the sort of counter-intuitive wisdom he found funny.

She smiled a little in return, though he was walking ahead of her and could not see it. The smile did not last.

"I guess so," she replied glumly. "It's like we haven't gone far enough, or something."

Andy stopped walking and faced her.

"*Do* you want to head north instead?" he asked. "This is your trip."

Elzy found his comment very odd. Andy was capable of altruism, but this journey of theirs was not an example of it. He needed to wander, both professionally and personally, and it wasn't safe to wander alone. A minor injury could become deadly on an isolated road. Criminals and predatory animals alike were more likely to target solitary victims. A student companion or two made Andy's journeys possible. He had chosen the route before he had chosen Elzy.

As much as Andy seemed to need to be in control, he had an equal need to pretend that he wasn't.

"No, heading south makes sense," Elzy reassured him. "I just don't like it, for some reason." She set off down the trail, ahead this time. She didn't want to worry him or get into a big discussion about feelings that neither of them would be comfortable with.

Their way ran through dense, broken forest and low but curiously rough terrain. The high, erosion-resistant granite of Mt. Katahdin lay behind them, to the north-east. Here, slate, ancient volcanic rock, and a more erodible form of granite built hills and occasional rocky ridges dissected by fast-moving streams and rivers and many small ponds. The Trail twisted up and down, never gaining much elevation but rarely on the level, either. Few of the streams had bridges, nor even a log to walk across, and travelers rarely kept dry feet for long.

The forest appeared broken for good reason. Winter ice, erratic summer storms, and various exotic pathogens had left fallen limbs and standing snags everywhere. Even aside from the damage, the woods were dense and chaotic with ecological youth. Inland Maine had been logging country, the domain, most recently, of paper mills. Overgrown dirt roads cut across the Trail here and there, and from high points Andy and Elzy could see the land as an archipelago of re-growing clear cuts of differing ages.

From one such ridge, over a break for water and a snack, Andy explained that the mosaic below them was not precisely arbitrary. First, the cuts had not been made at random, but planned according to whatever economic, political, and ecological reality applied at the time. Second, the size and shape of each cut, and its proximity to various other communities, influenced how and how quickly the patch regrew. The physical distribution of all the different patches dictated how animals, including humans, used the land. The wind that day was hot and fitful, the clouds streaked and clumped in a high, blue haze. The green world spread out below Andy's hand like a map and suddenly it made sense, she could see it, a giant pattern stretching out in both space and time. Elzy, suitably impressed, offered him the bag of butterscotch chips and pretzels.

Logging was more than a major driver of patchiness. Had they explored the region further, had Elzy taken the time to read the landscape as she had done so often earlier in the trip, she would have encountered logging as a major character in every story she read. The remnants of logging camps, the signs of rivers engineered for use in log drives, the histories of towns and cities originally founded and sustained by the logging industry, all told different parts of the same story. Like agriculture and sheep husbandry a little to the south, and even like the glacier itself, logging had shaped New England and lingered visibly in its eternally present past.

But the logging industry had followed the sheep and the glacier into history because there was no money to be made anymore by shipping trees long distances. Plenty of salvaged wood and fiber was coming out of abandoned buildings and landfills. And by the time recycled materials started to run low, most communities would have their own local forests—every town with the climate for it was busy planting trees for carbon sequestration and flood control.

The only people who had a use for the Maine Woods now were those who lived there. Most of them were families, both Waponahki and Yankee, who had taken refuge in the forest during the early transition and never left, like Hope's parents. They lived largely on what they could hunt, fish, and gather, though many kept small gardens as well. To keep the forest free and productive, they managed it collectively through a complex system of mutually enforced traditions and agreements among neighbors. Andy called it deer-ranching country and said it reminded him of home.

Andy explained all this, and much else besides, narrating natural history and quizzing Elzy constantly, just as he always had. Most of the time he preferred to walk in silence, but when they stopped to eat or to rest he would talk or entertain questions. If something caught his attention as they hiked he would take the time to explain it. And yet he seldom supplied the identity of a plant unless asked. He was one who could miss the trees for the forest, not the other way around, and he was far more interested in animals than plants anyway. Elzy knew the trees already, but there were shrubs here she did not remember seeing before.

And yet she knew them. Not all of them and not well, but the plants here were more familiar than they should have been.

Once, she paused at the crest of an open, treeless ridge to examine some leathery little shrubs. The place had an appealing, almost alpine character, thanks to the shallow soil and the exposure, and its small, deceptively delicate-looking plants and lichens must be incredibly tough. Like the spruces back on Monadnock, they couldn't grow just anywhere. All the easier places were taken by the more conventionally successful, the more softly ruthless species. Elzy thought the shrubs, all knee-high or smaller, must be heaths of some kind—members of the same family as blueberry and azalea—but they hadn't been on any of her plant lists for school. She couldn't remember ever having seen or heard of them before. And yet, she knew their names, not their botanical names, but childish, descriptive nick-names—*wrinkle plant, spring pretty, pale leaf.* They were familiar. As she turned to take a better look, a darkness loomed in her peripheral vision. She glanced up and made a small noise of shock and wonder. Andy turned back to see what she had seen.

"Mt. Katahdin," he said.

"Yeah, I know," Elzy told him, not taking her eyes off the wall of gray rock and green forest. She'd been walking away from it for days and yet it still filled a quarter of the horizon. Mt. Katahdin is not tall, as mountains go, but it rises dramatically out of a low, rolling plain, an imposing complex of ridges, peaks, and cirques. It looked oddly like an island to her, rising so abruptly and so high. That she was walking away from it seemed unbearably, unaccountably sad.

That sadness stayed with her, a regret or a longing for she knew not what.

"Why did the pandemic have to happen?" She asked, days later. They were walking now through a dark, mixed conifer forest over rocky, irregular terrain still soggy with yet more rain. In the gaps where trees had fallen in storms, the hot sun streamed through and set the ground literally streaming. She stopped at the top of a little rise and waited for Andy to catch up to her. She was faster on short slopes, though he had more discipline and hence more stamina.

"Why did the pandemic have to happen?" he repeated, when he came up alongside her. "What do you mean? I don't know that it did have to happen."

"I don't know. Maybe it's an irrational question. It just seems so meaningless for all those people to have died."

"Maybe nothing has meaning unless we decide to give it some."

He leaned on his hiking poles for a moment, puffing his breath out. Whether he was physically tired or simply emotionally so, Elzy couldn't tell. Either way, he walked on, conserving momentum. He would not risk resting for long.

"I just keep thinking," Elzy began, picking her way downhill after him, "why couldn't everything have stayed the way it was? But I don't suppose that's an answerable question."

"On the contrary, that one is answerable. Humanity's energy use was unsustainable. It literally could not be sustained. However the change happened—pandemic, climate chaos, or a deliberate transition away from fossil fuel—radical change was inevitable."

"Climate change would have changed things already? I mean, if we hadn't transitioned?"

"The climate was changing noticeably when I was a *kid*."

"No, I mean fallen apart. The collapse of the networks you talked about. The end of the old civilization."

"Maybe, but maybe not, unless you lived in Manhattan, or Boston, or Miami, or Mobile." He was referring to cities whose ruins had been raked by major hurricanes and which, presumably, would have been destroyed either way. "But generally? It's hard to say. Our climate now is about what it would have been if the old system hadn't fallen, because of atmospheric lag. I guess the question is whether civilization could have survived this climate for this long? Even before the pandemic, heat-related illnesses and deaths were rising. There were a lot of droughts and floods and heat waves and so on. Food prices were starting to rise globally, politically destabilizing some of the poorer countries, which then exported extremism, terrorism, and huge numbers of refugees to everyone else. But you could still ignore all of that, if you were wealthy and lucky, and many people did."

Andy's voice grew distant while Elzy climbed over and through a fallen maple. When she caught up to him he was waiting for her beside a soft little low point in the trail. She could see where water had coursed here, muddy and foaming, when Data came through. Wrack-lines of needles and leaves ran along some two or three feet above where clear water now trickled in braided beds of mud and sand.

"If we say for the sake of simplicity," Andy continued, "that those trends would have continued...would the rising costs of national security and natural disaster between them have bankrupted the country already? Our descendants would be pretty well done for, if we hadn't stopped using fossil fuels yet, but it's possible the lucky and wealthy would still be able to pretend otherwise. Except--" and he hopped lightly across the water, turned, and faced her again. "Nothing is ever simple." His eyes lit. All hint of exhaustion was gone. His grin was a dare and an invitation.

"How so?" Elzy asked, from her side of the little stream.

"You remember bifurcation points?"

"Yes."

Andy had covered the subject briefly in class, years earlier. Complex systems, such as organisms, ecosystems, or the biosphere, can change suddenly, like a switch being flipped, and thereafter follow a completely different set of rules. A hollow ball of identical cells folds into itself and becomes an embryo with the beginnings of organs in a matter of hours. A forest that has been sequestering carbon suddenly starts to shed it. An ocean current slows, rewriting weather patterns around the world and starving or drowning millions. Bifurcation points aren't random. That a fetus becomes a baby at around nine months post-conception surprises no one. But the shifts cannot be predicted from prior conditions alone, and no one had ever watched rapid anthropogenic climate change play out before, so no one knew where the bifurcations in this process would be. Anything could happen.

"So, you mean we could have passed a tipping point by now," Elzy asked, "some kind of runaway positive feedback loop that would make everything horrible?"

"Or made everything better. Don't forget, human societies are complex systems, too."

Elzy hopped across the stream and landed beside him.

"You mean—we might have done it. We might have gotten off

173

fossil fuel on our own?"

"Yes."

Andy and Elzy had backpacked together before, walking from Pennsylvania up to New Hampshire. They fell back into the familiar rhythm easily now, making and breaking camp, hanging bearbags, and cooking over the little alcohol stove. But now, there was nothing but hiking. They didn't even need to leave the Trail to shop, since locals happily resupplied hikers at reasonable prices.

Walking long hours every day, they burned calories faster than they could possibly eat. Even monstrously large meals disappeared in minutes and left them only slightly less hungry than before. Elzy, already slim and strong, simply became more so. Andy, like the male thru-hikers, grew gaunt. He had to punch new holes in his belt with his folding knife just so his pants wouldn't fall down. Elzy guessed that the constant hunger stirred bad memories for him, but of course he never said so. When he woke both of them by crying out in his sleep, he blamed the nightmares on dehydration.

Dehydration can cause bad dreams, and Andy, who had a weak thirst mechanism, did sometimes forget to drink. He was almost telling the truth.

An extra share each, above the price of whatever supplies they needed, bought a night in a real bed, a shower, and some home-cooked food from a local family. The beds were hard and narrow and the showers often cold, but Andy and Elzy sprung for a home stay every week or so anyway, so she could meet people. Future bookings in the area might depend on someone remembering her name. To that end, she made herself charming and memorable.

Andy, too, made an excellent house guest. Children especially found him fascinating, since he was a *real* scientist, and because he listened to even the youngest with the same grave, undivided attention he offered his own students. But he had no real business among these people. Whatever he'd been planning on doing in inland Maine, present circumstances precluded his doing it. He spoke as little as he had to. When no one seemed to be watching, he sometimes literally curled in on himself, abandoning his confident, masculine body language for what looked like a fair imitation of a turtle. Elzy wondered if perhaps he had somehow grown shyer of late.

She brushed the concern from her mind and threw herself into socializing. She felt comfortable with these people. Their daily rhythms felt natural to her and she volunteered to help with chores without even thinking about it.

"How did you know we haul water?" demanded the first woman they stayed with. "Everybody outside the Woods has pressurized pipes!" Her name was Crystal and she was as tough and prosaic as salt. She and her three young grandchildren lived in a ramshackle system of little burrows built of ax-cut branches, mud, and sun-brittle tarpaulins. Crystal and her now-late daughter had built the thing in a hurry twenty years earlier and she still lacked the money or the skill to renovate. They had no solar cells or wind generation, so obviously they had no water pump. Except in all the years she'd been renting out her daughter's old bedroom-burrow to hikers, none had ever noticed the obvious without being told.

"Not everyone outside has pressurized pipes," countered Elzy. Technically true, but the houses without water pumps were few and far between. Certainly, her mother's farm back in Octorara had running water, and the people there took it completely for granted. So why had she simply assumed this family's chores included hauling water? She didn't know, either.

That she didn't know was itself a clue, one not lost on Andy, who caught her eye as she headed out towards the stream. But, like her ability to climb rocks or her strange almost-recognition of the coastline, the new clue raised more questions than it answered.

The next place they stayed seemed centuries away from Crystal's burrow, though it too lacked road access and had not changed much since the pandemic. It had been built Before as an off-the-grid *bug-out*, a place designed specifically as a refuge just in case civilization collapsed. A tiny water-wheel provided electricity, a stockade provided defensible security and discouraged bears and coyotes, and the snug little house even boasted a well-appointed library. Four people lived there, a middle-aged sister and brother, plus the brother's grown son and daughter-in-law. All four, on the day of Andy and Elzy's visit, were upset, arguing shamelessly in front of their guests. Andy absented himself almost immediately, but Elzy thought someone should stay and guard their belongings. She had no sense of these people yet. And so she was more or less forced to listen.

"I'm telling you," insisted Mason, the grown son, "it wasn't any of the neighbors. Six trees felled, limbed, and bucked right by the river? Some outsider came in and floated them away. Most of them weren't even harvest size yet. What a waste. Who would do something like that? None of us would. Forest people would know better, or they'd know someone would make them know better!"

"This isn't the old days," objected the father, Jered. "Nobody comes in and just takes somebody else's stuff. Why would they? Don't outsiders have their own trees? It's probably Nathan's family. They were short on wood last year, and their kids don't have the sense God gave geese. Probably sent out Phoenix and Hope to get some wood and the little idiots didn't know what to cut. I'll talk to Nathan when I see him at August market."

Elzy's ear pricked up at the name *Hope*, but it obviously wasn't the same girl. When people started having children again after the pandemic, they overwhelmingly chose optimistic names. Half of all the children now between ten and fifteen years old were named Hope, Phoenix, Joy, or Health.

"Oh, don't bother Nathan," protested Theresa, the sister. "You know how rough it's been since Ari had his stroke, and with Jason drinking…"

"Six trees? Six trees?" This was Mason again. "Jason's drinking has nothing to do with it. Hope and Phoenix did *not* cut and drag off half the God-damned forest last week while no one was looking. And if it was anyone local, where are the skidder tracks? Where is the horse dung? The only place that wood could have gone was down the river and we all know what kind of people live down there. I should get a few of the guys together and…."

"Mason Dexter Swenson, you will not!" half-shouted Mia, Mason's wife. "You get yourself shot up or locked up and what am I going to do? You want our baby to grow up without a daddy?" Evidently, she was pregnant.

Elzy spoke up, more to preclude the ridiculous spectacle of a semi-public family argument than anything else.

"Um, I don't mean to butt in," she began, and they all looked at her, "but why don't you just call the cops? Let them handle it?"

"We can't *call* anybody," explained Theresa, in a friendly tone. "We don't have a phone. There's no coverage within five miles of here."

"Cops would screw the whole thing up, anyway," said Mason. "*We* know who has a right to that wood and when it's OK to cut it, but damned if we can figure out how to write a law about it. If we called in the cops, say it *did* turn out to be one of us. Say the cops decide somebody broke a law and they make an arrest, it'll be the wrong person arrested or the wrong sentence carried out—calling the law in is like trying to filet a fish with a hammer. And then we'll never hear the end of it. You know how it is. It's a neighbor thing."

Elzy did know. For all the violent crudeness of vigilante justice, she remembered its political finesse.

"The job of a cop is to arrest people who need it," said Theresa. "We don't necessarily want anyone arrested over a couple of trees. Unless it's an outsider, we just need to figure out who's responsible and go talk to them about it. But realistically, that won't happen until August. We don't have the time to go visiting everybody. It would be nice to have someone *like* a cop who could look into this sort of thing, but who wasn't so focused on whether or not to arrest someone. Someone who really knew about trees and everything."

"Like a naturalist-vigilante?" hazarded Elzy. "But it would have to be someone local, right? You wouldn't want an outsider."

"You got it."

When Andy returned that evening she told him about the conversation and her idea.

"You mean a forest ranger or a caretaker," he observed.

"Yeah, I guess so. But these people don't have the money to pay for anything like that. If they did, they'd have hired one already."

"Don't be too sure. You can't be certain which ideas are original if you don't check."

"OK, maybe. But some of these people can't afford proper walls for their houses, let alone paying for full-time rangers."

"What about part-time? You could make the balance of your income as a traveling environmental educator."

Elzy stared at him.

"*Me*? But I'm not local," she protested.

He stared back at her. He was in his professorial mode again, reclining on a couch, casually taking up space, supporting his head with two fingers at his temple. He waited.

"Wow," said Elzy at last. "That's not the kind of police work my mother trained me for."

"That's the point, isn't it?"

She stared at him again.

"You tell me, it's your idea," she countered.

"It's not mine, it's yours."

Elzy didn't reply, but, after a few more seconds of staring, abruptly got up and went to help their hosts with the chores. Andy remained on the couch, staring after her, almost but not quite smiling.

He knew he was right. Andy thought of himself as more or less socially oblivious—which was why he worked so hard to understand people—but actually he could be quite insightful, except as regarded his own relationships. He had noticed that as much as Elzy identified herself as a cop, that identity was actually someone else's creation. She could neither leave it behind nor wholly claim it as her own, and he'd been waiting for her to come up with some creative way out of the impasse. He knew she was probably correct about this community needing a local for the job, but the idea would percolate and become something workable eventually. He thought she was doing well.

He was not.

The uncontrollable weight-loss, the hunger he could not eat

enough to still, was part of it, but so was his continual talk about the past. For months, now, he had been dipping regularly into memories perhaps better left buried, for Elzy's sake. While his story was more or less finished, he continued to tell her about the lost world she had been born to. Here in the woods, just the two of them, day after day, there was nothing else to do, nothing else to think about, except walking and talking with his one ever-present companion. The world had become a hypnotic, green tunnel without end and memory and the terror of hunger walked with him.

There were mornings he awoke unsure of where—or when—he was. There were days when the sound of birds or of running water would become his children's voices. The scent of his first wife's shampoo would follow him for miles for no clear reason. Sometimes, just on the edge of perception, he thought he heard sirens deep in the woods. Elzy said she heard nothing. There must be a riot somewhere, the police responding, the fires, the pandemic, he had to get out of Phoenix—

After a few seconds he would shake his head, right himself, keep walking. He was not losing his mind, not truly. The sirens could have been real, there were occasional roads within a few miles of the Trail, even here. Except for Jen's scent, it was all disorientation and fancy, not true hallucination, and he was perfectly clear none of it was real. But it scared him.

Probably all of it would clear out of his head once he got off the trail, got enough to eat, and got a break from Elzy's charming but insistent company. All he had to do was hang on until they got to Pinkham Notch, in New Hampshire. But every day in the green tunnel was so like the last, and so unlike anything else, that he frankly had trouble believing anything would ever change.

In the meantime he would continue to answer Elzy's questions. He would be her rock, if she needed him to be. Anything else would have struck him as selfish and self-indulgent. He would be useful, he would do his job, and he would not need to ask for help from anybody.

The terrain was growing higher now, more frankly mountainous, each hill and ridge larger than the last. And yet the rock here was basically the same as it had been since Millinocket. The flat country to the east was the same, too, the same patchwork of granite, gabbro, metamorphosed mudstone, and ancient volcanics as everything else this side of the Norumbega Fault. The difference was pressure.

When the separate pieces that became Eastern North America assembled themselves long ago, the force of their joining drove up mountains, mountains since ground down again by time and grit as the land itself ripped apart again, leaving ragged, incomplete edges. Here, oceans washed between outcrops that had once belonged to the same body. There, faults sutured together the beds of strangers.

But the traces and signs left by that violence and tumult were not everywhere the same because the merging and tearing had happened in multiple stages, from multiple angles. Along an arc from Mt. Monadnock to Katahdin, the land had been baked and transformed by the unrelenting heat and pressure of nearby upheavals. Southwest Maine and northern New Hampshire had been baked most thoroughly of all, and the stress had strengthened the land here. When time eroded down the ancient mountains and then just kept on grinding, it was these rocks, the ones that had been most harshly tested, that resisted, standing up thousands of feet above the flat and fertile woodlots and potato fields that shared the same origins.

And on top of Bigelow Mountain, one of the tallest, most intensely metamorphosed peaks in the region, and the fourth highest in Maine, a small patch of alpine tundra, a community of tough, little plants that could grow nowhere else but the harsh places, found refuge. There, Elzy found mountain cranberry, a dark green shrub no larger than her hand, flowering.

In a nearby col she found an encampment of hikers, some of whom she knew. Tank was hiking back south until she reached the Hudson River where she would catch a river boat home. Loosianer was doing the same, except that he intended to turn off to the west in Pennsylvania and catch a boat down the Ohio, and from there down the Mississippi. Several others were familiar from the hostel too, mostly southbound thru-hikers. They weren't hiking as an organized group, but they deliberately kept to a similar pace for safety and for company. Business travelers and weekend hikers could come and go from the Trail, but at every tent site or lean-to, the thru-hikers could be assured of seeing someone they knew. Andy and Elzy, hiking fast, had finally caught up with them.

Elzy immediately immersed herself in gossip. Cup-o-Chowder had last been seen in Millinocket, getting ready for a date with Adric, who had confessed to Loosianer that he had a jar of canned clams he'd been saving for a special occasion. Evidently, the special occasion had arrived. The two women preachers had made the same mistake about market schedules that Andy had, and likewise decided to just hike through. They had gotten a faster start and kept up with the thru-hikers for a week until the Methodist developed blood poisoning from an infected blister and had to be hospitalized. Her prognosis was excellent, though. And Hope had traded email addresses with Tank and had recently sent a message boasting about seeing a moose. She said she would have been able to kill it if only such animals weren't too rare to hunt.

The unexpected meeting felt almost like a homecoming to Elzy, for although these people were not really her friends, they might as well have been. All her relationships except one were superficial and transitory anyway, and these hikers were happy to see her. Andy consented to stay the night so she could socialize, and then he hid from the crowds with all the dignity of an old tomcat. Elzy, understanding, covered for him so that the others never realized they were being deliberately avoided.

Andy had never told her that he disliked crowds. He certainly never asked her to help him do anything about it. But she had learned to watch the curve of his shoulders, the tension of his jaw, and the quality of his silences. She knew when he needed something and knew that she wasn't supposed to know. So she pretended not to know and looked after him anyway.

He needed looking after. She didn't know why, but he seemed

to be wandering.

Back on campus, Andy had had a reputation for absent-mind-edness, but that was mostly because he ignored details he didn't consider important, a habit that bothered people who did not share his order of priorities. As Elzy had discovered, his memory was actually good enough to keep track of an extraordinary number of projects without mishap. If he lost his keys or forgot to buy salt more often than most people, the difference was of degree, not of kind. Only now, deep in the woods of Maine, he had started to live up to his reputation.

There was the day he misread the map and led them forwards towards a spring that really lay behind them. Elzy found the thoughtlessness frighteningly out of character, but he seemed unwilling to talk about it. She figured everybody makes mistakes and let it go. But the next day he walked off down a side trail without noticing he'd left the main path. Two days after that, when he switched water filter cartridges, he put the new one in upside-down. He couldn't understand why the cap wouldn't go on until Elzy said something, and then he muttered about poor design. A day later, when he left his water filter behind—and didn't even notice until Loosianer caught up and returned it—Elzy finally admitted to herself that something had changed.

It wasn't that he forgot everything. Most of the time, he was still his normal, highly competent self. But suddenly he seemed able to forget *anything*, and some of his mistakes, like losing the water filter, could have been serious.

On a practical level, Elzy could pick up the slack. Even if the unexplained deterioration got much worse, she knew she could get both of them out of the woods and home safely. But there were days when she wondered what would happen to her career if he couldn't act as her sponsor anymore. She could not work without guild membership, could not join a guild without the signature of a sponsor, and could not get a new sponsor because such relationships take time, and time takes money, and she had none left. She felt stupid for having allowed herself such uncharacteristic vulnerability.

Other days, she worried about Andy's condition for reasons that had nothing whatever to do with her career.

The worst part was that he would not acknowledge that anything was wrong. When he couldn't ignore a mishap, he would insist that she had misunderstood his intentions or that badly-designed equipment or the Trail itself were actually to blame. He sounded so understanding and reasonable about all of it that she sometimes doubted herself. Maybe she was the one going crazy.

Then one evening, she went to fetch something from her pack. Andy had helpfully moved it over next to her hammock, which he had hung for her while she made dinner. Standing up too quickly from rummaging in her pack gave her a head-rush, so she grabbed her hammock-rope to steady herself and felt it give oddly. She inspected the line and realized it wasn't tied, just wrapped around the tree a few times and looped over itself once.

"Andy, you didn't tie my hammock," she called. In his look of blank shock, she saw that he'd forgotten about the rope utterly. Something had distracted him, and he'd just wandered away from it. The friction of rope on rough black cherry bark would have held just long enough for her to get in the hammock before dropping her almost three feet onto rocks and roots. She could have broken her tailbone or worse. "Andy?"

Already he'd pulled himself together and covered up his surprise. He calmly walked over and examined the hammock, fingering the rope and the place where the knot should have been but wasn't.

"I had intended to double-check this," he began, and then went on for about a minute off the top of his head, clearly trying to pretend that he had a well-thought-out explanation, while Elzy listened to him carefully.

Why, she wondered, was his explanation pissing her off? His voice sounded so friendly, so reasonable and supportive, as though he were sharing some fascinating professional secret with her. His words....

She couldn't quite figure out what he was talking about. There were digressions and diversions and subtle inversions and implications, and following it all felt rather like trying to solve some complex algebra problem in her head which, fortunately, Elzy was able to do. After a few seconds, the pattern suddenly jumped into focus and she realized he was lecturing *her* on the importance of clear communication. When he offered to help her improve her knot-tying skills, she boiled over.

"I did *not* sabotage my own hammock!" she shouted at him. "*I was not unclear!* Andy, you volunteered to hang my hammock, and you *said* you did it! How the hell am I supposed to trust you if you don't do what you say you're going to? What the hell?"

What the hell is wrong with you? She almost said it. Weeks of mounting frustration were venting themselves at once, startling both of them. She bit her lip. She had never raised her voice to him before.

He didn't shout back, but his features hardened and he raised his chin slightly. In the end, she was the one to apologize.

She knew Andy could not be doing any of this on purpose and that his loss of control must be mortifying him. Perhaps he was ill. She knew he still was not sleeping well, still having the nightmares. If he was dehydrated, that plus sleep deprivation could explain his poor performance. When she awoke at night for whatever reason, she would look over at his hammock and see the glow of his headlamp leaking through his tarp. What was he doing rather than sleeping? Was he reading? Composing more secret messages to his wife? Staring at the underside of his tarp, second-guessing all the decisions he'd ever made while searching fruitlessly for his son?

Then, in the morning he would be helpful and friendly and cheerful again. He would know everything and be able to do everything, the unquestioned and unquestionable captain of their little voyage. It was almost as though she had two separate, simultaneous, and mutually contradictory relationships with him, as though there were two Elzys and two Andys, and neither version could know anything about how the other pair got along.

She shook her head. She was getting tired, too—not of hiking, but of looking after Andy, of the green tunnel, and of having nothing whatever to do but walk and daydream about all the food she planned to eat when next she saw what passed these days for civilization. She had never starved, so the constant hunger didn't upset her, but she had become completely obsessed by food. *I want to go home*, the thought appeared in her mind without volition. When she remembered she didn't even know where home was, she almost wept.

And still the Trail grew rougher, finally culminating in Mahoosuc Notch, reputedly its single most difficult mile. As the name implies, the Notch is a valley, not a mountain, but its narrow floor is entirely filled with large boulders, some the size of small houses, like a dry, pebbly streamed as perceived by a couple of ants. If the pile has a bottom, dirt or bedrock, anything other than boulders under boulders forever, it is nowhere visible. The path wound over, between, and even underneath the smooth stones. Sometimes Andy and Elzy actually had to take their packs off to pass some narrow tunnel or high rock face. Then she would go first, and he would push or hand both packs through or over and follow. Then they'd have to do it again for the next boulder.

Not that either of them exactly minded rock climbing. The strange little valley was a welcome change of pace as well as a truly ridiculous place to put a footpath, and so first one and then the other began to giggle and then to laugh. Elzy said she thought this section had been routed by a couple of fourteen-year-old boys with something to prove, and Andy took the joke and ran with it, explaining with a straight face exactly how each turn and twist would "definitely stick it to those yuppie geezers" until Elzy's belly hurt from laughing. She still could not clearly remember what it was like to have a brother, but she thought it must be something like this.

Not long after, in a quiet, smooth-bottomed little valley, they crossed the state line back into New Hampshire and headed for the famously difficult White Mountains.

Local people boasted that the Whites had the worst weather in the world. Generally speaking they were correct; the mountains thrust upwards into the convergence of several major storm tracks. But that week, the weather was uncharacteristically perfect for hiking—dry and relatively cool, for August—and Andy and Elzy joked that they must just have bad timing, to have missed the famous storms. They made good time across the Carter-Moriahs and the Wildcat Range and down into Pinkham Notch.

The notches of the Northern Appalachians are high passes between higher mountains, glacier-carved, U-shaped, with flat floors watered by streams and beaver ponds. Pinkham is typical, except that its west wall is defined by the massive Presidential Range whose greatest peak, Mt. Washington, looms over four thousand feet above the valley floor. When Elzy followed the Trail across Route 16, she found herself already in the mountain's shadow. It wasn't even five o'clock yet.

There was no town center in the Notch itself, only a complex of travelers' facilities and a museum, but the complex could change money and had a media center with a fast Internet connection. Down the road in either direction there were farms and orchards and busy little towns with regular weekly markets. Andy had finally given Elzy full authority over event scheduling and she was eager to set up a new round of gigs.

The main display house of the museum doubled as a front office for the entire facility, which was owned and maintained by the Appalachian Mountain College. Andy perused the exhibits while Elzy approached the desk.

"Hi, we have open reservations at the hostel?" she began.

The desk-person looked through his list.

"Diana Cartwright?" he asked.

"No, Elzy Rodriguez."

He looked over the list again and found her name. *Open reservations* meant not setting an exact arrival date. It was a good option for some travelers, but since hostels wouldn't turn away customers in favor of someone who might not show up, the reserved bed sometimes turned out to be a cot in a closet. For that reason, open reservations were not popular, and Elzy had assumed hers would be the only name on the list. While she checked in, Andy came over, suddenly interested.

"Did you say Diana Cartwright?" he asked.

"Yes," said the desk attendant. "She's due in sometime this week."

"The climatologist?"

"Yeah, I suppose so. She's going to stay the night here, then go up Tuck's to the Observatory for a few days." *Tuck's* was short for Tuckerman's Ravine Trail. The Weather Observatory at the summit of Washington also belonged to the College. "Why, do you know her?"

"Yes, I do." Andy didn't elaborate. He waited until he and Elzy were out on the porch sharing a bag of trail mix to explain. Diana was a friend of his whom he rarely got to see because life, as he put it, was simply too crazy. He spoke briefly and glowingly of her work—she was developing a protocol for measuring trace atmospheric gasses by using drone networks. Quite plainly he wanted to wait for her. He would not say so. It would be unlike him to admit wanting anything for himself, and he had already caused Elzy enough delay.

She passed him the trail mix bag and he looked away from her, staring out through the dark timber of the porch to the green world it framed, mostly maple forest interrupted by spires of dark spruce, the loom of mountains, and in the middle ground, the paler sweep of beaver marsh on the other side of the road. In casual, relaxed moments, Andy tended not to bother so much about eye contact. If they did look each other in the face he would meet her eyes, but he seemed to prefer that they take turns regarding each other. Regarding him now, Elzy could see that he looked bad. He was freshly shaved, of course, but he had not had an opportunity to wash or cut his hair, which hung in his eyes like so much greasy, dead grass. His weight loss showed in his face and there was something dreadfully wrong with his eyes that had nothing to do with vision—he was either very sad, or exhausted, or both.

187

"Andy," Elzy began, as though she were asking for a favor for herself, "is there any way we could wait a few days? I'd really like to meet this Diana Cartwright, and I've been hoping to climb Mt. Washington, since I didn't get to do Katahdin. It's right there. I could go up and back and you could stay with our stuff. Unless you'd rather climb it with me?"

Something about Andy's face changed for a moment. He might have been surprised, or even grateful, but by the time he turned to face her he was in charge of himself again.

"No, you're right," he answered, as though Elzy's interests were the only thing on his mind. "You really could get a lot out of meeting Diana. Why don't you traverse the Northern Presidentials? It's a nice, challenging hike, even if you break it up into two or three days. If Diana gets here and leaves again before you get back, you'll meet up with her at the Observatory."

Elzy liked the idea. She *had* been being kind, but not, at the moment, altruistic. She really did want to meet the climatologist. She also did want to hike Mt Washington, and since the Appalachian Trail had been moved off the Presidential Ridge in recent years, the mountain would require some kind of side-trip.

She bought a topo map and jumped straight in to planning. Andy had hiked the Presidentials before and recommended a route that would take her over some half-dozen peaks and then back to Pinkham in a big loop. He also suggested she stay at the Observatory, if she needed to stop for a second night. The facility didn't rent rooms, but he was friends with some of the staff. Neither of them mentioned the possibility of him actually going with her again. They both knew he needed to vanish.

The next morning she set out, carrying only a few essentials. The abnormally light pack felt strange on her back and the trail seemed too easy. The way ran relatively level for a few miles through mostly sugar maple, beech, and yellow birch, then rose steeply over rocks and roots into the dark, mossy world of red and black spruce, balsam fir, and the occasional mountain ash. And then there was the tent site, just a couple of wooden platforms and a bear box among the trees. She didn't want to stop so early, but there was nowhere further on to camp legally.

She spent the rest of the afternoon eating most of her supplies and thinking of nothing in particular. She went to bed around sunset, hoping to get as much sleep as possible so she could get on the trail again early in the morning, but she couldn't sleep through the night. Instead she woke spontaneously and lay there for an hour or so, staring at the stars through the lattice of fir twigs and thinking how strange it was to be all alone. She wondered why she was awake, but eventually decided it was just a nap. If a puddle could be an island on land, then a period of wakefulness could be a nap at night. The thought made her smile and she slipped back into sleep, waking again only when the alarm on her cell sounded just before dawn. Without stopping for breakfast, she packed up her things and followed the trail steeply uphill, out of the trees, into sunshine, and up the narrow, exposed pyramid of Mt. Madison.

She could not see most of the rest of the Presidentials from the summit because massive Mt. Adams stood in the way, but she could get an impression of vastness. Fog, or maybe low clouds, streaked the valleys below her and climbed the lower, green feeder ridges here and there. The rising sun lit the tops of those cloud banks a rosy gold.

Between Madison and Adams lay a narrow col, its rocky floor green in places with low plants but otherwise open. A little stone building squatted there, too, and Elzy made for it, scrambling down over slabs and blocks of broken, blond schist daubed black and red and green with lichen.

The hut had potable water and a composting toilet to share, the last such facilities until the summit of Washington. Also, there were people. Once, paying overnight guests had stayed here, but that kind of tourism had all but dried up and the service was no longer available. Instead, the place housed six guild applicants who served as guardians of both the mountains and the few people who still hiked upon them. They had charge of all the trails in the Northern Presidentials, led search and rescue missions, and conducted field research and environmental education besides. They were, in fact, rather like the naturalist-vigilantes Elzy had been imagining, except they had no law-enforcement powers. She chatted with them for a few minutes about their duties over a belated meal of dried fruit, nuts, and pretzels before she went on her way.

The knee-high plants outside were actually a full-grown forest of black spruce, balsam fir, and the occasional heart-leafed birch. Against winter cold and ice-blast, the sturdy little trees had been forced to bonsai themselves for survival. As she left the col, even the tiny forest lost its grip on the ground and only sedges, lichens, and little crawling or cushion-shaped plants, like diapensia, Lapland rosebay, and Robbins' cinquefoil persisted among loose rock. Everything Elzy saw around her suggested—practically screamed—harsh conditions, but the actual weather of the day was clear, still, and now growing almost hot despite the elevation. From the summit of Mt Adams, she thought she could see the sea.

The view was like nothing she'd ever seen before, not so much in the largeness and distance—she'd been atop mountains before, after all—but in how much of it was treeless rock. Peaks and sub-peaks rose one after the other from the bare, gray-blond, rocky ridge for over ten miles up to the imposing summit cone of Washington, then five miles more of descending peaks behind that, all of it sedge and tiny, ground-hugging shrubs and little else. Only on the side slopes, a thousand feet below the highest peaks, could even the dwarfed and twisted firs and spruces cling. The sky was an absolutely perfect blue. Nothing made any noise at all.

Elzy stood on the summit, troubled by an odd sense of double vision. The view before her was utterly new and yet completely familiar at the same time. Or rather, something else was utterly familiar, something similar to this but not the same. For every peak and col and rock and gulf there was another one in her mind, but the picture wouldn't come clear. She couldn't tell what she was really seeing.

And there was nobody to ask, nobody to talk to, just the mountains and, beyond them, the lower slopes and hills like a rumpled, green carpet spreading out at far as the Green Mountains of Vermont on the one side and the Atlantic Ocean on the other. No buildings, no roads were visible. She might have been the only human being on the Earth, except that the dark conifer forest near tree line was marred by white blotches and smears of death and blast, much of it filling in with pale green hardwoods. The curving lines of dead firs were natural, a product of the wind, but the large patches of beetle kill and the invasion of hardwoods were new. Wind and ice would keep the summits open a while yet, but global warming was happening here, too.

There was nothing she could do about climate change, nothing she could do about her past, and nothing she could do about her faulty memory. Sometimes she felt as though she were pushing against a door, trying to get through, only there was no through to get. And Andy couldn't help her either. He wasn't here.

She spread her arms outward like a bird and touched nothing but sky, as viscerally amazed by his absence as by the lightness of her half-empty pack. Today, she lacked ballast. She lacked nearness and weight and the direction of someone else's judgment. A moment of something like agoraphobia came to her, as though the world were really too big, but it passed. Over the last few months, she had gotten so used to his presence, his warmth and solidity—and the luxury of a companion who really did know what he was doing most of the time. But her own judgment, though fallible, was as good as anybody else's, and it was good enough. She was Elzy Rodriguez, the best shot in Lancaster Valley and the most decorated cop her age in Octorara Town. She raised her arms again and whooped, knowing that there was no one around to see or hear her, no one who could laugh or question or mind.

But a little bird did hear her, a little dark-eyed junco who had been hoping she might drop some trail mix, and when she whooped the bird flew away, heading down off the ridge, into the valley, towards Andy.

Hours later and well past dark, Elzy stumbled into Pinkham Notch, her knees aching from the four-thousand-foot descent off

Mt Washington. She had been hoping Andy would wait up for her, as she had always waited up for him, but the college hostel was silent. She unlocked her empty room and fell into bed.

In the morning, she found the hostel abuzz with activity, but Andy had evidently gotten up already because she couldn't find him. She pushed her way through the crowd in the bathroom, used the facilities, and went to breakfast, finally spotting him a few places ahead of her in line.

"Andy!"

He jumped and she smiled, because usually it was he who snuck up on people, but he recovered himself and turned, showing her a rare smile of true social pleasure.

"Elzy! How was it?"

She changed places in line to join him, ignoring the frowns of the two people she cut in front of, and rattled off a long description of her adventures, very much in ten-year-old mode. She rarely acted that way anymore, and Andy, obviously fondly amused, let her chatter. He guided her ahead of him in the line, his hand almost but not quite touching the small of her back.

They both loaded up their trays with bowls of oatmeal, fresh fruit, and cottage cheese, all drizzled with honey, and found a table. Andy dug in, but Elzy paused, on the point of asking him how his time alone had been. Spoon halted in mid-air, he looked at her and raised one eyebrow. She did not ask.

Instead, he had more questions for her.

"You said something about the table-land seemed familiar?"

"Yeah, but I can't place it. It's almost right, but it's wrong. I don't know what it's reminding me of. I don't even know what *about* it is reminding me of something. There are too many variables. It's useless."

"*Everything* has too many variables. The art of science is picking the right ones to focus on."

"I'm not much of an artist." Elzy stabbed at her cottage cheese with her spoon. Her mood seemed to be rising and falling as violently as the trail she had hiked the previous day. "Andy, what if I *don't* get my memory back?"

"Well, what if?" he answered. "Say you don't get it back. What's really wrong?"

"The whole *point* was for me to remember, to get it back."

"Was it?"

"You said so yourself!"

"Did I?"

"Why do you always answer questions with more questions?"

"Do I do that?"

"ANDY!"

Their laughter startled some of the other patrons, who glanced over and then politely went back to eating.

"No, seriously," began Andy, trying to recover himself, "I've been thinking about this. I don't know how much more of your memory is *missing* so much as never there to begin with. A lot of people don't remember much of their childhoods. I can remember being a toddler, but none of my friends in college could. A lot of them really didn't have much from before they were eight or ten years old. And nobody remembers everything. I certainly don't. You aren't trying to achieve total recall from the moment of your conception, so what is it you're looking for? What do you hope to achieve if your memory of certain things comes back?"

"Wholeness," Elzy responded without hesitation. "I feel...like I'm cut off from my roots. Conditions and events shaped me, but I don't know what they were. I don't understand who I am or why. I want to."

"You're looking for your niche, your habitat."

"Yes. I want to be native. I want to know where I belong."

"You don't need memories to know that."

"Oh?"

"No. You only need to know where your habitat is and how you lived there. Those are the conditions and events that shaped you. They probably still exist. And your shape still exists. Bring them together and they'll match, you and your home. You're not really looking for the past. You're looking for the *present*."

"But I don't know *where* it was! I need my memory for that."

"Not really. You don't need full, vivid recall, only a few more clues. And we already have a lot."

"Just a few more clues." She said it as though he might as well have announced they needed passenger pigeons or rhinoceroses. Something there just wasn't any more of. If Andy noticed her hopelessness, he deliberately ignored it.

"Yes. Just a few more," he agreed.

They finished their meal and were just leaving the dining hall when Andy recognized a woman coming in the building.

"Diana!" he called over the crowd, and the woman gave a start, looked around, and spotted Andy—and startled again, as well she might. As Elzy knew, he seldom bothered to tell his friends even what state he was in, let alone sending anyone his itinerary. The woman pushed her way through the crowd to greet Andy warmly with a kiss high on one cheek. Elzy hadn't known such liberties were possible, but he accepted the affection without reservation.

Dr. Diana Cartwright was a very slight woman, perhaps in her mid-sixties, with long, very straight pepper-and-salt hair and skin almost the color of strong iced tea. Despite the rather Anglo-sounding name, she spoke with a slight Hindi accent. She wore an unusually loose and flowing version of the guild tunic and trousers and had a precise and gracious manner. If anything, she seemed even more self-assured than Andy.

If Diana was a small, authoritative bird, her guild-applicant assistant was a bear, or possibly an extremely large puppy. He was not tall, but broad and square, and so boisterous that he seemed to take up more space than his body actually occupied. A thick, black beard covered half his chest and a full mane of narrow dreadlocks hung just past his shoulders. The dark brown of his skin set off his startlingly green eyes handsomely, and something in those eyes looked slightly out of control. His name was Dashawn Harris, and Elzy liked him immediately.

Diana and Dashawn agreed to meet for an early lunch after they'd checked in and gotten settled in their rooms. That Andy and

Elzy had just eaten posed no problem, since both still had hikers' metabolisms and could happily eat almost constantly. An hour later, all four reconvened and Elzy and Dashawn split off to let their application sponsors catch up in private.

The weather had turned overnight, and while they ate, a thick, driving rain blew in and thundered on the roof. Occasional rumbles of actual thunder added to the noise, but Dashawn could talk over the din without effort. He ate much, with much enjoyment, and told a long series of wonderfully horrible jokes that made Elzy blush and choke on her food. She didn't blush over such jokes easily—she could be pretty ribald herself, when not around Andy. Besides being very funny, Dashawn was a self-taught roboticist. Diana Cartwright was not his mentor. Rather, she was his partner and supervisor in the project that he hoped would make him a real professional. He was going to design and program a fleet of drones for her.

"I make things fuckin' *fly*, dude," he explained, then remembered his audience and amended his phrasing. "Oh, sorry—*dudette*."

After the meal, the gusty rain continued. The dining hall mostly emptied out and the four of them collected at the same table and chatted through the afternoon. Andy spoke little but watched the conversation with a hint of a smile. Diana happily bubbled forth, mostly about her work and how she hoped to develop some kind of partnership with the meteorologists at the Mt Washington Observatory. Hours went by.

At a break in the weather in the late afternoon, Andy announced he had some work to do and excused himself. Elzy knew he probably did have work, but was also tired of company. He seemed much more focused and energetic than he had a few days earlier, but she guessed his reserves were still low. Since Diana and Dashawn planned to head up the mountain very early in the morning, he said his goodbyes, taking leave of his friend with his customary casual professionalism. Diana's amused fondness told Elzy she was used to it.

But in the morning Diana and Dashawn appeared at breakfast.

The weather was perfect for hiking, cool and foggy, with little wind, so their continued presence was puzzling.

"I thought you were going up Tucks this morning?" Andy asked conversationally, over a large plate of eggs.

"That was the plan," said Diana, "but you know what they say about making plans."

Andy smiled a little, clearly getting the joke, but Elzy must have looked quite blank.

"Plans make God laugh," he explained, making it sound like a well-worn folk phrase. "I take it the Deity is amused?"

"Yes, well, I broke my pants," she asserted, then laughed merrily at Elzy's confusion. "My dancing pants!" And she pulled up the hem of one pant-leg to reveal a slim, metallic bar anchored to a screw implanted in her visibly atrophied flesh. Evidently, she wore loose clothing to hide a robotic exoskeleton.

"You're going up Tucks in an *exo*?" Elzy exclaimed. She had just come down that trail, and knew it to be almost cliff-like in places. Exoskeletons were no longer uncommon, but most were awkward and cranky. Older models required the use of canes or crutches. Anyway, paraplegia is a pretty serious disability to just not notice in one's breakfast companion.

"I told you I do good work," Dashawn said and winked.

"Yes, Dashawn does very good work," Diana confirmed. "But unfortunately, not even he can make a machine impervious to damage. There is a stress fracture in one of my ankle-struts. I can still walk, but I do not trust it for climbing. We had ordered the part to be shipped here, but it did not arrive yesterday."

"The shipper said it would be here yesterday at the latest," Dashawn explained, "but now they're saying today or tomorrow. Jack-offs." When Elzy looked at him in surprise, he grinned and rolled his eyes. "What? You know they do it. Quiet stretch of road, no one coming…." He mimed looking both ways to see if the coast was clear, made an obscene gesture, and then snorted with laughter and glanced, perhaps self-consciously, at Andy.

Elzy was not surprised Dashawn would make such a joke—

she'd heard him say much worse. But she hadn't expected him to talk that way in front of his supervisor, let alone in front of Andy, a potential professional contact he didn't even know. She looked over at Diana, expecting to see disapproval, but the woman wasn't even looking at Dashawn. She was watching Andy. Elzy followed her gaze and saw that while he was trying not to, Andy was laughing.

She looked back at Dashawn, who was still giggling helplessly, but he made eye contact with her and she saw a deliberate intelligence there. She wondered if he had just performed an experiment and, if so, what he had learned from the results.

"Listen, you'll be here through tomorrow, too, right?" said Dashawn, when he had calmed down. It wasn't really a question. He was addressing Andy. "How about we hitch a ride into town today, give the girls a chance to, I dunno, get all *girly* and shit. There's a Greek place with an all-you-can-eat buffet, it's supposed to be pretty decent, and it's Riddle Night at the Prancing Pony. Drinks are half-price and you can win some serious shit, riddling."

"'Prancing Pony'?" asked Andy. "That's a Tolkein reference, right?"

"Yeah. Total geekapalooza. I have a friend who runs a role-playing game there on Saturdays, except he's out of town now. But Riddle Night is fun. It's like they take it seriously, but not at all seriously, you know what I mean? It's, like, actual fun for smart people and shit."

Andy considered the proposal.

"Elzy, this could be a good time for you to talk further with Diana. You mentioned having some questions for her." Of course, he couldn't just agree to run off and have fun without some pretext of organizing an educational activity.

Ten minutes later, he was standing on the edge of the highway with his daypack slung over his shoulder, pointing his thumb towards a riddling contest with Dashawn. From inside the dining hall, Elzy and Diana watched a teamster with a horse cart of mail pick them up and move off at a good clip.

"So, now we're supposed to 'get all girly and shit'?" asked Elzy, over a cup of chicory. She noted that Diana didn't seem to mind the language from her, either.

"He said it backwards," Diana explained, with more than a hint of humor. "He has been spending altogether too much time in the company of women lately."

"Does Dashawn not like women?"

Diana made a dismissive noise.

"I would not choose an assistant so idiotic as to categorically reject over half the human species. Dashawn likes and respects women, but he needs his 'man time.' Also, I do not think he is comfortable getting drunk around me. He feels the need to act as my aide." She meant that he assisted her when her disability proved troublesome.

"Andy seems an odd person to choose as a drinking buddy," Elzy commented, then chuckled. "Of course, some people say he's odd in general." She was performing some experiments of her own.

"I am not certain he or Dashawn are entirely sane," Diana mused, looking out the window again. Elzy looked at her, startled, and the climatologist glanced back, then smiled into her chicory cup. "At least their insanities are entertaining," she continued. "Perhaps they will be friends."

"I'm not always sure Andy has friends," Elzy admitted and worried as soon as she said it that Diana would feel slighted. But the woman seemed only amused.

"Yes, you do know," the older woman said. "You are just not certain he is *your* friend."

Elzy could not speak. Seen through, put in her place with more finesse than even her mother had ever managed, she abandoned all attempts at experimentation. Diana would provide the information she wished to provide, no more. Elzy swallowed hard and then took several sips of chicory.

"He is your friend," she acknowledged, at last. She tried to gather her dignity. "How long have you known him?"

"Since our undergraduate days" Diana explained. "We had several classes in common. We used to go rock climbing together."

"You knew him Before?"

"I did."

Elzy realized that Diana probably knew Andy's first wife and children. What were their names? What were they like? What was Andy like before he lost them—and what did *not entirely sane* mean? Elzy wanted to ask questions. Her impulse was to trust, to unburden herself of worry, to ask Diana what she thought Andy's recent muddle-headedness meant, whether he was sick, whether either of them could do anything to help.

And yet none of those questions came out. Andy's privacy was at stake, not merely hers, and she knew nothing whatever of his relationship with Diana, other than its length, nor could she get a clear read on the woman. Andy was a mystery, but he was a straight-forward mystery. Diana seemed to be operating on a whole other level.

Elzy decided to change the subject and started asking questions about the drones.

As Andy had mentioned days earlier, the climatologist had developed a protocol for measuring trace atmospheric gasses with drone networks. The idea was to address a problem Elzy was already vaguely familiar with—the loss of most research satellites and the fact that new launches were prohibitively expensive meant that climatology was essentially flying blind. As Diana had explained the day before, a number of research stations had brought trace gas detectors online over the last five or ten years, and the carbon dioxide concentration seemed to be falling steadily at last. But other greenhouse gasses, such as methane or the hydrofluorocarbons, were harder to track. Releases from ruined industrial facilities and landfills almost certainly continued, which meant that these gases were still concentrated in large release plumes. Since no one was entirely sure where most of those release points were, researchers were almost certainly underestimating them. Without those data, the climate models couldn't approach accuracy.

What had jumped out to Elzy the previous day was the size of the network Diana's plan called for—literally hundreds of drones flying transects through thousands of miles of airspace. Where was she going to get the money to build all of them? How was she going to get permission from hundreds of county air traffic control boards? Most people were still highly suspicious of unmanned vehicles. Even search-and-rescue fliers sometimes got shot down.

"That is where meteorology comes in," Diana explained. "Climatologists and meteorologists used to use many of the same satellites and research stations. Without the right data, the weather forecasts are not as accurate as they could be. Every time there is an unexpected storm or a long drought, political pressure rises to put more resources into weather prediction. I am hoping that the weather services will fund my drones in exchange for data."

"You're assuming ordinary people will accept a fleet of drones flying above their heads day and night."

"The drones will not normally be visible from the ground."

"Even worse. You have to explain the need for the drones to the general public in terms that really resonate emotionally as well as being scientifically sound. Do you have a public relations director?"

"No, I do not."

"Do you want one?"

They spent much of the rest of the day brain-storming. By the time Andy and Dashawn returned, late in the evening, Elzy had Diana's contact information and tentative plans to do a lecture circuit on her behalf the following summer.

The two men arrived slightly tipsy but laughing and bearing Diana's new ankle piece in a little cardboard box. It had been mis-delivered to an inn in town.

The next morning the sky was still cloudy but dry and calm. Diana and Dashawn had gone. It was time to approve the next batch of event bookings and get back to work.

Except there was no next batch to approve because Elzy, now entirely in charge of logistics, had yet to send in their expected arrival dates. She hadn't told Andy she had neglected the task, nor had he asked about it. Perhaps he assumed she was waiting for the guild's reply, but she wasn't. She was still dragging her feet.

First, she had been worried about Andy, eager to give him as long a break as he would accept. Now that he seemed clear-eyed and rested, she had a new reason for delay. She kept hoping he'd ask to take more time so he could go up the mountain and see his friends again. Of course he suggested no such thing. She didn't know why she constantly wanted him to show more interest, to place a higher priority on his friendships than he actually did.

After breakfast, they went outside to sit in the grass on the lawn and enjoy the air before the day got hot. Andy read through and answered a new batch of emails while Elzy texted with a couple of friends, got bored with that, and stared at the sky for a while. Eventually, she got up and wandered around the campus, then returned to Andy's side to stare at the sky again for a bit. A couple of flies joined them. Elzy flicked the insects away with a swish from a branch she'd picked up along the way. It caught Andy's attention.

"What have you got?" he asked, looking up from his computer.

"White pine. I guess it fell in the storm? Unless it's a nip twig." She meant that it might have been broken off by a feeding animal.

"Too big for that," he replied. "You were probably right the first time."

Elzy fingered the developing pine cones and then swished the stick around playfully.

"It's funny," she said. "I keep thinking it's strange that there's only *two* rings of closed cones on these branches. There should be more. But of course there isn't."

"Pitch pine has *serotinous* cones in the southern part of its range," Andy commented, frowning. Serotinous, as Elzy knew, meant that a cone stayed sealed closed with sap until released by a forest fire. Since a new group of cones grow every year or two, trees with the serotinous habit do have more closed cones on them than other pines.

"No, no, no," Elzy complained. "Pitch pine is *whisker tree*. I'm thinking of *claw tree*. But of course—"

She and Andy stared at each other in mutual shock.

"Only my brother came up with names like that," Elzy whispered.

"What is claw tree?" he asked.

"I don't know its real name—it wasn't on the list at school. It's a pine, but fairly small, with very short needles. Almost like a spruce, except the needles come in pairs. The cones are sometimes serotinous, but not always, and they're small, curved like claws, like this," and she held her crooked finger up to illustrate.

"Jack pine! That's jack pine. We have two more trees then, jack pine and pitch pine. Did you see both of them with and without your brother?"

"Yes, I think so."

"So they grew near each other? Or...wait! Did they actually grow together? In one community?"

"Yes, sometimes."

Andy seemed to find that significant.

"Wait here!" he half shouted, jumped up, and ran off towards the museum.

For what seemed like a long time but wasn't, Elzy sat alone on the lawn wondering what Andy could possibly have run off for. She came to no useful conclusion before he returned carrying a large cloth basket full of rocks. He was positively buzzing with excitement.

He set the basket down before her and moved some of the stones around so that none covered any of the others up.

"Pick which ones are *right*," he said.

"Right?"

"Yes. You said the coast of Maine was almost right but not quite and that the tundra up on the ridge was also almost right but not quite. Both those landscapes are dominated by exposed rock. What if it's the rock that is almost but not quite right? Which of these rocks would make those places *right*?"

Elzy considered. There were ten rocks, each just a little too large to fit comfortably in her hand—but she had small hands. She picked them up, one after another, and examined them. Five were granite, although of different colors. Three were swirled and banded metamorphic stones, but, again, each of a different kind. One was an irregular chunk of quartz, and the tenth was a sandstone cobble. Each had a little white, numbered paper circle glued on. They were samples from the museum's mineral collection.

"These three," she said, finally, choosing several colorful granites.

"You're sure? Not any of the others?"

"Yes."

And Andy erupted.

"I knew it! I knew it!" he crowed, pumping both fists in the air then drumming the ground with his palms. "I knew it!"

"Knew *what*? Where are those rocks *from*?" Elzy cried, feeling lost.

"The same place you are," he told her. "Mount Desert Island. Maine."

Chapter 8
Disturbance Histories

"Wait, what?" asked Elzy.

Andy had just told her the one thing she'd most wanted to know for as long as she could remember, and she had no idea what to do with the information.

"You're from Mount Desert Island," he reiterated. "It's an island off the coast of Maine, a bit farther north from where we were. It's the only place I know of where pitch pine and jack pine grow together. That you chose these rocks as *right* confirms it. They're samples of the dominant bedrock types exposed on the island."

"So, what, if I'd just said *whisker tree* and *claw tree* to you from the beginning you would have known where I'm from five months ago?" Of course, she had only remembered those words a few minutes ago, but she'd still feel pretty silly if the answer turned out to be so simple.

"Not necessarily," Andy answered. "There could be another pitch/jack community that I just haven't heard about. Or you could be conflating two memories or remembering family vacations far from home. But with the other things—Mount Desert Island *does* have stands of balsam fir near sea level. Parts of the Island *did* burn in the June fires. Its shoreline is rocky, like that of Casco Bay, and it has large areas above tree-line, like the Whites, but in either case the rock is a different color and texture—colors and textures that you recognized as *right*. All we need to do now is *go* there, test our suspicions, and find out where on the island you actually lived. We're really not that far away. We can take the Saco River down to the sea and catch the ferry."

"*We?*" asked Elzy, bewildered.

"Well, yes, if you want my help, that is. Although honestly, I'm not sure you need it. You're really coming along." His manner had completely and suddenly changed. He seemed no less friendly, but it was a professional friendliness for a mere colleague.

Elzy looked at him sharply. Evidently, he'd misheard her mono-syllabic question as an arch rejection, but instead of expressing anger or hurt—as he'd have every right to do—he was carefully letting her choose her own company, unhindered by what he might want. He was cautious of his own power, always, like a great cat with its claws sheathed, but this seemed excessive.

"Oh, I want you to come whether I need help or not," she told him. "I'm just surprised you offered. I'd expected that to be a trip I'd take after we were done."

If Andy felt reassured, he gave no overt sign. But then, he wouldn't.

"No, if you don't go now, something will come up and you might not get to it. We're really very close to the island. Now is the best time," he told her. "Anyway, I'm a scientist," he added, with a bit of a laugh. "I'm curious. I want to see how it turns out."

Elzy suppressed a smile. Of course, she didn't believe he was merely curious, nor did she believe he had not felt hurt. *What is with him not admitting anything personal?* she wondered. And yet she could not be sure. She still didn't know which of the several possible meanings of his behavior were real. Maybe he was only professionally curious.

"But you have plans for New Hampshire," she protested.

"Never make plans you can't alter if circumstances change,

Elzy," he said, his eyes dancing again, daring her to come with him on a fresh adventure. "Because," and he almost giggled, "circumstances change."

Organizing the new travel plan took several days. There were tentative plans to bow out of, new lodgings to find, ferry tickets to reserve, and the guild needed some lead-time with which to book a new list of events on Mount Desert Island. Fortunately, itinerant guild members often had to alter their plans, so no one would think poorly of Elzy for canceling. Finding work as a last-minute replacement for others would not be difficult, either. Finally, almost two weeks after their arrival, Andy and Elzy checked out of Pinkham and climbed Tucks together, bound for Mt Washington. A traverse of the Southern Presidentials would not take them out of their way, and Andy did not want to miss the mountains entirely.

The trail rose gradually along the length of a narrow, U-shaped valley for several miles, then launched itself up the almost vertical headwall. The trail gained over two thousand feet in less than a mile, working left and right across black, wet rocks. Andy and Elzy each carried almost thirty pounds of gear and supplies on their backs.

But false hellebore, mountain avens, Lapland rosebay, and other small plants, some of them in flower, grew beside the path and in pockets in the rock wall, and there were no trees to block the view of the long, intensely green glacial ravine. The way seemed easier because it was lovely. Then, less than a third of the way up, they climbed into a cloudbank as distinct as a cotton ceiling. Above the cloud lay a cool, wet otherworld cut off from both earth and sky.

"It's *cold* here," Elzy remarked, picking her way along.

"There's probably ice in among the rocks." Andy's voice drifted down to her, oddly muffled by the fog.

"Ice!"

"Snow builds up here against the headwall. It can get hundreds of feet deep and takes *months* to melt. I've skied here in August. There was an ice bridge across that stream. We went right over."

"*August!*"

"Yeah. Of course, that was thirty years ago…."

"Even thirty years ago…wait, how *big* was that patch of snow?"

Andy chuckled like he'd been caught.

"Oh, big enough to keep our beer cold."

"Ah. Everything makes sense now," Elzy commented dryly. Andy laughed, as intended, and she looked up at him. He clung to a ledge on the switchback above hers, twisting around so he could look at her. Distinct, luminous droplets drifted between them. The air smelled almost of snow, but wetter.

The fog was starting to condense on Andy's eyebrows and his hair clung to his forehead in the damp of exertion, but the hawk-look, the grin that lived more in his eyes than his mouth, was back. He was still too thin, but he moved again with that casual, power-ful grace she associated with him. Her fear for him was starting to ease.

At the top of the cliff spread a broad table-land of loose rock. On a clear day, they could have seen the summit from where they stood, but in the cloud they could see almost nothing. They walked in a sphere of visibility just twenty feet across and followed the trail trustingly. Finally the radio and microwave towers and the scientif-ic instruments of the Observatory complex loomed out of the gray mist. That Andy and Elzy now stood six thousand, two hundred and eight-eight feet above sea-level, on the highest point in New England, was a matter of faith.

They had lunch at the Observatory with Diana and Dashawn and Andy's friends on the staff, all of them but Elzy talking shop and trading stories about mutual acquaintances and the resident "Obs" cats. Diana reclined in a window seat, her exo in a heap near-by, its battery plugged in to a charging socket. She said she needed a break from it, that it pinched her ribs. She could barely sit up, let alone walk, without the machine, but the others clustered around her and gladly fetched anything she needed. She accepted their help like a queen.

Elzy had expected Andy to take some time after the meal with Diana, but instead he went off with Dashawn and one of the staff to find a cat rumored to have had four testicles prior to being neutered. The others returned to work.

"It's not like the cat will look any different," Diana commented, once they were gone. "It does not carry its extra organs around in a *jar*."

"The anemometer down in the museum doesn't look any different from other anemometers, either," Elzy pointed out, referring to the famous instrument that had recorded a particularly high wind speed. "Sometimes you need a physical representation to make something seem real."

"Boys being boys," concluded Diana, and turned her head to watch the cloud roil and rend on the other side of the cold glass.

Elzy sat down and watched the clouds with her in silence. Sometimes she could catch glimpses of the green valley thousands of feet below. She imagined, for a moment, only ever knowing the ground that way, and what it would be like to try to understand something only through such glimpses. For some reason, the daydream made her think of Andy.

"They seem to get along," she commented, remembering the excursion to the Prancing Pony.

"I am not surprised," Diana replied, in an odd voice, and Elzy looked at her, suddenly wondering if that day had been a deliberate intervention.

Deliberate or not, the intervention had seemed to help. Solitude and food and rest had clearly helped, too, but Andy had come back from his day with Dashawn seeming much more himself. Should she thank them? But what would she say, *thank you for fixing my friend?*

"He cannot be fixed, you know," said Diana, looking at Elzy now.

"What?"

"He cannot be fixed. None of us who lived through the pandemic can. We are all a little bit crazy. But that is not the important thing."

"Oh?" The cold gulf of air on the other side of the glass seemed to claw at Elzy. She felt a little dizzy. The conversation was getting away from her somehow.

"No." Diana was almost smiling, but not quite. "The important thing is whether we get what we need to go on in spite of being damaged."

"I don't know what he needs," Elzy admitted, and then wished she hadn't.

"I'm not so sure of that," Diana replied. "Understanding human beings is not rocket science—humans are much more complex than rockets." Her eyes twinkled. "But, being more complex, we also do not break the same way that rockets, being *mechanisms*, do. We are more like the sky—the climate system—or perhaps like one of Andy's landscapes. The sky *is* damaged, but would you speak of fixing it? Would you say you cannot help just because you do not understand it entirely?"

Elzy opened her mouth to speak, but then closed it again.

Diana's precise accent and the frank, steady focus of her large, dark eyes gave an impression of sharp intelligence, of laser-like control. Being the object of her regard felt uncomfortably like being naked before the impeccably dressed. Elzy felt torn, as she had in their earlier conversation back at Pinkham. She had no reason to distrust the older woman, and every reason to ask for her help, but her cop's caution rebelled against playing any game when she did not understand the rules. It came to her now that she never would understand, and that whatever choice she made with such inadequate information was going to feel like the wrong one.

Diana looked at her expectantly, clearly waiting for the questions they both knew Elzy had to ask. What did all that stuff about Andy and complexity and the injured sky mean? What sort of friend did he need now? Would he be OK? But Elzy said nothing, just looked out the window, and after a moment, Diana looked out the window also.

Andy returned with Dashawn (but without the Obs staff-member), both men in high spirits, talking fast and excitedly, not about polytesticular cats, but about the problems of teaching fully autonomous drones to evade attacks by predatory or territorial birds.

"You ready, Elzy?" Andy asked, beginning to re-layer himself with clothing. She looked at his flushed and happy face, at his still visibly haunted eyes, and wondered whether she had betrayed him by talking about him at all or by not saying enough.

Stepping outside, Elzy found that she'd forgotten the pitiless-ness of the mountain in the hour or two she'd been sheltered from it. Her blood shrank back away from the inhuman monochrome, the white wind that had risen while they were inside. The temperature hovered just below forty degrees, and the wet air invaded jackets and collars. A lone hiker who turned an ankle in this weather would hemorrhage body heat before help could arrive. The fog swallowed the summit, its buildings, and all signs of civilization, and Andy and Elzy picked their way downhill across the loose rock alone together.

In a col at the base of the summit cone, they came to a pair of large puddles which Andy called the Lakes of the Clouds. Elzy thought he was joking at first, but the names were on the map. Beside the lakes crouched another former tourist hut, this one abandoned, wind-damaged, and covered with graffiti. The gray cloud roiled. The wind was picking up.

"It's too bad you don't get a view," Elzy said, thinking of her crystalline traverse of the northern range.

"There is always a view," Andy told her, "even if it's only five inches."

Elzy circumnavigated the old hut, looking for a sheltered place to pee, and Andy closed his eyes and inhaled the mountain air. Everything smelled intensely of cold chamomile tea. The incongruous scent came from the pineapple weed growing near the hut—the plant is a close relative of chamomile, an exotic species brought accidentally on hikers' feet. But neither chamomile nor pineapple weed is an especially aromatic flower, and Andy had never before been able to smell them just by walking by. He concluded that the fog itself must have somehow steeped the flowers. He was inhaling aerial tea, a whole category of weather that had not arrived here until the alien pineapple weed did.

Elzy reappeared and he followed her up Mt Monroe, its summit only a few hundred feet above the old hut. Near the top, he turned to look back the way they had come, expecting to see only white blankness, but the fog was blowing again and a great, ragged bubble of clear air came up out of the valley and the entire summit cone of Mt Washington, a thousand feet of rock and gravel and blowing sedge, appeared above them and then disappeared again, all without a sound.

"Elzy!" he shouted, hoping she turned in time to see it. When he looked around, she was staring, open-mouthed, at where the mountain had been just a moment ago. There was no sign of it now.

After a moment, she turned to hike on and Andy followed her, scuttling like a beetle in the wind.

"Monroe was a president, right?" she asked, when the breeze died again.

"Yes."

"Which one?"

"Fifth, I think? Maybe sixth."

"And Washington was first?"

That Elzy wasn't sure on this point shocked Andy, but then she had never been to school before turning up in his classroom. She was knowledgeable, but there was no pattern to her knowledge, no sense that there were some things that everybody was just supposed to know. Political history was not exactly his strong suit either, but he told her what he could remember of the various presidents as they walked along. When she asked, he also gave her the names of the plants and lichens they passed. She took it for granted that he would have all of the answers to all of her questions, and he was relieved to find that, today at least, he happened to.

At a bump in the ridge line called Mt. Franklin, they abruptly walked through the bottom of the cloud and the view opened up clear and green for miles. On the summit of Mt. Pierce, the last peak before the trees began again, they turned and looked back.

"Mt. Eisenhower looks a lot like Eisenhower, the man," Andy

commented. "Bald and round on top."

"Do you remember his presidency?"

"He died long before I was born."

"Oh," said Elzy, clearly embarrassed. He knew she knew better, but in unguarded moments she tended to mentally homogenize the entire twentieth century. "All this looks so familiar," she added, surveying the open, rocky ridge they had just traversed. "But—not. So, Mt. Desert Island looks like this?"

"Parts of it do, a little. You'll see."

And they turned and walked into the stunted black spruce forest.

A mile or so on they stopped for the night at an established tent site beside another college staff hut, the southern counterpart of the building between Madison and Adams. The sun still had at least two hours left in the sky, but Andy was tired. Even Elzy was glad to stop. When she sat on the tent platform to take off her pack, she sagged for a moment, then rubbed her knees.

At this lower, gentler elevation, the evening was merely pleasantly cool, the air still and dry. They strung their hammocks from trees over the tent platform and hung up their wet things. Later, they cooked artichoke noodles and instant bean chili with sheep's milk cheese and ate out in the clearing in front of the college hut where they could watch the sky change colors at sunset.

Elzy watched Andy eat. By the leisurely way he addressed his food, she could see that the starvation-hunger was gone. He seemed normal. She had left behind the white, chill violence of the summit and could no longer believe what Diana had said about Andy being crazy, about his being beyond help, if that was even what she'd said. He was OK now, he had to be. Watching the sunset, he seemed as happy as she'd ever seen him.

And yet that night, Andy cried out in his sleep again.

The next day saw them through a lovely alpine bog, up and over two small peaks, and then down into Crawford Notch. Once a large hotel or similar structure had dominated the flat valley floor, and its foundations and fragments of its parking lots were still visible.

Now the Notch hosted a dairy farm with a small store front. Andy and Elzy ate lunch there and then walked for several miles along the creek that would become the Saco River. They camped for the night by its banks.

In the morning, they continued along the widening creek and came to the ferry dock in the late afternoon. They put up in a hostel there. Early the next morning the ferry pulled out with them on it, bound for the sea.

The ferries of the Saco River were of a different design than those of the Penobscot, being smaller but with cloth awnings for shade and shelter. The benches faced each other in pairs across little tables that could fold down to convert to bunks. A few passengers napped in sleeping bags as the ferry hummed along. If hungry, one could buy meals from carts and stalls at any of the stops. The food came in little rush baskets with cloth napkins, and later the ferry collected baskets, napkins, and empty drink bottles and returned them all for re-use. The entire river thus became a giant restaurant with multiple kitchens and multiple mobile dining rooms.

Near noon, Elzy and Andy stepped off the boat to buy lunch. The cart at the dock sold fries, pretzels, and apparently every possible sort of sandwich filling that could fit inside a toasted hot dog roll—beans, grilled vegetables, cheeses, even egg salad made to order from whole, unbroken eggs stored in a jar. The day was growing warm again and there was no easy way to keep an opened egg cool. A painted wooden board listed all the options in neat charcoal lettering.

"Andy, what's *inland oyster?*"

He peered through the glass lid of the warming table at the stringy fried stuff indicated by the sign.

"I don't know," he murmured. "It doesn't look like anything's testicles." He was thinking of prairie oysters, of course.

Elzy smirked. The proprietor laughed, then hastened to explain.

"Oh, no, no. Everything here is vegetarian. It keeps better. This is oyster *plant.* You know—it has a long root like a white carrot? The flowers are like giant dandelions."

"Oh, salsify!" Elzy recognized the description. "I've had that before. It's good."

"Well, you can have some now for three tenths."

She and Andy each got an inland oyster roll and a bottle of root beer, plus a basket of fries with ketchup to share, and got back on the boat.

"It *is* good," Andy pronounced. "Does it actually taste like fried oysters?"

"Sort of," Elzy replied. "A little. You've never had oysters?"

"No." He obviously thought the answer self-evident.

"Have you *ever* broken Jewish dietary laws?"

"I break some of them often. But the laws I do follow? I haven't broken those since I rode east the first time."

"Why not? Why follow some laws and not others?"

"I don't know."

"You're like my mother," Elzy commented, and took a bite of her roll.

"Excuse me?"

"You're religious the same way. She says I was christened, and she crosses herself sometimes, but she didn't object when I didn't want to be confirmed. She only goes to Mass on Christmas and Easter. I don't think she prays anymore. So she's like you. She's religious out of *habit*."

Andy leaned back and folded his arms over his chest.

"In my case it's a little more than that," he said, after a pause. "I'm Jewish because my mother was Jewish. She was because of her parents. One of my grandfathers had the numbers, you know, on his arm. If I assimilate, if I start thinking and acting like everybody else, then for what did they survive? Why did they come to America, if not for me to be able to live as a Jew, here?" And he went back to eating his roll. The boat started moving again with a small jolt.

Elzy exhaled, blowing the hair out of her face. She was used to the shadow of the pandemic, but this? She'd read about the Holocaust in books. She'd never thought to find its legacy sitting across the table from her sharing a basket of fries.

"Your family has been through two tragedies, then," she said. "I hadn't thought of that."

"Everybody goes through something."

"It's like hurricanes," she said, after some thought.

"Oh?"

"Yeah. The Great September Gale, the Hurricane of 1938, Tropical Storm Irene, Hurricane Odette, you've told me how to find sign from all of them. But those scars don't *mar* the landscape, do they? They create it."

"What you're talking about is disturbance history," Andy told her. "Say, fire. People look at a wildfire, they think it's the end of the world."

As he spoke, he noticed he had a blob of ketchup on the back of his left hand. It looked almost like blood. He put his roll down and used his ketchuped hand as a sort of palette, daubing a violently red spot into the middle of the table with his right index finger.

"And it *is* the end of the world," he continued, "if your world happens to be encompassed by the particular patch that burned. Animals and plants die in fires. Sometimes people do. That loss is very real. But it is local in both space and time. If you pull back, if you look at the bigger scale, you see there are lots of little burn patches in various stages of recovery." He began dotting the table with a lot of little ketchup-blobs. "Pull back far enough and you see the fires are just part of a larger, complex pattern—like the logged patches in the mountains, if you remember." He surveyed his work and Elzy laughed to see it. He'd made a rather crooked and pointillist smiley-face.

That evening the ferry pulled into port at the mouth of the river just as the shadows of sunset started to stretch over the water. They were back on the Maine coast. Andy and Elzy checked into an inn, changed their money yet again, ate a late dinner, and got online. As promised, Andy's guild had sent them a list of possible bookings. After a brief discussion, Elzy emailed all the relevant market coordinators and event directors with arrival dates. She also arranged reservations at an inn in Bar Harbor and applied for a permit to camp in any of the game reserves on the island.

Elzy had mixed feelings about her new, expanded responsibilities. On the one hand, she was pleased to have won Andy's confidence. On the other hand, now that she was more nearly Andy's equal, she found herself playing the little kid much less. She missed it. She had been an adult for so long already and she frankly doubted that she'd ever get another chance to be anything else.

She did not have mixed feelings about taking the coastal ferry again. Although five different boats made the coastal run, she'd happened to land on the same one she'd been on the first time, and the crew remembered her. Almost as soon as she and Andy had stepped aboard she heard voices happily call her name. She ran to stow her pack below, claimed a bunk, and then joined the crew to help cast off and set sail. As she coiled a mooring line, the bosun's mate, whom she had always found attractive, told her he wanted her email.

Andy spent most of that first evening aboard on deck reading, but as shadows started to stretch over the water, he got up and looked out over the starboard rail. Few birds flew between him and the horizon, but he spotted a gannet and two gulls. Dolphins examined the boat and he said nothing about them that might alert the other passengers. The starboard rail watch saw the dolphins too, but he wasn't going to say anything either. The two men made eye contact and nodded at each other, sealing their pact for peace and quiet.

Once, two adult dolphins, swimming close with a calf between them, came straight towards the boat. Andy concluded that he was watching an educational field trip—the dolphins were human-watching. The trio surfaced together just long enough to breathe and then, in unison, arched back under the waves and down towards the boat's keel.

The cloudless sky turned yellow, then dark blue, then the almost-full moon washed the sky silver. A steady breeze pushed the boat along in silence, the captain having ordered even the softly-humming motor shut down to conserve battery power overnight.

Andy realized he was alone on deck, except for the bow and rail watches, the helmsman, and the officer of the watch. If other sailors remained on duty, they were elsewhere, attending to the needs of the ship below decks, where artificial lights were allowed. The other passengers had gone below, too, to play cards and to read. Elzy had gone off watch with her friends hours earlier and was doubtless asleep. He turned and looked up at the mains'l, belled out taut by the wind, its solar coating almost black against the silver sky but shining a little, there at the curve, a pale electric blue of reflected moonlight, and the various lines of the rigging pale and vague as spider-web.

He sat down with his back against one of the wooden life-jacket lockers and took his little computer pad out of his knapsack and thumbed on its audio-record function without activating the screen. Then, eyes on that taut sail, he whispered his secret words to his wife, his beloved, in the privacy of the dark, as he did every night. The slight rocking of the boat upon the waves comforted him and he fell asleep with his tablet still recording.

He woke an hour or so later when the sailors furled the sail and dropped anchor outside of Portland. The breeze was dying anyway. The moon stood high in a sky now just slightly hazy, and Andy went to below deck to sleep.

By the time the ferry motored into Portland the next morning, the haze had thickened. On their way back out to sea, they found waves rising, although the air hung almost still. The captain explained that there was a tropical storm offshore, but it was well to the south and no direct threat. An hour or so later, the wind began to wise and the sea grew choppy. The captain ordered the motor shut down again to let the batteries charge faster, and the ferry flew northwest on wind alone.

Andy settled himself on the deck with his book. The day was heating up quickly now, despite the smart breeze, and he heard some of his fellow passengers express the hope that this would be the last heat wave of the summer.

"It's almost *September*," one of them said. "What kind of weather is this for Maine? It's not normal."

Andy wondered what the man's basis for comparison was. Even in a statistical sense, normality had been a moving target for generations now, and yet the general public had gone straight from doubting global warming was real to believing it to be over. He shook his head slightly and wondered what it had been like to live in a world without such a constant sense of dislocation, one where *normal* meant something. Most of the other passengers went below deck where a heat pump kept the air cool. Presently, Andy's head nodded forward in sleep.

When he woke, Elzy was sitting next to him. The watch had changed and she and her new friends were off duty. He hoped she would not realize he'd been sleeping.

"Do you read and reread that book from beginning to end, or do you keep starting over again randomly?" she asked, without preamble.

"Randomly, for the most part," he told her. "Though it's hard to say what's random, for things like this. I should flip coins, like for the *I Ching*."

"How could you derive page numbers with coins, though? You'd need dice."

"That *is* a problem," he conceded. "Pick a number between one and one hundred and ninety-eight."

"One hundred thirty-five."

Andy turned to that page, glanced over it briefly, and read aloud.

Doaist philosophers tell us that surprise and subtle instruction might come forth from the Useless. So it was with the wastelands of the American West—inaccessible, inhospitable, arid, and forbidding to the eyes of most early Euro-Americans. The Useless Lands became the dreaming place of a few nineteenth- and early-twentieth-century men and women...who went out into the space and loneliness and returned from their quests not only to criticize the policies and assumptions of the expanding United States but, in the name of wil-

*derness and the commons, to hoist the sails that are filling with wind
today.*

Almost reflexively, he looked up at the literal sails, dark blue
now in sunlight, filling with real wind. It occurred to him that the
entire exhausted planet had become a dreaming-place.

"This doesn't look right," complained Elzy. Andy looked over
at her and saw that she had been practicing sailors' knots with a
length of rope while she listened.

"What knot are you trying to do?" he asked.

"Rolling hitch."

"Huh. I don't know that one."

"It's the knot holding down that tarp over there."

"That's a tautline hitch."

"It's a rolling hitch."

"Well, a knot by any other name….See how there is space inside
and outside the loop? Take your first two turns inside the loop, the
last one outside. Two in, one out."

"Oh, OK," Elzy acknowledged, finding that his tip helped. "How
do you *know* so much?"

"Same way as you," he told her. And indeed, she was busy expanding her own eclectic knowledge base at that moment.

"Speaking of which, what is this?" she asked, handing him a
coin. "It says *one dollar*, but I thought dollars were made of paper."

"Most of them were. They made exceptions for coin-operated
machines and for collectors. Where did you get it?" The coin was a
Susan B. Anthony dollar. He hadn't seen one in thirty years.

"Ian, the bosun's mate, gave it to me. He says it's good luck."

"I hadn't heard that one." He wondered uncharitably if Ian
hoped the gift would help *him* get lucky. Then again, rare objects
collect superstitions. It occurred to him that Elzy had probably
handled very few metal coins in her life. The new money was always printed on paperboard or cloth, even the smallest denomina-
tion, the hundredth-share. There was no point in making durable
cash because shares expired after only two years. You couldn't have

a currency based on food if its specie lasted longer than preserved food did. He and Elzy were separated by a single generation but also by an entire world.

She must have been thinking along similar lines.

"How did it all change so fast?" she asked. "It's only been twenty years. And I *remember* fifteen years ago, and everything was pretty much modern already."

"I think you're remembering more modernity than there actually was," Andy told her, with a bit of a smile. "Society stabilized at the smallest scales first. Farms and even some towns established within a year or two. As a child, it is the farm and the town you would have noticed."

"They did only organize our police force eight years ago," Elzy conceded. "I guess a town without its own police wasn't very modern."

"There you go."

"OK, but still. You told me how civilization collapsed. Why didn't it stay collapsed, like in *Mad Max*, or *The Book of Eli*?" These were movies she had seen online, full of sere, post-apocalyptic landscapes and thrilling action sequences.

Andy shrugged.

"Nobody wanted to live in *Mad Max* or *The Book of Eli*," he explained. "The United States had been orderly for a long time. For better or worse, people wanted to reestablish something like normalcy as soon as they could. Maybe civilization is a matter of habit." The idea struck him as funny.

"How?"

"I told you about Chevron," Andy began.

"Yes."

"Most towns were like that, as far as I know. Farms or ranches formed treaties with each other so people could come together to socialize and barter. Then the towns came together to form counties a few years later. Some of those towns were basically modern from the beginning, but there were hundreds of other variations—theocratic enclaves and miniature empires and isolated, unaffiliated farms, and all kinds of other things. Once we got radio and cell coverage up again they all started to converge pretty quickly, though. America is still more culturally and economically diverse than it used to be, and there are the tribal areas and the autonomous nations, but most Americans don't really want to live in theocratic enclaves or autocratic empires. So we don't."

"And theocrats and emperors can't force us to?"

"Not yet."

"Why not?"

"That's the advantage of local economies. If I don't need anything from you and you don't have any power I don't have, then you can't force me to do anything I don't want to do. I expect inequality will develop again, simply by chance, and then start to build on itself—communities will start to dominate each other and then take control of each other's resources."

"So we're back to islands again?" Elzy suggested, referring to their earlier conversation around the tide pool. "Locally-based economies provide some protection against *both* resource over-exploitation *and* inequality?"

"Well, they're the same thing. Nobody's going to knowingly over-exploit their own environment, not if they know they can't move away afterwards. You over-exploit someone else's. And with the money you raise that way you go on to exploit more people and places so you can raise yet more money. You make yourself hard to stop."

"Another reason for people like me to do what we do." Elzy was quiet for a moment, thinking. "You said Keene didn't fall apart like so many of the towns and cities did. How did it transition? You never told me what it was like when you first got back there."

Andy assumed that the two statements must be connected. Elzy had an orderly mind, even a too-orderly mind, in his opinion. And yet he could not follow her from one topic to the next. He considered.

No, he hadn't told her what it was like, only what he had done. He hadn't meant to leave that out. What *had* Keene been like?

Images of the city before the pandemic rose spontaneously in his mind. The flowers and toys and notes lain in memorium beneath the ersatz shoe advertisement the summer that actor died. A bicycle, its blue frame rusting, left chained to a metal rail—no one knew who owned it, and then one day it vanished. The way the light shone lemon yellow on the snowy, wooded hillside of Robin Hood Park on a cold afternoon in February. From the corner on West Street he could look up over and between the buildings and see that hill, before the traffic light changed and he went on his way.

Andy had never liked Keene all that much and he hadn't intended to stay, yet somehow it had stayed with him. Maybe it was because he'd been a young father there. He remembered the daily rhythm of trying to sort out who would pick up Jordan from soccer practice, who would take Sarah to the dentist. Trying to plan next year's family vacation around both Jewish Youth Camp and that conference in Tuscon he might or might not be able to get to. Weighing the relative merits of local versus organically grown apples or whether either was really better than the ones on sale at Hannaford's for seventy-eight cents a pound. Why could he remember the price of Red Delicious apples for twenty-five years when he couldn't recall whether he'd eaten breakfast yesterday?

Elzy seemed to be getting better at handling her memory flashbacks, but despite the rest at Pinkham, Andy was still unquestionably getting worse. She could say a word or a phrase now and he would fall into the past almost totally.

What was it like when he returned to Keene?

And suddenly he was back in his old house, his wife's houseplants all dead, his books all molded and mildewed, holding the empty shell of his pet tortoise in his hands. Poor Chunk, left waiting patiently in an abandoned house and found too late.

He should have told somebody to go save his tortoise. As soon as he learned his wife had died, he should have called someone. But he'd been crazy with grief, and anyway, if he had arranged for a friend to get his pet, someone else would have eaten the animal. They ate most of the town's other pets.

He hadn't asked for any of these memories to rise. It wasn't that they were all bad, they weren't. Some of them were heart-warming, or even funny. But if the past was lost to him then it should stay gone. He didn't want his memories, any of them, but they would not leave him alone anymore. He would have pushed them all back down again, regained control, but Elzy had asked him a question. He had to remember in order to answer her.

"What was Keene like when I first got back?" he started, his voice even, his face and body casually neutral. "It was messy. You've seen the town, it really came through quite well, but it had a kind of awkward adjustment. For example, the traffic lights—they all had their own little solar panels, so even when most of the town lost its power, they all kept going. There was no reason to turn them off, so nobody bothered. There were no cars, so no traffic, but the traffic lights kept going just fine."

"I've seen Keene, and there's plenty of traffic," Elzy objected. "Without traffic lights, you'd get run down by an ox cart."

"Yes, but back then there were no ox carts. Not enough oxen. It takes a couple of years to raise and train an ox team, and there just weren't enough. A few people had horses, but there really wasn't much wheeled traffic on the roads for the first five or ten years."

"So, what, everybody just ignored the lights?"

"No, that was the thing. Half the time, we obeyed them. There was no traffic, it was all gone, and we crossed at the crosswalks and we waited for the *walk* signal anyway. It was familiar."

"That's kind of funny," Elzy commented.

Andy, lost in the past, gave a single grunt of rueful laughter. Then his expression cleared and he smiled.

"Did I ever tell you about the Free Keene people?" he asked. If she wanted to talk about funny....

"No. Was Keene imprisoned?"

"Not exactly. This was before the pandemic. The Free Keene group was concerned about government imperialism and over-reach—basic Libertarian thinking." Elzy nodded. Libertarian values were popular. Modern state governments were minimal. "Ex-

223

cept they thought that the most egregious local example of state imperialism was parking meters."

"No."

"Yes! So they'd go around, harassing meter-readers until the meter-readers quit, one after the other. Eventually the town just put in a computerized system, meters that could identify the car parked in the spot and mail a ticket to its owner automatically."

"How did the Free Keeners like that?" Elzy was starting to smile, too, seeing where the story was going.

"Oh, they hated it," Andy told her, already starting to giggle. "But then the pandemic came. Everything shut down. Abandoned cars everywhere. About six weeks after I got back to town, they got the first hydropower plant online. Before that they'd had some solar power, but it wasn't enough for even a basic town grid. Anyway, so when they switched on the power feed to the police station, the whole parking meter system activated itself and started spitting out parking tickets and late-payment notices and late-late-payment notices *for everyone in town.* All those abandoned cars!"

"No!"

"Yes! It was all automatic, and there was no way to turn the damn thing off—there was no off button, no cancel function, nothing. Eventually they had to cut the power back off and cut the machine's wires."

All of this had to come out through giggles and wheezes, and Elzy was laughing so hard her belly hurt and her cheeks cramped up. Sailors going about their business on deck stared at them.

"What did they do with all that paper?" Elzy asked, when she could breathe again.

"Oh, there really wasn't all that much. When the paper feeder emptied, the police reloaded the printed tickets to keep the machine from jamming."

"Did Keene really have all-local food production before the pandemic? Because it was a transition town?" Elzy asked, more seriously.

"No, though they were better off than a lot of places. They had built a lot of *regional* food capacity, but that didn't help Keene directly when fossil fuel ended. What they did have was a core group of people who thought a lot about food, fuel, and fair economic distribution. When the pandemic began, they realized pretty quickly what was about to happen. They bought plants, seeds, top soil, chickens, sheep—stockpiling the *means* of food production. And they started organizing people."

"And that was enough?" Elzy sounded doubtful.

"No, but remember, Keene was a college town with a large population of current and recent students. Most of those went home to their families very early in the pandemic. Then about a fifth of the remaining population died from the pandemic itself. So, only about ten thousand people really tried to survive in Keene. And they planted gardens, and raised chickens and sheep, and gathered nuts and crab-apples from street trees. They ate acorns and squirrels and fish and deer and most of the dogs and cats. And most of those people survived."

"They ate their *dogs*?" Elzy's shock was not sentimental, Andy knew. She wasn't a sentimental person, but as both a policewoman and a farmer, she would regard dogs as necessary tools, not something one could easily get by without—and of course, when she was a kid, dogs must have been hard to come by.

"Most of them wouldn't have been any good for work," Andy explained. "They were pets, and there was no food for them." Ah, but Chunk. He had been even more useless, but Andy would have fed Chunk, if he could have. "When I got back to town, the people were thin. Some were very thin and they had been thinner. Not all of them had made it. But they shared their food equally. No one was well-fed while anyone starved. And they welcomed me back."

He remembered the young orchards, the rapid recycling of buildings and lawns and parking lots back into farms, how proud everyone was to be able to grow food.

Back in the present moment, the captain shouted a command, and Andy and Elzy looked up to find the ferry heading in to Harpswell. Elzy ran to help handle line. Andy stayed put, out of the way, and watched the bustle. The dock at Harpswell Neck Marina was newly built and stood well above even the modern high tide line—all new construction gave the sea room to rise. But at present the tide was low and so even the ferry, a large and tall craft, rode its moorings with its rail some eight feet below the deck of the wharf. The crew configured the gangway as a ramp up and instructed the passengers to please watch their step.

Privately, Andy thought the looming dock and the swinging tides somewhat excessive, though Elzy clearly didn't give it a second thought. ten-foot tides were normal for her.

The ferries didn't serve regular meals except to the crew—passengers staying aboard more than a few hours brought their own—but sometimes businesses near the ports donated food to passengers and sailors alike as a public relations measure. Today, one of the restaurants at the marina sent aboard a small army of smartly-aproned men and women to set up a massive and gorgeous buffet. The restaurant staff did not stay but left the buffet set up. Everyone ate at their leisure as the ship motored away and then caught the wind out in the bay and sailed off. The sailors would clean up and when the ferry returned heading south it would return the trays, plates, and sealed canisters of compost.

There were three hundred and eighteen people aboard, counting the sailors and officers, but the buffet was big enough for everybody to have a light lunch. It was probably as much as the restaurant served in an entire day, yet here all of it was, for free—eggs and fruit, fish and cheeses, pan-fried new potatoes with rosemary, tomatoes sliced, salted and layered with fresh basil, and mountains of buttered sweet corn. All the restaurant had asked was that its name, *Anne's Farm and Seafood Café*, and logo be displayed on small cards next to every platter.

Andy selected a deviled egg to start with and reflected that for him, and for everyone anywhere near his age, probably all over the world, there was no better way to demonstrate good will than to offer someone something to eat.

That afternoon, Elzy learned how to climb the rigging and what sort of work a sailor could do up there—*skylarking*, or climbing just for fun, being strictly prohibited. Andy returned to his book for a while, ate again, and then watched the sea go by. The water was a dark, almost jade green, dotted here and there with lobster buoys, free-floating shreds of seaweed, and groups of moon jellies white as sea-glass tumbling slowly in the bow-wave of the ship. He made a game of counting the jellies but lost track quickly. He found having nothing particular to do glorious. His body was starting to recover from the hike, though he still felt hungry most of the time. The cloud thickened throughout the day and the ferry stopped in Boothbay Harbor, New Harbor, and then again on the other side of Muscongus Bay. After sunset the sky cleared again, the clouds scattering as the off-shore storm broke up and dissolved. The moon, full now, rose in glory, and again Andy could record his daily message to his wife in private.

He woke suddenly the next morning to the ship's engines starting. For a few seconds, he did not know where he was or why. The cool, dim passenger's compartment, lined with rows of closely spaced bunk-beds, smelled of oak and pitch and other people's sleep. Gradually, orientation returned to him and his dreams evaporated, leaving only a vague and ugly miasma in his mind. He'd been having the nightmares again.

He drank water from his canteen. The ship had anchored outside of Rockland, and must be heading into port there now. Later, it would stop again at Camden, and then head out among the six major and many lesser islands in and beyond the mouth of Penobscot Bay—a busy day for the ferry. His head began to clear.

Andy watched the other passengers get up, some of them repacking bags and preparing to disembark. He stayed in his bunk. He wanted to avoid the chaos on deck of a ship in port. He heard and felt the ship docking and activated his tablet. As expected, there was a Wi-Fi signal drifting in from some facility on shore. He uploaded his backlog of emails, video messages, and other work and had downloaded about half of the new material in his in-box before the ship pulled out again and the signal faded. He wished he had time and space to watch his wife's messages now, but he did not. He stood and smoothed his slept-in clothes. He saw that Elzy's bunk was empty and guessed her watch was on duty. He visited the head and went up on deck.

He found the morning extraordinarily bright. The dry, clear air was still relatively cool, the sky a hard blue with white streaks. A breeze tossed the ship and the sea prettily, and he realized he'd been right to come on deck when he did. Sitting below decks could make a person seasick on a day like today.

Elzy lay asleep on the galley hatch. Her ability to sleep just anywhere charmed him utterly. He stepped past her and took his accustomed place at the starboard rail. The sun-hard sea glittered blue and huge and something inside him swelled almost unbearably taut with the beauty of it. On one level, he felt entirely and indolently happy. But on another level, he was still conscious of being all broken inside. He thought now he might feel that way forever.

He thought back to his conversations with Elzy over the past few days. His grandfather, Zalman, had been only twelve when the Nazis came. Leibel, the great-uncle who didn't make it, had been even younger. Andy wondered what kind of life those boys would have lived if war had never come, if the Poland of the early 1930s had continued to exist. His grandfather's life had been interrupted, preempted, disturbed, just like his. Andy thought about wounds that would never heal, places that could not be rebuilt, and children who would not be coming home—and the one who still might, if he could arrange it.

And he turned and looked at her while she slept, her hand curled near her mouth, her dreams flitting visibly across her slack face.

"She did a shift and a half yesterday," said a voice next to him. Andy jumped. It was Ian, the bosun's mate. "And she learned the night watch last night."

"She does seem dedicated," Andy agreed.

"Captain would offer her a job, if she'd ask, but I don't think she will."

"She's an environmental educator," he explained, feeling an odd, possessive twinge.

"Is she? That would explain her talking to Cappy about whether we ever do interpretive programs." The sailor looked at him and saw, perhaps, something of that twinge. "She's keeping her options open," the man said.

"She is wise," replied Andy.

At Camden, Elzy woke, helped the other sailors dock the ship, and then went below to sleep again. Some hours (and several stops) later, she came back up and joined Andy at the port rail. The ship had just rounded Deer Isle. Lifting one finger, Andy indicated that she should look east.

"Is that...?"

"Yes."

Mount Desert Island loomed tall as a giant molar, black against the glare of the sun. And now Elzy knew exactly why looking at Katahdin from a similar distance had made her so sad—this sudden granite looming, this dark height so out of place among the lower, rolling hills of the other islands and nearby coast, it was the same view. She had seen this before, receding, the same way Katahdin had receded, but from the deck of a ferry like this one. She didn't remember, precisely, but she knew.

The island was still several stops and many hours away. The breeze died between Deer Isle and Isle Au Haut, and the ferry hummed along on its electric motor, its solar sails hanging slack. Elzy worked with the other sailors, repairing and refurbishing gear or cleaning when there was no line handling to do, but she kept coming back to the port rail.

After Swan's Island, the breeze picked up again, and the crew kept busy trimming and re-trimming the sails to catch the varying breezes, but Elzy no longer worked with them. The ship was within five miles of the big island now, almost paralleling its southeastern coast but gradually closing the distance. She could not look away. From the deck of the ship Elzy could see north up the length of the island's glacial valleys. From this angle, the solid black wall was gone, replaced by a family of separate mountains rising green in the sunlight, the tops of the highest domes dotted and speckled blond with acres of bare granite.

Sometimes she could see an orangish line where the water met the land, interrupted here and there by tiny sprays of white—surf. The tide was low but the waves were high. The wind was rising out of the south, the air crisp underneath a streaky sky.

Elzy stood at the rail with Andy, watching the waves break on the coast of her homeland. She had never quite believed him that she was from Mount Desert Island. Not that she'd ever known him to lie, or even to be wrong, but she had wondered about her origins for so long that they felt like the subject of myth, of dream, a reality without literal fact. And yet here was the island. From the minute she'd seen it, she had known it was real and that it was hers.

The ship would turn again soon, following the shoreline as it curved north to Bar Harbor. They would dock in just over two hours and Elzy would gaze at the island the entire time. Everyone knew it, and the sailors left her alone. Andy gazed not at the island but at Elzy.

Presently he borrowed a pair of binoculars from the rail watch and handed them to her. She steadied her elbows on the cap-rail and focused the mechanism.

The orange headlands and tossing spray jumped and jerked with the movement of the ship and the swell of the sea, but Elzy ignored the dizziness and kept watching. Six gannets and one gull passed through her field of vision, but she ignored them, too. Through the lenses the forests resolved into masses of narrow spruce spires and the occasional taller, broader spreading—a white pine. The longer she watched, the closer the ship came and the more detail she could see, sloping jumbles of fallen granite slabs, miniature coves backed by nests of smooth gray and pink cobbles, and all the rest of it burnt orange or brown-black and ringed by reddish-brown seaweed just starting to float again on the rising tide.

"How does it look?" asked Andy.

"*Perfect,*" said Elzy.

Chapter 9
Wildness

Bar Harbor was a lively little fishing village slightly over-run with ferry passengers. Two- and three-story buildings lined a loose grid of somewhat hilly streets, most of them ending at salt water. A very green and grassy main square featured a cheery, white gazebo and a couple of tall, columnar trees. Shops, restaurants, and little art galleries served crowds swollen by travelers from out of town.

Andy said the place didn't look very different than it had before the pandemic. Aside from minor renovations, the buildings along the main streets were all the same. Passersby strolled along eating French fries or fried oysters from recycled paper cones. The streets were clogged by traffic, and bright flags and banners flew from balconies. Awnings bearing business logos undulated in the breeze.

And yet there were major, less visible differences. A slight aroma of draft-animal dung, not car exhaust, mixed with the salt air, and the traffic mostly had hooves. The storefronts included the standard tannery, blacksmith's, electronics repair shop, and bakery of any modern town, not the t-shirt shops and tourist trinket places of old. Most of the buildings along the side streets had been converted into warehouses, or demolished and replaced by apple orchards and vegetable gardens. The place owed its busyness to the ferry terminal, the nearby college, the county high school, and its status as county seat, not to tourism. Bar Harbor was not a resort town anymore, only a fishing village. Just three hundred people lived here year-round. The seasonal Waponahki community and a few Yankee families escaping the heat of inland Maine swelled the town to nearly six hundred in the summer.

The place would be Andy and Elzy's home base for at least the next ten days.

That evening, over drinks and a late dinner on the inn balcony, Elzy broached the subject of her future.

"Andy, if I applied to a guild tomorrow, would you sponsor me?"

"*Are* you applying to a guild tomorrow?"

"No. Just suppose."

"Yes, I would."

"Good," Elzy replied, feeling a kind of warmth spread through her chest. She said nothing about her feelings, though. The moment was ordinary, anticlimactic.

"Do you know yet what guild you'll apply to?"

"No, but I do know how to find out. I want one that focuses around here, but has some regional and even super-regional reach. I want to be able to travel, but I don't want to be stuck doing introductory acts for strangers all the time. I want to come back to the same audiences over and over so I can build on my work with them, like offering real classes instead of just workshops. And I want to do that *here*. So tomorrow at the market I'll start asking around and then go to the library, see who contracts with these towns."

"Good."

"I'll probably wait to actually apply till this winter—I'd like to get my portfolios from school together, and they're all at my mother's house. But I'll make sure, before we leave, that the people here accept vidchat interviews."

"That's a good precaution."

"I've already set up a possible partnership with Diana Cartwright, to do outreach to towns for her drone project. And the ferry captain is checking with his supervisor if they can hire me to do interpretive talks in the off-season when they need more business. Do you think a guild would mind that I've been setting up paying work on my own?"

"On the contrary, showing initiative will make you more valuable to them."

Elzy had never doubted that Andy would say yes eventually. He wouldn't have taken her on in the first place if he weren't sure she was worth his investment of time and energy. Applicants were sometimes rejected by the guilds, but seldom by their own sponsors. And yet success had been far from certain.

There was the bandit attack, when Elzy hadn't been sure she or Andy would live to September. There were the weeks in the forests of Maine when she'd doubted Andy's health, even his competence. There was the sheer weight of a process that, counting coursework, had stretched on for years. Anything could have happened, and most of it hadn't. She felt that there should be some kind of celebratory or congratulatory note to the conversation, but she couldn't think of anything to say. So she said nothing.

Night had fallen and now the tempo of the town changed. A dozen different bands started up in tiny venues all along the streets. Drunken laughter rose here and there from balconies and porches and isolated pools of sky-shielded electric light. The balcony of the inn faced away from town, but from its side a person could lean across the railing and look over to the Village Green where revelers strolled among LED footlights bright as stars. The night was warm, almost muggy, with a slight, uncertain breeze.

The thing she and Andy had come all this way to do was done. A few more weeks of work here on the island, the still almost-unbelievable search for her home, however that turned out, and they would head south. Andy would start his winter classes and she would no longer be his student.

She wondered if she would be his anything. Sometimes she had thought he was reticent with her because he was her teacher and that he would open up more afterwards. But really she knew better. Maybe he was reluctant to treat a student as a peer, but teaching also gave him a reason to interact with her at all. Andy kept in frequent contact with many people, but that was because he worked with them. It hadn't escaped her attention that his purely social meetings were few—and all accidents.

It wasn't exactly that she pined for his attention, she told herself, but knowing how this adventure would end, and that it would end soon, made her sad.

Elzy sipped her wine and ignored the mosquitoes in silence.

That night, a vicious little squall line hurried through between three and four in the morning and swept the hot, humid weather away. By dawn the sky was clear, though no one in Bar Harbor could see it through the ground-level fog. Before the fog burned off, the weather changed again. The sky curdled, and a long, slow, wet period settled in. For days the temperature barely rose above sixty degrees. Locals announced that fall had arrived at last.

In the morning, Andy and Elzy began a solid week and a half of continuous work, making up for the weeks without income. Andy received a steady salary regardless, but his guild did need money with which to pay him.

Elzy was the opening act at the market on Saturday night, and she and Andy both led workshops Sunday and Monday. During the week, Andy had an engagement as a guest lecturer at the college and both of them were special guests in separate classes at the high school. Actually, the high school had asked Andy in as part of a series on "People Who Made/Witnessed History." His private feelings about such a request were distinctly ambivalent, but he agreed to do it anyway. The following weekend, Elzy opened on Saturday again and she and Andy repeated their workshops.

Then, that Monday afternoon, after the market closed, the two of them paid a visit to the County Land Records Office.

Elzy wasn't sure what to ask the clerk. She did not know her father's name or even whether he had ever registered legal rights to the land. Also, she was well-known in town by now, and did not want the details of her life to enter the town rumor-mill. Andy guessed the reason for her hesitancy and spoke to the clerk himself.

"Hi, we're looking for uninhabited or abandoned plots of land?" He was wearing his guild member garb, so an obscure—and perhaps nosy—question would not arouse comment. He was clearly a scientist, and scientists ask questions.

The clerk cheerfully unfolded a large paper map of the island.

"These green areas," she explained, "are all uninhabited now, classed as game reserve or water supply protection. You can hike through them, but you need a permit to camp. These orange areas are wild resource lands—like national forests, if you remember those, but they're owned and managed by the Waponahki, so you'll need a permit from them just to enter. Still, no one actually *lives* there, so they might count as uninhabited. Does that help?"

"Oh, yes, thank you." He examined the map carefully.

"Now, I can't promise," interjected the clerk, "that there weren't forest families in any of these areas the first few years After, but there are none there now."

"Forest families?" Andy remarked, sounding mildly interested. "Do you have any records of where they might have been?"

"Sure, some," the woman replied. "Anyone who made it through the first two or three years would have been entered in town land records. We have copies of those here. But we don't have property lines for most of those claims because the towns didn't start surveying until six years After. Most of the forest families had gone by then."

"Gone? That's interesting. We've just come from inland, and there are still families in the forests there. Do you know where they went?" Andy still sounded casual. He didn't want to give the clerk any reason to start gossiping.

"No, mostly we don't," the clerk told him. "But if any of them come back, we've got their land claims waiting for them. If you're doing some kind of survey, you'll want a hard-copy map. They're six tenths each."

Andy bought two, thanked the woman, took his hat and his

rain poncho from the hook by the door, and stepped back outside into the cold fog. The rain had stopped overnight, but the thick sea-fog still trended gently downwards. Elzy followed him out.

"If you can't identify where something *is*," Andy remarked, with some satisfaction, "start by identifying where it *isn't*."

"At least I'll be able to claim the property if we find it," said Elzy. "But I don't understand how this helps. How do we know where my family wasn't?"

"We know yours was a forest family, because of how you reacted to the families inland. If your father took you to hide in the woods, that would have been somewhere in Acadia National Park, and all of that land is now protected resource land of one kind or another. So, land that is occupied now is where your home isn't. That narrows our search down."

Back at the inn, Andy opened up one of the maps.

"Let's start looking *here*," he said and pointed to a water-protection zone on the western half of the island. "It was the largest roadless area in the park that wasn't visible from a treeless mountain-top. Anyway, our next booking is in Seal Cove, so we can search all week, if we have to. We won't need travel days to get to work."

"I don't know," Elzy said. "That's a lot of land to cover."

"It is, but we've narrowed it down a lot from where we started. And you might remember something more when we get in to the right area."

"OK."

They took a local ferry to the town of Flamingo, on Southwest Harbor, and made it to the town dock by four-thirty. From there, the walk to the southern end of Long Pond ran just two miles up and down low hills through woodlots, blueberry orchards, and the occasional rocky pasture. The way was frankly lovely and had once been a popular place to live, judging by the many old gravel driveways that now went nowhere.

Then the agricultural character faded out in favor of dark spruce forest, and the neatly graveled street reverted to pot-holed and weed-cracked asphalt. Near the bottom of a steep hill the road turned abruptly and stopped at the narrow tip of Long Pond. Just before that last turn there was a flat area off the side of the road that might once have been a parking lot. Now it held three wooden tent-platforms, two metal bear-boxes, and a nice view of the pond through a loose screen of good-sized aspens. Andy and Elzy strung their hammocks from the posts provided and walked down to the water to eat their dinner of trail mix and apples.

"How deep do you suppose that pond is?" asked Andy.

Elzy frowned. She assumed he was quizzing her, as he so often did, and that there was some way to calculate the depth of the body of water. Perhaps it had to do with the wavelets on the pond's surface or the steep slopes of the valley's sides. But if there was such a method, she did not know it.

"I don't know, Andy, how deep is it?"

"It's *tarn* deep," he replied, straight-faced, and then chuckled. A *tarn*, as she knew, is the flooded bottom of an alpine glacial notch. Long Pond's basin is the product of a *continental* glacier, and hence not actually a tarn, but the joke worked anyway.

She rolled her eyes and laughed.

"That's terrible," she told him. "If I tried that on stage, they'd pull me off. They'd take one of those big hooks from back in vaudeville and they'd pull me right off."

"Made you laugh, though," Andy pointed out. "I had a teacher who used to tell that joke."

The pond was, true to its name, quite long. From where Andy and Elzy sat in the grass beside a water-pumping station, they could look north along the axis of the pond a couple of miles. But east to west, the place was narrow as a river valley and bordered by steep, rocky walls clothed in forest. Already the shadows of the western ridge reached across the water and up the side of the opposite hill. Where the sun still fell on the upper ridge-face, the trees and a couple of exposed rock ledges glowed golden. The sky was clear and cold-looking. The rain and fog seemed not to have fallen here, for the sand of the lonely little boat ramp was powder-dry. Besides the quiet hum of the water-pump and the murmuring of the water in the rocks on the shore, there was almost no sound.

"This is so *wild*," Elzy commented, and then laughed a little. "In both senses," she added.

"What's 'wild'?" asked Andy.

"I'm not sure," she admitted. "I would have said it's some place untouched by humans, but there aren't any. We've *touched* the whole sky. But this is wild anyway. What else would you call it? Maybe wild is a place where humans aren't *in charge*? A place where we neither plant nor weed?" Andy nodded and she continued. "But it's not just that. I mean, it's like what you said, humans are natural, too...and there are wild people, wild thunderstorms...the word has to mean something else, something bigger."

"You're on to something there," Andy said, nodding again. "Abandoned urban lots are wild, soil is wild, dreams are wild—these are processes without deliberate control from the outside. These systems create their own order from within their own processes, their own wholeness. Gardens have their advantages, but a too-tightly managed garden cannot create its own fertility. For that, you need wildness."

Elzy looked at Andy sharply for a moment. It was unlike him to speak of dreams. She'd expected him to define wildness technically, in terms of soil bacteria to fungi ratios, or something. But she knew there were depths to him he did not normally discuss.

"When I was a little girl," she told him, "at my mother's farm, I would go out into the woods sometimes. It was dangerous—there were bandits in the woods still—but I went anyway. To get away from people who bothered me. I felt free there."

"It was your refuge."

"Yes. And my father's, if he brought us to a place like this."

"That's traditional. There's a long history of people throughout the world reverting to dependence on wild places in times of need—political refugees flee to it, rebels rally in it, and the starving hunt there. And even before the pandemic there were people in the United States who relied on deer meat to get through the winter."

"How is it," Elzy asked, "that wildness seems to recede when humans show up, if we need it so much?"

"It is a paradox," Andy acknowledged, and then went on, obviously thinking aloud. "Maybe the need to try for control is too ingrained? However wild the soil in a vacant lot may be, a landscape that still has its wolves and lions is more so…and living with predators capable of killing you if they want is no joke. But we need it. We more than need it, wildness is essential to who we are. Your home is a wild place, Elzy, it's your inheritance, but to an extent the same is true for all of us."

"'Home is the place where, if you have to go there, they have to let you in,'" Elzy quoted from some half-remembered poem.

"Soil to soil. Wildness thou art, and wild thou shalt remain," paraphrased Andy, in a similar spirit. "But the receding you alluded to is quite real. There's *less* wildness than there used to be even fifty or sixty years ago. Not simply in terms of acreage, but the wild places that remain are thinner. Less diverse. The entire biosphere *weighs less* than it did when I was a kid."

"Weighs less?"

"Yeah. Photosynthesis captures carbon and releases oxygen, right? Every carbon atom in all the living or once-living matter on the planet, including fossil fuels, was once sequestered by a plant. The ratio of free oxygen to carbon dioxide grew as the biosphere grew. When we measure the proportion of carbon dioxide increasing again, that means the biosphere is shrinking.

"But it's not just size, it's energy. All those carbon compounds—in fossil fuels, in these forests, in my body or yours, the energy stored in those chemical bonds is all sunlight, embedded *sunlight* harvested, at one time or another, by plants. That's all the energy we have here on Earth. Remember that energy, complexity, and stability are connected? The more energy is in a system, the more complex, the more stable, the more *resilient* it is. But burn that fossil fuel, release that energy, and the whole system just winds down. That's why the weather isn't stable anymore. That's why we've lost so many species, why the stocks of what's left are so low.

"You can't destroy energy, but you can't recycle it, either. The incredible power of the Industrial Revolution, the Age of Coal, the Age of Oil and Natural Gas was energy *going away*. And we can't get it back. Even if the loss is over, now, it's irreversible. We can only wait for plants to collect more energy over deep time."

"I remember," said Elzy, a little stunned. Andy had covered all this in class years ago, and she did remember, but that was before she'd realized climate change still mattered. She hadn't been paying much attention. She hadn't made the mental connections. "I just can't picture it. This—and so much of what we've seen, traveling—*looks* perfect, just...beautiful."

"It *is* beautiful. But it's also degraded. *Everywhere* we've been is. Even since I was a kid—there used to be more birds, more insects. You can hear the difference. Wildness was louder."

And indeed, no autumn bird tried its voice, no predator howled. A single late-season cricket began to sing in a tuft of grass, but he was the only one.

"That's weird to think of, the experience of just sitting outside, *hearing* things, changing."

"Every generation thinks what it has is normal. It's hard to wrap your head around how fast things are changing, how much has been lost, because our baselines keep moving. When Europeans first came to North America, they saw this great, unsullied wilderness, but even then a lot of species had already been hunted to extinction. There used to be *elephants* in New England."

"Elephants?"

"Yeah, elephants. Woolly ones."

"Oh, yeah, mammoths."

"Mammoths *are* elephants. And they belong here, or used to. A lot of animals do."

Elzy tried to imagine a mammoth making its way through this little valley, along the narrow rim beside the still water, and she couldn't. Such an animal would just be too big.

"If so much is gone, do the relationships that make something be native still exist? Do places still exist to be native *to*? If a place is a family, not a location, with so many species dead, are some families just *gone*?" Elzy had meant the question in the abstract and realized, too late, that there was no way Andy could hear words like *dead, family,* and *gone* abstractly. She put her hand to her mouth as though she could catch her words.

He closed his eyes a moment and something like a fast-moving shadow crossed his face.

"Some don't. Some places, some...contexts, are gone," he admitted. "But some are still around. Wildness persists. There's always hope." His voice sounded quite normal, as though he talked of nothing of more than intellectual import, except for the way he said *hope*. Sisyphus might have spoken of his rock in just the same tone. But then he brightened, quite deliberately. "Don't worry. The place you were born to is still here. We'll find it."

She smiled gratefully at him with equal deliberateness.

The light had vanished from the clifftops and the few clouds glowed tangerine. They both checked their headlamps, just to be sure. The cloud faded to purple and then to a pearly grey. Two bats hunted in the sky over the water and a loon called. Andy watched the bats and Elzy watched him.

"Andy?" she began. He turned his head a little towards her but kept watching the bats. "I don't think I'm going to remember any more. We could see the place where I lived, but I don't think I'd recognize it."

"Elzy," he said, turning to look at her now, "if you can't remember the land, find the place where the land remembers you."

And that's what they did.

The area they had come to search was an oval of about four miles by two between Long Pond and Seal Cove Pond. A couple of old forest roads, no longer maintained, crossed through to the north and south, but in the middle there were no roads and only a few marked trails. There, in the shelter of low, forested, but rugged mountains, a family might well have hid from the chaos of the early transition and survived. Rather than wander around searching, Andy proposed a more methodical approach. He used the trails to divide the area into manageably-sized sections and then sketched a series of transects, west to east, across each of the sections with a pencil and the straight edge of his orienteering compass. By hiking the transects, they could be thorough without fear of redundancy, and if they saw no sign of habitation, they could move on without worrying any more about it. Again, he was trying to establish where Elzy's home wasn't in order to find out where it was.

"There is really no such thing as *no* information," he pointed out. "Every attempt to learn can teach you something."

"What about a poorly-designed study?" she asked.

"Those teach you how to design better studies," he replied.

That night, by the light of a candle-lantern, Elzy made an improvised tape measure by tying their extra bear-ropes together and knotting them at intervals, while Andy worked out the details of the transect pattern. He wanted the lines to be close enough to ensure good coverage, but far enough apart that their total mileage would still be manageable. Finally, he decided that they could do all of the section defined by the Long Pond Trail and the Great Notch Trail the first day, if they left out the more nearly perpendicular areas and divided the transects between them. Elzy would take the even-numbered lines while Andy took the odds, so they'd always be walking adjacent transects.

In the morning they set out, carrying only their day-packs, following an easy foot-trail along the water to the beginning of the transect pattern, where they stepped into the woods and turned uphill.

It was slow going. The terrain was steep, sometimes very steep, with little rocky ledges and cliffs here and there, and they could not choose an easier path but must walk straight ahead, following their compasses and counting their paces, to stay on the transects. But the way was blocked every fifty or a hundred feet by uprooted trees or by thickets of spruce saplings. There was no *straight ahead* to walk. Instead, they used their compasses to choose a landmark—an oddly-shaped tree or a large rock—on the correct heading, made for that, estimated the step-count, and then choose the next landmark. The forest floor in many places was only a thin skin of spruce needles, twigs, and moss stretched across a hidden jumble of loose rock and downed, half-rotted trees. Any step might discover a void capable of snapping an ankle or sheltering a hive of yellow-jackets. And always they had to keep an eye out, searching the land left and right for the clues they had come for.

And yet Elzy felt very much in her element. She had no trouble picking her way through the forest and her mind did not wander but instead fell naturally into the same alert presence she had relied on as a cop. She could not see Andy, most of the time, but she could hear him off to her right through the trees. She would hear him if he called to her and she kept her ears open in case he needed something. She knew, without knowing how she knew it, that if one of them was going to make a mistake, fall in a hole or walk eye-first into a tree-branch, it wasn't going to be her.

Because this was home. She could not have said if they were near her actual homestead, but if not, then the place must be very much like this one. She was sure of it. Her body simply knew.

The forest was dominated by white spruce and Northern white cedar, with minor notes of red spruce, yellow birch, red maple, and big-toothed aspen. Where the deciduous trees were many, enough light made it through the canopy to support an understory of spruce and balsam fir saplings, ferns, and small striped maples, while several different kinds of moss, plus bunchberry and clubmoss, spread over the ground. Elsewhere there were only the spruces and cedars, and nothing grew beneath their shade but the carpet of dry needles and broken twigs. Unlike the red spruce forests of Monadnock or the Whites, this forest looked relatively intact. Many of the trees showed insect damage, and there were worrying clusters of dead spruces here and there, but the young trees coming in to replace them were mostly more spruces. The wholesale switch to hardwoods had not begun here. White spruces are lowland plants in New England, favored not so much by the temperature as by the shallow, rocky soil. Climate change touched them too, but only up to a point. So far.

Elzy saw very few balsam firs, the *sap trees* that had triggered her first memory flashback, but Andy had told her they were common on other parts of the island. Here, the forest was older and the spruces had had enough time to shade the firs out. The rugged landscape seemed dark, close, and private.

And there was no definitive sign of habitation. At the end of their first transect pair, they stopped at the trail that marked their section boundary and used Elzy's measuring cord to see how far off the transect pattern they'd gotten and where the correct beginnings of their next transects were. Elzy recorded the discrepancy on her phone, and they set out again. And found nothing. She knew intellectually that by ruling out places where her home wasn't they were, in fact, making important progress, but it felt like they were making no headway at all. At the shore of the pond they measured and turned again.

Their first few laps were only about a quarter mile long, but as the upland arm of the Long Pond Trail curved further and further away from the shore, the transects grew longer and the terrain more varied. Groves of nothing but hardwoods suggested pockets of deeper soil below. Dramatic age discontinuities split the spruces into distinct neighborhoods. Here lived twisted, sap-dripping ancients, there, young, pole-straight trees raced for the sun. Sometimes tangles of saplings or knee-high seedlings crouched below their elders and sometimes they didn't and Elzy could not figure out why. Ridges of all but exposed bedrock supported fairy gardens of cryptogamic growth—reindeer lichen, gray, white, and green, and moss beds six inches deep, or clusters of ferns. No good naturalist would set foot in such a delicate place, so the lichen patches, too, became obstacles to navigate around. The slope on the pond side grew steeper, and there was the narrow valley of the Great Brook to cross and cross again. They rested, ate a mid-morning snack, and then began their fifth pair of lines.

Almost immediately, they began noticing scattered hints—an old cedar game-pole, a stone fire circle choked with fallen needles, the stump of a tree felled by an ax. But all those were inconclusive.

They could be the work of poachers, people wandering far from home. Elzy carefully noted the location of each by transect number and pace count number and tried not to get her hopes up.

Then, near lunchtime, she crossed a trail and stopped a moment to look at it. It definitely was not on her map, but she could not tell, at first, whether this was a game trail, a hiker's shortcut, or something else. It had a disused look but had obviously once been deliberately cleared.

Just as she was about to call out, she heard Andy shout her name.

"Did you find the path?" she asked.

"What?"

"The PATH?"

"What? I found a trail!"

"Me, too!"

"What? Elzy, there's a trail here!"

Andy eventually figured out what she must mean and followed the mysterious trail around its bend to meet her.

"It's not on the map," he told her.

"I know. And nobody's used it in a while. But maybe it's one of the older trails, something the Park Service abandoned even Before?" Elzy was still being cautious.

"Unlikely," he said. "See that steep section? If this was ever a Park trail, there would be steps there. And the treadway would be eroded from use."

Elzy looked around for more signs.

"This was maintained recently," she said. "Look, somebody cut those branches with a saw."

"It's not that recent." Andy fingered the bark where newer growth bulged around the base of the dead stub. "And how far this sticks out? No professional or professionally-trained volunteer would leave something like that at eye level. A non-professional cared enough about this trail to carry a hand-saw up here."

"Not within the last fifteen years," Elzy added, from somewhere behind and off to his right.

Andy looked over to see what she had noticed. A young spruce tree grew in the middle of the treadway near a bend in the trail. He had walked around it on his way over to her without thinking about it much. Trails often split around trees. But looking again, he saw what Elzy meant—the path didn't actually go around the tree because the treadway did not widen at all. In fact, the spread of its limbs had forced him to step off the trail when he went by and there was no sign that any shoes besides his own had done so. That meant the tree had sprouted in the middle of the already-existing trail, which meant the trail wasn't in regular use at the time—and had not been in regular use since. And obviously, the trail maintainer hadn't returned to cut the obstruction away. Spruces, like firs and pines, grow one whorl of new limbs per year, and Elzy had counted twelve whorls, plus the scars of three more low on the trunk where the tree had shed branches as it grew. The trail maintainer had left the same year she had.

The only remaining question was in which direction to follow the trail? They knew the main homestead could not be anywhere they had already covered, but obviously the path curved and either direction could lead anywhere in the remaining territory. Elzy chose to head right because it felt correct, knowing that her choice might be no better than flipping a coin. Andy tied his handkerchief to a tree branch to mark the spot, in case they had to return and resume the survey—it could still be a false lead, after all. They set off.

Following the trail proved much easier going than walking the transects had, as it more or less stayed on the same level whenever possible. And while fallen trees or the occasional new sprout blocked the way here and there, the path was mostly still clear. There were no weeds or undergrowth, thanks to the dense canopy overhead. And then the trail vanished. Thinking the way had been obscured somehow, Andy and Elzy searched around and found themselves standing in a Park Service path, probably the Great Notch Trail. Elzy guessed, or maybe knew, that the trail builder had deliberately hidden the intersection. She searched for and found where the mystery path picked up again on the other side.

As they walked, they spotted more and more signs of former human habitation. Ax-cut stumps all had about fifteen to twenty years of decay on them. Crudely built, dilapidated tree stands and blinds perched here and there, some with a few old-style shell casings lying around them. And, once, they found a strangely shaped tree, a small red spruce.

The tree split into multiple trunks about three feet up, each of them bowing far out from that central point before turning and growing upwards, so that the separate trunks enclosed a space between like a small chair.

"If I *was* here as a little kid," Elzy suggested, "I probably made this into a fort." Even as she said it, though, she realized the tree would have looked very different when she was a child. She schooled her mind back into forensics, not whimsy.

Spruces and other conifers split into multiple trunks only when something interferes with the main stem. A deer or a porcupine or a budworm might kill the tender, young leader, or deep shadow might slow it while a patch of sunlight nearby allows a side branch to become dominant. Which is the most likely explanation depends on species, circumstance, and the shape of the tree, but none of the possibilities seemed quite right to Elzy. Something looked off. Andy stared at the mutant tree and considered.

"This wasn't a killed leader," he concluded. "The sizes of the upper and lower parts are too different. The spread of the trunks is too broad. Somebody cut a sapling and took away the whole top. Why?" He looked for and found the scar from the original trunk, confirming his suspicions—it had been about two inches across and sawed off smooth. He used the span of his hands to measure the current diameter of both the lower trunk and the upper ones and he counted the limb whorls above where the upper trunks turned towards the sky. "This tree was cut...the year of the pandemic."

Elzy tried to imagine the tree as it had once been, a young spruce sapling, a man cutting it off at a convenient height with a handsaw, not bothering to even harvest all of the wood....

"Oh!" she exclaimed. "It's a Christmas tree!"

"Of course," said Andy, as though he should have thought of it. He looked at the plant thoughtfully. They were both thinking *what is the chance that all of this could be a coincidence?* Not zero, not yet, but how long do you delay reaching a conclusion? If Elzy and her father had not lived here, someone an awful lot like them had.

"This is so weird," Elzy said. "I wonder what I got for Christmas that year, and whether I liked it?"

"You got a father who wanted you to be happy despite everything," Andy said, and for a moment he could not look at her.

Less than a quarter mile more and a brightness appeared ahead in the gloom. Elzy's heart beat faster and she wondered whether she were about to drop into one of her fugues. She'd never had any warning before, and anticipating the disorientation frightened and excited her.

And yet, when she actually arrived, everything was only vaguely, intensely familiar. No fugue, no new, clear memory.

The place was not bright because it was open, though obviously it had been years earlier—a low rectangle of logs showed where a raised vegetable bed had sat in sunlight. But since then the logs had begun to rot and the bed and the clearing had filled up with young trees, some now twenty feet tall. The reason for the brightness was that about half the saplings, especially the ones growing in the garden, weren't spruces—they were apples. Apparently, in the latter years of her family's occupancy, she and her father had been going somewhere else to collect apples and they had tossed the cores all over. Some of those seeds had sprouted and survived.

Further back, under the older canopy, Elzy saw several small, strangely-shaped buildings. Two were low A-frame tunnels, heaped with soil and covered with needles, moss, and apple-leaves. Spruce seedlings grew from the sloped roofs, but without direct sunlight they had grown slowly and were still very small. There were also a tall tipi-shaped structure made of sticks, some of them fallen in, and a low, round thing of stone and wood. It came to her that these were the privy and the food-cache, respectively. She knew this place. She didn't remember being here, and yet she knew it, unequivocally. That haunting, absolute familiarity erased any possibility of doubt. And there were the graves.

Elzy found them towards the opposite end of the compound from where they'd come in. There were four of them, the ground sunken in and piled with rocks over the shallow burials. Each was marked by a crude wooden cross inscribed with the name and the dates of its occupant.

Four graves. Who were the other three? Elzy could not read any of the names well, since lichen and rot had erased most of the lettering, but the dates were clear enough. Two of these people were adults when they died, two were children. Evidently, Elzy's family had fled to the woods with another family, and the others had not made it. She couldn't remember them at all, though she must once have known them well.

One of the graves, of course, belonged to Jamie. Besides his dates, cut into the now rotting wood with a knife, there was the name—hard to read, but that was definitely a "J" and several more, somewhat ambiguous letters. The last name was even harder to make out, but it wasn't Rodriguez. It started with a C. It didn't matter. It was her brother's final resting-place.

She tried to picture him and managed a vague image of a dusty, light-brown boy, the sunlight behind him streaming through one almost comically large ear, turning it pink. His short, frizzy hair was light brown, not black—he took after their pink-skinned father more than she did—and the sun lit it up like a caramel halo. But his face was in shadow, the features blurred. In memory, she looked up to him, both literally and metaphorically. He seemed mature and supremely competent.

What had he been like, really? She tried to recast what she could remember of him, all the little bits and pieces, from the viewpoint of an objective adult, a stranger.

He had been only eight years old when he died, that was undeniable. He was a little kid. And he was illiterate—she could remember reading his homework aloud for him, though she must have been only four or five at the time. It had seemed utterly unremarkable to her then that she could read and her big brother could not. Now, for the first time it occurred to her that her brother might have been one of those children adults worry about.

And yet…he had been able to recognize almost every plant on the island. And he must have learned most of it on his own, because he'd had to name most of the plants himself. Jamie was not a fanciful child—he would not have made up new names for the pleasure of invention but only to fill in for what adults could not tell him. Elzy remembered her surprise, in college, when she'd learned that most real naturalists identify trees by leaf and twig characteristics—she'd always relied on bark appearance. Bark, after all, is always visible at eye level, while the leaves of a tall tree are not. Andy relied on bark as well, but she hadn't learned the habit from him. She'd never thought about where she could have picked it up. She guessed now that Jamie had taught her, and that he had focused on bark because no adult had taught him the official way plant ID is done.

Jamie had not just taught himself to identify plants. He had been able to recognize entire plant communities. He'd had no names for those groupings, no language to discuss them, but he kept track of which plants grew together under which conditions. He could navigate across the wooded parts of the island like that, off-trail, when the family went camping. The different types of forest were distinct but interlocking places to him, landmarks. He could see a coherent rhythm and logic where most people saw only trackless woods. Elzy had never feared getting lost in his company—nor had their father feared for her. In most of her little memory snippets, she and her brother were alone together in the woods or on the rocks of the sea shore, no adult in sight. She understood now how few parents of their father's generation would have permitted that.

Jamie had used to drill her on all he knew and loved to teach, much as Andy did, except the boy did it with the innocent impatience of the very young.

"Look, dumbass," he had said to her, with no malice intended or perceived, "this is a *swamp*, so that *can't* be sugar maple. Figure it out!" And she had—the tree had been red maple, or *pointy maple*, as he called it, for the angular leaves. But she'd felt so dumb. She'd been five.

She could not in all honesty think of her brother as *just* a little kid. Little he had been, but at eight years old he had known more about his corner of the world than most adult naturalists—and he had mostly taught himself. What might he have become had he grown up? And how much of her life did the fact of his existence explain?

Why had she always considered plant identification so intrinsically important? Why had she always loved science, even before she'd harbored any hope of ever going to school? Was it something she had in common with her brother, or something she had learned from him? There was no way to know.

Why had she felt so immediately drawn to Andy? He was well-respected on campus, certainly, but no one back at school had ever really seemed to *like* him. He did not encourage personal connection, for one thing, and there was his intelligence, his quirkiness, itself. He was too distant, too different, to like. And yet Elzy liked him. She always had. He made sense to her in a way that the rest of humanity did not. Had she learned this, too, from Jamie?

The boy had been her first teacher, her first hero, her first genius companion.

And yet, while Elzy could recognize the tragedy of her brother's death as a loss for humanity, she had no sense of loss for herself. If anything, she had just now found him. She was happy about that. It was in another life, under another name, that she'd loved and lost a big brother. Standing by his grave she could feel no grief. She wandered away to examine another part of the compound.

The house drew her attention. She knew that the building was *the house*, and not, say, a storage shed, and that the similar small building some distance away was the new chicken coop. New? Why *new*? She didn't know. Those were simply the words that appeared in her head when she looked at it. Perhaps it was newer than the house, and indeed it looked slightly less crude.

She marveled at the curious x-ray sensation of knowing exactly what was inside the little building, the objects it contained and the internal structure its skin of soil hid. She knew that the heaped dirt was for insulation, that the triangular design was supposed to be bear-proof, and that there was no hearth inside, only a pit lined with rocks and sand. In the winter, her father would bring in shovel-fulls of glowing hot rocks from the fire-pit outside, to heat the house like a sauna through the long, dark nights.

Her narrative memory, the kind that plays like a movie in the mind, might be missing or never formed in the first place, but there are other kinds of remembering. Everything she had learned as a young child, all the plants, how to shoot a bow and fire a gun, how to catch and clean a fish, all that knowledge was safe and sound in long-term storage. Her body remembered how to move through this clearing. Her hands remembered how to live here.

She stepped forward, moved to open the door, and a wasp flew out at her belligerently. The little animal was defending a nest built under the narrow eve in the apex above the door. Elzy backed off, leaving the insect to her claim.

In backing away and looking around, she saw Andy. He was standing in front of Jamie's grave, apparently transfixed by it. What was he doing? Elzy stepped towards him a little. He could not see her. She stood behind him by about twenty feet.

He knelt by the grave and reached out to touch the wooden cross for a moment, his fingers lingering on the carved dates. After a moment his hands came up to hide his face and his body curled, collapsing forward into an almost fetal position. He began to weep.

No mere decorous tearfulness, Andy was bawling, full on, spasmodic sobs. Elzy hadn't even known an adult man could make that noise. It sounded odd in the deeper register. *What was going on?* He could not be crying for Jamie's sake, and yet the boy's marker had clearly triggered him. What did the marker say to him?

Really, it said only J... C... and the dates. *The dates.* She remembered, suddenly, that he had once referred to his son as an eight-year-old. That was during the pandemic—he and Jamie shared a birth year. She didn't know what the C. stood for, but it could as well stand for Cote. Not that it did—Andy was not their father—but she realized that if the other little boy, J. Cote, had a grave, it would look like this.

Elzy felt torn. Her impulse was to run over and comfort her friend, and yet she knew he might not thank her for doing it. Having a witness to his tears was probably the last thing in the world that he wanted right now. What she should do, she thought, was to creep quietly away and later pretend she had not seen. And yet she could not do that either. In the end, she compromised by doing the worst possible thing, which was to stand there and just watch him cry. But Elzy had never claimed to be any good at any of this.

Finally his sobs subsided and then ceased. He started to sit up, to lower his hands from his face—and stopped, frozen there awkwardly, almost like someone kneeling in prayer. Elzy realized that in crying, his nose had run. He'd covered his face and hands in snot.

Ah! Now, she could help! She walked forward, dropped her handkerchief across his steepled hands, and then retreated a couple of feet back out of his field of vision. If he wanted to pretend she was not there, she would let him.

"Thank you," he said, his voice sounding watery but otherwise surprisingly normal. He cleaned himself up, stuck the cloth in his pocket, and rubbed his hands in the duff as a final cleansing. "You can have mine, when we get it back. We'll trade."

Ah, Andy, Elzy thought, fondly. *Are you ever not a gentleman?*

Dry-eyed now, he resumed his staring at the grave marker. Elzy sat down next to him, close but not touching. She still didn't know what he wanted from her and she did not know how to ask. He reached out an arm and pulled her into a sideways hug and her ear come to rest on the textured cotton at the hollow of his shoulder. She wrapped her arms around his middle and his sweat-damp shirt felt cool on her skin. They sat like that for a long time.

"Why did they have to die?" Elzy asked. It was a child's question, but it was not for her own child-self that she asked it.

"It's a disturbance," replied Andy gently, his voice a sigh.

Finally, Elzy felt the moment ending. Andy loosened his grip on her shoulder, and they sat up, away from each other.

"There. Do you feel better now?" he asked and Elzy had to stifle an incredulous laugh.

Could he really think *she* had been the one whose sorrow had started all this? Could he expect her to think that she was? No, he could not, by no reasonable stretch of the imagination—and yet, this was Andy. For Andy, she could engage in some polite fiction.

"Yes," she assured him. "Yes, I feel OK now, thank you."

Having found the place, Elzy did not want to leave. She knew she had to get back to Bar Harbor to register her claim, and then there was the show in Seal Harbor coming up in a few days. But tonight at least she wanted to stay at the homestead. Andy agreed and volunteered to go get the rest of their gear from the campsite so she could spend the afternoon exploring. His offer was generous, but he also clearly wanted time to be alone and to think for a while. They ate lunch together and then he walked off down the trail.

What, exactly, had happened there by the grave? Elzy still was not sure. He could not think he'd actually found his son, could he? She knew from experience that memory could overwhelm a person, unmoor a mind from both space and time, but when the fugue-state ended ordinary reality returned—unless a person was delusional, which she was sure Andy was not. And yet something seemed to have changed for him. Of course he had seemed unsteady and quiet over lunch. Crying hard like that exhausts and alters a person, just as rage does, and, being Andy, he would feel a need to withdraw. Elzy had learned that he used interpersonal distance somewhat as a turtle uses its shell, and she let him be. But something, something besides his mood, was different, now. Something about him had changed.

After he left she did nothing at all for a while except to lay on her back with her palms pressed, root-like, into the duff and watch the sunlight filter through the apple leaves. Despite the growth of the new trees, the rot of the buildings, and the absence of her father, the scents and the shapes, the occasional sounds of mosquitoes, cicadas, and birds, they were all *right*. She could cut the trees and rebuild the gardens, if she wanted to. She could mourn her father afresh, if she needed to. Whatever was wrong with the home site, whatever didn't match her memory, could be either fixed or understood, because this was the right place. And that familiarity itself felt so odd. She couldn't get over the strangeness of knowing herself at the center of the world, rather than at its edge.

It was rather, she reflected, like when she'd had a badly decayed molar extracted just before she went off to school. How she'd woken from the anesthesia and felt the pain *missing*, pain that she'd long since learned to ignore, even largely ceased to notice, and yet its absence was a blessing, a soothing silence where she had grown used to noise.

She was home.

Elzy had not meant to spend several hours staring upward like that, but that was what she did. She roused herself only when a raven called out from somewhere and another, much farther away, replied. She wondered how long ravens lived and whether these could remember her. They might be telling each other *hey, Elzy's back!* The thought reminded her that before long it would be Andy who would be back, so she got up and set about documenting the site with her cell's camera and fixing its exact location on the map with her compass.

Also, she knocked down that wasp nest. This was *her* house.

When Andy returned, carrying her big frame-pack lashed to the back of his, he acted as though nothing remarkable had happened to him that day. She did not press him, but cleaned out the old fire pit, set their little alcohol stove in the middle of it, and cooked their meal. Through dinner and afterwards they chatted a little but mostly sat with their own thoughts, each in silence but with the other for company. Everything seemed normal, except that Elzy felt more relaxed, more comfortable with Andy than she ever had before. She knew she was feeling the echo of some shift inside of him. Perhaps he had finally set his child down.

The next morning, Wednesday, they broke camp early to return to Bar Harbor. They had to get back to Seal Cove by Saturday, and weren't sure how long the registration process would take. They didn't know if perhaps Elzy might have to prove her identity, or how she would go about doing so given that she still didn't know her original last name.

In order that Elzy might seem as authoritative and trustworthy as possible, they both dressed in professional garb before leaving the woods.

"Why," she asked, as Andy zipped her up for the thousandth time, "do guild members wear clothing they can't get into by themselves?"

"Not all of them do," he answered, and turned so she could zip him. "Tunic designs vary, and some people can reach even these zippers." Then he looked at her over his shoulder. "What we do, we cannot do alone anyway," he added, in such an altered, gentle tone of voice that afterwards Elzy was never quite sure she had not imagined it. Then he busied himself straightening his hood and attaching his little silver pin as if he had said nothing remarkable.

A few hours later, they pushed open the door of the Land Office in Bar Harbor. They needn't have worried about identification, as it turned out. A different clerk waited for them, one who recognized Elzy almost as soon as she walked in.

"*Elzy? Elzy Cruz?*" she exclaimed. "You're back!"

Elzy stood mute in shock, not knowing how to react. The clerk, a heavy-set blonde woman of maybe fifty or sixty, peered at her cautiously.

"Why, sure, it is you, isn't it?" she asked, perhaps trying to reassure herself. "You were friends with my daughter, you and Jamie. It was such a shame about him. And then your father got sick....Oh, it's so good to see you again, Elzy—but you probably go by something more grown-up now, don't you?"

"No, I'm still Elzy," she replied, finding her voice at last. "But I'm Elzy Rodriguez now."

Surprise lit the woman's face. Although she apparently hadn't been to any of Elzy's events, she recognized the name. Next, her eyes shifted to Andy, obviously wondering if he were Mr. Rodriguez.

"I took my Mom's name," Elzy explained. "I've been living with her."

Andy introduced himself, somewhat self-consciously, as Elzy's application sponsor. The clerk reciprocated, calling herself Mandy, which saved Elzy from having to ask. But then Mandy launched into a long series of gossipy updates on dozens of supposedly mutual acquaintances and Elzy finally had to admit she didn't remember who any of those people were. The older woman clucked sympathetically and filled her in. Apparently, ecological relationships weren't the only kind she had on the island. When she told Mandy about her father's death, the woman's eyes filled with tears.

"Oh, I'm so sorry. I had so hoped he would find the medicine he needed in Pennsylvania."

Part of Elzy had been waiting to hear just those words for sixteen years

"Mandy, I want to claim my father's land," she announced, finally. "I don't know what kind of proof you need of my identity and ownership."

"You?" Mandy exclaimed. "You brought me two ducks you'd shot yourself the first time you and your father came to visit me after the pandemic. You don't need to prove anything. Where, exactly, did you folks live?" And she activated her tablet in order to look up the plot and edit its legal status. But when Elzy told her, she started clucking sympathetically again. "Honey, that area's got an easement on it. You couldn't start a farm there, it's a water supply protection reserve. You might be able to appeal the zoning, since you do have prior claim...."

"But I don't want to start a farm," Elzy interjected. "I'm going to have my own income, assuming I can get a guild to represent me."

"That's not going to be a problem," said Andy.

Elzy looked around at him in surprise—she had almost forgotten he was there. The warmth spread through her chest again, folding itself around his words.

"Can I at least hunt for my own use and have a garden?" she asked Mandy. "There's got to be some sort of provision for minimal use, if you have it listed as private land with an easement on it."

The clerk checked her records.

"It's listed for four people, maximum residency, but that's not enough for—"

"It's enough for me," Elzy insisted. "I just want some place I can be rooted. I don't need to be able to grow crops for a living. Maybe I can work at least part-time as a caretaker of that complex of reserves?"

"We already have a crew that does trail maintenance in there a couple of times a year."

"I know," said Elzy, who had noticed the well-kept public trails. "But do any of them live on site and have eight years of experience in security and law enforcement and four years of coursework in environmental education?"

"You do?"

"Yes. So, is the job open?"

"I'll check on that for you," Mandy said.

Elzy left the Land Office that day with, as her mother would have said, all her ducks in a row. Her father's land was now in her name. She could survey the exact property lines when she returned next year, since none of them were contested by anyone. She knew how to present her proposal to serve as caretaker for the area. She knew what guild she wanted to apply to and how to do so. And it was still only Wednesday.

She and Andy didn't have anywhere to be for a few days. She proposed using the unexpected opening in their schedule to walk to Seal Cove and see some of the island, rather than taking a boat. Andy accepted the idea and suggested they route the first part of their way down the length of the Champlain Mountain ridge, so Elzy could get above tree line for a while. It was already mid-afternoon, but the island was thick with campsites and hostels, so they simply set out.

It took several hours of walking along the road to reach the Black and Orange Trail, which they followed through an aging aspen grove up to the shoulder of the mountain. Beyond the aspens, much of the land was exposed bedrock, the soil having eroded away after a big fire about a century earlier. Islands of pitch pines persisted here and there, literally holding their ground with stubborn, shallow roots. Some of them were even collecting new sand and organic matter around their margins. Depressions in the rock collected sand as well and most supported moss, reindeer lichens, and sprawling shrubs, such as three-toothed cinquefoil and lowbush blueberry. But mostly it was just smooth, undulating stone tinged pale green by crustose lichen as flat and hard as paint.

The trail rose higher and crossed some kind of invisible divide beyond which the crustose lichen was almost entirely black. Elzy asked if it had died and Andy said no, it was just a different species, one that took longer to establish. They now walked over ground that had been exposed for centuries rather than decades, above the old, pre-fire tree-line.

"We're not over two thousand feet, though. How can we be at tree-line?"

"We're not even over a thousand feet yet," replied Andy. "Tree-line here is just very low. It's a combination of harsh weather and frequent fires. Once granite loses its soil, it takes a long time to regain it."

"Why?"

"Look at it! Very few cracks, very few of those depressions. Nothing to retain sand. The soil has to build up from lichens onward. It takes hundreds of years. And then there's another fire."

"Why does it burn so often?"

"*Often* is relative. The Fire of 1947 and the June Fires burned different areas. I'd say each part of the island burns only once every few hundred years. But granite-derived soils don't retain water well, so, relative to other parts of New England, the island is fire-prone. Hence the excellent berry harvest." As Elzy knew, blueberries and their relatives do well in the same kinds of conditions that foster frequent fires.

The trail turned left along the base of a rock ledge and Andy called a break. He still wanted to rest more often than he had earlier in the trip, and he also seemed to be making a greater effort to stay hydrated. They took off their packs and sat down with their backs against the two-foot face of the ledge. Elzy dug out the trail mix bag while Andy drank deeply. From where they sat, they could see the blue ocean speckled with solar sailboats and, beyond them, a group of smaller, outlying islands.

"See this lichen?" said Andy, indicating a large, green, peanut-shaped growth on the wall behind him. "It has to be around two hundred years old, to be this big. Think about what it's seen, sitting here for that long?"

"Did you call a break here because of that lichen?" Elzy asked. "Did you know it was here, individually?" If anyone knew lichens individually, it would be Andy.

Uncharacteristically, he ignored her question. He ate a handful of trail mix and then pointed towards a large building in the lowlands.

"See that building? Now it belongs to Atlantic College, which is named after the old College of the Atlantic because it took over some of their facilities. But that building used to be Jackson Laboratory, where they bred mice for research. It's been rebuilt *three* times. What sounds you can hear from up here, the look of the forest there, that building, it's all changed, changed multiple times, since this lichen has been growing here."

They sat in silence for a while. Andy did not usually speak so fancifully as to talk about what a lichen could see.

"Jordan would have loved this," he said, finally, and the hair on the back of Elzy's neck stood on end. He had never before spoken the name of any of his family in her presence. "He loved *narrative*. I was planning to take him up here, that summer."

"What was your son like?" she asked him.

"Like me, but more so." Andy laughed a little at his own wording. "He looked like me, in the face. He thought the way I do. When he was very little, I could almost always predict what he was going to say because I knew the brain he used to say it. He grew out of that vulnerability, of course. He was a little shy, like me, but give him time and he'd make friends with anybody. Boys, girls, it didn't matter, even when he got to be seven or eight years old. Not many boys that age are like that."

"Did you read to him, too? Like you read to your daughter?" Elzy remembered Andy saying *I used to read to my daughter* and had always thought it strange he had not said *children*.

"No! He told stories to *me*. That is one way we differ. Differed. He could tell the most extraordinary stories. He told me a bed-time story every night I was at home, almost from when he first learned to talk. I remember them all."

"Maybe you can tell me those stories next," Elzy suggested. "Then I can remember them, too."

And Andy looked towards her, his eyes very wide and as blue as the shining sea behind him, and he did not speak.

They walked onward, following the curving ridge of the mountain. In its openness this landscape was indeed very much like the tableland of the Presidentials, with the islands of small, twisted pines standing in for the clumps of dwarfed spruce and fir of the New Hampshire krumholz zone. The next ridge over, and the one on the other side of that, were taller, rockier, and more open, and resembled the Presidentials even more. But the colors and textures of the rocks and vegetation here on the island seemed warmer somehow, coarser yet more welcoming. And where the Presidentials comprised a single curving ridge, here there was a whole, neighborly row of linear, steep-sided ranges, each separated from the next by great gulfs of air and light reflecting off the pale rock and off the surface of the lakes and ponds far below.

And Elzy asked questions about all of it as they walked, just as she always had. And Andy answered them or admitted that he didn't know, just as he always had. And she never knew how that normalcy in her behavior sustained him, made the bedrock they traversed seem safe and stable after all. It would never occur to her to doubt his expertise or his authority just because she had seen his tears.

A damp wind blew and as the hours wore on, it grew damper, stronger. By the time they reached the southern end of the ridge, shreds of fog rode that wind and spit rain occasionally. They could no longer see the ocean, only the blowing wisps of white. In the wet, the lichens crusting the rocks came alive, filling the strange gray world of the cloud with color. Elzy's fingers grew cold, then numb, and she pulled them into her sleeves as best as she could while still holding her hiking poles. She had no gloves, and her spare socks were at the bottom of her pack, which she could not open without exposing everything inside to the damp.

Then they climbed down the steep, rocky hill known as the Beehive, a curving vertical face fitted with iron ladders and hand-holds drilled into the reddish rock. The way was totally exposed and dangerously slippery, yet slim little Juneberry trees clung to the rock here and there like a detail of some Chinese landscape painting.

At the bottom of the Beehive they dropped abruptly out of the storm. The air near sea level was clear and dry and almost still. The sky was partly cloudy and the peaks invisible, but there was no sign of rain. Out of the wind, the air was comfortably warm.

The trail wound down through airy groves of aspens, around a paddock full of bored-looking horses, down a few flights of old wooden steps, and out onto a crescent-shaped sand beach with a freshwater marsh behind it. Sunset wasn't far off, and they'd planned on camping on the sand, but unfortunately dozens of other people had had the same idea. A beach party was in full swing. The horses had apparently been used to haul in fire-wood, a whole hog, and a huge quantity of alcohol. Teenagers shrieked and flirted with the frigid waves, and a pair of shirtless young men spotted Elzy and beckoned her to join the festivities. She could almost feel Andy tighten up uncomfortably beside her.

There was still no way he was going to admit to her that today he couldn't handle the crowd.

"Is there anywhere else we can camp?" she asked, rescuing him. "I really don't want to stop hiking yet."

"There are trails over on Great Head," Andy said, pointing at the forested arm of land to the east of the beach. "It's public land, so we can camp wherever we want, when you're ready. Hardly anyone ever goes there anymore."

They filtered drinking water for the night from the marsh, then spent the next hour exploring a series of neatly graveled footpaths that looped through mostly spruce and pine forest. In a grove of oak and aspen they dropped their packs and set up camp. The place was a trail junction near an abandoned asphalt parking lot, but the open forest let in a lot of light and when a light breeze sprang up the quaking aspens shivered almost musically. The sound of surf was lost to them, as were the noises of the partiers on the beach, but a distant buoy dinged with some unseen swell. There was even a flat stone block perfect for the alcohol stove.

As Elzy waited for the water to boil, she looked around the little junction with interest. Coltsfoot and wild sarsaparilla grew thickly in places, the latter yellowing towards fall. Old stems of wildflowers gone by stood, brown or golden, in the sparse grass and leaf litter. A little moss clung to the bases of some of the trees. White ash trunks, mostly dead, stood as minor accents among the other century-old hardwoods. Young spruces were just starting to take their places in the overstory, but gaps in the canopy and the white bark of dead and fallen paper birches kept the feeling of the woods light and airy.

Mentally, she stripped back the years as Andy had taught her. She watched the spruces shrink back into saplings, saw the fallen and rotted paper birch trees reassemble themselves and reach for the sky.

That was odd—some of the birches were recently dead, perhaps as little as five or ten years ago. If she ever came this way as a child, she would have seen them alive. Elzy could not remember ever seeing a living paper birch grove, only unhappy specimen trees hanging on through human intervention. Rising temperatures and exotic pests had killed off the lovely plants in all the forests south of Canada, but they hadn't died everywhere all at once. Most of Mount Dessert Island had been bad for them, but here in this grove they'd had a refuge for a while. Paper birch shares a lifespan with human beings, and some of these on one side of the trail had made it into old age. None of those on the other side had. The curls of rot-resistant white bark over there were all much smaller, torn by time, the wood all long-gone.

Elzy frowned.

She could see no difference in history or topography between the two adjacent forests, and yet for certain plants the trail had followed the line between life and death. Why? In a moment she worked out that the soils must be different. From what Andy had told her of the island's geology, she guessed that the trail junction lay on top of a boundary between granitic and metamorphic bedrock. The latter produced sweeter soil, more wildflowers, and, once, a temporary haven for paper birch.

Once she had solved the puzzle, she could all but see the difference in the bedrock, just as she could see the history of climate change in the scraps of white bark or the older history of fire in the presence of the quaking aspens. A year ago, even eight months ago, she wouldn't have noticed any of these patterns. She would only have seen a pretty collection of trees. Reading the landscape was not something they taught at school but a skill particular to Andy. She had learned from him as they traveled.

Nature's secrets had been revealed—she smiled at the cliché. Nature had no secrets. The dead birches were there for anyone to see. Even what the naked eye could not discern, the mycelia, the cyanobacteria, the rotifers and nematodes in the soil, the tardigrades among the lichens and mosses, all of that was perfectly available to anyone who cared to use a microscope. But without knowledge, all of it was strangely invisible.

The forest was rather like a man who in all sincerity insisted that he had nothing to hide, yet volunteered almost nothing about himself. You could understand him quite well, if only you already knew him.

Elzy looked over at that man, tapping away on his little red notepad, like he always did. She still didn't even know his age.

"What was this place, this spot, like, Before?" she asked. "I mean, aside from the trees and everything." She meant aside from the ecological changes she could read around her. Andy nodded, understanding, and considered.

"Not much has changed here," he said finally. "There would have been contrails above—linear clouds that condensed around the exhaust of jet planes. The air smells better, cleaner, now, though I never noticed it smelling bad except in retrospect. You might have been able to hear the hum of traffic or boat or airplane engines. The parking lot was in use. There would have been more hikers, mostly tourists from off-island. They would look different—people dressed differently back then."

Elzy had known about contrails and private cars and older clothing styles, of course, but the sense of normality in Andy's voice, the way none of what he described seemed exotic to him, was shocking.

"I was born to that world, and I still don't remember it changing."

"I've seen the world change twice," Andy told her. "When I was a child, most people didn't have cell phones. I didn't have a computer of any kind until I was a teenager, and then I had to share it with my whole family."

"You all had your own cars but not your own phones? What, did you drive over whenever you wanted to talk to someone?"

"Sometimes. But we did have landlines—phones that connected by wires. You've heard of them, right?"

"Yeah, of course, but I thought they went out in the 1980s or something."

"No, we still had some landlines up until the pandemic."

"Whoa!" exclaimed Elzy. Andy smiled.

"Hey, I have some pictures here, if you want to see them," he offered.

"Did you take them? Before?"

"Oh, no. None of my pictures survived. I got these from the library in Bar Harbor. I thought you might want to see what the island used to look like."

"Oh, yeah!" Elzy moved over eagerly to sit beside Andy and his computer. He scrolled through images of cruise liners, motor-powered lobster boats, and hikers wearing Gore-Tex and brightly colored polypropylene. Sometimes she asked questions and he answered them. "That was my world," she reiterated, "and I remember none of it."

"I still sometimes catch myself thinking that the future I imagined was real," Andy confessed. "I expected so much. I expected to see my children grow up. I expected to get tenure somewhere. I expected the world I knew to continue, even though I knew better. One way or another, I knew the world was going to change. It had to. That's what *unsustainable* means. The only question was how it would change and when—and what would come after. Do you feel deprived, Elzy?"

Her brow furrowed. It wasn't the sort of question Andy normally asked—nor was it the sort of question she normally answered.

"No. Should I?"

"There's a lot you won't get to have or be, because of what my generation and the ones before us did."

"No," she told him. "Maybe some people my age do, but I don't expend much energy on what I can't have."

"That's wise."

"What about you? Do you miss any *thing*?" Her emphasis on *thing* was deliberate. She didn't doubt he missed people. Andy caught the distinction and smiled briefly, with one corner of his mouth. But it took him a while to answer.

"It's silly," he said, finally, looking away. "I had a motorcycle. It was very loud and it could go really fast...for no reason at all. Nobody does that anymore." His smile faded. He looked down and fidgeted with his hands.

Of course people still enjoyed going fast, when they had the means to do it. People who lived among hills where it still snowed regularly loved their sleds and skis. And everyone wanted a fast horse or an excuse to ride in a car. What people did not do was willfully forget what going fast—what any expenditure of energy—cost. Elzy, and people like her, wouldn't think of a joyride as power and fun. She'd think of it as foolishness and waste. And she'd be right.

And yet, in the foolishness of the past there had been an innocence. Andy shook his head. He knew she wouldn't understand.

But Elzy was looking at him oddly, almost impishly, her head cocked to one side.

"Get yer motor runnin'," she sang, in as low and tough a voice as she could manage.

He stared at her a moment, shocked that she even knew the song. He hadn't known it survived. But then the corner of his mouth turned up, the beginnings of a smile.

"Head out on the highway," he replied, in a wobbly tenor.

"Lookin' for adventure," Elzy continued. Andy grinned widely. "*Whatever comes our way!*" It was a duet, now.

Hey, darling, gonna make it happen
Take the world in a love-embrace
Fire all of yer guns at once and
Explode into spay-ace!

Like a true nature's child
You were born, born to be wild
Fly so high, yer never gonna die-ie!

Dancing around now, singing slightly off key, the eminent scientist and the hardened warrior goofed off together. They sang the whole song, even singing nonsense syllables through the instrumental passages. And for a moment the words of the song felt true. No one would ever have to die. The fun would never have to stop. And a road trip with a friend really could last forever.

Appendix A
The Science of
Ecological Memory

Ecological Memory is a novel grounded in science, but it is not intended to be a textbook; so where scientific explanations did not contribute to the narrative, I left them out. This essay provides some – not all – of those missing explanations.

On language and metaphor

Scientists and laypersons use language differently. Besides the obviously specialized jargon, scientists use their own definitions for common words such as "theory". When scientists talk with non-scientists, confusion often results. It is no good asking scientists to talk "normally" because it is not like they are talking in a code, where one word stands in for a word in Standard English. Scientists use words differently because they say things for which Standard English has no words.

Each branch of science includes ideas and ways of thinking that are foreign to laypersons or even scientists from other specializations. A new way of talking follows automatically. Anyone who does not realize words can have other meanings is likely to miss the new (sometimes very interesting) ideas scientists are trying to convey.

For example, people often use the word "energy" to mean any intangible experience, like the "happy" energy of a room. The room could have a happy *something*; but, in a scientific context, "energy" is not the word for it. Energy is, roughly speaking, the capacity to do something. Heat is one form. Movement is another. Energy has to come from somewhere and go somewhere. It is measurable and can run out. Many people do not understand these concepts but think they do, because the words are familiar. Maybe that is why the US still (as of this writing) does not have a sustainable national energy policy.

I am not providing a glossary, since any necessary definitions are worked into the story. I am simply reminding the reader that familiar words can hide new concepts—a warning that applies in many other contexts too.

A related point and source of potential confusion—new ideas hiding in plain sight—has to do with the popular, metaphorical use of terms from ecology: cities are "concrete jungles", aggressive CEOs are "at the top of the food chain", and so on. Metaphors are fine, but it is important to recognize that ecology also applies to humans literally.

At several points, Andy and Elzy use the language of ecology to talk about themselves and their relationship. In a way, they are indulging in metaphor—but in another way, they are not. They are not saying that families are the human equivalents of ecosystems. The human equivalent of an ecosystem *is* an ecosystem. There is no human world separate from the natural world. There is just the world.

At the same time, certain principles apply equally well to many kinds of systems—whether ecological, biological, or social. Andy and Elzy are using the familiar (to them) language of ecology to talk about relationships that are not ecological but work much the same way.

The post-petroleum world

Ecological Memory depicts a world that includes both ox-carts and robotic exoskeletons. Some readers might ask why. Yes, this is a world without fossil fuel, but it is clearly a technologically advanced society, so why are the people stuck using ox-carts? Why not use renewable energy?

The short answer is that they can and do, but if they used enough renewable energy to replace fossil fuels fully they would just wreck the world again. Where energy comes from is generally less important than how much is used.

People are used to hearing, and telling, the story of technological progress in terms of innovation. Cars are more advanced than ox-carts because they go faster. The other—often forgotten—side of the story is energy. A car that ran on a few bales of hay could not go much faster than an ox, no matter how advanced it was. Advancing technology has allowed the use of more and more energy, and that—not innovation alone—is what gives us our unprecedented power.

Fossil fuel has made increasing energy consumption possible because it is energy dense, easily portable, and abundant (or, at least, used to be). Fossil fuel also causes climate change and ocean acidification; and it indirectly causes several other ills, such as loss of biodiversity. The mechanisms involved should be roughly familiar to most readers. The surprise is that drawing the same amount of energy from other sources would likely cause similar problems; only the mechanisms would be different. Understanding why requires exploring the science of complex systems.

"Complex", here, has a specific, technical[1] meaning: a system is complex if it has certain properties, such as self-organization and a nested or hierarchical structure (complex systems can have other complex systems inside them). I am a complex system, and so are you. So are cells, ecosystems, and entire biospheres. Books have been written about these systems, and they are worth a read, but the important thing to know is that systems science is all about the flow of energy. Complex systems can fight entropy and win. Readers may remember that entropy is the tendency for everything in the universe to run down as energy dissipates. Complex systems do lose energy to dissipation, but they do not run down, because they actively draw in energy from outside themselves. If a system is drawing in more energy than it loses, it is *anti-entropic*. Think of a baby, eating and eating, turning all those calories into growth and development, or a young forest, rapidly increasing in biomass

---

1 The presentation of complex systems here and elsewhere in the book is adapted from in-class and one-on-one discussions with Tom Wessels and Charles Curtin. Both cover some of the same ground in their books; see "Suggested readings".

and biodiversity. Eventually, the complex system reaches a point of equilibrium where energy inputs equal losses, and growth stops: that is *maturity*. From the standpoint of systems science, individual human beings remain mature only briefly. Almost as soon as people reach full size, our metabolisms slow and we start losing energy. We enter what is called the *entropic* phase. More colloquially, it is called aging, though injury or illness can trigger an entropic phase before maturity, too. A system that stays entropic long enough will cease being complex. That is death.

All complex systems go through these phases, though not all become entropic automatically with age. Forests never die of old age, but they can become entropic. A forest on fire, for example, is losing energy (in the form of heat and light) at a fantastic rate. If the fire is not too severe, the forest will survive and become anti-entropic again as it regrows. As Andy explains in the story, size, complexity, and stability increase and decrease together. A mature forest has more biomass and is more complex than either a young, recently-sprouted forest or the pile of ash and cinder left behind by a forest fire. Similarly, adult people are not just bigger than babies; they are also smarter and more resistant to disease. There is a reason people sometimes call the latter part of the human entropic phase a *second childhood*: bodies shrink, becoming less capable and less healthy as they lose energy.

All this energy must come from somewhere. Complex systems draw energy from the larger systems they are nested within. My cells draw energy from me. I draw energy from my society by working for a living and buying things. My society draws energy from the biosphere. The catch is that if the smaller system draws too much energy, it can force the larger system into an entropic phase. The larger system can even collapse—cease to exist—leaving the smaller system floating loose in whatever system the larger one was nested within. Think about why cancer kills if it is not successfully treated. Think about how unsustainable logging kills forests. Think about what follows from the rapid burning of fossil fuel.

The biosphere, too, is a complex system, and it, too, has had

272

anti-entropic phases when it was actively growing, becoming more complex and more stable. The biosphere draws its energy (mostly) from the sun, through the process of photosynthesis, which gives us all our free oxygen and most of our biomass as well. And the carbon at the heart of that biomass remains part of the biosphere as long as it is part of chemical compounds that store energy captured by plants—which means that fossil fuels still count as biomass. When Earth was young, the growth of the biosphere, including the growth of its fossil fuel deposits, drew down the atmospheric carbon dioxide concentration. When the biosphere entered its mature phase, the carbon dioxide level more or less stabilized. Now that we're burning fossil fuels, we're liberating that stored energy and the CO2 concentration is rising rapidly as carbon leaves the biosphere—this loss of both biomass and energy means that the biosphere is now entropic.

Let me repeat that: Earth's biosphere is currently entropic *because of human activity.*

Loss of stability, complexity, and size always accompany loss of mass and energy as a complex system starts to die. In human beings, that means poor health, increasing disability, and the wasting away of various tissues. Erratic weather, changing climate, and loss of biodiversity are simply the same pattern applied to the biosphere as a whole.

That burning fossil fuel should trigger a global entropic phase should not be surprising, given that the whole point of fossil fuel use is to access *a lot* of energy, quickly. Earth receives a certain limited amount of solar energy every year, and plant and animal life, as well as the movement of wind and water, takes place within that energy budget. If the human species confined itself to the same annual budget, living on sustainable forestry, agriculture, and renewable energy sources, most of the consumption that people take for granted today would simply be out of reach. Fossil fuel makes the *more* we want possible, and does so by delivering energy at a higher rate than the biosphere receives. Biospheric entropy is the inevitable result.

If the human species stops using so much energy, the biosphere will re-enter an anti-entropic phase and recover—though it will take a very long time for full recovery, possibly millions of years. That's better than not recovering at all, and the sooner we reach carbon neutrality, the more likely we are to have a livable planet during the recovery period. Hope remains, though time is getting short.

Giving up fossil fuel entirely is probably a necessary step towards sustainability. What is the alternative, some complicated global carbon rationing system? Who would administer or enforce it? And why would anyone bother? Truly sustainable fossil fuel use would—*by definition*—yield no more energy than renewables can.

But the end of the Age of Fossil Fuel alone will not rescue us. Should we ever find and use an alternative way to draw more energy than the biosphere has to spare, the system will be back in the same entropic muddle it's in now. Imagine replacing a Stage Four cancerous tumor with a six-mile-long tapeworm. The patient still dies; the only difference is the mechanism.

Energy is energy. Using too much has consequences.

One way or another, human over-use of resources will end. Unsustainable processes do end, by definition. We can survive only by shifting to an energy budget similar to what existed prior to the Industrial Revolution—a change that will impose real limitations on what the species can do and how it can do it. But a return to pre-Industrial limitations need not mean a return to pre-Industrial life.

An energy budget is not a time machine. There is no mechanism by which limitation alone can erase scientific and cultural advances or prevent further advances. Where those new advances might lead, I cannot say. I have simply imagined one possibility—one that includes both exoskeletons and ox-carts.

Predicting the future of the climate

Readers familiar with New England may notice that the weather in this book seems odd. It is hot in May, the people are preoccupied with the possibility of flooding, and there are a lot of storms. The characters think it all normal. Am I, the writer, trying to depict climate change? Yes and no.

Yes, I had climate on my mind when I wrote this book. The New England climate in the story is not the one that exists today, and I wanted readers to notice. Fiction in the present Age of Rapid Climate Change needs to acknowledge climate as a function of time as well as space: no writer would give Seattle the same climate as Miami, so why depict the past or future with the same climate as the present?

Climate is the set of patterns that weather makes over time, and this story takes place over less than a year: not enough time for any patterns to become clear. That the characters think hot weather in May is normal—not the hot weather itself—suggests the climate has changed, and even that is a poor indicator. Humans are notoriously bad at identifying trends based on personal experience; that is one reason why record keeping and statistics were invented.

It is just as well that the story does not give the reader a good view of the climate. Constructing a scientifically plausible fictional climate—which I would sorely like to have done—is fiendishly difficult if not ultimately impossible. The problem is that climate cannot be predicted by ballpark estimations and back-of-the-envelope calculations. One of the curious traits of complex systems is that no detail can be guaranteed to be too small to matter. The phrase "butterfly effect" describes how the flap of an insect's wings could cause a hurricane on the other side of the planet. In a picturesque way, the phrase describes a problem that cropped up with the earliest weather simulations: two simulations with nearly identical starting numbers often yielded radically different results (Curtin & Allen 2018). Attempting to simulate a climate without the aid of a supercomputer and *a lot* of data is, at best, an exercise in fantasy.

If the story were set in a version of the future that climatologists consider likely, my job would be rather more straightforward: just look up the climate projections that have already been done and attempt to synthesize. I did just that for a piece I published online several years ago. But the abrupt, near-term end of fossil-fuel use in my novel has not been subject to much in the way of simulation because no one thinks it likely.

Since I could neither invent nor look up a scientifically plausible climate to use as setting for the story—and since the plot does not allow for depicting the climate directly anyway—I simply wrote any scenes involving weather with three adjectives in mind: "warmer", "wetter", and "more extreme". These are consistent with contemporary predictions for the region over the next century (see e.g. van Oldenborgh *et al.* 2013), as well as loosely plausible for the various scenarios implied by my story.

Science can't tell us what the climate for the setting of the book should be, but it can shed light on what Andy thinks it is doing—an important part of his emotional landscape, given who he is. Remember that the field of climatology in his time is very limited. Most of what he understands about the climate is what he remembers from Before.

The reader might think that, since fossil fuel use has stopped, levels of greenhouse gases and average temperatures should both fall—but what might seem obvious is not necessarily true.

As of 2010, combustion of fossil fuels was responsible for about two-thirds of total greenhouse-gas emissions by weight. There are other sources of carbon dioxide however, and there are other greenhouse gasses: notably methane (a much more powerful greenhouse gas than carbon dioxide), but also nitrous oxide and two related groups of gases, the chlorofluorocarbons (CFCs) and hydrofluorocarbons (HCFs) (Edenhofer *et al.* 2014). In my scenario, carbon emissions from fossil-fuel use are over and have been for twenty years. That does not mean, however, that other kinds of emissions, such as methane from landfills or melting permafrost, stop – at least, not instantly. For reasons I will go into later, some could increase.

To understand the total concentration of each gas in the atmosphere—and how it is likely to change over time—it is not enough to know emission rates. One must also look at rate of loss, which will be different for each gas. Picture running a bathtub with the drain open; whether the tub fills or empties depends on inflow versus outflow.

For most greenhouse gasses, loss ("outflow") is primarily by chemical degradation occurring at a more or less set rate per gas (Ehhalt 2001). Carbon dioxide is a little more complicated, because it does not degrade this way. Rather, it is absorbed through a number of processes, each with its own rate and capacity.

The fastest way for carbon dioxide to leave the atmosphere is absorption by the oceans' surface waters. A large amount can be absorbed in just a few decades. Unfortunately, water can only absorb so much, and the oceans' surface waters have already absorbed a lot; that is why they are becoming increasingly acidic. Of course, a lot more water lies beneath the surface, but the ocean mixing required for it to absorb carbon dioxide does not happen on a human timescale.

After ocean surface waters reach capacity, the next fastest way out of the atmosphere is the chemical weathering of rock, but that, too, does not play out on a human timescale. A big carbon dioxide spike takes tens or even hundreds of thousands of years to flatten out (Ciais *et al.* 2013).

Scientific articles on potential recovery from climate change tend not to mention absorption of carbon by organisms, even though it is organisms that sequestered the carbon in fossil fuels in the first place. I would guess this is because the sequestration process—including the accretion of new oil, gas, and coal deposits—is so very, very slow.

Andy confidently asserts that carbon dioxide levels are falling—quickly enough that he expects to be able to study the ecological results of the change himself. He is very excited. Presuming he is right, that could be taken to mean that ocean surface waters have not, in fact, reached capacity; but another possibility presents itself.

While the formation of fossil-fuel deposits takes place on a geological timescale, living plants are a different matter. They, too, sequester quantities of carbon, and many of them, including large trees, can grow relatively quickly. Individual plants are not considered carbon sinks because, when the plant dies, all that carbon is released again; but entire plant communities can, indeed, be carbon sinks. Where one tree in a forest dies, another can grow and take up the carbon in turn. Indeed, deforestation is considered an important source of carbon dioxide emissions—so, logically, the growth of large, new forests should have the opposite effect.

I have never heard reforestation suggested as a way for carbon dioxide levels to drop, but perhaps that is because relevant discussions typically assume that the human population is going to stabilize—not fall. With so many people and associated agriculture and infrastructure in the way, there is not much room for new forests to grow. But Andy has experienced a radical reduction in the population—the reader learns that, at least in the US, the population is about one tenth of what it had been; the rest of the world is presumably similar. *Per capita* resource use also appears to have fallen. That leaves a lot of room for new trees.

Could continental-scale reforestation cool the climate? There may be precedent.

When Europeans first came to the Americas, they brought along diseases to which the Americans[2] had no immunity. This was not germ warfare (that came later), but the result was dramatic, continent-wide population loss and widespread societal collapse (Wessels 1997). Forests grew in places that had previously been cleared. The idea that North America was a pristine wilderness prior to European conquest is partly due to the overgrown, depopulated mess that colonial explorers found in the wake of the terrible pandemics (Wessels 1997).[3]

The post-contact pandemics are history's closest analogue to the present story. Contagious disease really did cause the end of a world. It also caused a large-scale reforestation event coincident with changes in atmospheric carbon-dioxide levels and a global drop in temperatures (Dull *et al.* 2010), the second, more severe,

2 I did not write "Native Europeans," so why should I write "Native Americans"?
3 Their misinterpretation of what they saw is understandable. The *persistent* belief that a continent inhabited by humans was an example of *untouched* nature is racism.

phase of the so-called Little Ice Age. The first phase may be partially attributable to the Black Death in Europe, another pandemic that triggered large-scale reforestation (Hoof *et al.* 2006).

The timing of events does not support either pandemic as the sole cause of cooling. Other explanations and possible contributing factors have been advanced, and it is far from clear what role—if any—each played. Nevertheless, respected experts have taken seriously the idea that continental-scale reforestation could be enough to cool the planet, suggesting that global reforestation now could change the climate.

Of course, carbon sequestration by reforestation only works if the forests that once existed *can* grow back. History offers examples of cleared forests that did not return, despite apparent opportunity, for reasons like soil loss (Curtin & Allen 2018), and forests all over the world are starting to die from climate change itself, or from stresses made worse by climate change. Some forests—notably in the tropics—already have become net producers of carbon dioxide, and many more across the world may follow suit as climate change worsens and dieback exceeds growth (Allen 2009). Dying forests could even release enough carbon dioxide to speed climate change and kill even more forest, but whether we have reached that nightmare bifurcation point, or might reach it soon, is unclear.

So, in Andy's time, the global greenhouse effect may or may not be weakening, depending on various interacting factors—some of which I have mentioned and some not. Several of the relevant questions might well be answerable by anyone with the appropriate mathematical skill and enough data. Others are only answerable with a supercomputer. Still others might not be answerable at all.

Even assuming that the greenhouse effect is weakening in Andy's time, whether the planet is cooling yet is another question. If greenhouse gas levels simply stabilize, warming will continue for several decades, perhaps 30 to 50 years (Mann & Kump 2015), because the climate needs time to adjust to a stronger greenhouse effect. If the greenhouse gas levels then drop, cooling will occur—but I have not been able to learn how quickly that cooling happens.

Logic suggests that if the greenhouse effect weakens *before* the temperature stabilizes, cooling will begin sooner than it otherwise would, but I have not found confirmation of that principle, either[4].

But even the onset of cooling will not necessarily undo the damage done by rapid warming. In fact, Earth may continue to deteriorate for some time. Biodiversity loss, like climate change, has a time lag. Evidence from Europe suggests that extirpations peak at least a hundred years after major habitat loss, a delay referred to technically as *extinction debt* (Curtin and Allen 2018). Ice, likewise, requires time to melt, as anyone knows who has ever enjoyed a drink with ice on a hot day. Big chunks of ice take longer than small ones, and so the massive glaciers of Greenland and Antarctica could go on melting for a very long time before the "melting debt" already accumulated is paid. Undoing such damage might not be possible on any time-scale—when complex systems change, the change is often permanent.

But the irreversibility of change is not the same thing as hopelessness. The sooner the greenhouse effect weakens, the less debt will accumulate and the sooner the new anti-entropic phase can begin. We cannot go back, but we can go on.

So here is Andy, twenty years after the collapse of the world he once knew, in a climate that seems vaguely consistent with the predictions he remembers, but it's hard to be sure. He knows that soon the world must diverge from prediction, if it hasn't diverged already. Perhaps the planet will cool, wildlife habitat will expand dramatically, and he will live to see the beginnings of regrowth. Then all Andy's losses, all the personal tragedy and tumult he has been through, will mean something: the unavoidable side effects of repairing the world that he loves. Alternatively, forest die-back, or some other destructive feedback loop, could render rapid climate

---

4 Search engine algorithms seem to be organized in such a way that infrequently-asked questions are almost impossible to find answers for, even if the information has been published. Since Andy has a friend in climatology and isn't dependent on search engines for answers, he may know more about the mechanics of cooling than I do. Unfortunately, given the other things he doesn't know, he still can't say whether cooling has begun or when or if it might start.

change self-perpetuating. The sacrifice of nine-tenths of humanity might yet prove to be too little, too late.

Andy is aware of these possible alternatives, but in the year in which we meet him, he does not yet know which scenario is playing out.

The specific case of hurricanes

Two tropical storms occur in the course of the story. Mention is also made of several catastrophic hurricanes that occurred some years before. Readers might conclude that I am trying to show how climate change has increased tropical cyclone activity (hurricanes and tropical storms are both tropical cyclones). Indeed, I had something like that in mind—but I also intended a certain ambiguity.

I intended ambiguity both because personal experiences of climate change *are* subjective and therefore ambiguous—as noted earlier—and because there is no way to be certain what climate change will do to hurricanes (Mann & Kump 2015). While it may seem obvious that warmer surface waters will lead to stronger storms, the history of science is full of ideas that seemed obvious but turned out not to be true.

Climate change has doubtless affected tropical-cyclone behavior already, but it is hard to be certain how. Most of the tools used to study hurricanes, such as weather satellites, did not exist before humans started influencing the climate. Before-and-after comparisons are difficult without a clear "before" picture.

Readers should not conclude that climatologists are ignorant of what is happening with tropical cyclones, only that prediction is more difficult and less certain for tropical cyclones than for other aspects of climatology. Indeed, my story is consistent with the tentative predictions that were current when I wrote the book. New research methods and better computer models may soon lift some of the limitations I had to work within.

Epidemiology and real-world pandemics

Ecological Memory is hardly the first story to involve a civilization-ending pandemic. The theme is a popular one because people are worried, and with good reason. Widespread ecological upheaval makes it easier for dangerous new diseases, such as Ebola and SARS,[5] to jump from other species to humans (Quammen 2012). Modern transportation technology means that an outbreak could conceivably go global within days (Quammen 2012). The type of worst-case scenario that makes a good disaster story is possible.

But there are good reasons to think a disaster-story-come-to-life highly unlikely (Quammen 2012).

First, health authorities are very concerned about the possibility of pandemic and can respond very quickly to any emerging disease. In most cases, new diseases enter humans through contact with an animal our species not usually encounter. Such contact is most likely in remote, isolated areas, meaning that (with rare but important exceptions) outbreaks begin far from large population centers with airports. The isolation gives epidemiologists time to study and learn to control the disease before it can spread beyond the region.

Second, most outbreaks would stop without causing global pandemic, even if doctors did nothing. Most diseases leave survivors who are immune to re-infection, so as the outbreak progresses, the proportion of immune people in the population rises and the less likely it is for a sick person to have contact with anyone who is vulnerable. Infection rates slow and the outbreak ends.

Third, not all pandemics—not even all horrific pandemics--threaten civilization. The flu outbreak of 1918-1919, for example, killed 50 million people, a significant fraction of all humans then alive, yet civilization went on.

Three barriers to civilization-ending pandemic—can each fail? Yes, they can and they all have, at one time or another. But for the doomsday scenario to play out, all three must fail together—the bad-luck equivalent of the same person winning the lottery three times in a row.

Fear of the worst case is by no means stupid. Indeed, such fear

---

5 Severe acute respiratory syndrome.

helps keep society safe by ensuring that public health agencies get the funding and other forms of support they need. But the possibility of civilization-ending pandemic is not a reason to stay awake at night worrying.

But a careful reader will notice that in my story the pandemic is only the trigger; the actual cause of societal collapse is something else, something we are currently not at all prepared for.

How to build a fictional virus

Most people who write about killer viruses do not seem to care about realism. Neither do their readers, who just want a good story. The results make virologists twitch. But narrative and realism are not actually at odds; to be great, a story should not make any expert twitch, so I consulted Kevin Egan, a student of virology.[6] What follows is a summary of what I learned.

Viruses are just one type of potentially infectious agent or pathogen. There are many others, including, but hardly limited to, bacteria, fungi, amoebas, and certain worms. Infectious agents can cause diseases, but they are not diseases themselves. Not only is it possible to host such an agent without being sick, but some disease symptoms, such as fever, are activities of the immune system. An infectious disease is not an entity but a relationship.

Viruses are odd in that they have some characteristics of life but not others. They are segments of DNA or RNA in a protein jacket able to gain entrance to a cell and control it. The hijacked cell then stops doing its regular job and starts making viruses instead. All living organisms, including archaea and bacteria, can contract viruses. If a single-celled organism contracts a virus, it usually dies. In multicellular organisms, viruses cause damage when enough cells have been hijacked that body functions are impaired.

The immune response to viruses is two-pronged: killing hijacked cells before the newly-constructed virus particles can escape; and destroying the virus particles themselves as they circu-

---

6 My consultant, along with several of his colleagues, also reviewed this section of the essay for accuracy.

late through the organism, using antibodies specially developed for each virus. The body keeps antibodies for every virus it has ever encountered, which is why many viral diseases can only be contracted once.

In fact, a functional immune system can prevent a second infection by any virus. When viral diseases recur, it is because a new strain causes the same disease, or because the original infection persists and then reactivates, or because the immune system itself was compromised. The principle of acquired immunity is how vaccines prevent disease: a weakened or killed virus is introduced to prompt the creation of appropriate antibodies.

It may seem counter-intuitive, but disease is not the goal of a virus, nor of any pathogen. They are not capable of malice, and fighting the immune system costs energy that could otherwise be used for something else. If a pathogen can be said to have a goal, it is simply to replicate and to spread, and most can do so more easily if they can minimize conflict with the host. Most pathogens are thus under selective pressure to evolve ways to treat their hosts more gently.

Host organisms, for their part, are also under selective pressure to evolve more efficient means of defense. In some cases, efficiency means total immunity, but in others it can mean tolerating the pathogen.

Over time, pathogen and host species can evolve a kind of truce; as their relationship becomes less conflicted, the disease becomes progressively less serious and may disappear. When a species is an asymptomatic carrier for a pathogen, as certain bats are for the Ebola virus, it is because the two have extensive evolutionary history together and have a truce. Exposed to a new host species, the virus may fail to gain entrance at all, but if infection occurs, it is likely to be highly destructive.

The principle is the same as the definition of "nativeness" discussed by Elzy at the beginning of the story, where non-native organisms cause problems because their relationships are all new. In general, organisms that lack evolutionary history either do not interact at all, or they interact in destructive ways.[7]

To cause a disease capable of triggering the end of global civilization, a virus would have to be one with which humans have no evolutionary history, and hence no truce. New diseases emerge regularly, but as already discussed, the chance of a natural disease causing a doomsday scenario, while not zero, is implausibly small. To avoid resting my plot on too long a chain of coincidence, I opted for a genetically engineered virus.

Genetic engineering does not involve creating something from nothing. My virology consultant suggested I choose a real virus that my imaginary genetic engineers could alter. The fictional disease would then be shaped by both the range of possibilities for viruses in general and by the behavior of the template virus specifically.

I chose measles.

Measles is highly infectious and can be dangerous, but has several characteristics that prevent it from being a doomsday trigger. The fictional disease needed to have a higher mortality rate, needed to be universally infectious in humans, and it also had to be harder to contain through quarantine.

To defeat containment, I had initially wanted the disease to begin with an infectious, but symptom-free period. Real viruses, however, cannot spread to a new host until the first host has a sufficiently high viral load—and that viral load also triggers an immune response, which manifests as symptoms, such as fever or lethargy. While there are diseases that have symptom-free infectious periods, such as HIV/AIDS, these periods are preceded by a bout of flu-like symptoms. Measles itself suggests an alternative: *a prodrome*, or period of vague malaise, slight fever, and tiredness prior to the onset of definitive symptoms. It is possible to be in a prodrome and not realize one is sick. My fictional disease has a longer, more infec-

---

7 Tom Wessels explored the progression, through co-evolution, from a destructive relationship to a benign or even mutually beneficial relationship in his excellent course, Principles of Sustainability, and, to a lesser extent, in print (Wessels 2006). For further discussion of the principle as applied to diseases and herbivorous insects, see Quammen (2012) and Tallamy (2009), respectively.

tious prodrome than measles.[8]

Natural measles is highly infectious among unvaccinated persons, but some people do have natural immunity, and most acquire immunity through either vaccination or infection. To defeat both natural and acquired immunity, the new virus must have different proteins in its outer jacket, since these proteins are how the virus attacks host cells and are also the means by which antibodies recognize and destroy viruses.

Measles is part of the morbillivirus group, meaning that the proteins in its jacket do not mutate readily. Although multiple strains of human measles exist, all can be defeated by the same antibodies, which explains why no one gets measles more than once and why the measles vaccine is so effective. The fictional virus, while no longer measles, is still a morbillivirus, so survivors acquire lasting immunity, explaining its apparent disappearance after the pandemic in the story.

Natural measles is only lethal in about 1% of cases. The fictional disease must be more severe, but in a way that reflects its origin as measles, since the progression of a viral disease depends, in part, on which types of cells the virus attacks and in what order, and cell preference is a genetically determined trait.

Measles attacks the skin, conjunctiva (mucous membrane covering the exposed surface of the eyes), and linings of the lungs and intestines. Besides high fever, definitive symptoms include a distinctive rash that starts on the face and spreads; red eyes; a persistent cough; and, often, diarrhea. Opportunistic bacterial infections can cause complications, such as pneumonia.

For my story, genetic engineers alter the speed of progression so that the prodrome appears sooner but lasts longer. They also reduce the virus' affinity for the skin and increase its affinity for the lungs and digestive tract. The resulting new disease involves only a subtle rash but causes pneumonia directly in every case, along with

---

8 Infectiousness can and generally does vary over the course of a disease. It is often low during the prodromic phase; but there are diseases, such as influenza, with highly infectious prodromic phases (Quammen 2012).

diarrhea and vomiting—bringing the mortality rate up to 20%. The reduction of the rash is important to how the medical establishment responds.

For the genetically engineered virus to reduce the human population in any significant way, it must outmaneuver the Centers for Disease Control and Prevention, analogous agencies in other countries, and the World Health Organization. Simultaneously deploying the virus at multiple locations helps, as does giving the disease a long prodromic phase. Still, if every case of the new disease were misdiagnosed as familiar measles, the public-health response would be immediate and quite possibly successful.

That is because—at least in the United States—measles is a "reportable disease": any doctor identifying it is legally obligated to report it, which triggers an investigation. A dozen or so cases of "measles" in people who have been vaccinated against it would certainly draw authorities' attention. Reducing the rash makes misdiagnosis as fifth disease (a mild illness that produces a red rash on the face) or even flu more likely, and neither are reportable. Of course the disease could and occasionally would be mistaken for ordinary measles, but chances are excellent that the first few cases escape being reported, giving the rapidly spreading pandemic a head start. Even when a few "measles" cases are reported, their small numbers would likely cause epidemiologists to underestimate the problem badly.

Since no comparable pandemic has occurred in modern times, determining how society responds to the pandemic (which helps determine its rate of spread) lands more solidly in the realm of imagination. My virology consultant does assure me, however, that the timeline I imagined does give virologists enough time to complete basic research before the collapse, meaning Andy can explain to Elzy (and the reader) what caused the pandemic and how the virus spread.

From moose to jellyfish

Throughout *Ecological Memory*, there are references to animals that might strike the reader as odd. Shellfish, it seems, have become rare in Maine, as have moose. Jellyfish are common. These are references to environmental problems, largely related to climate change.

Rising carbon dioxide levels alter not only the climate, but also the chemistry of the world's oceans, since carbon dioxide, dissolved in water, becomes carbolic acid. Enough carbolic acid can dissolve the shells of oysters and other mollusks, or interfere with shell formation in the first place (Barton et al. 2012). New England's lobsters prefer colder waters and have already started moving farther north (Albeck-Ripka 2018). The book simply assumes a continuation of trends already underway.

Climate change is only one stressor on marine ecosystems, along with over-fishing and other factors. Some researchers anticipate that as marine ecosystems collapse, jellyfish populations will increase dramatically; already one finds stories appearing of strange and dramatic jellyfish blooms (Trotter 2015). I witnessed such a bloom myself: 52 lion's mane jellyfish washed up together on a short section of Maine shoreline. Several passersby commented that they had lived in the area their entire lives and never seen anything like it. But while anecdotes are suggestive, they are not conclusive. There simply has not been enough research yet to determine what is going on.

Moose are not, so far as I know, suffering from rising temperatures directly; but calf mortality is increasing across much of their range, in part due to massive infestations of winter ticks. Warmer spring weather allows more ticks to survive and lay eggs (Dell'Amore 2015). In ecology, simple answers are, more often than not, wrong, so the climate-moose connection may not be as straight-forward as it seems. With no pre-global-warming tick census to compare against, it is difficult to be sure how much tick populations are really changing. But while whitetail deer have an instinctive ability to remove ticks, moose lack that instinct (Holyoke 2016), suggesting moose evolved with fewer ticks.

Readers may ask whether moose will not simply evolve to deal with ticks now. Unfortunately for moose, evolution takes time, and climate change is progressing too rapidly for most species to keep up. Besides, moose are so intimately adapted to their habitat that they help define it: the so-called *spruce-moose forest*. Even if the tick problem could be resolved, climate change is gradually undermining other aspects of moose habitat. The spruce-moose forest is shrinking, retreating north. At some point, moose will indeed become a rare visitor to Maine.

References for Appendix A

Albeck-Ripka L. 2018. Climate change brought a lobster boom. Now it could cause a bust. New York Times, June 21.

Allen C.D. 2009. Climate-induced forest dieback: an escalating global phenomenon? Unasylva **60**: 231—232, 43—49.

Barton A., B. Hales, G. G. Waldbusser, C. Langdon, R. A. Feely. 2012. The Pacific oyster, *Crassostrea gigas*, shows negative correlation to naturally elevated carbon dioxide levels: implications for near-term ocean acidification effects. Limnology and Oceanography **57**: 3, 698—710.

Curtin C.G., T. F. H. Allen. 2018. Complex ecology: foundational perspectives on dynamic approaches to ecology and conservation. Cambridge University Press, New York, NY.

Dell'Amore C. 2015. What's a ghost moose? How ticks are killing an iconic animal. *National Geographic*, June 1.

Dull R.A., R. J. Nevle, W. I. Woods, et al. 2010. The Columbian encounter and the Little Ice Age: abrupt land use change, fire, and greenhouse forcing. Annals of the Association of American Geographers **100**: 4, 755—771.

Edenhofer O., R. Pichs-Madruga, Y. Sokona, et al. 2014. Technical summary. Pages 33—108 in Edenhofer O., R. Pichs-Madruga, Y. Sokona, et al, editors. Climate change 2014: mitigation of climate change. Contribution of Working Group III to the Fifth Assessment Report of the Intergovernmental Panel on Climate Change. Cambridge University Press, New York.

Ehhalt, D., M. Prather, F. Dentener, et al. 2001. Atmospheric chemistry and greenhouse gasses. Pages 241-280 in Houghton J.T., Y. Ding., D. J. Griggs, et al, editors. Climate change 2001: the scientific basis. Contribution of Working Group I to the Third Assessment Report of the Intergovernmental Panel on Climate Change. Cambridge University Press, New York.

Holyoke, J. 2016. What is a 'winter tick'? And why does it matter to moose? Bangor Daily News, July 14.

van Hoof T.B., F. P. M. Bunnik, J. G. M. Waucomont et al. 2006. Forest re-growth on medieval farmland after the Black Death pandemic: implications for atmospheric CO2 levels. Palaeogeography, Palaeoclimatology, Palaeoecology **237**: 2—4, 396—409.

van Oldenborgh G. J., M. Collins, J. Arblaster, et al, editors. 2013. IPCC, 2013: Annex I: Atlas of global and regional climate projections. Pages 1313—1390 in Stocker T. F., D. Qin,   G.-K. Plattner, et al, editors. Climate change 2013: the physical science basis. Contribution of Working Group I to the Fifth Assessment Report of the Intergovernmental Panel on Climate Change. Cambridge University Press, New York, New York.

Mann M. E., L. R. Kump. 2015. Dire predictions: understanding climate change. 2nd American Edition. D. K. Publishing. New York, New York.

Quamman, D. 2012. Spillover: animal infections and the next pandemic. W. W. Norton & Company, New York.

Ciais P., C. Sabine, G. Bala. et al. 2013. Carbon and other biogeochemical cycles. Pages 465—544 in Stocker T. F., D. Qin, G. -K, Plattner, et al, editors. Climate change 2013: the physical science basis. Contribution of Working Group I to the Fifth Assessment Report of the Intergovernmental Panel on Climate Change (465-544). Cambridge University Press, New York.

Tallamy, D. W. 2009. Bringing nature home: how you can sustain wildlife with native plants. Timber Press, Portland, Oregon.

Trotter, B. 2015. Jellyfish jamboree on Maine's coast back for second summer. Bangor Daily News, August 7.

Wessels T. 1997. Reading the forested landscape: a natural history of New England. Countryman Press, Woodstock, Vermont.

Wessels T. 2006. The myth of progress: towards a sustainable future. University of Vermont Press, Lebanon, New Hampshire.

Appendix B
An Annotated Reading List

The following list includes some books that I used in researching this story you have just read, but I have also included several that cover topics I studied by talking to people or by taking classes. Those of you who want to learn more about the ideas and information behind this story can start here. This list is not alphabetic but rather thematic—books adjacent to each other on the list have something in common in terms of how they relate to *Ecological Memory*.

Spillover: Animal Infections and the Next Human Pandemic
2012. David Quammen
W.W. Norton & Company
The scenario in my story departs from real pandemics in several important ways—but pandemic is still an important concern. Here, David Quammen describes how real pandemics work and how they are yet another symptom of our ongoing global ecological crisis. Like everything Quammen writes, it is highly readable and even entertaining, despite the scary subject matter.

Dire Predictions: Understanding Climate Change, the Visual Guide to the Findings of the IPCC, 2nd Edition
2015. Michael E. Mann, Lee R. Krump
DK Publishing
This book provides an actual ink-and-paper summary of our knowledge of climate change as of its publication, written for a general audience. Folks who want the scientific nitty-gritty can get it by reading the IPCC reports themselves. They are available both online and in print.

The World Without Us
2007. Alan Weisman
St. Martin's Press

Literally a description of Earth without humans, as though we had all suddenly vanished one day—what would happen to the stuff we left behind? Although the premise of my book is quite different, I used Weisman's work to get a sense of how the abandoned and ruined areas might be faring twenty years out.

Roadside Geology of Maine
1998. D.W. Caldwell
Mountain Press Publishing Company

Roadside Geology of Vermont and New Hampshire
1987. Bradford B. Van Diver
Mountain Press Publishing Company

The Roadside Geology books, though in some cases a little out of date (new discoveries are made in geology all the time) are a great place for interested non-geologists to begin. The basics are all explained, and as the name implies, the books are organized by highway. If you're going somewhere by road, just look up your route and follow along to find the geologic description of whatever you can see out your window. As a non-geologist myself, I tend to find geologic descriptions hard to visualize. Being able to see exactly what the writers are talking about helps.

Guide to the Geology of Mount Desert Island and Acadia National Park
2016. Duane Braun, Ruth Braun
North Atlantic Books

As of this writing, the Brauns' book is the most up-to-date treatment of Mount Desert Island's geology around. The couple also runs a small museum on the island dedicated to both geology and the local history of mining. I heartily recommend both the book and the museum.

Bark: A Field Guide to Trees of the Northeast
2011. Michael Wojtech
University Press of New England

The recognition of trees by their bark is important in my story. As the characters observe, this is a skill that some naturalists learn, but very few ever teach—leaf and twig characteristics are just much easier to describe unambiguously. But the leaves and buds of a tree might be forty feet off the ground, whereas the bark is at eye level. *Bark* is the first field guide to teach this very practical form of tree identification.

Newcomb's Wildflower Guide
1977. Lawrence Newcomb
Little, Brown, and Company

There are a lot of field guides out there, and for the most part I leave readers to find their own favorites, if they even want field guides, which not everybody does. I recommend *Bark* because it is particularly relevant to my novel. I recommend *Newcomb's* because it is head-and-shoulders above any other wildflower guide I've found. There's a bit of a learning curve for Newcomb's system, but nothing a motivated beginner can't handle, and it will teach you a better way to look at—even think about—flowers. If you want to see New England the way my characters do, learning to "think like a Newcomb," as one of my own teachers put it, is a good way to start.

The Book of Forest and Thicket: Trees, Shrubs, and Wildflowers of Eastern North America
1992. J. Eastman
Stackpole Books

The Book of Swamp and Bog: Trees, Shrubs, and Wildflowers of Eastern Freshwater Wetlands
1995. J. Eastman
Stackpole Books

The Book of Field ad Roadside: Open Country Weeds, Trees, and Wildflowers of Eastern North America
2003. J. Eastman
Stackpole Books

These three are not field guides. Instead, they are collections of essays on the principle ecological relationships of various plants. Once you can identify a plant, possibly with the help of a field guide, you can look it up here to find out what it's doing. Alternatively, if you notice something happening, say, an odd sound coming from inside a tree, you can look up the plant and possibly find out what organism is making the noise. I really did this—it was a sawyer beetle. Again, this is knowledge that my characters have and it informs the narrative voice of the story.

Reading the Forested Landscape: A Natural History of New England
1997. Tom Wessels
The Countryman Press

Forest Forensics
2010. Tom Wessels
The Countryman Press

Several times, my protagonists deduce the history of a place by observing what grows there. You can learn to do the same thing, as these two books explain. In *Reading the Forested Landscape*, each chapter focuses on a single illustration of a forest scene and what can be read from the evidence in the picture. The text is clear and readable, an excellent introduction to a whole new way of seeing the forest. *Forest Forensics* covers similar material but uses a field-guide format so you can quickly look up the evidence you find in front of you.

Bringing Nature Home: How You Can Sustain Wildlife with Native Plants
2009. Douglas W. Tallamy
Timber Press

The purpose of this book is to aid homeowners in creating wildlife-friendly landscapes. Doug Tallamy's advice is based directly on his own research and his text is excellent by both academic and general-readership standards—that's no mean feat. His research, described here, shows that the best definition of belonging to a place is not the length of one's history but the intimacy of one's (ecological) relationships. His insight became one of the primary metaphors of my book.

Becoming Native to This Place
1996. Wes Jackson
Counterpoint

A thorough exploration of the idea that each human culture needs to adapt to the reality of the place it inhabits. The book is not well-written, but the dense and erratic text hides some important material that is worth reading several times, if that is what it takes.

Song of the Dodo: Island Biogeography in an Age of Extinction
1997. David Quammen
Scribner

Biogeography is the study of what lives where and why. In extremely readable and often entertaining text, David Quammen explains why so many species don't live in various places anymore. As the reader might guess, the several discussions of various kinds of islands in my novel refer here. And yes, there's a note of hope at the end.

The Geography of Childhood
1997. Gary Paul Nabhan
Beacon Press

Gary Paul Nabhan is one of my favorite writers, both for his ideas and for his ability to evoke a place in full sensory detail with just a couple of words. He is an ethnobotanist by training, and writes about the connections between humans and their landscapes. Here, he discusses the connections of very young humans, arguing that there is a distinct developmental phase when children bond with their land—and that the loss of a place a child learned *during that developmental window* can cause lasting psychological scars. Of course I wrote the timeline of Elzy's childhood with Nabhan's argument in mind.

Our Ecological Footprint
1996. Mathis Wackernagel, W. Reese
New Society Publishers

An "ecological footprint" is the area of our planet's surface that you, personally, use. While it is not possible to determine where exactly our footprints lie—which fields grew the wheat that made our daily bread—it is possible to calculate how big the footprint must be. Although the book is intended as a practical guide towards personal sustainability, I'm including it here as an excellent introduction to a way of thinking developed more fully in the next three books. Also, if anyone ever accosts you with "where did you get *that* idea?" you can retort "Mathis Wackernagel!" without missing a beat. It's a name you won't soon forget.

The Myth of Progress: Towards a Sustainable Future
2006. Tom Wessels
University of Vermont Press

My characters' discussion of complex systems theory and related topics are rooted in a class Tom Wessels taught, which I frankly wish everyone could take. This book, together with the next one, served as textbooks for the class and present most of its ideas. Tom wove together several different bodies of scientific thought to produce the clearest, most coherent vision of what sustainability is and why it's important that I have ever found.

The Web of Life: A New Scientific Understanding of Living Systems
1996. Fritjof Capra
Anchor Books

This book, together with the previous one, explores a lot of the conceptual material discussed by my characters—and *Web of Life* presents a unifying, and very nearly magical, vision of science quite different from the reductionist version most of us are more familiar with.

The Science of Open Spaces: Theory and Practice for Conserving Large, Complex Systems
2015. Charles G. Curtin
Island Press

Complex Ecology: Foundational Perspectives on Dynamic Approaches to Ecology and Conservation
2018. Charles G. Curtin, Timothy F.H. Allen
Cambridge University Press. New York, NY.

Neither of these books is written for a general audience. The latter is more or less a textbook for people who already have their PhDs, and the former is an instruction manual for large-scale environmental conservation—and instruction manuals never make a lot of sense if the reader isn't in a position to follow the instructions.

But I'm recommending both anyway, at least to my more adventurous readers.

Most of us encounter science only as it is "translated" for us by science educators, documentary makers, and journalists—many of whom are not scientists. Something is inevitably lost in translation. Too often, science ends up seeming settled, finished, and rather joyless, a mere list of facts, instead of the messy, human, and challenging thing it really is. One of the reasons I wrote a novel about a scientist and his student was that I wanted to show science from the inside. Recommending these two books is another attempt to tell readers about the world of my characters.

The Practice of the Wild
1990. Gary Snyder
Counterpoint Press

This is one of those texts that will reward careful, repeated study with deeper and deeper insight. It's the one Andy reads constantly as a kind of secular bible. Might I suggest following his lead?

Appendix C
A Glossary of Sorts

Here is a list of the species pictured in each of the illustrations that start the chapters. Not everybody has to be a botany geek.

Chapter 1: Pathogens

Eastern hemlock (*Tsuga canadensis*) with hemlock woolly adelgid (*Adelges tsugae*) infestation.

Chapter 2: Native Organisms

Black cherry (*Prunus serotina*) with unripe fruit and a cecropia moth caterpillar (*Hyalophora cecropia*) in its fifth instar. Cecropias are native and do not threaten their food plants at all.

Chapter 3: Differential Survival

Twigs of balsam fir (*Abies balsamea*) and red spruce (*Picea rubens*).

Chapter 4: Novel Ecosystems

Twigs of pin cherry (*Prunus pensylvanica*) and quaking aspen (*Populus tremuloides*).

Chapter 5: Islands

Flower head rugosa rose (*Rosa rugosa*).

Chapter 6: Migrations

Monarch butterfly (*Danaus plexippus*) and milkweed plant (*Asclepias syriaca*).

Chapter 7: Bifurcation Events

Twigs of jack pine (*Pinus banksiana*) and pitch pine (*Pinus rigida*).

Chapter 8: Disturbance Histories

Flower of oyster plant (*Tragopogon porri-folius*).

Chapter 9: Wildness

Twigs of northern white cedar (*Thuja occi-dentalis*) and white spruce (*Picea glauca*).

CPSIA information can be obtained
at www.ICGtesting.com
Printed in the USA
BVHW041402150719
553472BV00003B/90/P